PLAYING
WITH
MONSTERS

AMELIA HUTCHINS

PLAYING
WITH
MONSTERS

Copyright © June 28, 2016 by Amelia Hutchins
ISBN: 978-0-9970055-2-3

ISBN-10: 0-9970055-3-X   ISBN-13: 978-0-9970055-3-0

Authored by: Amelia Hutchins
Cover Art Design:Vera Digital Art and Photography
Copy Editor: Gina Tobin
Edited & Formatted by: E & F Indie Services

Published by: Amelia Hutchins
Published in (United States of America)
10 9 8 7 6 5 4 3 2 1

STOP!

Read the warning below before purchasing this book.

TRIGGER WARNING: This book includes scenes of graphic violence and sex does have scenes that might affect sensitive readers. Rape isn't a joke, nor is it used for titillation in this book. If you know someone or have been a victim of rape yourself, get help. Don't let this asshole get away with it because chances are, your attacker will do it to someone else. You're not alone in this. Thousands of people are raped daily; there are hundreds of people who go free after attacking their victim because the victim is afraid to report or discuss the crime for a variety of reasons. No means no. If you or someone you know has been a victim of rape, get help. **RAINN** is available in many countries, and is a free confidential hotline. It is free to call and available 24/7 call

1-800-656-HOPE

WARNING!

This book is **dark**. It's **sexy**, hot, and **intense**. The author is human, as you are as well. Is the book perfect? It's as perfect as I could make it. Are there mistakes? Probably, then again, even **New York Times top published** books have minimal mistakes because like me, they have **human editors**. There are words in this book that won't be found in the standard dictionary, because they were created to set the stage for a paranormal-urban fantasy world. Words such as 'sift', 'glamoured', and 'apparate' are common in paranormal books and give better description to the action in the story than can be found in standard dictionaries. They are intentional and not mistakes.

About the hero: chances are you may **not** fall instantly in **love** with him, that's because **I don't write men you instantly love**; you grow to love them. I don't believe in **instant-love**. I write flawed, raw, caveman-like **assholes** that eventually let you see their redeeming qualities. They are **aggressive**, **assholes**, one step above a caveman when we meet them. You may *not* even like him by the time you finish this book, but I promise you will **love** him by the end of this **series**.

About the heroine: There is a chance, that you might

Warning! (cont'd)

think she's a bit naïve, or weak, but then again who starts out as a badass? Badasses are a product of growth and I am going to put her through **hell**, and you get to watch **her** come up **swinging** every time I knock her on her ass. That's just how I do things. How she reacts to the set of circumstances she is put through, may not be how you as the reader, or I as the author would react to that same situation. Everyone reacts differently to circumstances and how Magdalena responds to her challenges, is how I see her as a character and as a person.

I don't write love stories: I write fast paced, knock you on your ass, make you sit on the edge of your seat wondering what happens next books. If you're looking for cookie cutter romance, this isn't for you. If you can't handle the ride, *un-buckle your seatbelt and get out of the roller-coaster car now*. **If not, you've been warned.** If nothing outlined above bothers you, carry on and **enjoy the ride!**

There's an exclusive sneak peek at the end of this book!

S.L. Jennings has added the first chapter of her highly anticipated Paranormal Romance from the book BORN SINNER of the SE7EN SINNERS Series at the end of this book!

Make sure to read it and add that bad boy to your Goodreads! It's coming this summer! Are you ready to lose your religion?

I am.

DEDICATION

To my fans: Thank you for understanding that
life happens and isn't scripted. Thank you all for
understanding that it takes time to write, and sickness
doesn't care what you have planned, or what is going on
in your world, it just happens.

To Gina: Seven books. That should say it all. Thank you
for sticking it out with me no matter how crazy I get,
because that's what friends do. We've been through a lot
together, so here's to more shenanigans, and characters
bickering!

To my team: To my street team who rock my world,
pimp my books, and keep the word going while I write,
I couldn't do this without you. To the roleplaying group,
who keep the team entertained while I write, thank you.
To the beta group, who stays up late to make sure I get
the feedback back on time. To my editors, Mari, Gina,
and Terri, thank you for understanding that I have no
perception of time when I pick a release date. David and
Chelsea, thank you for the amazing covers you two put
out, and do for me. Thank you to everyone for keeping up
with me while I run for the finish line.

Dedication (cont'd)

To my friends, and family: You all may be batshit crazy, but even if I got to choose, I'd still choose to be with you. Life is fragile, and tomorrow is never a sure thing, so thanks for sharing your lives with me. To my husband, I still love you the most, always and forever. **To my daughter, if you ever date anyone like the men I write, I will kick your ass up between your ears and you will walk sideways for a month, but I'll still love you.**

Also by Amelia Hutchins

The Fae Chronicles

Fighting Destiny
Taunting Destiny
Escaping Destiny
Seducing Destiny

The Elite Guards

A Demon's Dark Embrace

A Guardian's Diary

Darkest Before Dawn

Monsters Series

Playing with Monsters

PLAYING
WITH
MONSTERS

CHAPTER one

I've been told that I am a survivor, tough, beautiful, and quirky, but the truth is, it's my disguise; my shield. I'm mostly broken and I've tried to hide what I feel, but failure has been all I've known on that accord. I've experienced death, love, and now life. I don't know where I went wrong, or how I allowed the darkness inside of me to grow. I know only that instead of fighting it as I should have, I poked it, prodded it, tried to see what it was made of…And now it's slipped beneath my skin and I can't seem to eradicate it from my soul. *Can't eradicate self*, is what it whispers to me in the silence of the night.

Is the darkness a part of me? Have I allowed myself to become the darkness? Why does it whisper such things, so seductive and exhilarating? Why do I listen to it? Maybe I am beyond redemption or saving. But if I am; from what I've been taught, that would be the end conclusion. If someone like me can't be saved after what I've endured, then maybe we are all beyond redemption. Maybe none of us deserve to be saved.

Whatever it is, I'll face it head-on. He says he can save me, but what if I don't want to be saved? What if instead of saving me, I want him beside me? I don't need him to save me, if that is even possible; I have to save myself. I just need to know that when I do, it won't cost me my soul.

I don't know if he's my savior, my enemy, or the reason I've embraced this darkness, but I do know I can't live without him. He brings out memories that don't feel right, memories that might be stolen from someone else. I'm not what he thinks I am, and he's not what he portrays himself to be. I can feel his darkness feeding from mine and it scares me. There's something inside of me that screams to be set free. If I fall for him, I fear that the monster that sleeps within me will awaken, and I'm scared that if it does, I won't recognize myself anymore.

I'm in control for now, and I will do everything I can to remain that way. With the past coming back in patches and glimpses, it's easy for now. What scares me is I know that I could be the same woman whose life is unfolding in my dreams…or, more to the point, nightmares.

Can't eviscerate true self, but what if you could? What if you could erase the past and take control of the future? Oh, but what *if*.

＊ ~＊~＊~＊

-Magdalena

I awoke from the nightmare covered in a cold sweat. My hair clung to my neck and I couldn't shake the remnants of the dream. I knew that they'd been getting a lot more frequent and vivid lately, and although I couldn't remember much about the details of the dreams, I did know that in each one of them, I died. It wasn't supposed to happen in dreams; you just didn't die. You woke up before you did. Everyone knew that. So why did I get screwed? Not only had I died in every dream I'd had recently, but the other consistent thing I remembered was that I'd allowed the monster in my dreams to seduce me right before he'd snuffed the life out of me, literally!

Tonight's dream felt so real, to the point I'd woken up wet in more places than I wanted to admit. I showered and sat down to recall the details in the journal I'd kept since my senior year in high school. I wasn't sure I wanted to write this one down because I knew it was worse than the others had been.

He'd been with me, and the next moment I'd been running through the forest holding some kind of large trinket box covered in strange writing—one I'd accidentally opened. I'd awoken on the floor in his estate, and the events and reason leading to my arrival at the estate were spotty at best. It had seemed a blur, but I'd felt it, as if it had been me inside the dream; but that was impossible.

I'd gone to his house on behalf of the coven, with their warnings ringing in my ears, but the actual details seemed to escape me. It was foggy, and I was pretty sure I'd gone there to kill him. I'd felt fear, mixed with the knowledge that I was supposed to do something bad to protect the coven, to keep them away from the monster who had infiltrated our tightknit group with his story of being an outcast warlock.

He'd been so much more, and I'd fallen in love with

him. He'd been everything I was looking for, and now I knew he hadn't felt what I did. He hadn't loved me. Instead, he'd used me to get to the others; to try and harness and use our powers for his own. I swallowed past the bile that rose in my throat as I stumbled through the forest. I knew I had to abandon the plan and get away from his house before he came back, yet whatever had been inside the box was making it impossible to even focus on what I was doing.

I took off at a run, only to fall and hit the ground with a deafening thump. My dress caught on a bush, tearing it as I rose. I looked for the box, but my vision doubled and his voice screamed my name from the direction of the manor house.

I turned and made my way through the thick, winding forest, escaping the monster. *What had I done?* I kept whispering it, as if I could find the answer within me. I fell again, and again, my legs too weak to support my flight. The earth rose to meet my fall, and eventually I could run no more. I hid behind an ancient oak tree, whispering prayers to the Gods to aid me in my escape.

I heard a branch snap beneath his weight and I refused to open my eyes to meet his angry stare. "What did I do, what did I do," I repeated over and over again numbly.

"You know what you did," he whispered as his hand touched my cheek. His palm cupped my chin and I felt the tears that fell for what I had done. I was in love with this man, this monster who had fooled us all.

My body trembled from the simple touch; anticipation from what we'd both denied each other was there in my mind. I knew now why he didn't come to my father with a marriage proposal. This man was wicked, and his seduction was part of his play; another stepping stone to his endgame.

"What did I do," I whispered brokenly.

I hadn't expected to be pulled into his arms, or for his mouth to crush against mine with his sinful kisses, but both of those things happened, and before I could protest, he'd taken us both to the ground. I could feel the proof of his arousal, and the sound of fabric as it was ripped apart should have scared me.

"You forced my hand, remember that," he whispered barely above a breath. His mouth left mine and heat sailed through my body as his mouth clamped onto one nipple and then the other. I was voiceless, and only simple moans and whimpers would leave my lips. "You shouldn't have been the one to come; it wasn't supposed to be you," he said as he lifted his mouth from my breasts and gave me a prodding stare. Those eyes, as beautiful as the wild dark ocean, could see through me.

"I loved you," I whispered brokenly as I tried to remember who I was with. He kissed me, and this time it wrecked me. I didn't care that he was my enemy, or that he was the purest form of evil. In this moment, he was the man I'd fallen in love with.

I felt his hands as they lifted the skirt and petticoats of the dress I wore, and his long fingers entered my slick flesh. A scream ripped from my throat as they plunged through my flesh into my heat, and the noise of anguish that sounded from his throat brought fresh tears to my eyes.

"Don't do this," I pleaded, rocking my hips, enjoying the feel of his body connected to mine intimately.

"This is mine, just as you will always be, sweet girl," he murmured as I rocked my hips clumsily while he used his fingers wickedly. "What you opened wasn't meant for you, but it can't be allowed to grow," he whispered as his mouth rained kisses over my jawline down where my pulse beat wildly. "You won't believe me, but I did love you, until you betrayed me."

He pulled away from the kisses, and his fingers left the warmth of my body. I cried out with regret at losing the drug-like state and wept. "*You* betrayed *me*," I choked out. "You lied about everything, even what you were. I trusted you, so you're my demon to slay!" I screamed as he pushed his fingers back inside of me, stretching me. The knife he produced with his other hand came up and sliced through my palm, taking my blood. "No," I whispered, shocked as his eyes began to glow and his smile turned cruel. "I curse you on this night. Before the first light of dawn you shall be returned to the fires of hell from which you came. My brothers and sister will finish what I have started, and you will be sent back to where you belong!"

His features twisted angrily. "Hell cannot hold me, witch. I will return to complete what I have started, and you will die knowing that nothing you or your coven does will prevent me from succeeding."

"I will be reborn, and I *will* remember you," I whispered with enough force that his smile faded.

"You're a fool if you think you can stop me, Katarina. You set forth your own doom, along with those who follow you. You will all be cursed to relive your failures, over and over again. From this day forth, any rebirth you have will be drawn to me. I will allow you to fall in love with me every fucking time. Your coven will watch it happen and they will be unable to help you. The evil you consumed will follow you as well, because of what you've done. Not even I have the power to undo what you've unleashed. So with every new life, you'll be cursed to relive the past in your dreams—only, when you awaken, the dreams will become elusive. At the first sign of dawn, you will only remember fragments and never see my face until I allow it; but by then, it will be too late," he finished.

"Isn't it enough that you plan to kill me once?" I questioned even as my traitorous body lifted for his touch.

"One lifetime with you would never be enough," he said with remorse in his eyes. "I was sent here follow a specific course, one set long ago; you were not supposed to be in my way. You were as much of a surprise to me as I was to you. That's how you fooled me, though, wasn't it? You used my need for you against me, and I promise you this, my little witch. It will never happen again," he whispered as he sat up on his knees and looked down at me from above. "I really wish you hadn't opened that box."

His hand cradled my face as I watched his eyes. He was eerily beautiful, and yet I could sense the power that oozed from within him. I was so lost in his beauty that I didn't realize he'd still held the dagger until it was lodged in my heart.

Shock registered and I grew cold and, thankfully, numb as he whispered his goodbyes.

"I will kill you for this," I whispered as blood filled my lungs. A smile formed on my lips as blood escaped and slid down my chin. "I won't let you win."

I'd awoken from the dream, and he'd been there. He'd been on top of me, watching me as if he'd been flesh and blood. He'd smiled coldly and whispered the words that had turned my blood to ice. *The game's in play, sweet witch.*

Needless to say, sleep eluded me after that. I remained awake and as the dawn broke, I watched as the words disappeared from the journal and my mind.

CHAPTER
two

I sat in the window seat as the storm rolled in off the Pacific Ocean. The storm warning sirens had been going off all morning, and yet the storm comforted me. Thunder clapped from high in the sky as lightning crashed against the waves before they rolled and smashed onto the shore. I'd spent the rest of my morning trying to recall the details about him, my dream lover. As his dire warning had predicted, only wisps of the dream memories of him remained as the sun rose in the red and orange sky.

I could remember the feel of his flesh, and the rush that his touch had sent through me, but not a single detail of his features remained. The journal didn't have a single reference to any dreams over the past year, even though I was sure I had written them down as soon as I woke from each nightmare. My chest had felt bruised this morning, and a quick shower hadn't stopped the pain, or removed the feel of him from my flesh.

Checking my voicemail, I winced when the elder from the coven notified me in a crisp, businesslike voice that my presence was required in Haven Crest. The Awakening was coming up quickly and I had a big choice to make, one that would shape my future forever.

I'd screwed up on enough of my choices before I'd left home that I wasn't sure this choice should be left up to me. For starters, I'd almost gotten married to Todd, the supposed love of my life, who had romanced me into agreeing to be his wife, only for me to find him in bed with the biggest skank our coven had ever spawned—one week before our wedding, no less.

It had taken me a month to get out of bed after that, and nothing seemed to dull the wound to my heart or my ego. The only thing that had gotten my ass out of bed had been the arrival of the United States Army, who had brought us a flag. One week after that, the body of my brother Joshua had been brought home for burial.

I'd been the one to tell him to go; that if he wanted to go, who could stop him? He'd told me that he couldn't stand being around the coven anymore and he wanted to make a difference, and I got it; I understood it. What I didn't understand was how someone could put a bomb in a public place that was frequented by children. One hundred and forty-two people had died in the attack, and I had tried to figure out what could push a person to do something so horrendous and ruin peoples' lives for a disagreement of beliefs.

I often wondered if he would have been able to save himself and the others who had died in the explosion if he had waited for the Awakening before enlisting, or if he could have returned for the ceremony.

Our coven's elders had decided centuries ago that it would be best to bind our coven's power until we came of age and were eligible for our first Awakening ceremony. They said it protected our coven as a whole from unwelcome attention from the outside world due to irresponsible young witches and warlocks. Until both events happened, the youth of the coven were unable to do much more than the weakest of charms or blessing spells. The last Awakening ceremony was a little over a year after Joshua had enlisted and I knew that he had tried to come back for it, but his commanding officer had declined his request to return home. Instead of abandoning his unit, he had deployed to Afghanistan powerless, and as mortal as the men he fought beside. He'd died mortal as well.

My grandmother had begged me to stay after that, but I couldn't. It was the last straw in a long string of unhappy events. Everything inside of me needed a time-out away from that world. A scholarship to one of the colleges that offered a botany program had cemented my decision that leaving was the right thing to do. It was a way to get out and see the world, and to learn how to better the family business in Haven Crest if, or when I decided to return.

My mother hadn't blamed me for leaving, but I had for a long time. My grandfather once said that you can't change the past; you can dwell on it, but eventually you need to let it go. Look to the future, and remember the past when you need to, but lock it down and don't dwell on it because it is the past, and you are already in the future. He was a very smart man.

My grandfather died when I was fifteen, and I missed him every day since. I hugged my knees tightly to my chest as I remembered better times. I needed to put those thoughts behind me, because the moment I got back to

Haven Crest, the festivities for the Awakening would be in full swing.

The idea of going home was overwhelming, and, while I had my reasons, I could have left under better circumstances, or given more warning than I had. There's a limit to what the heart can endure, and what the mind can absorb. My heart had shattered at the loss of my brother, but it had already been broken when my father left us and the love of my life slept with Cassidy Smithers. I had become numb, and I'd begun building a wall around me. I didn't let people in anymore, but I continued to live and get by. I took everything one day at a time, stopped looking to the past, and focused on my future.

If you could call what I was doing living. I'd had a meaningless one-night stand with the man who had done my tattoos. I'd kicked myself in the ass for allowing it to happen, and in the back seat of his car outside of a bar, no less. It had been more than a letdown, and for a long time afterwards, I'd hated myself for doing it. I'd promised myself, as most girls had, that the first time would be something special, and it hadn't been. I'd asked myself for a few weeks afterwards if I'd been punishing myself or Todd. I'd moved on, though, and gotten myself tested for STDs after seeing him take another unlucky girl out to his car. A girl needed to protect herself, and I was no different.

Whatever; I'd lost my virginity, which Todd had treasured. I'd done it because it was something I could control, and because it was an act of revenge against him, which only ended up hurting me. I'd been at a low point in my life, and on a downward spiral. After a few mishaps and picking fights with the wrong people, I'd realized that my self-destructive path was only hurting one person: Me.

At least by the time I'd finished this phase of acting out, I'd only had a single one-night stand, seven fights, several stitches, one broken nose, and an attitude adjustment.

It was out of my system after six months, and by the seventh month I'd settled into a routine that I could comfortably do with my eyes closed. I'd given up working at nightclubs to avoid temptation, and started working a safer job. I worked a nine-to-five in a floral shop during the summer months and part-time during school, putting my green thumbs to use. Since it was kinda what I had done at home, it was familiar.

After work, I'd pick up a bottle of wine and head home to my empty apartment. The only person who missed me through the day was Luna, a small cat that I'd found with silky black fur and a crescent patch of white on her chest. She'd been left to die at one of the many rest stops between here and Haven Crest.

I'd used the milk that was supposed to be for my coffee for her, and nursed her back to being a healthy kitten, and since that day three years ago, I'd become her mother. We were both alone, but only one of us had chosen it.

I looked around the small apartment and noted that for being here for three years, I had nothing. Sure, I had a few new pieces of clothing, and a lot of shoes, but other than that, I had nothing. I hadn't made any new friends, and I'd kept to myself. Hell, my neighbor had spent weeks pestering me with her suspicions about me being in the witness protection program, and for a brief moment, I'd thought about going with the story but it would have been a lie, and I'd told enough of them to myself that I didn't need another one on my conscience.

The thunder cracked across the sky, drawing my attention back to the storm, and I smiled sadly, since the storm matched my emotions perfectly. I didn't want to go home, but I did miss my family.

I stood up and stretched out, tossing the empty journal on the bed. I moved to pick one of the near-dead Gerber daisies from the fire mantel and brought it back to life with a simple touch of my finger. I plucked the bud from the stem and held it to my nose.

"I'm coming home, Kendra," I whispered to the flower. I moved to the window and opened it, allowing the storm into my apartment. Rain pelted my face as I held the flower in my palm and whispered the words that would take the message and flower to my twin sister.

I didn't wait for the storm to pass before I quickly packed my meager belongings into the old Toyota four-door I'd picked up in high school for a steal of a deal, and then returned to force Luna, who wasn't a happy camper about being placed in her carrier for the long car ride home, into the car.

I looked around the apartment and blessed it for the next lost soul who was searching for whatever they'd lost, and headed home to face the past head-on.

I knew there would be mixed feelings when I got home because I had left in the middle of the night without saying goodbye to anyone. Goodbyes were hard, and I'd been an emotional wreck with the weight of leaving everything I knew behind. It was just easier, and so I'd left without a single word to anyone. I'd prepared them in my own way, dropping hints, and speaking to my grandmother of what I had planned. She'd explained it to them after I'd been on the road and in the wind.

On the voice message this morning, the elder had left a summary of the upcoming events, which was how I knew that when I got home I'd be coming back like a thief in the night. And, knowing my mother, the manor house would be filled with witches, male and female, who would be participating in the Awakening. It would also be the opening celebration, so it was a required meet-and-greet along with welcoming those who had travelled here for the celebration.

I entered town with a sense of dread, but ignored it as I continued down the country road to home. Haven Crest was a small town of close to twenty thousand residents. Most were scattered in the woods, or on Witching Hills, which was where my family had settled down in the late 1800s.

It was past eight, which meant that I'd missed the opening of the party but would be able to enter unnoticed, or so I hoped. I parked the car in the back, behind the little guest house, quickly unloaded my things and Luna from the car, and lugged all of it up to the quaint little cottage my grandparents had lived in before my grandfather passed away. I'd moved a lot of my things into it, expecting it to be where Todd and I would stay until we could afford to get our own place.

It was less than a ten-minute walk to the main house, and had actually been the main house at one point in time while our great-great grandparents had built the larger manor house. Mom had redone it, presumably after a little too many DIY shows and entirely too much wine.

I deeply inhaled the air around me. I'd always loved it here. The fresh jasmine blooming in the gardens and the herbs that grew wild around our place had been a huge draw for our ancestors, and in this moment in time, I could understand it. I closed my eyes, sparing a moment to get lost in the scents and the natural buzzing of the leyline which ran through this town.

I used the key I still had and entered the silent house, knowing my dress for the opening celebration of the Awakening was waiting inside, because it had been one of the first things I'd moved into the cottage before I had left. It wasn't a formal dress, but it had been a perfect fit.

The dress was beautiful, handmade by a woman named Athena. At one time, it had been a part of her dowry, but according to my grandmother's story, she'd never married. Her fiancé had been murdered and then she, too, followed his fate. It was a shame the poor woman had never worn the work of art, but lucky for me, since men back then were basically one step up from cavemen—who knew what would have happened to the dress on their wedding night?

I was sure Cassidy would be decked out in couture and her group of friends would be dressed in whatever was trending, but I hadn't wanted my mother to fork out hundreds or even thousands of dollars for a dress. She had probably paid for Kendra's, and had most likely ended up donating a kidney to pay for it.

Showering quickly, I did my hair and make-up in record time and slipped into the dress. For a brief moment, I was elsewhere. I could see glimpses of things I didn't recognize, and worse off, I couldn't breathe. As reality came rushing back, I considered taking the dress off, and had to mentally calm myself.

"What the fuck," I snapped, and Luna's purring was the only answer.

I moved to the oval shaped stand-up mirror and my breathing stopped. The dress was more than beautiful. It was a work of art. The Grecian style dress was a smoky taupe tulle evening dress that had a V-neck and pleats that gathered down the front on each side of the V. It had a spray of tiny beaded embellishments that dotted the pleats of an elaborately beaded piece cinching the gown tightly at the waist. Floral accents peeped from the neck and sides of the dress, created in expensive lace.

My light blue eyes and caramel blonde hair shined and were a perfect contrast for the dress. My light skin tone accented it perfectly. The only thing missing were the perfect breasts to fill out the bodice, and a waist that could give the right curve to the dress. Yup, hello low self-esteem, how I've missed you in the last hour.

What woman doesn't want a boob enhancement at some point? I stared at my reflection and wondered if they'd recognize me, and then cursed myself for being an idiot. It's not like I've been gone a decade, and they did have my identical twin with them for the past few years.

"Get it together, Magdalena Fitzgerald. There's going to be a ton of eyes on you tonight. You can do this, you can. So what if your ex-fiancé is in there, probably with his new skank-friend, and everyone in town knows what happened? You need help, probably in the mental department," I whispered to the mirror.

Flipping open a small wooden box, I pulled out the domino mask that I'd bought before my life had gone upside down, and looked at the silver mask with its cubic zirconia accents before returning my eyes to the stranger in the mirror. I could do this. Wine would help, but I wouldn't get that until I got inside the main house, and then it would defeat the purpose.

I slid the mask into place and tied it quickly before I slipped into my lace-up heels. I tied them and headed to the door. With one last look around the room, and a warning for Luna to behave, I left the safety of the guest house.

CHAPTER three

Outside the old Victorian style house that I'd grown up in, I paused. I could hear the music floating through the open windows, and the sounds of laughter and people lost in conversation. It had been so long since I'd been home, and the nerves and doubts were pushing to the surface.

I reminded myself that I wasn't the same girl who left this estate three years ago. I'd changed, not because I'd wanted to, but because I'd been hurt enough that I had to, just to survive. I'd run away because I'd been unable to process the losses, and knew now that while I'd been strong enough to deal with it, I'd needed time and space to learn how to face it. I'd picked myself up, and I liked the woman who'd I'd become. I built her from scratch, and she was independent and stronger than she could have ever been if she'd stayed here.

I looked at my home. *Home.* It sounded so easy to just

come back, and yet it wouldn't be. I looked around at the elaborate decorations that gave an elegant, festive look to the entryway, and the trees.

The lanterns that hung from the weeping willows had fireflies inside of them; of course, the bugs weren't a natural inhabitant of the Pacific Northwest, but it wouldn't have been hard to get some delivered. In addition to the lanterns, there were ribbons that hung from the branches of the smaller trees, and attached to them were floating candles. The ground was covered with rune-carved stones to keep any evil out of the house itself.

I reached down to pick one of the runes up and ran my thumb over the smooth surface. I replaced the rune where it belonged in order to keep the warding spell up, and moved up the path to the manor.

With my mask in place, and my walls erected around my emotions, I focused on the entryway of the house. I was so focused on the house that when a dark shape moved from the shadows I almost didn't see him. I felt him, though; my heart raced and my stomach did a somersault as my eyes met his. I could feel immense power as it pushed from him and wafted over my body.

He stood with the lights behind him, his face masked by the shadows. Instincts said to turn around and back away from this man slowly. He wasn't from around here, but with the Awakening looming in the near future, there were bound to be those from outside of our coven in town for the celebrations.

It wasn't until recently that our coven had begun interacting with the other nearby covens. I'd heard rumors of it before I'd left. The elders had been entertaining the merit of allowing witches and warlocks from other covens to the Awakening celebrations; something about new blood in the coven or something like that, which was pretty liberal thinking for our very conservative coven. Of course, they'd accepted outsiders before, like Helen.

The man in front of me was thirtyish, six and a half feet tall, if not more, with dark hair which lightly dusted over his shoulders, impeccably managed, with not a single strand out of place. He had well-defined features chiseled into masculine perfection, with eyes that didn't just look into your soul. No. His eyes slipped inside, took notes, looked at all your darkest secrets and erotic fantasies, and then brought them to the surface when he was finished.

He was decked out in an expensive black suit, probably Italian, tailored to fit his massive size perfectly. A crisp white shirt peeked out from beneath the suit, and a tie, crimson in color finished off his ensemble. This man didn't occupy space; he consumed and dominated it.

This wasn't a man I wanted to know; the lethalness that I felt from him set all my warning bells off, as well as every part of me that was woman. My girly places perked up, as if they sensed just how fucked they'd be if he tried to get too close. It was downright embarrassing that my body was itching for him to soothe its needs. This man was the type you stayed away from; that predatory gaze promised that he could chew you up, and little would remain when he was finished.

He watched me silently. It unnerved me, and the moment I took another step closer to the door, so, too, did he. I paused, watching as he closed the distance between us. My mind tried to remain focused on him while my body heated up like a volcano ready to erupt. My cheeks turned crimson to match his tie as I realized that even though he was a total stranger, my body didn't care. He hadn't spoken a single word. He didn't need to; the look and heat banked in his eyes said it all. I swallowed air, needing it in my starved lungs, unaware that I'd stopped breathing as I watched the man.

The way he was watching me was unsettling, as if he had X-ray vision and could sense my response to him, and that, too, was not comforting. I retreated a step, trying to remain at a safe distance from him, to no avail. He closed the distance easily, until he was standing right in front of me. My body trembled, shaking like a leaf in a storm.

He still said nothing and the instant his hand lifted and his thumb trailed over my bottom lip, I knew I was in trouble. A smarter person would have stopped him. A smarter girl would allow self-preservation to take charge and run from whoever this man was. Obviously I'd lost my self-control along with my brains, because I stood rooted to the ground, as if I'd exchanged my feet for actual roots.

Something about him was familiar, but even as my brain itched to remember, his mouth lowered to mine and all coherent thoughts went out the window. Flesh to flesh, his power slithered over my body, and the moment his tongue pushed past my lips, I was lost.

It was like being woken up by a power line that fell on my house. There was the electricity that shot through me, the multitude of emotions that roared to life as his kiss deepened, and then there was my primal response. It felt as if he was the conductor and my body was the symphony that he controlled. Like an out of control train, he derailed my mind. Cataclysmic event of a major catastrophe, his lips rocked my world and made my knees weaken, and just from a kiss.

Lights flashed behind my eyes, awareness dawned, and I pushed his massive body away. Shock and awe woke me up. "You kissed me," I whispered breathlessly.

He smiled, but it wasn't the kind that pulls a smile from you, as it was faintly mocking and challenging. I've seen men look at women as he was looking at me right now. As if he was the hunter and I, his kill. I looked at him, really took him in.

He was letting me size him up and I wondered why. I couldn't look away from him. It was as if I was watching a car racing to cross the tracks with a speeding train coming right at it. I knew I shouldn't watch it, but the brain is a morbid thing; it needs to see it. Needs to watch what happens, learn from it. Fucked up thing, the mind is.

A couple walked by us, either so enamored of each other that they didn't see us, or they were ignoring us. Stupid asses; love was the one thing that could tear you down and cut you open. I knew that helpless, cold, detached feeling that she'd soon feel. If this means I'm screwed up for thinking all men are dogs, I don't care. I was a brick house. Brick houses were me. Walls have been built to protect me, brick walls with mortar that was infallible. Or so I had always believed. Why did I *feel* him?

I turned my eyes back and watched him. I didn't know what to make of him, or how he'd dented my walls, or why. Who walks up to a total stranger and kisses them? He does. I tried to move past him, but his hand slipped up and touched my cheek and I stalled. Like a car on the freeway with others rushing by me.

I was thankful for the mask, and all that it concealed. I reached up to remove his hand and sparks flew. I hissed at the array of emotions that ran deep inside of me. I pushed him away, hand and all, and moved to the door. I had things to do, and he wasn't on that list.

Who was he? Why did he kiss me? Questions without

answers always drove me insane, but I didn't have time for him, or those questions. I was late and I told myself I could do this; I *was* doing it. I entered through the doors, made my way to the grand staircase, and paused hesitantly.

It was my last chance to turn around and leave town before anyone realized I was back. I stiffened my spine, pushed my arms back, shoulders high, and moved down the stairs to the lower level where the ballroom was. I could already sense Kendra's presence, which meant she sensed me as well. Twins have a bond, one unlike anything else in this world.

I missed her, like the forest missed rain in a drought. She was the sun to my moon, the one I shared a womb with for eight months; was supposed to be nine but we broke out early together. My eyes drifted to the candle in the window, and I smiled.

They hadn't given up on me; I often worried that they would. I might have, had it been they who left me. Three years would feel like a lifetime without them. I lifted my hand, blew towards the candle, and watched as it flickered and went out. I saw her before she saw me. She was wearing a shimmering white dress that made her caramel colored blonde hair pop in contrast. Good choice, almost as good as silver. Light blue eyes the color of the ocean in a turbulent storm drifted to the stairs where I stood, waiting.

Twins are an anomaly in our world, but identical twins are unheard of. The elders worried that one of us only held minimal powers, and thought we were wild cards. Wild cards need to be played, that's what my grandfather always said. Wild cards could be a good thing. He'd told me when the elders had come to the estate and what they had said.

I'd been terrified of what they'd had to say, and for the first time in my life, I knew what it felt to be afraid of losing her. What if I had all of the magic and she'd resented me for it? Or vice versa? Could the bond we shared make it so that we had to be together to cast? So many questions had been posed that day when they'd paid my mother a visit and voiced their concerns.

It wasn't until our twelfth birthday that I got my first result with magic, even though I'd spent years before it trying to figure out if I was going to be powerless. I had been upset about something my mother had said and I threw a huge fit, one that made the lights fizzle and blink on and off. Three days after that, Kendra blew the electrical panel of the manor house.

Those little incidents had the elders predicting that she held more power, and while I held some, it wouldn't be enough for the ancestors to bless me with a strong mate for the Harvest. The ancestors would choose the strongest pairings which resulted in lifelong arrangements occasionally. Married couples were exempt from the ritual. It was why I'd first decided to marry Todd, since his bloodline was powerful, and we'd already liked each other. Falling in love with him hadn't been hard, either.

"Lost inside your head?" Kendra's words pulled me to the present and I smiled as I hugged my sister.

"I've missed you so much," I whispered.

"I thought we'd lost you, but somehow I knew you'd come back to us when you were ready."

"Magdalena," my mother whispered through thick tears. "Oh, you're home!" she cried as she hugged both me and Kendra on the stairs, uncaring that we could all teeter and fall down.

I pushed up my walls to hold back the emotions, but

held on to them as if I was afraid I'd wake up and be back on the coast, alone. I finally pulled away as I felt eyes on us. Up at the top of the stairs, in the shadows, was the man who'd kissed me. Below us was an entire room full of onlookers, most already knew who I was.

Our eyes locked, and for the briefest moment, his eyes flickered even though he was in the shadows, and I blinked. Ocular illusion? I wasn't sure, and I normally tried not to assume anything, but something was bothering me about him, and I couldn't put my finger on it.

"You outdid yourself, Mother," I said without looking away from the stranger.

"It's an honor to be chosen to hold the opening celebration of the Awakening, so we went all out," she admitted. "Cost a pretty penny." A penny she probably didn't have, but she wouldn't have turned down this honor.

"It's beautiful," I replied, wondering what the others were thinking of us, and, as if she noticed it too, my mother indicated that we should join the crowd with a wave of her hand.

"You're just in time for the unmasking," she announced. "I'd been holding it off in hope that you'd make it here before we did it."

"The unmasking?" I asked, as I held both her and my sister's hands as we walked to where the crowd had gathered. I looked at Kendra and smiled.

Normally, I'd know everything about the ceremony, but I wasn't old enough to participate when the last one happened. I knew the important things, and had kept a mental checklist, but this was new to me, and the elder's longwinded voice message hadn't mentioned this. Obviously I should have come home early to make sure I was ready for everything.

My mother dropped my hand as she clapped loudly to gain the attention of the large crowd. It took her a few moments, but eventually they quieted, and the other girls joined us on the large hardwood floor of the ballroom.

"I'd like to welcome the witches and warlocks who will lead us into the next generations and wish them fertility and powers from the Goddess Hecate. Blessed be," she said and the crowd repeated her last words. "I'd like to call those who are eligible to participate in the ritual this year to the floor for the unmasking of the postulants of Haven Crest who have joined us for the Awakening this year."

I watched as about thirty young men and women stepped onto the floor with me and Kendra, and noted that Cassidy, Kat, and Sophia were all eligible as well. My eyes searched the crowd for Carolina, but she wasn't here, or she was out of sight. Todd, however, was right in front of me. His gentle brown eyes watched me with something that was akin to regret.

I mentally slapped more mortar on my mental bricks. *Walls don't fail me now!*

"Without further ado, I give you the postulants of the Awakening," my mother said before she moved into the crowd and stood right next to the man who was watching us. Luckily, his eyes weren't on me this time.

I reached up and released the bow that held the silver mask in place and turned to watch as Kendra did the same. A semi-hush fell over those from out of town as we returned our focus to the men who now crowded the front of the group.

Mystery man looked confused; his eyes slipped from me and then to Kendra a few times before they settled back on me. I wondered if he searched for the difference between us. There was a physical difference, but it was almost imperceptible.

"Who do you like?" Kendra asked as her eyes searched through the men.

"No one," I announced with a sideways glance at the man who'd kissed me.

"Not him," she whispered in a hushed tone. "That's Lucian Blackstone, and he's not here to make a match with any of us. He's doing business with the coven, and the elders. Draven is looking good," she continued.

"Then why is he here?" I asked as my eyes locked with his and a shiver trailed down my spine.

"He owns some exclusive club right outside Metaline Falls. It's a little crazy; the thing went up basically overnight. The elders have seemed to accept him, though, and you know the rules."

"You don't question the elders," I mumbled.

"Todd's been asking about you, and he and Cassidy never dated," she whispered as she placed a hand to comfort me on my shoulder.

"Todd isn't anywhere on my list," I stated.

My eyes landed on Lucian and my pulse leapt. His eyes remained on me as well, and right beside him was Todd, with his eyes watching my every move as he anticipated what would happen next.

CHAPTER four

I had expected Todd to be here, and I'd expected that slice of pain to rip me apart, and yet I felt nothing. I waited, expecting it to come. Any moment now I would feel that cold, gutted reaction that I'd felt when I'd caught him screwing Cassidy. Only it never came.

My eyes left him and settled on Lucian, who watched me intently. My heart skipped and restarted with an alarming beat that I was afraid he could hear from where I stood across the room from him. I felt his eyes as they slid over me without even bothering to hide the hungry look in their inky depths. His eyes reminded me of a wolf who was sizing up its prey.

A soft blush spread across my face as I realized my eyes had been doing the same as his, sizing him up and finding nothing lacking. He wore the suit perfectly; each well-defined curve of his body was visible even in the dimly lit room.

I was so caught up in this man that I didn't realize Todd had moved until I felt his hand on my cheek, and turned to look at him. His mouth crushed against mine before I knew his intentions, and instinct—or self-preservation—kicked in and I pushed him away.

"What the hell?" I whispered angrily. I wiped my mouth off with the back of my hand and felt angry tears as they started to rise with the knowledge that half of the room was now watching our exchange. Including Lucian.

"I fucked up, Magdalena, I know it, but not a day has gone by since you left that I haven't thought about you."

I waited for my heart to ache, or shatter, but nothing happened. The only emotion I felt was anger, and that was because he'd kissed me. Here, in a crowded room with men I could potentially be paired up with at the ritual.

Before I could reply, he'd dragged me out onto the dance floor as hushed whispers went up at the sight of us together.

"This isn't a good idea," I hissed beneath my breath.

"I don't care what they say," Todd replied as he tried to lower his mouth to mine. I turned my head away from him.

"Kiss me again, Flanagan, and I'll cut your lips off," I warned.

"I'm a good choice for the ritual, Lena. Your mother will approve of me, and I am sure our ancestors will bless us as well," he assured me.

"I don't want you back," I said after I'd managed to shut down the anger. I looked at him and shook my head. "You didn't just screw up, Todd, you lost me forever. Doesn't matter what the ancestors say—you and I? It's never going to happen, ever. I think the ancestors will take that into consideration during the ritual; they wouldn't be that cruel, I'm sure."

"No, I'll fight for you; you will be my wife."

"You lost that chance when you screwed someone else on my bed. You'd be fighting me, Todd, because I'm the only thing that stands between us getting back together. It took me a long time to figure it out, but the truth is I don't love you anymore. I thought if I faced you tonight, that it would hurt. It doesn't, I feel nothing. The pain isn't there anymore, so maybe you saved us both from making a big mistake."

"We weren't a mistake," he growled as his fingers bit into my sides where he held me to dance around the floor. "I won't give up on us, as you apparently already have."

"I forgive you, Todd, but listen to me. I don't want us back. You and me? We were done the moment you slept with Cassidy. You made a choice, and it is okay now. At first, I admit, it broke me apart. If you had loved me enough, you wouldn't have slept with her, but you did. It's in the past, so leave it there."

I pulled away from him and headed to the doors that led into the garden. I could feel him watching me, and I needed to get fresh air, and distance from him. Whatever I had once felt for him was now gone; there were no butterflies when his lips touched mine, no overwhelming need to hold on to him. I felt relief. I almost felt sorry for him, and, in a weird way, thankful that he'd done what he had.

If he hadn't slept with her, we probably would have married, only to discover that we were just stupid kids who thought we'd been in love and we probably would have separated once reality set in. I smiled as I pushed through the crowd and headed to the doors.

Outside was beautiful. The sky was clear, allowing the stars to shine brightly from their lofty perch in the midnight sky. The air was cool, but after being inside, it was welcome. My eyes found the overgrown hedge maze and misted at the memories of my brother that arose.

We'd spent an entire summer redoing it since we hadn't been able to afford for it to be done by a real gardener. It was well over a mile long, and a mile wide, and was situated between our property and the abandoned mansion that belonged to the connecting property.

In the middle of the maze was a fountain, which had been beautiful once upon a time, but hadn't been maintained since the other property was now empty, and we didn't have the knowledge or money to have it refurbished. Josh and I had carried buckets of water from the lake to fill it, after we'd managed to clean it up. My arms had never hurt so bad in my entire life once we'd managed to fill the damn thing.

Slipping out of my heels, I walked to the high arch that signaled the beginning of the hedge maze, and ducked beneath an overgrown limb that cut off the entrance. The sides of the maze stood a lofty six and a half feet tall.

I wiped at a tear as I entered the shadow-filled maze. Once, when I was about six, I'd gotten lost in the maze and at the time I'd been terrified of it. It had felt like forever that I'd been lost in the overgrown, unkempt thing. What felt like hours had merely been minutes, but the feeling of being lost and alone had made me thankful when Joshua had found me, not too far from the entrance, crying as if the world had just ended. He'd swept me up and carried me to the house, assuring me that he would never leave me and if I was ever lost again, he'd be here to find me and bring me home.

We finished the maze a week before he'd shipped off for boot camp, and I'd spent countless days afterwards planting flowers and herbs inside the maze to impress him when he returned home.

He'd never come home, though. Straight from boot camp he'd been stationed in Georgia, and from there he'd been shipped overseas. I wouldn't see him again, until he was brought home in a casket for burial. I missed him, and everyone had said that with time, the pain would lessen. They lied; it didn't get easier. In fact, some days I woke up missing him and went to bed still missing him. Time didn't heal shit. I adapted, learned to handle the pain better, but it was always there. Occasionally it would become so suffocating that I thought it would consume me, but I didn't let it. Time didn't heal the loss of death; you either learned to manage it and accept it, or you didn't. You either lived with it, or you didn't. Life was about choices, and the big ones always sucked.

I swallowed past the memories and stopped to look around. How long had I been walking, lost in my head? I spun around, looking for any of the herbs or flowers I'd planted; since they were annuals, they'd return the next year. I couldn't see any of them, and the maze was bathed in shadows that fueled my imagination.

I heard a twig snap close behind me and turned to see who had wandered in after me. My hair flew up as a gust of wind filled the maze and I felt a prick against my flesh and then pain. I cried out and moved my hand to where I could feel the drop of blood as it slid from my arm. I looked around slowly and then took off in the direction I'd come from, only to round the corner of the maze and slam into something hard.

My face ached, and I fumbled on the ground where I'd

fallen in the collision. My hands lifted to feel whatever had smashed my face, and touched something thick and soft. I felt it and pushed my hand around it. My sight finally came back as the stars dimmed; I looked at what my hand was holding, and swallowed a gasp that was stuck in my throat.

"That's mine," a deep growl resonated, along with a familiar voice.

My eyes darted to the penis in question, which was making its presence known through his slacks, and it was favoring the right. It hadn't felt like a dick; it felt more like a freaking snake! A *giant* one. I blushed as I backed up, still on the ground, aware that he was watching my clumsy effort to gain some semblance of dignity back.

"I'm so sorry. I didn't mean to grab your…penis."

Seriously, of everything I could have grabbed on to, it had to be his penis? This world was cruel. I slowly got to my feet and dusted my dress off as I looked up at him.

"You shouldn't be alone out here; there are hungry wolves in the woods," he purred, and as his lips curled into a smile, I shivered. It wasn't a friendly smile, more like the Big Bad Wolf's smile right before he ate poor Little Red Riding Hood in one swallow.

"Is that so?" I asked with a guarded look.

"What are you doing here?" he asked, his eyes raking over my bust line, which was doing little to hide the girls thanks to the fall I'd taken.

I could have fixed them, but I didn't want to turn around and give this man my back. Something inside of me was terrified of him, and I wasn't sure why, or what it meant.

"I own it; why are *you* here?" I countered.

"*I* own it," he said with a narrowed glance at me.

"Don't think so; the property line is split with the maze. Half is on our side. The other half is abandoned property," I said, my voice trailing off as he started walking around me, forcing me to turn with him to keep my back away from him. "Like what you see?" I asked when he stopped and lifted his hand to my cheek, or I thought it was to my cheek; instead he pushed a stray tendril of hair away from my face and tucked it behind my ear.

"I assure you, Lena, that I do in fact own the maze," he said with a confident smirk that I wanted to slap off his face as his words repeated in my head. "Are you as innocent as you look, or is that just an act for all the boys who want to plant their seed this year?"

"I never said or did anything to lead anyone to that conclusion. I'm not a virgin. Not that it's any of your business," I murmured angrily. *Seed*, who the hell called sperm *seed* in this day and age?

"Good," he said with a look that squashed and devoured any objection or argument I might have had.

"Good?" I asked as I crossed my arms over my chest and glared at him.

"Is the boy in line to pluck your petals?" he asked with a look that said he already knew the answer, but wanted to hear it anyway.

"Todd and I have history," I whispered, unsure why I felt compelled to divulge anything to this man. He did as I was doing, and kept his back to the maze wall. Where I probably looked small and insignificant against the wall, he ate up the space with his presence. Making it to where he dominated it with his presence.

"You fucked him," he announced with a narrow-eyed look of annoyance.

"No," I said as I shook my head. "I was going to marry

him, but it never happened."

"Because a woman like you needs a man who can control her?" he snorted.

"No one can control another human being," I snorted right back.

His mouth curved into a sexy smirk and his eyes smiled as if I'd just presented him with a challenge that he thought funny. "No?"

"No," I repeated. "No one can control someone else."

"Control is easy to obtain," he stated as he stepped closer to the spot where I forced myself to stand my ground.

Everything inside of me wanted to haul ass back to the party. To find safety inside the house cluttered with people. A sane person would have played it safe and run when faced with a man who was talking of control. Me? I remained rooted to the spot, knowing that if I gave an inch, he'd take a mile.

"Is that so?" I uttered as I adjusted my head to follow his eyes as he moved closer.

He took another step, and I tried to remind my legs that now would be a good time to beat feet and run home. Was I scared? Fucking terrified. My heart was beating hard; my chest would probably bear proof of it in the morning with bruises from the continual assault of it tonight. My body reacted, and he hadn't even touched me! I felt a moan slip from my throat and I fought to hold it in, to never let him hear it escape from my lips.

His eyes demanded obedience and something else, something dark.

"I know what you need, little girl," he said roughly, as if he'd swallowed gravel.

"And what's that?" I whispered.

"You need someone who isn't afraid to give you what you need, what you crave. What you yourself are afraid to ask for. Any real man would have felt that need; I did. It's why I took your lips without asking. It's why I kissed you. You needed it, that subtle reminder that you're a woman, and you're confident, aren't you, Lena? You let it slip, though, ever so slightly. You're not looking for romance, are you? No, didn't think so," he said as his hands cupped my breasts and I looked down to watch him as his thumb deftly lowered the top to expose a nipple. I gasped as he rolled it between his fingers, and my eyes moved to his as his mouth lowered to press his hot breath against my ear. "Sometimes we don't care about the romance; it's the sex we are after. The feel of flesh against flesh, and the intense need to soothe the ache," he hissed as his teeth bit my ear gently.

I moaned, unable to contain it. I felt the sensation in my stomach as it swirled to life, hot and untamed. My panties were getting wet from his words alone, but his touch, his touch made me wild with need, a need I had never felt before. I bent my neck, giving him more room to work with even though I knew I should stop him.

I wasn't this girl, the one who came to the party and lost her morals. I'd been there, and done that. The moment his thumb trailed across my lips, I opened my eyes to find him watching my horrified reaction to his seduction. Still, I didn't stop him. Not even when he started lifting my dress with a cocky smile on his face.

His hands on my legs turned them to boneless flesh, but a well-placed hand on my back seemed to work well enough to hold me up. I knew what he was about to do, right here in this maze. Anyone could catch us, and it excited me.

"You have a dark side, little witch; let it out to play," he demanded in a deep growl of authority, and two things drew me back to reality. One, I didn't even know him. Two, I wasn't about to let my dark side out to play with anyone. It was like a splash of cold water.

"Stop," I whispered as I struggled to get my bearings. I pushed away from him and he let me with a cocky smile, as if he knew I would. "I can't do this."

"That's because you're not ready for something like me yet. You'll get there, Lena. No one else could handle the fire in your eyes. Unless I'm wrong about you," he said, and his tone was almost insulting as his eyes trailed over my exposed nipple, which just happened to be hard and throbbing, as was my wet pussy. "Go back to the party; be young for a little while. Have pretty babies and live a boring life, as is the coven's decree."

His sudden change in attitude brought my anger to a rolling boil. "Screw you," I whispered angrily as I righted myself and fixed my dress.

"I almost screwed you just now, little girl," he growled back.

"Maybe, but you didn't succeed, did you?" I said in challenge. I regretted it instantly when I caught the look in his eye. He had just become someone else; cold, detached, and confident.

"If I wanted to fuck you, I would have. You're ripe for the taking; this body? It's pent up from being denied what it needs the most, which is to be fucked hard and relentlessly for hours until you're nothing but a quivering mess. Right now your mind may not like the idea of fucking me, but your pussy does. Judging from how wet it just was, it seems to like the idea of being fucked by me a lot."

"Go to hell," I said through clenched teeth.

"Can't face the truth?" he asked softly.

"I don't have to tell you shit," I growled. "Why are you so sure that I want you? Maybe I just wanted to see how far you would try to take this?" I challenged.

I had one touch of his hand and I'd been a goner.

"You weren't here this summer; why?" he asked, changing the topic.

"Personal reasons," I answered.

"Was it because the boy who kissed you fucked someone else?" he asked with a look that said he already knew. What an asshole! He'd known all along what had happened with Todd and was playing with me.

"Rumors," I whispered as I felt the embarrassment that came with him saying it out loud. "They're like a cold; once you catch it, it's already evolving into something else. A new strain," I whispered.

"So he didn't fuck someone else right before you were supposed to marry him?" he asked with a curious look in his eyes.

"So what if he did?"

"He's a fucking idiot," he growled. "As I said before, he couldn't have handled you."

"Like you know me?"

"No, but I've met enough women to know which ones can be handled, and which ones need to be handled with care."

"And which am I?" I asked carefully.

"Neither; you're the kind people kill to own. You're the rarest breed; the one who can't be owned unless you are willing. You're not even close to being ready, so go back to the party, and grow up."

"You're an asshole," I whispered. "People don't kill

to own women," I argued.

"In my world, they do," he warned.

"Do you always kiss strangers?" I pulled his own switch of subject, watching as his eyes smiled, even though his lips never moved.

"You're one to ask, since tonight I know you've at least kissed two men here."

"Maybe I wanted you both," I said flippantly, and heard how hollow it was before the last word was out.

"You're naïve. Go back to the party, find a nice boy and settle down. Live your life; it's more than some people ever have the chance to do."

"I'm not here to become someone's wife. You were right about a couple of things, though," I said, and wondered what he was thinking behind those obsidian eyes.

"About?"

"I'm here to get fucked, shake shit up a little bit. Get my powers, and take my place. I'm not naïve, I just know what I want, and that's not children. I have no intention of having pretty babies, or a happy ever after. Love's destructive and nothing more than a lie to make people think there's some great force out there waiting for them. So here's a thought: Why don't you go home, settle down, have some pretty little heartbreaker babies, and get lost."

He laughed and shook his head. He moved incredibly fast, and before I could react, he had his fingers threaded through my hair, holding and controlling my head as he yanked it back and pressed his mouth to mine, crushing and dominating it until I opened willingly for his kiss. He didn't ask permission, nor did he need it. His kiss was earth-shattering, devastating. I didn't need to breathe; it was overrated anyway, right?

Just as suddenly as he kissed me, he was gone. The only thing that lingered was his spicy, masculine scent, and the swelling of my lips.

What *the* fuck? He just fucking disappeared!

I was still looking around for him when I heard Kendra's panicked voice as she called out my name. I had to remind my feet that they were connected to my legs, and my legs to my hips, and up the anatomy ladder.

How the hell had he done that?

"Lena!" Kendra's worried cries were joined with my mother's.

"I'm here," I shouted as I started towards the front of the maze, oblivious to the creature who watched me from the shadows.

CHAPTER
five

*Hell is empty. All the devils are here. – **William Shakespeare***

~Lucian

I watched her from the balcony of the newly-renovated Blackstone manor. She was on the deck, staring up at the stars as if they held some fucking answer. Human emotions ran through her. Conflicted, and yet not. She wanted me, sure as fuck. Her spine curved, pupils dilated, and she'd been drenched in need. Of all the things I could control, a woman's reaction to me wasn't one of them.

She's young, pliable, breakable, and naïve as a newborn. Humans, by nature, are weak, and witches are no different. I'd felt her inner conflict, and yet she'd allowed me to pursue her, to taste her. I'd felt emotion for the first time in eons, and it had been addictive. Why? Why her? Out of all of the willing pussy I had, why did my cock react to her? Why did I feel something for someone who didn't even understand she was flirting with death? She's a good girl. All pretty parts that I'd fucking shatter into a million broken pieces just to watch them break. So what the hell was wrong with me?

Bodies react when chemistry is active, but mine? Mine doesn't react to shit, and it hasn't for a long time. Not until it found *her*, but passion was always short-lived with me. My body didn't react to Kendra; in fact, it felt about the same thing as it would for a fucking statue. Nothing. Nada. Zilch. Magdalena? My cock stirred, and worse, the dark dead place inside of me felt something, and *it* stirred. Un-fucking-believable.

In the garden she was more aware, but the first time I kissed her? Her lips moved, and yet no sound had come out, fish out of motherfucking water. She wasn't even my type. I liked my women fast and easy, disposable. And I didn't fucking kiss; kissing insinuated feelings. I didn't feel. Not anymore. I laughed silently. *I* kissed *her*. I didn't break my own fucking rules, ever, not for anyone, no matter how much I wanted them.

The last woman I kissed and felt something for was dead; her portrait hung above my mantel. A reminder of the fucking monster I'd become. I was more than she could handle. I fucked like I fought: Dirty, ruthless, and without a single ounce of mercy.

I was the person you don't want to get close to. I wasn't a good person, and didn't fucking care to be, either. I was the one you called when you want something done without question. Don't ask, I wouldn't fucking tell. I could make people disappear without a fucking trace. I was the creature that the other monsters feared. I was the one who hid in the shadows, tracking my prey and killing them before they even knew I was there. They didn't see me coming unless I wanted them to. I enjoyed killing; that subtle rush of adrenaline reminded me of who I was, *what* I was. It was the only emotion I could feel. Until her.

She had darkness inside of her that I'd only seen a few times before. A darkness that slithered just beneath the surface, and was deadly once it had been released. She was a little broken, and yet there was a light in her eyes that I couldn't ignore. She'd looked unsure standing at the entrance to the party. I'd felt her fears; known the moment she'd been about to run. I couldn't let that happen. Not without tasting her first. She was fire to my ice, sun to my moon, lace to my leather. Polar fucking opposites that shouldn't attract.

The moment I kissed her, I forgot where I was and what I was doing. I was gentle with her, and I wasn't fucking gentle. I broke bones, killed worlds. I was the villain, not the fucking hero. I didn't even taste her blood yet; fucking idiot. I walked away, confidence in check as I moved inside. She was unaware that I'd followed close behind her, stalking my prey.

When she'd gone out to the garden, I followed her. Watched her. The moment she left the party, she became my prey. Hunted. It should have ended at the first kiss. Instead, I needed another taste, and once I'd sampled her blood in the garden, and knew she wasn't my target…that should have settled it. It didn't. I needed to own her, to hear her scream my name. To feel her flesh pound against mine; continually pounding it until she was nothing more than a hot, quivering mess.

Her sister hadn't been a match either, but twins were irregular in covens. I needed to know why they'd been born now, and why they bore such a resemblance to *her*.

Katarina loved games, and she loved her pathetic coven more. She'd included them every time she was reborn in our twisted game of revenge. I'm almost positive that it was one of her family's descendants who built this estate, and the maze that I'd almost fucked Magdalena in.

Somehow, I knew once wouldn't be enough with her. The moment she had pulled back, I got cocky, watched her eyes become aware of the prick in front of her as her inner bitch unsheathed her claws. I'd smiled, knowing she'd want distance, and I needed it. My cock needed distance from her supple curves, and inside the house was far enough. It would give me enough time to remind myself of what was at stake.

I didn't show anyone the monster I'd become. Instead, I projected formality and civility. It placated the witches. It gave them a false sense of security to think a being such as I could merely be human. I was so fucking far from it. Most thought I was Lucifer's right-hand man, but I was so fucking much more. Time had no meaning for me, or my kind. Worlds died. We didn't. We moved on to the next, evolved, dug in, and repeated the cycle.

I was fucked if I wanted this little girl. Me, the scariest fucking monster currently residing in this world, with some sweet little witch, one who hasn't even been awoken to her powers? Fucking pathetic. I chose to believe it was that scent of hers that was drawing me in, making my dick sore with how fucking hard it was. She needed to be thrown down and fucked until she's reduced to nothing more than a hot, trembling mess. Until her mind could no longer determine where pain ended and pleasure began. In the end, they always screamed and begged for more, and I loved it when they begged me, bartering with me.

I didn't have any mercy and I didn't pretend otherwise.

I watched her as she left the porch, unaware that a monster was watching her every move. Barefooted, skirt hiked up enough to reveal cream-colored flesh as she walked to the small cottage alone. She stopped at the midway point to the cottage and looked around as if she could sense she was being watched. Could she feel me? Impossible. Her head tilted to the side, listening. Eyes glanced at the spot where I stood, bathed in the shadows.

What. The. Fuck. She had not been through the Awakening; she couldn't fucking sense me. I watched her scan the shadows where I stood. It would be so fucking easy to crook my finger and whisper the words of dark compulsion to bring her right to my front door.

She was different from the others I'd encountered so far in the coven; smarter. She pulled away first. She had a strong moral compass buried inside of her. I liked to own things, make them mindless, and mine. This one, she'd be wild to own; she'd put up one hell of a fight before ever allowing another to own her submission. Tonight she wanted to throw that moral compass out the window and fuck like animals on the dirty ground of her own estate; I'd felt it. She pulled away. It pissed me off. No one has ever denied me; they all ended up exactly where I wanted them in the end.

She started to move again, eyes open wide, watching, looking for something. Me? My eyes traced the lines of her supple body. She's slender, petite even, definitely not my type, she's fucking breakable. I liked my women hardy, able to handle what I gave them without the fear of breaking them, not that I bloody fucking cared if they broke in the end. Her breasts were small, at best a handful for my large hands. I liked them bigger, liked to watch them bounce as I pounded into their body. Rock-fucking-hard from a single pinch. Fuck. Her hips were slim, too slim. Not nearly as full as they should have been. Yet my mind played out a vision of her, ass up, head down, and me fucking pounding her sweet flesh, why? Head case much?

Would she be like the others I fucked, and lose a little piece of her soul when she shattered at the end of it? Would she even realize what she'd lost by fucking someone like me? The others never had; clueless as fuck. Only one had felt my invasion, and she'd paid for it. Turned against me, and ended up hunted down and…

Don't go there. Dick gets hard, the fiend stirs. It's dark in there.

Witches are different than human men and women; I liked their breed. Ethics, bitches didn't have them. They were as fucked up as I was. They bred and would often kick their partner out like fucking trash on garbage day. Witches were smart, they got to the point. No fuss, no muss. Spread those pretty little legs open, fuck for days to breed the next generation, and then it was over as quickly as it began. Power received for those of age, baby in the oven, and they moved on. Even the mated ones moved on.

Maybe it explained why this little wisp of a girl had the balls to look me in the eyes when most full-grown men couldn't do it. Most knew they looked upon death in human form, and yet she held my stare without fear. Ballsy, even for a witch.

I liked the way her body moved, the way she moved. Slow and sure of her surroundings, she was searching for evil in the shadows, her eyes looking around, carefully taking everything in. Most wouldn't notice it, but I did. She was careful with her life, and yet so weak in my presence.

She grabbed my dick.

There was more than chemistry there. Explosive, cataclysmic events unfolded before she released it. I'd let it happen; I got hard before she released it…she'd felt it. She didn't flinch from the size; she flinched because of what she was holding. I'd discovered several facts in those seconds as her hand gripped my dick. One, she wasn't skilled at fucking. A dick's a hard fucking thing to not notice. Literally. Two, she's not a virgin like half the whimpering bitches at the party. She got fucked, but it was probably one hell of a letdown. I'd find him, and end him. Do the women of this world a kindness. No one touched what I wanted, or what I planned to own, even if I didn't plan on keeping it.

I'd set myself directly in her fucking path. Head-on collision, same as she did to me at the entrance of the maze. Tit for motherfucking tat. I needed to know if she felt me as strongly as I felt her presence. She didn't. Head slammed against my chest, teeth chattered, and I let her fall to my feet. Bastard that I am. It took a lot not to follow her to the ground and take what I craved and needed more of. And I needed her in a room, with no escape, willing, and no fucking witnesses.

A weaker being wouldn't have won that silent battle. Most didn't have the patience or the time. I had time, and I had patience in spades. I knew where she slept, where she ate, and she had my scent all over her. Not by accident, by design. No other creature would dare to fucking touch her with my scent on her. It's certain death if they even fucking tried.

I inhaled her scent before she could slip inside the house; again, she paused at the door.

I learned it.

Knew it.

I could track her for miles; so could my men.

She was so fucked.

I smiled coldly, knowingly. Images of her body covered in sweat, twisted in sheets, me on her, under her, inside of her. I growled; imagining everything I planned to do to her excited the monster that I was, but her body? It was exciting the man I once was, before I became this thing.

"You're mine now, little witch," I purred, and watched as she moved inside and slammed the door. As if it could keep me out? She had protection set up around the cottage. Black salt circled it, while white salt lined the window sills. Normally it would hold the monsters at bay and protect her from those wishing to do harm. Normally.

"Claiming her?" Deviant asked carefully, his eyes on the woman visible now only through the window.

"She's off limits. What did you discover?" I asked, turning to look at my men who watched the girl with open curiosity before they dismissed her.

"She's been out of town for a good amount of time. Off the grid. The timing was before we moved in and set up shop, probably why we only got bits and pieces of the story. Most I assume are nothing more than rumors. It's too bad they forgot to mention the identical twin part in their incessant yapping. She moved to Pacific City soon after the passing of her brother, who died in Afghanistan in a bombing, but we already knew that based off her sister's profile. She studied alchemy guised in agriculture and shit, basic witch-off-the-grid tactics. She was pretty active in the party scene in Portland about three years ago, and then she just wasn't."

"What else did you learn?" I asked, taking note that

she'd moved into the bathroom, and was removing her clothes. *Easy, way too easy, Lena.* I turned away, allowing her privacy as she bathed.

"She pretty much kept to herself, didn't try to make friends, and everyone I talked to barely knew she existed. Not even the men; it was as if she was so plain, that they didn't even notice her. Explain that one, because she's anything but plain-looking. One neighbor thought she was there, hidden in the witness protection program."

"She had to use magic; at least it would be my guess. It would allow her to live amongst the humans without the need to interact. She'd be almost invisible, and no one would remember much about her. It would have also kept her off the Guilds' radar. Her coven is one of the original covens, but you already know that. These assholes lock up their children's powers to fly under the radar; they have for centuries, and I still manage to find them every time. Knowing that, how did she manage to cast that strong of a spell?" I mumbled.

A woman who purposely didn't want to be seen by others? Most would add the components to be noticed by men, and yet she'd purposely included both men and women. Why?

"This coven looks like the others, same shit as the fucking Guilds," he noted and I turned to look at him.

He was younger than most of us, and hadn't been present for most of this fucking mess.

"This coven was started by one of the most powerful witches in creation. Her offspring cursed us, don't forget that. The moment you forget, you become weak. These people may look weak, but they're deadly. They hide it well, but that's why they're easy to find. They stick to traditions. I want to know why she left here. Something drove her away from her coven and their protection."

"Her father left her mother a few months before Magdalena was supposed to get married. Her fiancé fucked Cassidy Smithers; cold bastard did it right in her own bedroom too. A couple weeks later, she and her family were informed about her brother's passing, and she stayed just long enough to see him buried but was gone by the following week. I'm guessing she was too weak to withstand it. Took off instead of dealing," he concluded.

"She's not weak," I growled in warning. "There's more to this, even if she didn't realize it at the time. Witches band together; they seldom ever stray from their coven. In grief, they band even closer. Something made her break tradition; something she may not even have known was pushing her away from them. I want to know why. Tell Devlin to get credentials, and a full background secured. I want him here to attend the functions that I cannot, and he's to watch her. He needs to get her attention and hold it. He's not to fuck her, or even look at her wrong. She's mine, I've already marked her. Make sure he knows it."

"Is she the one we seek? If so, shouldn't we be ending her existence?" he questioned.

"Do you give the orders, or do I?" I growled coldly, a warning; I wouldn't give a second one.

"I'm only asking. We have to find your girl, and fast. We got less than two months to hunt her down and kill her before shit gets twisted. We know she's here, so where the fuck is she? It's not like they have a whole lot of places to hide her."

"It's your first game, and if there's one thing I can tell you, it's never expect it to be as easy as walking in and ending her life. She's a master at hiding, and we usually identify which one she is after the Awakening ceremony.

She'll be found when it's time. I've never failed yet, and I'm not about to. I never lose. Until then, do as I ask."

My eyes moved to the candle that flickered in the small bathroom as Deviant left me to my thoughts. I could hear the music she'd turned on; it was muted, probably earphones. I closed my eyes, picturing her naked, running soap over her soft curves. I'd be slipping on a mask of civility to get closer to her, which wasn't my favorite thing to do.

I could easily fuck her and get her out of my system, but I wanted her to know what was happening. I wanted her to be willing, and to understand just who she was fucking when she did it. I wanted her permission before I took what I wanted from her. It would be a first for me, since I was used to taking what I wanted with no fucking conscience or consequences.

Humans were always oblivious to the evil that walked among them. Most couldn't fight or fuck their way out of a wet paper bag, and yet I somehow knew she was different. She'd fucking told me to go have pretty babies.

Breeding wouldn't happen for her, not this go 'round. She was going to be in bed with death, and getting her pregnant wasn't an option. I just needed a few hours with her, uninterrupted. It would have to be enough, because we had a game to play. If she wasn't the one I was looking for, she would be a pleasant diversion. If she was, the game would be far more interesting this time.

"Lucian," Spyder growled as he moved onto the balcony.

"Spyder," I mumbled as I continued to listen to the music. Humans and their fucking music; some I could handle, some, not so much.

"What about the girl?"

"Which one?" I asked.

"The job; she's in the basement."

"Finish it," I whispered, not bothering to turn around. "A life for a life," I growled, low and deep. Sometimes it was good to be the monster that I'd become.

CHAPTER
six

I lowered my body into the old fashioned claw-foot tub. After travelling to get here and what happened at the party, I was drained and exhausted. There wasn't a part of me that wasn't achy. There was a fire in my lady parts, caused by a certain male who had started a blaze and hadn't extinguished it. I rested my head against the tub and closed my eyes as I placed my earbuds in, and tried to find some semblance of the peace I was used to living alone.

Images of Lucian and his hands touching me in places, brought them right back open. I growled as I removed the buds and slipped beneath the water. I wondered if anyone would notice if I drowned from my absolute embarrassment at my behavior tonight.

I'd kissed a total stranger, which, since I'd had a one-night stand with my tattoo artist, technically wasn't a completely new concept for me, but I'd at least known his damn name before I'd kissed him. With Lucian, he'd taken total control of me; his mouth touched mine and I didn't stop him, didn't question it. I kissed him back! Not just once, but twice, and I'd allowed him to almost seduce me in the maze. I'd been more than tempted to let it play out.

Right up until he'd told me to go make pretty babies like some breeding cow. Men sucked, no matter how hot they were. No, the hotter they were, the more they sucked.

Lucian, though…The man was more than just a pretty face. He was lethal to a woman's senses, and wickedly good at kissing. In fact, I'd never been kissed as he kissed me tonight. The first kiss was soft, yet conquering. My senses had gone down in flames, and he'd made them his bitch. There was no white flag being waved around in surrender, just scorch marks left behind wherever he touched me. The second kiss was controlled, precise. He'd left me breathless and boneless. Obviously brainless as well, since I'd almost let him take me in the maze. I'd felt him all the way to my soul, and I was pretty sure he'd left a mark there, somewhere on it.

I wrapped a towel around my body and headed into the bedroom, where I pulled on a pair of soft baby blue lacy boxers, and a white camisole. It took about twenty minutes to finish unpacking and right the bedroom, and after that was finished I spread another layer of salt, and black salt I'd made before leaving Pacific City, around the house. The layer Kendra had drawn around the cottage would have protected the occupant; this one was more specific to protecting me.

Salt was big in our community, and had many uses. We dyed it black, yellow, green or blue. Each color had a different spell associated with the magical properties of the salt, which was excavated from the earth; the closer the salt deposits were to the leyline, the better. The black salt I placed would ward off any evil that wished to do me harm, and the white salt would pack an ass-kicking if anyone with evil intent neared the house. I used the last of the black salt around my bed, and pushed a small packet of black salt under my pillow.

I moved around the room, doing mundane things, until I heard Luna mewling in the front room. I walked into the room and bent down to pat her back, making sure she had food and water. I was about to turn off the light in the front room when I heard a scratch at the door. I moved closer, peering through the curtain to see what was there. I'm not sure what I expected, or if I expected an actual answer when I asked who was there.

Eventually I opened the door to get a better look and Luna darted out through the small opening. I opened the door further and called for her, and noted a branch that I would have to step over if I was going to catch her. Luna was a city cat, and we were deep enough in the woods that it wasn't uncommon for mountain lions to be near. There was no way in hell I was letting my baby become mountain lion chow.

"Luna!" I snapped as I strained my eyes to see her through the darkness of the night. Most of the property was lit up by the moon. However, this area was shaded by the trees and bushes. I caught a glimpse of her as she darted towards the edge of the property and headed into the heavily wooded area.

"Damn, damn, damn," I growled, wincing as I stepped on a twig as I started after her.

I'd taken a few steps before I felt the taint of darkness; an all too familiar rush of power pushed through me and

I froze in place. I'd felt that familiar power a few times, once when I lost my grandfather at fifteen. I'd been grieving, and I'd had felt the first pull to the darkness that most witches denied easily. The second time was when I'd found Todd in bed with Cassidy, and I'd almost let it have control. I won those times, and had somehow managed to push it down and deny it the use of my anger for an entry way into my soul.

I'd lost the third battle, but I'd somehow managed to push it down after the fact. The day they'd brought my brother's body back home to be laid to rest, I examined it. The magic, not the body. I poked it, and played with it to see what it was made of. I'd kept it a secret, which in this coven was against the rules. I'd won in the end, and lifted the taint of darkness and the seductive call of evil, and now I had the knowledge that I'd bested it.

The wind picked up and I felt a chill in the cool night air. I moved forward, instinctively looking for my baby, who was probably lost in the woods and scared by now; after all, she'd never been outside a day in her life since I'd found her.

I pushed through the bushes, and winced when they scraped my arms as I came out the other side. I could make out muffled voices asking questions about depth and the temperature of the soil. I started to take another step closer to the voices and paused. I blinked as I watched men with shovels, and Lucian, who appeared to be holding…a body? My hand slapped over my mouth to stifle a scream as the scene unfolded.

Men were digging in the ground, and one was so deep into the hole they had dug that only his head was visible. I watched in horror as Lucian turned enough that I could see his expensive suit, covered in blood. The moon lit up the surreal horror show and I silently stepped backwards, only to close my eyes against the deafening sound of my foot crunching a pile of twigs.

All eyes turned to me and I spun on my heels and hauled ass back towards my mother's house. I screamed as my foot hit a hole, and I landed on the ground hard. I rolled and got back up, and didn't plan on looking behind me until I hit the property line.

I ran like there was a crazy group of serial killers chasing me, because the reality of it was there actually *were* killers chasing me. I ran through tree branches and bushes and the memory of seeing it before hit me like a train, as if it had happened to me before. Running for my life shouldn't have felt familiar, right? I turned and looked the moment my foot hit the property line, hoping that they wouldn't be able to pass over the runes that were buried in the property lines, but no such luck.

They didn't even slow down. I screamed, knowing my sister would be able to feel the terror I was experiencing, and relief washed over me as the porch light came on at the main house. I continued until she opened the door and I slipped inside and slammed it closed again, throwing the deadbolt and the other steel lock into place.

"Call the cops," I wheezed, trying to catch my breath as my legs gave out and I fell to my knees on the floor, breathless. "Dead body. Lucian. Bury."

I sucked in a deep, shuddering breath and shook my head. "Oh God, they were burying someone."

"What are you talking about?" Kendra asked as she kneeled beside me and touched my arm comfortingly.

"Girls? Is that you?" Mother called from the stairs at the same moment a knock sounded at the door.

I jumped to my feet and slammed my back against the

door, as if my slight weight would keep him out. Another knock sounded and I screamed for them to call the cops or the coven, someone who could actually save us. I'd counted at least four men chasing me, and they weren't average sized by any means.

"What?" Mother said as her blue eyes took in the sweat that covered my brow and the dirt all over my hands and knees.

"He was burying a dead body, call someone! *Anyone.* They killed someone!"

My mother, God bless her, reached behind the coats on the rack and retrieved the shotgun, then cocked it to ready with one hand as she pulled the cordless off the shelf and dialed the number for the coven.

The knocking stopped and I moved to the window, just in time to watch Lucian as he disappeared into the shadows. I turned around as my mother set the phone down.

"What happened?" she asked as she moved to the window and stood guard.

"Luna got out, and I chased her. I made it to the edge of the property and into the woods. I came out in time to see Lucian holding a dead body, and his friends digging her grave. They were asking about the soil temperature and depth."

"Are you sure it was a body?" my mom asked as she set the gun down and moved towards me.

"Yes, it was a body! He was covered in blood. I think I'd know if it was a body, right?"

"Calm down; Kendra, put some tea on while we wait for the coven to get here."

Fucking tea? Was she serious? Was that supposed to make the murderers disappear? I'm sure they'd pause for a cup of tea before murdering us, sounded legit…*Not!*

My mom held my hand and shook her head. She pulled me in and hugged me tightly as I felt the first hiccup before the waterworks started up. I wasn't sure what was worse; that Luna was gone, I'd made out with a serial killer, or that someone was being buried in an unmarked grave. Probably the last one, but the fact that I'd made out with the number one suspect who'd killed them didn't help my conscience any.

"If it's true, they'll send him away."

"What about the body?" I whispered as I pulled myself together.

"It will be sent to the sheriff anonymously. He'll know what to do to find where it belongs."

Kendra entered the room and I shook my head as she offered me a mug of hot chamomile and peppermint tea.

It took the coven exactly thirteen minutes to make it to our house, and since most of the elders were located close to each other, it was easy enough for them to make it to our home in a timely fashion. I was questioned and then as a unit, with the Awakened witches at the front line, we made our way across the property lines.

When we got to where I had seen Lucian standing with the body in his arms, I gasped. The entire yard was covered in grass. There hadn't been enough time for them to lay all that sod, let alone have it look as if it had been there for weeks. Lucian and his friends were there, and they greeted the coven and heard the suspicions.

I kept my eyes to the ground, trying not to panic as he moved closer until I was forced to make eye contact with him. I swallowed the panic, and fisted my hands tightly at my sides to hide the slight tremble that had yet to abate.

"A body?" he asked and moved his arm to indicate the

yard with a sweeping motion. He was calm, much calmer than someone who had just been holding a bloody body should ever be. His suit was crisp and clean; the white shirt didn't have a speck of blood on it. My eyes locked with his and I stepped back, away from him.

"I saw it," I whispered.

"Magdalena, we don't accuse those who seek to help the coven without good reason," Helen admonished me along with a murderous look.

I chewed my lip and shook my head. "I know what I saw," I said firmly as I squared my shoulders.

"Everyone knows she's crazy, Lucian, we're so sorry to bother you in such a way," Cassidy cooed as she slithered over and rubbed her hand over his shoulder. He didn't look away from me, and in his eyes I could see anger. "Lord knows she has to be going crazy, just finding out her own sister's been warming her ex-fiancé's bed in her absence."

My head swung around to meet Kendra's gaze, and I blanched at the guilt I felt from her. I swallowed and shook my head. "I'm not crazy," I said softly. "Not yet anyway," I muttered as I took my eyes from Kendra and settled them back on Lucian.

"You just called us out of bed because you thought you saw a dead body," Cassidy said with a poisonous look.

"Mother," I said, ignoring the fact that everyone here was looking at me. I didn't break eye contact with Lucian. It was a battle of wills, and I sure as hell wasn't losing. I just needed to high-tail my ass out of here.

"Go home, Lena," she murmured softly and I glanced to where she stood, looking at me as if I was a stranger.

I turned on my heel and headed back through the

woods. My feet ached from the forest floor, and I could feel bruises forming on my hands and knees.

"Someone ought to lock that crazy bitch up," Cassidy sniped loud enough that I could hear it.

"Enough, Cassidy," Helen said. "Lucian, I'm so sorry. You know how kids are; their imaginations can be so vivid and wild."

"No harm was done," he replied, and I didn't bother to even turn and see if my mother was following me.

I moved through the woods and found Luna safe and in one piece waiting by the door of the cottage. I picked her up just as Kendra pushed through the bushes.

"We need to talk about this," she pleaded softly.

"Not tonight," I sighed as I pushed the door the rest of the way open and stood in the threshold as she mounted the stairs. The coven exited the forest; all of them seemed to be giving me heated looks. "I'm tired, and Cassidy is just praying we give her a show. Honestly, I don't care if you were with him. I really don't give a shit."

I walked inside the cottage and closed the door in her face, then set Luna on the floor. I moved through the cottage in a daze, my mind replaying the scene from earlier that I'd walked into. It was a body wrapped loosely in a bloodied sheet; a bloody feminine hand had escaped the sheet, and dangled lifelessly. Lucian had been covered in blood, which according to logic, would indicate she'd been alive not too long ago. Not that I was an expert, but I'd watched enough police shows to know that some of the facts had to match up.

I flicked off the lights in the front room and headed into the tiny kitchen. I rummaged through the cupboards until I found tea and the old kettle that my grandfather had used when he'd been alive.

Luna rubbed against my ankle and I looked down and shook my head. "You're a bad kitty. You know better."

She meowed and started purring. I reached down and scratched behind her ear before I lit the stove and retrieved the first aid kit to clean my wounds. When I'd finished with that, I moved to find the valerian root to add to my tea. It would help me sleep tonight.

I turned off the stove and moved into the bedroom. I slowly turned off the lights on the way while holding the steaming cup of tea away from my body. In the bedroom, I placed it on the side table as I pulled down the sheet and moved it aside. I managed to sit back up as I remembered the tea and took a small sip before I moved to check the salt around the bed, the door, and beneath the pillow. After what I'd seen tonight, I wasn't taking any chances.

Tonight had been a clusterfuck. I pulled my hair into a ponytail before bringing the cup up to my lips and blowing on the hot liquid before I took another drink, then sat back in bed. Luna jumped on the bed and moved to my side as I placed a hand on her and scrunched up my nose.

"I think I made a mistake coming home," I whispered to the cat, who ignored me as she cleaned her paw.

I felt the valerian root start its magic and my eyes grew heavy as I lay there. Eventually I pushed the cat over enough that I could lay on my side, while stroking her gently. I fell asleep with her pressed against me, her soft rhythmic purring the only noise in the room.

I'm not sure what woke me, but something had. My hand smoothed over the bed, looking for Luna, but it wasn't the cat that I felt. What I felt was hard and yet soft at the same time, warm. I whispered a name, and groaned as I opened my eyes a slit to see what my hand was touching, but the room was bathed in dark shadows.

My hand continued to explore the contours of whatever was in my bed, and then slowly, my brain kicked in and I lifted my head. I pushed off the bed instinctively, but before I could make it even an inch away from him, he was on me.

His hand captured my hands and pressed them against the metal frame of the bed painfully as his other arm pressed against my chest, pushing the air from my lungs and blocking me from being able to draw any new air in to replace it, or scream.

My lungs burned. I gasped and struggled against his unmovable body. He didn't look like he weighed that much, and yet I couldn't even pelvis bump his ass off of me. I moved my head and thrust my hips until stars filled my vision. I felt my pulse quicken as the reality of what was happening sank in. He was freaking killing me! In my own bed, why did the bad shit always happen in *my* bed?

His eyes watched me as if fascinated by me suffocating and the moment he lessened his hold and removed his elbow from the center of my chest, I gasped and sucked in air. I had planned to scream, but his hand covered my mouth, trapping it there.

"If you scream, you're dead. Don't be stupid. Don't scream," he whispered hoarsely. His hand lifted from my mouth and moved to my throat gently, the threat abundantly clear.

"Get out of my bedroom," I whispered through the pain of fire that filled my lungs.

"And miss hearing you saying my name in your dreams? I think not, little witch. Were you dreaming of me?"

"No," I whispered as I considered my options. They

were limited, and I was pretty much fucked.

"You called out to me; my name left your lips more than once while you slept," he argued as he positioned himself between my legs with finesse. I bucked my hips to move him and his lips curved into a wicked smile. "Is that an invitation?"

"Fuck you," I snapped. "If I was dreaming about you, it probably had something to do with dead bodies and you being covered in blood, asshole."

"Hold still, Magdalena," he said after I bucked wildly to dislodge him, uncaring of the hand placed strategically against my windpipe.

"Get off of me," I hissed and continued struggling to free my hands, right up until his hand left my throat and moved to my ass, lifting it to press me against his fully erect dick that no amount of clothing could hide.

"I'd stop before you drive me past the point of no return," he growled, and I went limp. No struggling here, calm is me. "Too easy," he whispered as he moved his erection away from me. "You're fragile," he noted. "You'll be bruised come morning."

"Proof that you're an ass?" I sassed, which probably wasn't the best idea, considering my position.

"What did you see tonight?"

"You and your sick friends burying a body," I whispered. "I'm not crazy, I saw it. You were covered in blood."

"You think you saw me covered in blood," he replied in a tone that struck a nerve, or every nerve.

"No…"

His eyes held mine and I lost all coherent thought. I felt like I was drowning in them, as if I ceased to exist without their heat. I tried to form words, but nothing came out, as if I was a fish out of water gasping for air. Only I was gasping for words, and I couldn't form any. What the fuck?

"Don't fight it," he whispered softly as his thumb traced my cheek and then my full bottom lip. "My men want you dead for what you saw tonight. I think you can be saved from that; what do you think?" he asked and smiled as I once again moved my lips as fear spread through me. It felt wrong, his magic, what he could do. I had no willpower, nothing. Words eluded me, and that scared the shit out of me.

What the hell kind of monster was he? I couldn't talk, and my mind was turning to fried mush. I tried to speak again, but only air escaped from my lips. Had I just moaned? Or was it my imagination? It was at least a freaking noise.

"You saw me tonight, but you were mistaken," he whispered hoarsely as he lowered his mouth to my collarbone and kissed it. My body responded, even though I begged it silently to ignore his wicked lips.

"I was mistaken," I parroted softly, and blinked at my own words. That hadn't been what I'd intended to say at all.

"Yes," he said as he lifted his hands from mine, releasing them. "That's a good girl, Lena," he muttered as his mouth touched the pulse that raced along the length of my neck. "You were mistaken; you saw me burying a dog in the back of my property, one who'd been struck by a car on the highway."

"I saw you burying a dog," I whispered breathlessly as he sucked on my neck. I could feel his smile curve against my flesh as he heard my heated moan in response to his mouth against my skin. His hand brushed the stray hairs that had been freed from my ponytail away from my face, his mouth pressed against my forehead, and a tear slipped from my eye.

How the hell was he holding me here? I couldn't move. He'd freed me physically, but something had replaced his hold and I was helpless to do anything but lay on the bed as he hovered above me, placing soft kisses against my flesh.

"I came to you after the others left, and you let me in to talk," he continued.

My chest heaved as I tried to force the right words out of my mouth, and yet I repeated his words verbatim. His eyes lowered to where my nipples had hardened as his mouth seduced my body, and my mind. One hand slid over the flesh that was exposed, and his fingers found and leisurely traced the outline of one nipple and then the other.

"Tell me to fuck you," he urged.

"Fuck me," I uttered to my own horrified amazement. I'd totally intended to tell him to get fucked elsewhere, by anyone but me. "No," I hissed somehow, forming the word my brain was screaming.

His eyes lifted to mine. "You want me buried inside of you, Lena. Invite me to fuck you. Part your legs for me, *now*," he growled as his tone intensified. "Show me how wet you are."

"Fuck me…" I whispered breathlessly as I stretched my legs open further than they already were. It was painful, embarrassing, and angry tears rushed to my eyes. I refused to let this monster see me cry.

"Good girl," he replied as he sat back on his knees and looked over my body that was spread open for him. At least I was dressed, barely, but it was something between him and my lady parts. "See, sweet girl, you see how easy it is for me? I have full control of you. I can make you do anything at any time. I can steal any memory from you and you'd not even miss it. The only thing I cannot make you do is respond to my touch as you are right now."

I trembled as his words echoed through my brain. My eyes took in his disheveled suit and noted the runes that glowed and pulsed just beneath the collar of his dress shirt. Death runes? Impossible. It was a dead language. No one knew how to use them, let alone control them enough to place them upon skin. I tried to focus on them, but unbidden, my eyes moved to meet his.

"You won't get in my business again," he whispered with a strange tone and cadence to his words as he lowered his mouth and nipped at my bottom lip. Pain shot through my body, and I moaned as he released my lip, only to capture it again and apply even more pressure. Pain mixed with pleasure, and I felt my body melting for more. "You like that, don't you, sweet girl?" he asked as he pulled away and looked my body over slowly. "You make it really fucking hard to walk away when you respond to me so sweetly," he rumbled angrily and I blinked in confusion.

As if I wanted this? I couldn't seem to control my body around him, and he had me at a huge disadvantage.

"What are you doing to me?" I whispered in a broken whimper as the emotions I had been holding back threatened to come out all at once.

"You'll stay out of my way, because killing you would be a waste of what I presume will be a worthwhile fuck. I won't take chances, not even for you, Lena. My men want you dead and they're not convinced you can be swayed to stay out of our way. You're too fragile in this state, too breakable. Do you understand what I am telling you?" he asked as his eyes lifted to meet mine. I inhaled a shuddering breath as I took them in. They were no longer inky black, but a striking shade of blue mixed with green hues. I blinked and they were back to normal, and I wondered if I had imagined it?

"I'm fragile, I need to stay out of your way," I replied through anger and disbelief. I was *not* fragile!

"I wish you weren't so fragile," he whispered ruefully as his fingers trailed between my thighs. "I'm not accustomed to waiting for what I want, and it's only going to be harder on you when I finally get it."

I narrowed my eyes on his and forced words out through my useless lips. "I didn't see a dog."

His eyes snapped to mine and narrowed. His body instantly pressed hard against mine and his hands captured my face and held it immobile between his large hands. His kiss was hard, punishingly so. I moaned and tried to remember why I needed to fight him.

"I came by the house to explain what happened tonight," he said insistently as he pulled his mouth away. "You let me inside. We talked for a while, and I told you about the dog. The one I discovered on the highway. It's what you saw me burying tonight. There was no body, just a dog. You thought it was a human, but it was an honest mistake. I left when you became tired, and you slept peacefully afterwards."

My lips moved, telling him exactly what he wanted to hear. After the words had left my mouth, I kissed him to shut him up. His words were ricocheting through my head, and it hurt. *Bad.* It was like compulsion, but I knew it couldn't be. Witches of our coven were protected from it, and yet whatever he was doing, I wanted to believe in what he was saying.

"You'll come to my club tomorrow. Your sister will bring you at the coven's bidding. You'll come to my office alone. I'll see you there, sweet witch."

I blinked and looked around the room. I sat up and looked at the floor where the salt was still in place around the bed. My eyes moved to the warding runes on the walls that had been carved there when the house was first built, and then I looked out the single window at the fading form of the man who I was pretty sure wasn't a warlock, because we couldn't do those kinds of tricks.

CHAPTER
seven

I pulled the teapot from the stove and filled a large mug to the rim with burning water. The earthy aroma of Earl Grey made my nose dance a little as I added the sugar and stirred the mixture together. I set it down briefly to pull on the knee-length weaved sweater, and headed to the porch.

I placed the mug on the white oak carved coffee table my grandfather had made so many years ago, and seated myself on the small porch swing. I'd missed home, and even though I'd enjoyed living outside of this place, I felt the call to come back the entire time. I'd actually had to force myself to remain where I was and on the path I'd chosen for myself.

My eyes traveled to the garden and I paused. The wind blew the overgrown herbs, sending wisps of the flowering plants into the rows around them. My mother had never let it become this overgrown, not even when

Joshua died. I'd been pissed that instead of screaming and crying, she'd gone to the garden.

I hadn't understood it at the time, but now I did. It gave her purpose, and was soothing, familiar. My hands itched to pull the herbs from the soil, to feel the familiar dirt beneath my nails. Normally the plants would be harvested and stored for winter. Some would already be in the drying hut, where they would be cured naturally for potency.

We used the herbs from this garden to do spells, ceremonies and, most importantly, to fill the shelves of our store and be shipped out to other covens. Yet it was in disarray, overgrown, and neglected.

The sound of boots hitting wood along with the associated sounds of creaking from the front porch of the main house pulled my attention from the garden, to where Kendra was moving towards me. Her shoulders were back, her hair up in a messy bun, and she had dark circles under her eyes that told me she hadn't slept much at all.

I squared myself for what was to come, and knew that it was better to get it out of the way than let it build. We were alike in that way; usually neither one of us could sleep if we'd had a fight with each other, but I'd been able to sleep just fine last night, why? Memories of flashing midnight blue eyes mixed with a soft hint of green came rushing back and I sighed. More nightmares I couldn't remember? Probably.

I remembered him being here, but it seemed off. As if it wasn't my memory but something else. I was catching flashes of other things, such as his hands against my throat, his lips touching mine. Nothing so simple as a nice little visit which was what my mind kept telling me it had been. My brain itched, and those flash backs kept happening the moment I stopped trying to remember. It also tended to make my brain fuzzy, as if something was preventing the memories from coming. Or maybe I was just wishing something more had happened, which meant I seriously needed to stop thinking about Lucian in a kinky-I-want-him kinda way.

"We need to talk," she said softly as she moved across the porch and sat beside me on the swing. Her hand slipped into mine and I continued staring out over the sprawling estate. I felt her eyes on me and after a few minutes of pulling up enough strength from the elements, I turned and looked at her.

"I need to get this out, and I need for you to just listen to me," she started.

I groaned inwardly and kept my eyes fixed on hers. Her jewel-like eyes sparkled with unshed tears as she shook her heart shaped face and sighed heavily. Or maybe I'd been the one to sigh. Her honeyed complexion was ashen today, probably because of the severity of where this was leading to. She pushed a stray lock of caramel colored hair away from her face and bit her lip in thought, as I often did. We were identical in looks, and still so very different from each other even in our similar mannerisms.

"Groan all you want, but I need to tell you. I need you to understand why I would do this, especially after what he did to you," she continued.

"I don't care why you did it," I whispered. Actually, I did. I cared because she was supposed to have my back. We were identical twins, and we had an unshakable bond. It was just weird that he'd go to her, when he'd had me. I didn't understand it at all.

"You were gone, and neither of us understood why you went through with it," she replied. "First he started coming around asking about you; what school you went to. I sent him away at first, but he kept coming back. We started talking, and we had something in common: You," she said with guilt buried in her feelings and tone.

Great, my sister, and my best friend, bonded with my cheating ex-fiancé over me? How sweet.

"Stop that," she said picking up on my inward sarcasm without me needing to say it out loud. Sometimes being as close as we were really sucked. "I didn't want it to happen, but I missed you so much. We missed you so much. Everyone else? They didn't notice. I mean, they did, but it was like you were a ghost around here. Your name wasn't spoken out loud; it was as if you'd died with Josh in Afghanistan. Do you have any idea what that was like for me? I couldn't bring you up, my other fucking half, and I couldn't talk about you. It made people uncomfortable; everyone except Todd. He wanted to talk about you, and it felt good. I had someone I could talk to about missing you. I couldn't even feel you! I was out of my head going crazy, and you didn't even call. Not even to return my calls. We'd never been apart, Lena, and then you were just gone from my life as if you'd cut me out like a cancer."

"I needed to get away, Kendra. I needed to figure out what was next, because being here was smothering me. I get that it was selfish, but if I'd tried to say goodbye, you'd have begged me to stay. I couldn't. I was a mess, and there were other things going on. I just needed to know I would be okay by myself, I guess. I needed to know that there was life outside of this town."

"You could have sent me a letter," she whispered as she turned her eyes away. "As I was saying, we got close and things just happened. I love him. I think maybe I always have, and that makes me suck big time, because you're my sister and my best friend. I know that if he'd remained yours, nothing would have ever happened."

"I sent you flowers, and I know you knew they were from me." I inwardly tensed.

She rolled her eyes in response and shook her head. "That's not the same and you know it." Her chest heaved as she expelled a deep sigh.

"I know you wouldn't have done this if I was still with him. I don't hate for you being with him," I sighed heavily. "I do think it's a little twisted that you and I are identical, and a piece of me wonders if he isn't using you as a backup." Based on his words and behavior last night, the scenario made perfect sense to me.

"I considered that, but he loves me, even though I broke up with him. He said we should play it out, let you think he hasn't been with anyone since, well, you know. I slept with him, though, and you coming back home hasn't changed how I feel about him. I guess I needed to be here for you, and I wanted to be the one who explained it. I didn't get a lot of time with you last night, which is probably my fault."

"Probably partly mine too," I said sheepishly. "I was too busy kissing Lucian before I accused him of clinging to a dead body."

"Shut the front door, you didn't," she laughed. "And then all this mess, shit, Lena. You're so wicked," she said as she leaned back and closed her eyes before she sat back up, smiling.

"Twice, and almost gave him a lot more," I admitted. "The guy can seriously work some magic with his lips."

"Speaking of Lucian, the coven has called you in to answer for what you did last night. Cassidy's mom isn't going to let it go. I can come with you."

I curled my fingers around hers and shook my head. "It was a dog," I whispered, even though something inside of me wanted to scream that it wasn't. *Weird.*

"Get dressed; I'll meet you out front in twenty minutes."

"Sounds good," I said, still puzzled by my reaction to the words. Why didn't I believe myself? I looked up as she paused.

"I'm really sorry you had to find out like you did. Unless the ancestors do a bit of intervening, I won't be with him for the Harvest; Mom says that after what happened with you, that it showed poor character and he might be one of the few that the ancestors don't bless during their first Awakening. I'm not sure what he feels for you, but I know he regrets what he did."

"I don't love him," I blurted, and smiled as she expelled a shuddering sigh. "I don't know for sure if I ever truly did. I think we were just moving onto the next step without any real understanding of what it would mean. We were kids, and it might sound crazy because only a few years have passed, but I guess I feel relieved that I didn't end up his wife. I might actually have to thank Cassidy for being a bitch, and sleeping with my fiancé. That really fucking sucks."

She laughed, and it pulled a reaction from me. I laughed and shook my head. "Why did you go through with it? I thought, or assumed it was because he cheated on you and you were heartbroken. I felt pain, I know it hurt you."

"It hurt me pretty bad, but I just thought we were cursed, or that I was. Every man I loved left me, all of them, Kendra, and in such a short amount of time too.

Dad, Grandpa, Joshua, and Todd. All fairly close to one another and I thought it was me. That maybe I was cursed, and if I could get away, you'd have a chance. At least when I was convincing myself to go it's what played through my head. Do you remember Grandmother telling us about the curse? That every man we loved would leave us, or die?" I whispered softly, as if someone would over hear us.

"I don't believe it. Joshua was killed by a bomb, Grandpa died of natural causes, and Dad left us all. Todd fucked up, he was an idiot. Dad, by the way, is back. He's with Helen. Turns out Cassidy is his, seems that even though Dad was paired with Mom for the Harvest, he was also sneaking off with Helen during the same time. He found out Cassidy was his, and left us. He made it look like he left town, because they needed time to figure out what to say. Like we wouldn't see right through what he wanted. Helen has a lot more money than Mom does and her standing in the coven is higher, even if she isn't one of the original bloodlines."

I felt my heart twist and closed my eyes. "That explains why Cassidy hates us."

"Not us, just you. I've spent some time with her."

"Thanks," I replied on a laugh. "Anything else I should know?"

"I was sneaking into the Guild, learning about our history. I'm a badass now," she snickered proudly as my stomach dropped.

My blood ran ice cold. "You did what?" It felt as if the floor had been knocked out from beneath me. No one was that crazy, surely not Kendra. Not my sister.

"Chill out, I was safe. They're not as bad as we've heard, either. Shady, but who isn't? I met Guild witches, and Enforcers outside the Guild. Even went on a date with one. They're not like us, but they are serious about their jobs, big time. Brainwashed to the mother-loving core," she said with an emphatic nod and a wide, naughty grin.

"That's insane! You could get in trouble, Kendra. Big trouble if the coven ever figured it out."

"Ask me what I got," she said, ignoring my words.

"Are you listening to me? What if you'd been caught in the middle of that fight between the Guild and Fae?"

"Didn't happen; in fact, it was actually boring in that place," she said flippantly.

"It got blown up!" I screeched at her.

"Yeah, but not when I was there," she pointed out. "Our family history was there, and I think the missing grimoires might be inside of the catacombs. They have our entire history inside their damn walls, while we have nothing!"

"We have them too, just not accessible for the average witch. They're off-limits unless you're an elder. What exactly did you risk your neck for at the Guild?" I asked, my curiosity piqued, even though my heart hammered with knowing she'd placed herself in danger's path, and I'd been clueless of it.

Going to the Guild was forbidden, always had been, so what was worth going there? My eyes took in her closed-off demeanor and I wondered what she was hiding. She had wanted me to ask what she'd found, but there was something else she was hiding from me, I could feel it.

"I found a few things out about demons, and other things about our line. Things no one else seems to know about."

"Such as?" I asked, and waited for her to answer.

"Later, I'll show you everything I have, and what I

learned from my visits."

"Visits, as in plural, more than once?" I snapped angrily. What the hell was wrong with her? Out of the two of us, she was the conservative, never got into trouble, always listened and followed the rules.

I stood up and retrieved the empty mug as I shook my head. "Stay away from them; they may seem decent, but they're deadly. They are nothing more than trained assassins."

"You're wrong; Olivia was sweet, meek. Nothing like we thought them to be, and she helped me."

"She helped you steal files?" I asked pointedly.

"Well no, but she didn't stop me either. I knew she suspected I was checking out things about existing separatist covens, and she didn't question it."

"That you know of, Kendra, she could have followed you, or sent an Enforcer to do so, how do you know she didn't report it to the Guild?"

"Because I've been going there since you left, and no one has come here, and nothing has happened. It's been months and they're a little busy with the Guild being attacked and blown up by the Fae, or whoever they're claiming did it."

"They're saying it was the Fae," I agreed. "That is yet another reason why you shouldn't have gone to the Guild. You could have led those creatures here as well."

"I needed answers, it's not like I went in there with my name on my forehead and handed them a DNA swab to test my genetic makeup."

"You might as well have," I said pointedly. "You do know that they keep track of every archive checked out, and if you looked into our history, and they have it flagged, you put a target on all of us. Who are you? When

I left here, you wouldn't have disobeyed anything that the coven said."

"I checked out a lot of random things as well, not just our history. I'm smart enough to cover my tracks. I grew up, Lena, just as you did. I'm curious about our history, and I want to know why they make us hide."

"Let's just forget you went there for now. I'm in enough trouble with the coven. You can show me what you found later," I mumbled as I moved to the door. "Promise me you won't go to any of the Guilds again. Ever. I couldn't live without you, Kendra. Kill the cat, no more curiosity. Got it?"

"I love you, too," she said as she blew a kiss and headed to the main house. "Hey, when are you going to move back into the main house so I don't have come all the way out here just to talk to you?"

I shook my head and met her eyes, not needing to give her an answer. I couldn't move back into my room, it was filled with items for my wedding, and pictures of the life I'd left. There was also Joshua's room directly across from my old room, empty.

I moved back inside the cottage and quickly changed into something conservative that I could face the coven in.

CHAPTER
eight

I sat outside the doors where the coven had assembled inside the Town Hall building, mortified that they'd called others in to witness my punishment. Obviously they had wanted them to observe the workings of the elders, which made sense, but sucked that it would be at my expense.

"Magdalena, they're ready for you now," one of the older ladies said as she placed the phone back into its cradle and went back to her work on the computer in front of her.

I swallowed and pushed off the chair as I moved to the wide wooden doors that led into the huge room I'd only been in a few times before as a child. The room was filled with people who were talking amongst themselves until the doors' hinges, which obviously needed a good oiling, announced my entrance.

I wasn't surprised to see my grandmother on the panel,

or Helen, but it was my dad sitting beside her that made me lose forward momentum as I locked eyes with him. He had no right to be here; he'd left us.

He'd gotten in a huge fight with my mother, and must have left us during the night. I'd waited an entire month for him to come home before it finally sank in that he wasn't coming back. He had abandoned us. The man, who sired us, had raised us and loved us since birth, had just walked away without a backward glance.

I'd told Kendra that he would come back, but like this, well that wasn't how I'd envisioned it. Cassidy was his blood daughter, and I could understand some of her anger if she'd known who he was, but like our own birth records, hers would have been blank if it had occurred during a harvest celebration.

"Magdalena," my grandmother's tone was firm, polite. "You have caused quite a disturbance."

I wanted to reply in my best Yoda voice, having caused disturbance in the force…young Jedi. Yup, that's me. Sign me up, give me the light-saber and I'd be good to go.

"It's more than just a disturbance," Helen said and as my eyes moved to her, I passed over my father's graying head that bobbed in agreement. "We do not make accusations against anyone without solid proof, which you lacked; much less those who donate millions into the community. What do you have to say for yourself?" she said with malice and a solid look of death in her baby blues.

"I made a mistake, and I'm sorry. I thought I saw something and I didn't. It was my impression that if we think harm has been done, we report it no matter how small of an offense it may be. All matters are to be reported to the coven, and to be handled within their ranks. I thought he held a dead body in his arms and I reported it. I now understand that it was a dog that'd been struck on the highway, but in the dark I misjudged it."

"I do not think you understand the severity of your accusation. Lucian Blackstone has helped this community out of a hole and has donated millions of dollars to the coven. Without him, we'd be in trouble."

"Bad investments?" I asked.

"That is none of your concern, child," Katy said sharply.

I turned my eyes to look at the fifty-something witch who hadn't been on the panel when I'd left town. She was friends with my mother, or had been when they were younger, but they'd grown apart soon after high school had ended. She frequented the store we owned since her own knowledge of potions and herbalism was lacking.

"You will not make the same mistake again," Helen continued, even though the others hadn't gotten a word in yet. "For the next week you will forfeit the right to participate in the Awakening celebrations, unless Lucian himself allows you to. You will go to Lucian and beg his forgiveness and offer your services to him in the upcoming events he has offered to hold for us. That is yet another reason why your crime is so severe. He has supported this community, and helps us with anything we have needed of him. You will do whatever he requires of you, as long as it is within reason. Do you understand what I am saying?"

"I understand," I mumbled. I got it, I was to do whatever he wanted. No matter what he asked, I had to do it. He could ask me to bark like a dog, and my response would be woof. I hated that if I wanted to attend anything,

I'd have to ask *his* permission.

Freaking great.

"Is that all? She deserves a more severe punishment," Cassidy pouted and I watched as my father turned and patted her arm lovingly.

"An entire week is quite enough," my grandmother said, her eyes daring Helen to challenge her.

A week in time-out during the Awakening celebrations was huge. It was an important time in the coven, one of the biggest things in a witch's life. A time when we would come into our powers, relieved of a curse by the witches of old to protect the young as well as the coven itself. Not to mention, they had discovered a foolproof safeguard that would continue our coven's existence through the centuries.

Our coven has its own brand of 'catechism' to teach the young and pass on what heritage the elders deemed that we can know. They taught us that we descend from a very powerful line of witches and our coven originally came from Aberdeen, Scotland in the sixteenth century, escaping in the chaos surrounding one of the witch hunts of the time. Back in those days it was a scary time to be a witch, let alone piss someone off.

Several actual witches were rounded up with many innocents in the hunt. However, there was a story about one of the witches of our coven dying a horrible death at the hands of a monster that triggered the actual exodus from Scotland. The coven took the first available ships they could find and settled in what is now known as Nova Scotia.

Our coven uprooted and moved about sixty years later and became part of a coven just outside of Salem, Massachusetts. With all of the dangers that humans, demons, and the Fae posed to our coven, it was decided that we would separate again to protect our coven and the elders came up with the genius idea of locking up the powers of the young so we couldn't give our coven away, and essentially make the coven harder to detect.

Eventually we moved to the west, an uncharted land at the time, rich for herbs and other things we needed to flourish. We survived, each family helping each other to make it to the next year. Sickness came, and with it, an entire bloodline was lost. The coven took matters into their own hands, and created the Harvest Celebration and ceremony that would ensure that the next generation would be born and the bloodlines would carry on.

During the Harvest ceremony that follows the Awakening, the ancestors are called upon to decide our mates if a witch isn't already married and in a permanent union. Those who have been through their Awakening are literally compelled to mate for days after the Harvest ceremony. Ancient thinking people they were, they named it the Harvest ceremony to symbolize fertility and planting of the new seeds within the coven.

Witches are sexual creatures by nature; many rituals call for nudity or sex as part of the rite, however the month of the Awakening ceremony is the only time in our lives where chastity is warranted as it was thought that the powers that were unlocked during the Awakening ceremony would be more powerful, as would the children that would be sired after the Harvest.

I however wasn't keen on the idea of creating life, but the call of the power that I could feel growing inside of me was addictive, and like the others, I was here to obtain my birthright and I'd be doing whatever it took to please the ancestors so my powers were awakened, even mating with whoever the ancestors chose for me as the mating part of the whole shebang was compulsory and not optional.

I wasn't sure why we needed a bunch of dead people deciding who we created life with, or if we deserved our powers. They were dead, and times had changed. I understood that back in the old days, sometimes unions had to be forced, but this was the freaking twentieth century and a woman didn't actually need a man to conceive a child. We had technology and we weren't sheep anymore! We could use a baster if needed!

"Magdalena, wake up!" Kendra's voice penetrated my trail of thought. *"Seriously, you scare me. A freaking baster?"* she snickered in my head.

"She's not even listening, mother!" Cassidy's high-pitched cry pulled my eyes to hers.

"I'm listening; I accept any punishment given. I will go to Lucian and apologize and offer my services for any event he needs help with."

My grandmother shook her head and I narrowed my eyes on her; she didn't look happy with me, but it had been dark. It was an honest mistake, and I'd really thought it had been a body, and not that of a dog.

"You are dismissed, and, Magdalena, see that you make no further accusations towards our guests," Helena sneered as she turned and smiled at my father.

He wasn't a guest; he was one of our own. I stared at him until his eyes rose to meet mine, and I watched as he lowered them with shame.

It was official; all men sucked.

CHAPTER
nine

I'd tried on nine outfits by the time I settled on a white wraparound top that exposed more skin than it concealed, and low hip-hugging jeans that fit like a glove. I slipped into the *Jimmy Choos* I'd found in a secondhand store in Seattle, and looked over my reflection. I wasn't sure why I wanted to look sexy, but I felt it was imperative.

Hands pushed around my throat and I coughed and blinked at my reflection. What the hell was wrong with me? I dabbed on some gloss and a little mascara, and headed to grab my purse. It was secondhand as well, but I'd found a thrift shop that had received a ton of donations from the well-to-dos of Seattle. I'd spent three paychecks there, and I hadn't regretted it one bit.

Being from a family that was careful with money, I made it work. I found bargains where I could, and I bargain shopped my ass off to stay in style. I wasn't afraid of working, nor was I afraid to get my hands dirty. I didn't have the luxury that Cassidy was born into; getting everything she wanted. Mom and Grandma always reminded us that you appreciated things more if you had to work hard for them, and I guess they were right.

The shop kept our family fed and covered the basics for us, including maintaining the bare minimum on the manor house. However, it didn't allow us to get too crazy. Kendra and I worked in Mom's shop until I left, and I have to admit that I'd learned a lot from it.

I headed out the door after ensuring Luna had food and water and looked at the map that Kendra had scribbled for me. The coven had forbidden her from going with me to make amends with Lucian, and that scared me; it seemed important for her to come in with me. Why? I knew there was something off about Lucian, so why would I want to bring her to him?

I moved towards the garage where Joshua's car was stored, and paused as I felt a sharp slice of pain move through me. I hadn't seen the car since the day I'd driven him to Spokane to catch his flight to Georgia and Basic Training at Fort Benning. It was the last time I ever saw Joshua.

I made my feet move, and pulled the keys from my purse. He'd left me it, his pride and joy. His baby. I'd helped him build her, and she was just another example of what made us close as brother and sister. I fanned the dust away from my face as I allowed my eyes to adjust to the dimness of the garage, which was really just a barn. Joshua had converted it into his own space, and used it to fix up his car with what he made from deliveries and working at fast food places while he was in high school.

My hands removed the car cover and came away

covered in a thin layer of dirt. I moved to the wide double doors and swung them open, letting the light inside. His baby was a beautiful candy apple red 1967 Chevrolet Camaro super sport, which somehow he'd made showroom floor ready again. He'd spent a pretty penny on the details, including a two-tone pleated interior. He'd rebuilt a mean four hundred and thirty horse power pace performing engine. It was a beauty for sure, with the voice of a V8 that purred to life through a Flowmaster exhaust system.

Joshua's best friend Bryce had kept the car in running condition, a small favor that he'd promised to do while I was gone. Cars need attention or they die, just like us. I made a mental note to drive up the border town where Bryce lived and thank him; I owed him that much. I hadn't been ready to take ownership of the car when I'd left, and he'd agreed to come every three months or so and do the maintenance.

I pushed the key into the ignition and closed my eyes at the familiar sound of the engine clicking and purring to life as it started up. "I miss you so freaking much," I whispered to Joshua, wishing for just one more moment to kiss his cheek, or hug him. All those simple things that I'd never get the chance to do, and had taken for granted when I'd had plenty of time to do them.

I revved the engine and made my way to the main road, then hit the gas, enjoying the rush that came from the power of such a big block engine. I'd gotten so lost in the drive that it was over too quickly. I pulled into the parking lot and took a look at the massive club.

Club Chaos was huge, bigger than any of the nightclubs I'd seen while I'd been in Portland and Seattle, and they had some pretty massively sized places. The outside was painted black, with a deep crimson red neon light that lined the trim and the doors. There was a bench outside the large club doors, but no one was taking up the space. My eyes moved to the sign again, Club Chaos, all sinners welcomed?

It didn't look like much from the outside, but as I moved to the doors and opened them, I was in awe. I didn't get long to look as a man with a man-bun stopped me from placing more than my foot inside the door.

"Invitation only, sweetheart," he growled as he looked me over with the bluest eyes I'd ever seen. I opened my mouth to make a comment about the bun he wore his dark blond hair in, and snapped my mouth closed. He was seriously working it, and by working it, I mean this guy made it look good. Normally I'd laugh it off; most men couldn't wear it and make it look anything but hilarious. It wasn't until he crossed his heavily tatted arms across his wide chest in an intimidating pose that I realized I was checking him out. My eyes lifted to his crystal blue eyes and an image flashed in my mind. Last night, shovel. He'd been digging the dog's grave. I hadn't gotten a very good look at him until he'd been behind me, chasing me through the woods.

"I'm here on behalf of the coven, to apologize to Lucian for my actions. Is he here?" I asked, and hoped to the Gods he wasn't.

Man-bun smiled and uncurled his arms as he stepped closer, forcing me to give ground and back up. His skin was a striking contrast to the salmon colored shirt he wore, and I wondered briefly if he was making a point, that real men did wear pink, they just didn't admit it. His smile was akin to Lucian's, wolfish with a hint of that whole *I'm-going-to-eat-you-alive-little-girl* shit.

"Boyfriend's ride?" he asked as he looked over my head, to where 'baby' sat alone in the parking lot.

My head turned and I took her in. She was a thing of beauty. "It's my brother's car, or was."

"Was? What'd you do little girl, steal it? Out for a joy ride?" he snickered.

"Actually, I own it," I mumbled and felt a small prick of guilt and pain.

"He get in trouble and you find out, use it against him as leverage or some shit?" he asked as those eyes moved back to mine.

"He died in Afghanistan," I whispered through the familiar lump that rose to my throat as I admitted he was dead.

"Shit," he muttered as he looked her over once more and then moved aside to allow me access into the club. "Boss man is in his office, interviewing people and shit. Go on up, little lady."

I moved into the club and paused, finally being able to look the place over. I'd worked in two clubs, but only until I'd gotten the job I wanted. I'd rented a hotel room, and had tried my luck in Portland while I worked at the nightclub, but the cost was a bit much considering we pooled our tips at the end of night. The first club had been smaller, and the tips pretty crappy, I'd moved on to the next one within a week and a half. The next one had more clientele, but the hours made it hard to do much of anything, let alone go to college and live in something more permanent.

Eventually I'd ended up in Pacific City. I'd been close enough to attend college classes and had landed a job at a florist while earning a degree. I'd attended evening classes at Tillamook Bay Community College, and paid for it with the wages from the floral shop and scholarships but still had a ton of debt for the degree that I still needed to finish.

Not one of those clubs I'd worked at was anything like this one. The room was larger than I would have thought it would be from outside. It had black lights that outlined the dance floor, above and below. There were other strands of lights as well as strobe and gel lights, but in the middle of the day, they were off, probably to save on the power bill. The ones at the bar were on, however, and blue and green lights pulsed beneath the glass which was mounted into the countertop of the bar. The place wasn't deserted; a few people sat at one of the larger booths and a couple sat at one of the corner booths, and I could barely make out their features as they sucked face.

My eyes drifted to a door that was labeled 'Sinners' Lounge' and my curiosity rose as I noted the huge beefy guy that stood in front of it, watching me. I ignored him as I continued to give the place a quick onceover until I found a staircase that led up to what I assumed would be Lucian's office.

I was about to step forward when a woman placed her hand on my shoulder. "You here for the interview, Sugar? Head down that hallway," she said, pointing a finger in the opposite direction from where I'd assumed his office should have been. "There's a staircase at the end of the hall; it will lead you to a set of rooms. His is the one marked 'owner.' Good luck!" she chirped as she took off towards the bar.

I followed her directions until I was in a hallway that was lined with dark windows on either side, and from where I was, I could see an entire wall of the same dark glass. My curiosity was fully piqued, but the huge door that said 'owner' on it was in the middle, so I stopped and forced myself to knock once I'd worked up the courage to face Lucian.

A woman answered the door. She was in her late twenties, early thirties. Perfect raven hair framed her face with delicate ringlets. Her face was oval, with a perfect button nose that made her look even more delicate than she probably was. Her skin was ivory, and smooth, without a single wrinkle, which made me think more in her twenties. My eyes moved to her violet eyes, and then to her perfect rosebud mouth which was smiling welcomingly.

"You must be Dana; you're late, but he is still willing to see you. Good help is hard find around this place," she said in a whimsical tone.

"Actually, I'm Magdalena, and I'm here on behalf of the coven," I corrected her. My palms were sweating and my heart hammered wildly as her demeanor changed from welcoming to venomous.

Whoa, what the hell?

"Lucian," she said his name with a tenderness that made my brow rise as she continued to glare at me. "It's a witch, want me to throw her out?" she offered.

"Let her in, and go get the others trained quickly. We need them ready for tomorrow," he said softly, with the same familiarity in which she had spoken to him.

She turned sideways to let me through and I felt something strange coming from her; hate? Jealousy? What the heck was her problem with witches? She moved back into the room, as if she intended to stay, but Lucian gave her a look that was filled with tenderness, and she returned it in spades.

"I'll leave you to handle your business, my love," she said, putting emphasize in her words.

The office was immense, with expensive furnishings I'd pinned a time or ten on Pinterest. Pinned under the board labeled *things to buy if I won the freaking lotto.* Lucian was seated behind a sizable desk, with a cool expression on his handsome features and I faltered in my confidence. I quickly got real busy taking in every piece of furniture in the room.

The office was designed in rich, dark mahogany and black leather furniture. It was pure masculinity at its finest. My eyes scanned the glass wall, which was tinted, and yet wasn't as dark as the others I'd seen. It took up an entire wall, much like the end of the hall that I'd been curiously interested in checking out. I skimmed over an old painting, and my eyes moved back to it as I took in the delicate features of the woman who had been painted.

I moved closer without even realizing I had until I was stopped right in front of it. She looked as if she could be my sister, or an immediate family member. She had the same heart shaped face and delicate features that both Kendra and I had been born with. Her hair was the same caramel blonde, with a few streaks of darker hair running through it.

I hadn't heard him move, but the moment I turned around to ask him about her, I was eye level with his chest. I looked up before thinking about it, and met his eyes.

"Why are you here?" he asked smoothly.

"I came to apologize about my actions and accusations last night," I whispered, and felt a fine bead of sweat forming at the base of my neck.

"The coven sent you here, alone?" he inquired as he took a step away from me, which eased my mind from wanting to run back to the safety of my car and burn rubber.

"I asked for my sister to join me, but she was instructed to stay out of it. She was also busy with preparations for the next event," I mumbled.

"You're not busy with them as well?" he asked as his eyes moved from me and flowed back to the picture behind me.

"I won't be attending them," I replied crisply, his eyes never leaving mine as I moved around the office, except to glance occasionally at the haunting picture that seemed to give me the chills.

"Why?" he asked as he moved away from me and turned back around to stare at me.

"I'm being punished."

His eyes flickered with interest at the word, and I moved away from him. My feet took me to the glass wall, the farthest place I could stand in the huge office away from him. My body was doing things, bad things. My nipples were as hard as pebbles, and there were butterflies playing keep-away in my stomach. There was a subtle arch in my spine, and if I wasn't mistaken, my hips had just spread in open invitation for this man.

The room below that the glass looked over was empty, for the most part. A few people were cleaning it, probably with bleach and a lot of other disinfectants. There was a raised stage that would be about knee level if I was standing in front of it. Not high enough to be used for a band, and the lack of speakers told me that it wasn't used for music at all.

There was a large wooden X, which had chains on it, but whatever was normally connected to it must have been removed for cleaning. Chairs were pulled off to one side, also being cleaned. *Weird.*

"What's that room used for?" I asked without thinking

it over. I turned to find him, once again, right freaking behind me. What the hell was he, a ninja? He made no sound whatsoever when he moved.

His smile lifted into a dangerous smirk that made me feel I'd just awoken something sinister inside of him, instead of asking a simple question. His eyes were basked in the shadows and today he wasn't wearing his suit jacket, just the white button-down shirt with the sleeves rolled up, exposing ink that had been tattooed into his skin. The brief glance I sneaked of his tats was sexy as fuck, even more so than when he had worn the entire suit. He wore slacks, and expensive Italian leather boots, which should have made more noise than they had when he walked across the expensive marble floor of the office.

"It's private," he said after a moment of me staring at him and him returning the favor. Suddenly I felt underdressed and exposed. This man's eyes were probing, intrusive. It was as if they could see beyond my skin and straight into the dark recesses of my soul.

"Private what?" I whispered breathlessly as my mind went back to last night, and replayed his mouth on mine, and other places. Moisture drenched my panties and his nostrils flared, as if he could scent the proof of my traitorous body's response to the memories.

"It's none of your business," he warned as he moved towards the desk and indicated with a nod of his head for me to follow him. "It could be where I murdered a woman last night," he replied with humor in his sensual tone.

Oh, he's got jokes! I wasn't laughing. Asshole.

Guilt washed over me and I blushed with it. I willingly followed him to his desk and watched as he leaned on it and crossed his muscular arms as he waited for me to take a seat. I wasn't sitting. It would give this man more power over me if I was seated and he was looking down. I remained standing, and placed my thumbs in the pockets of my low-fitting jeans.

It exposed more of my stomach and his eyes noted it. I smiled. I felt sexy in his presence, which I hadn't felt in a very long time. Not since I'd been cheated on. Even if I no longer felt the pain I had over Todd's betrayal, it had shaken my confidence, and removed any sense of self-worth for a time, but it was coming back. Slowly.

"Look, I'm sorry for what I did. I thought I saw a body; I had no idea it was a dog. I think the blood threw me, and I wasn't dumb enough to wait around to see what it really was. So I'm sorry that I assumed the worst of you."

He nodded but said nothing. His eyes just continued to stare at my own, as if he had some sort of x-ray vision that was allowing him to see inside my soul, to scan anything that I may have seen before I met him.

"I'm also here to serve you," I muttered and then blushed as my words played on a loop inside my head.

His brow rose and his eyes narrowed as his lips lifted into a wicked smile. "Is that so?"

"I'm to offer my services to you," I amended and blushed even more. *What the fuck was wrong with me? Of all times to make an ass out of myself, this was not it.*

"Tell me, Lena, what could you possibly do to serve me?" His eyes sparkled with a look that said he was entertaining himself at my discomfort.

"The coven wanted me to help you with any of the upcoming events you are hosting for the Awakening, however I can also help with the club, I have skills in that department," I said, and his lips tugged in the corners.

"You think I need help?" he asked as he took his seat

behind the desk and watched me closely.

"You're hiring. The girl said so when I was trying to find your office," I answered as I finally sat in the chair.

"Did she also tell you exactly what I was hiring for?" he countered effortlessly.

I felt my mouth go dry. "No," I said.

"Didn't think so, or you wouldn't be interested in asking about the job. So that leads us back to, the original question."

"Why don't we just cut the shit; what do you want me to do to make up for what I did?"

"You accused me of murder, and then hiding the body on my own property," he said as he touched the tips of his fingers together and watched me.

"Not technically. Technically I only accused you of burying a body," I said softly. My eyes were locked with his, and it wasn't hard to figure out what he wanted. I just wasn't willing to give that up because I owed some debt to him. That reward had to be earned.

"And if you were to choose to your own punishment, what it would be?" he countered.

"Three Hail Mary's, and some time on my knees..." I smiled and licked my lips seductively. "In the garden, of course, or praying for forgiveness," I finished with a voice I'd never heard come out of my mouth. Whoever's it was, it was sexy as hell.

He swallowed hard, his eyes narrowed and a muscle began ticking in his jaw. His hands lowered and he sat back as he watched me challenge him with nothing more than a look. I wasn't sure why I was flirting, but I was. *Hard.*

"What can you do that doesn't end with my dick exploring the depths of your tight throat?" he replied easily and I about swallowed my tongue.

"Pretty much anything except that?" I answered in a small voice.

"So I could bend you over this desk and fuck you? Is that a service you offer everyone you accuse of murder?" he continued.

I groaned and shook my head. "I get it, I shouldn't have gone there."

"Rightly so," he replied easily. "Tempting as it may be, I don't waste my time on those who have no experience."

"Who says I don't have experience?" Why did I ask that? Where the hell had I left my brain today?

"I ran a background check on you after you accused me of murder last night. You know, a little fill-in-the-blanks since you left the coven. Imagine my surprise when it led me to a few places in Oregon. Like Portland."

"I only accused you of burying a body," I mumbled as heat filled my cheeks.

"Turns out no one even noticed you existed there. You didn't sleep around with men as most witches do when they leave their coven, and the one time you did, you told the bartender after she asked how the guy was, that he was *fine*."

"You checked me out?" I asked in anger. *Un-freaking-believable.* He'd checked me out, and that shocked me.

"You accused me of murder, and I'm a very rich man. I check out those who accuse me of anything, and I look for a motive. I needed to know if you were on a witch hunt, to put it bluntly. I checked out every little detail of the time you've been away from home."

"You needed to know about my sex life to verify if I planned to accuse you of murder?"

"I told my people to find out everything about you,"

he replied easily as his fingers drummed on the wood desk. "Miss Fitzgerald. You told the bartender that it was *fine* when she asked about the sex you'd had outside of her bar. You were gone less than ten minutes, so I can only conclude that there was nothing *fine* about it. You wanted to know what the fuss was about. You needed to know what had driven your fiancé into someone else's bed, what could possibly be so good to ruin your picture-perfect relationship for. Only you didn't find it. You allowed some asshole who didn't even know you were a virgin to fuck you in his dirty car. He probably used that car with a hundred other women before you, ruining their expectations on being fucked as well. He didn't show you what all of the fuss was about, though. Instead you walked back into that bar, and had no further inclination about getting fucked again. You didn't even try again, because you thought sex was boring, painful, and just *fine*."

I felt my hands as they balled into fists as he sat behind his expensive desk judging what I'd done. I couldn't believe that he'd found out as much as he had in such a short time, but that he'd actually gone the lengths he had and uncovered what he did; it had been painful, and everything he was saying was true. How he had guessed I was still a virgin at that time baffled me; he must have been hoping that my face would give him the answer, or perhaps one of his people knew the art of divination. However, he had no business giving two hoots about my sexual encounters.

"You see, sex isn't just *fine*. If it's *fine*, the one who did the fucking…or both the people should be taken out and shot dead. Sex should be primal, downright fucking dirty. It should make you need it, want it. Sex with the right person makes you wonder how you've ever gone without it. It's addictive, and animalistic. Bare fucking bones, Lena, right down to the most basic needs of the human nature. He ruined your perspective on sex, and that needs to be rectified."

"And let me guess, you're willing to fix it for me? Thanks, but no thanks. What you did? It's called stalking. You had no right to dig into my life; I didn't dig into yours. I did what we've been trained to do. When we see something that we can't explain, or has to do with burying evidence, we call the coven. I didn't say you raped me, I didn't accuse of doing shit to me. I had no motive for what I did, other than I misjudged what you held in your arms. Was I wrong? Yes, and for that I am sorry. Never accuse me of having motives. You? You have nothing I want or need."

His eyes narrowed and he looked me over with an expression I couldn't figure out. His eyes moved to where my torso was exposed, and to the ink my shirt did little to hide from his eyes.

"You carry his ink," he said softly.

"Some of it, yes," I confirmed hesitantly.

"A constant reminder that sex is *fine*," he smirked. "Why didn't you try again with someone else?"

"I didn't need to," I lied. I'd been afraid to, since the first time hadn't gone so well. He was right about one thing; sex had been ruined for me. There had been a lot of blood, which had to do with the guy not bothering to get my body ready before he'd penetrated it. It hadn't just been painful, it had been horrible.

"You gave up so easily?"

"I didn't give up. I'll be trying again in a few weeks. According to the elders, my ancestors will pick out my perfect match, and I can only go up from where I was, so I'm not too worried about it. Now, if you're done prying into my disastrous sex life, I came here to offer my services which should have nothing to do with what I can offer you sexually. As you already know, it's limited. It's also none of your fucking business. To add salt to the injury, for the next week I can only go to the events of your choosing."

"If I make it my business, it is. If I offered for your body during the Harvest, what do you think they would say?" he asked as his eyes slid to where my heart was pounding painfully. "Helen is desperate for me to stay here and put more money in the coffers of the coven. What if my price was you?"

I blanched and shook my head. "According to the elders, it doesn't work that way. Even if it was the case, you are better off offering for Cassidy; she's experienced. I don't sell my soul for anything or anyone."

"Everyone has something they'd mortgage their souls for; it's only a matter of finding it and exploiting it."

"That's fucked up," I said, looking right at him, unwilling to look away while we dueled in a silent battle of wills. Being in a room with this man was like being in a cage with a wild lion; you knew that if you pissed it off, it would rip you apart, and yet I couldn't tear my eyes away.

"It's true," he said softly. "I won't keep you from many events, not unless you piss me off. Don't piss me off, Lena. You won't like me if you do so."

"You won't offer for me," I retorted, ignoring the fact that he'd just let me off the hook for the events…or most of them. "You need to conquer, draw blood. It's written in your eyes. You like the fight. You like to win. I'm not interested, nor am I on your menu, per se. And I like that perfectly fucking *fine*. Unless you or one of your people are adept at scrying, you have no idea if I liked it or not, but you want to know. You didn't go looking to see if I was after you, you went snooping into my life because you're some kind of control freak. You want the truth? I went out and I got fucked, I spread my legs for him and he accepted the challenge. It was *fine*. You don't know me, and yet you sit there judging me. Why? Why the hell do you care? Because you *kissed* me? Or because I almost got dirty with you in the grass?"

"If I'd wanted to fuck you in the grass, you'd have been fucked, and I promise you this," he said, standing up and coming around the desk before I could put distance between us. He lifted me up and held me against him, his hands grabbing my hair and my chin, forcing me to look up or break my neck. "It wouldn't have been *fine*. You wouldn't have been *fine*. You sure as fuck wouldn't have been out of your bed today. When I fuck, I own, I dominate, and I fuck without an ounce of mercy. I *claim*. When I finish with someone, they sure as fuck don't walk away saying it's *fine*."

I was trembling. The entire room was spinning out of control and my body, stupid fucking traitorous body, was on fire. I could feel the power he exuded, and being this close to him with walls around us was intoxicating. It was as if he was a freaking transformer, feeding all the lines around the city. His eyes watched mine, and I had to remember to breathe as his mouth lowered to mine, only he didn't kiss me.

"You need to get fucked," he murmured as his lips barely touched mine with each word he spoke. "You need to forget what *fine* is, and discover what earth-shattering-legs-shaking-can't-fucking-get-air-don't-fucking-need-it-to-live sex is. You're wet just thinking about it, aren't you, Lena?"

"I am not," I replied, enjoying the brief touch of my mouth against his.

"Pull down those panties, show me how wet you aren't, and I'll stop, right now. I won't bother you ever again."

"Go to hell," I whispered breathlessly as my body trembled for him to do more than just talk.

"Been there, it's not as hot as they say it is. Take your clothes off, and use me. Use me to discover what *fine* sex isn't," he rumbled.

"Not a chance," I replied, finding my brain. "If I wanted sex, I'm sure as hell not shopping for it in here. There are a lot of men just begging to be fucked in the coven, ones who won't try to own me in the process. I'm a butterfly, I fly free, asshole," I whispered and felt his lips curve into a smile as I closed my eyes.

"If you're a butterfly, then you're tripping over your god damn cocoon while trying to shed it, little girl," he said with a tone that sent a shiver up my spine.

"You're wrong," I replied shakily. "I'm just finding my wings. Spreading them wide, and getting ready to catch air. I don't need someone, *anyone*, holding me back. Now, let me go. I don't like you."

"I don't like you either," he growled.

"Good," I countered.

"Good," he said with silk in his tone. "Go find Daisy, tell her you will be working in the main bar for the next few days. Tell her the black outfit, and Lena, if you don't show up for work on time, dressed in that outfit, you'll spend the rest of the evening locked in here with me. I assure you, it won't be fun or *fine*."

CHAPTER
ten

Hours had passed since I'd left the club, and nothing seemed to get rid of the heat that his touch created in my soul. I had waited outside the cottage, expecting my mother and sister to return to the main house. Eventually, I grew restless and ended up dressed in a pair of shorts, a white tank top, boots and headed outside to take my frustrations out on the garden.

I didn't know how much time passed while I pulled weeds, removed flowering herbs, and planted new seedlings. My hands were covered in dirt, my nails ruined. I'd never felt happier than I did right now in this garden. Not in a long while.

I could feel the sting of the beginning of a burn on my shoulders, as it was blisteringly hot today. Considering it was late autumn, this could have gone either way and I regretted not putting on sunblock. I pushed on, intending to have the garden at least weeded enough that I could plant the start of new herbs for the greenhouse which would keep them protected from winter's icy fingers during the cold months that would be coming soon.

I felt eyes on me and looked up from where I'd just pulled out peppermint roots that could go from the ground straight into the greenhouse, and looked around. Sweat trickled between my breasts, so I reached up and swiped at it before pushing away the hair that clung to my face.

I couldn't see anyone around, and as I stood up to retrieve the basket of roots, I still couldn't. I looked around the garden and then gave myself a once over. I was literally covered in dirt. My knees were covered in it from where I'd knelt; my hands and arms as well. I could feel it in my hair and on my face and I didn't care.

However, it was disturbing that I could still feel the intense stare of someone watching me. I bent over and set the basket down as I made my way to where I'd forgotten the valerian roots. I heard a twig break and spun around as I made it into the next row of herbs.

Lucian stood on the edge of the garden, his dark blue eyes looking me over with something akin to horror. He was dressed in a pair of loose jeans that hung just below his hips and a white shirt that fit his body loosely, even though I could still make out the contours of each well-placed muscle.

I swallowed and scrunched up my nose as I stood, totally covered in filth. I didn't look away from him as he slowly took in my dirty knees, arms, hands and face. I wasn't sure why he was on our property; he sure the hell hadn't been invited by me.

"Do you plan on leaving any dirt in the garden?" he asked as a raven brow rose with his question.

"Oh look, he's got jokes," I mumbled as I wiped my

hands off on my shorts. "Need something, or did you just decide to come help me get dirtier?" I asked, and as his lips curled into a seductive grin; I rolled my eyes at my own words. "That's not what I meant, and you know it." Around him, what I meant, and what actually came out of my mouth were never the same things.

"I don't play in gardens," he teased as he made his way closer. "I know a lot of ways to get dirty, trust me, but rolling in the dirt isn't one I partake in."

"Of course not; rich guy like you getting his hands dirty?" I challenged. I didn't know why I kept opening my mouth, but I was about knee-deep in it.

"You think I don't know how to get dirty?" he asked, and I had a really bad feeling that he wasn't speaking about the dirt in the garden.

"No, I don't think you do. I bet you don't need to get dirty. Men like you? They have people, who have other people, who get the dirty stuff done. I on the other hand, don't mind getting on my knees and playing in the dirt."

He laughed and shook his head. He picked up my basket and moved it to the row I was about to start on. "I take it no one has told you that your mother's boutique is shut down, or that Cassidy took all the business when she opened her own store on Main Street?" he asked softly as he bent down and started pulling up a flowering stalk of valerian, releasing a whiff of cherry vanilla scent. The fragrance from the flowers was wonderful and could be used in perfumes; the roots smelled a bit like moldy socks, and was way better than Tylenol PM if you needed a good night's sleep.

"Cassidy wouldn't know the difference between valerian and peppermint, let alone how to use them for medicinal purposes," I said with more anger than I had intended to.

"Actually, she's doing pretty well. She's a good girl," he said as he lifted his eyes to mine, as if he were trying to see how I would react to his words. *Asshole.*

"You're wrong; good girls are only bad girls who don't get caught. We all have a bad girl inside, just scratching to be let out."

He laughed huskily. "Most don't admit it."

"Most are idiots," I mumbled as I knelt in the dirt beside him and started picking out the plants that weren't completely ruined. "Why are you here?" I asked.

"I saw some dirty little vixen playing in the dirt. Thought someone should have the balls to tell her she was fighting a losing battle. I know covens, and Cassidy's mother is trying to run this one. The others will all fall in line; that's also why your mother's store went ass-up."

"Ass-up," I snorted. "Hardly. One witch doesn't run a coven. It's called a coven for a reason. It takes many witches to cast spells, and a single witch is nothing without her sisters and brothers. What you're referring to is called sheep. Helen is a sheep dog, so she guides them. It's pathetic."

"And you're not a sheep?" he asked as he turned his head without pausing to check the plants he tossed into the overly full basket.

"No," I said. "I don't fall in line with the others. I tend to march to my own drum, I guess. It's probably why I have to serve you now. They say it's to set an example, but I think it has to do with how I behaved as a child."

"And what did you do as a child? Throw dirt at people?" he laughed, and I smiled.

"Hardly; I tried my first spell alone. Almost set the barn on fire. Next was when Ophelia wouldn't stop calling me a pyro, so I lit a few candles next to her, which unfortunately caught her hair on fire. How was I supposed to know she'd used half a can of hairspray on it? We were nine. Punishment was swift and severe. Cassidy and her gang were relentless, teasing me about it for years, trying to get me to step out of line so I could be punished all over again."

"You like playing with fire?" he asked, and it had nothing to do with what I'd just admitted to.

"Maybe I like the slow burn," I said as I bent over to pick a stray bulb of lavender that had seeded from a flower a few rows up. I wasn't prepared for the gentle slap on my rear, or braced for it. I ended up completely face down in the dirt.

I turned around but he moved closer, pinning me into the soft soil. "You look good in the dirt," he whispered as he lowered his lips and started kissing me.

I felt my blood ignite, but the moment he moved to deepen the kiss, the sky clapped with thunder, and rain was let loose from a storm I hadn't even noticed was coming. I squealed as he lifted his head to look up, and peals of laughter erupted from me as I took in his disgruntled frown.

His eyes came back to rest on me, where I'd remained on my back in the dirt. I closed my eyes against the rain that pelted me. I laughed harder as I struggled to get up, only to be pushed back down and kissed until my bones turned useless, and my mind turned dirty.

I was soaking wet, which had little to do with him and more to do with the rain that was coming down in buckets. He pulled away and looked in the direction of his mansion, and then to the cottage that was closer.

"Looks like you're going to have a houseguest until

the rain clears, little witch," he murmured as he stood up, pulling me with him as he moved with purpose towards the quaint cottage.

"I'm not inviting you in," I shouted over an angry crash of lightning followed by thunder that was closer than I'd originally thought. I took off towards the cottage, and didn't stop until we were both safely inside.

"You'd kick me out with the storm being what it is?" he asked and I scrunched up my nose and tilted my head considering it.

"Actually, I totally would, but only because I don't have anything that will fit you, and I don't plan to offer you a shower," I mumbled as I removed my boots. "I plan to get clean...shit!" I said as I moved to the door and swung it open as I scanned the garden for the basket.

I took off without waiting to see if he would give chase. The bulbs and seedlings wouldn't make it through the storm unless it rained enough, but I didn't plan to chance it. I made it back to the garden and slid in the mud. I landed with a hard thud, and lightning cracked across the sky and hit one of the trees close to the house. It split in half and hit the ground with a deafening sound. Another bolt hit, down closer to the garden, close enough that my hair rose in awareness as I snatched up the basket and slammed into a very solid form.

My teeth rattled, and I was temporarily woozy as strong arms carefully picked me up and moved towards the cottage.

"The basket," I cried to be heard over the raging storm.

"Stupid woman, it's only a few ruined bulbs," he growled angrily. "It's not worth your life."

"I need them," I said and held on around his solid neck as he reached down to retrieve it and moved swiftly towards the safety of the cottage.

He set me down inside and I felt my face for damage. My hands came away dirty, but luckily not covered in blood. I looked around the cottage for Luna, who seemed uninterested in my current state, or our houseguest.

"I have towels in the bathroom. I'll grab you one," I said, already moving in that direction. I opened the small towel closet and pulled out two towels as I caught sight of my reflection.

I looked like a crazy woman, covered in mud. It was in my pores, and pretty much everywhere else as well. I moved into the front room and looked him over. His shirt was brown, and clung to his body like a second skin. His jeans, which already hung low over his slender hips, were barely managing to stay up.

"Shoes off, and if you need another towel, there's a few more in the closet. There's a wood stove in the kitchen; if you start it, I'll make some tea when I get out of the shower."

"You get to shower and I get to stay dirty?" he asked with a look that said *are you kidding me?*

"I think I like you better covered in dirt," I laughed as I watched him hold his shirt out away from his skin. Pampered city boys could never handle getting their hands dirty.

"Is that so?" he countered. "You have something on your face," he murmured and held up his hand to his face. "Here," he laughed as he indicated my entire face which I'd already known was covered with smudges of dirt from pushing my hair out of my face as I worked. "Besides, you've no idea just how dirty I can be," he whispered with a sexy smile that begged for me to ask him to divulge exactly what he'd meant by it. I ignored it completely.

"Jerk," I replied as I moved into the bedroom, retrieving a pair of yoga pants and a shirt. I dug through the dresser, pulling out an old shirt of Joshua's.

I managed to find him a clean change of shorts that looked like they were from Joshua's senior year of P.E. He was a big guy, however the shorts and shirt would still be a little tight on Lucian, but that was just a bonus for me. Also the knowledge that he'd be going commando until the storm passed wasn't bad either.

I moved to the shower, fully intending to hand him the clothing, but I paused to watch him as he pet Luna. I shut the door as far as it would go, but it wouldn't fully shut because of the bad hinges. I made a mental note to stop by the hardware store in the morning and see if they had a set to replace them with.

I undressed and slipped into the shower, turning the water on and enjoying the feel of being clean again as it washed away the hours spent in the garden. Mom and Kendra hadn't made it home yet, which worried me with the ferocity of the storm that had come out of nowhere. They were in the Jeep, so luckily would be safe on a stormy road.

Seemed kind of screwed up that I just got home and they'd ditched me to go and do whatever. I felt eyes on me as the soap washed over my body, I turned in the shower finding nothing but shadows as the lights continued to flicker, until they fizzed and went out.

Great! As if this evening couldn't get any worse? I whispered a spell for the candles that were lined around the room to light. I could still feel the eyes upon me, and yet I couldn't see much past the shadows of the room.

I finished washing and exited the tub, making sure to turn the handles all the way until the water ceased to drip. I looked out the door, finding no one there, and then out the window. *Weird.* I dried off quickly and got dressed, then headed into the front room to find it empty. I continued to the kitchen where I found a very muddy man lighting the old cook stove. It wasn't fancy, but it was old and beautifully redone with love.

I'd helped my grandfather redo the rusted cast iron finish and clean it up to surprise my grandmother for her birthday the year before he'd died. I loved what it stood for: A love that even in their golden years had been full and as pure as the day they'd fallen in love with each other.

"This thing's an antique," he stated and I startled, yanking my mind back from where it had gone to.

"My grandfather fixed it up for my grandmother," I admitted. "She loved it. I love it; it's old, but it's beautiful and works just fine. Plus, it's pretty handy during a blackout."

I sat at the table, observing every sinewy muscle that worked beneath his shirt as he loaded it with wood and set fire to it. I could make out the runes that were tattooed all over his arms; they were old and no matter how much time I spent looking at them, I wasn't sure I could place what they stood for, or meant. Some looked like death runes, which was almost a forgotten practice. Others were even stranger; men with hands covering their eyes and women with hands covering their mouths, as if he had secrets he didn't want others to see or speak of.

I was lost in the wonderland that was his body when he turned and caught me ogling it. I smiled guiltily as a blush spread across my face. "I set clothes in the bathroom for you. The hot water handle sticks; you'll need to muscle it to get it on and off. I'll make some tea while you get clean."

"Thanks," he said as he pulled off his shirt before I could object. My traitorous eyes moved over his flesh hungrily. As if I was starving to death, and this man's flesh was the most delectable dish in all creation. I swallowed hard as my eyes latched on to the thin patch of hair that trailed low, into his jeans. I licked my lips and forced myself to look at anything except him.

I waited until he was out of the room before I moved into the tiny space to retrieve the teapot, and then filled it with water. I listened as the water turned on in the bathroom, and exhaled a heavy sigh of relief. I had Lucian in my cottage, and from the small kitchen window, I could see that the storm was only getting worse.

I pulled my cell phone off the kitchen counter and checked for messages and making certain that I hadn't missed any texts; I dialed my sister's number and got nothing. I pulled the phone away from my ear and looked at the *searching for service* icon.

"No service?" a deep voice rumbled behind me. I spun around to answer, but words didn't come out.

His hair was still wet from the shower, tousled to look as if he had just run his fingers through it instead of taking the time to brush it. The white towel I'd given him was wound around his hips, and that damn happy trail was back, wet, with droplets that seemed to flow down there, invitingly. My eyes gravitated to his pierced nipple and I couldn't tear them from it. It was as if they'd been superglued to the spot.

"I…I…what?" I whispered as I forced my eyes back to his in time to catch a smug look of satisfaction on his face, and the heat in his eyes that melted my bones.

The tea kettle let loose a loud whistle that made me

jump in surprise. I whispered a silent curse at my own behavior, moved to take it off, and poured the hot water into the waiting cups. With shaking hands, I scooped a bit of loose dried peppermint and lavender into two small infusers and dropped them into the mugs.

I knew he was right behind me; I didn't need to turn around to see that he'd come up behind me and was standing entirely too close. In a freaking towel…Gods, what the hell had I been thinking? *Here, go shower in my bathroom while I make us tea, and afterwards, you can bang me over the table, 'k?* Get a grip.

C'mon girl, you have brains. Use them. This guy? He's an egotistical asshole who flaunts his money around. You can't seriously like him. Women like you? They don't get men like him. You have nothing he could possibly want except *a quick fuck, and well, not going to happen.*

"Clothes didn't fit?" I asked as I put sugar in my tea and turned around, giving him a curious glance.

"I put mine in your washing machine. Should be done here pretty quickly," he said smoothly as his eyes lowered to my mouth.

"Sugar?" I asked as I danced around him and moved to the small table. This man exuded power, and worse, he ate up what little space was in the room.

"I'm about to get there," he whispered hoarsely.

"In your tea," I corrected him. My heart was beating wildly, and my pulse was probably visible to his eyes with how hard it was pounding.

I was stuck in a tiny cottage with him, in a blackout, with candlelight dancing on the walls and in his seductive eyes. The only thing that he had on was a flimsy Walmart-brand towel. One that did very little to hide that he was sporting a package that was more than ready to be delivered. I needed to move this into the front room, where at least Luna could back me up!

"Shall we take our tea to the front room?" I asked in a breathy voice which caused my eyes to go wide in surprise at the vixen's voice that had replaced my own.

A knock sounded from the front door and I all but tripped over him in my haste to get away from my own reaction to him, and his omg-he's-got-an-eight-pack-happy-trail-special-motherfucking-delivery-hell-nipple-piercing body.

CHAPTER
eleven

I stood in the doorway trying to figure out how to get Kendra's mouth closed as she ogled Lucian from the other side. He had no shame. Instead of hiding from whoever was at the door, he'd moved behind me, and was now giving my sister and mother plenty to look at it.

"Power's out," Kendra chirped as her eyes gave him a good onceover, and then another.

I knew her pain. One look just wasn't enough. Seriously. You needed to look at him, look again, visually touch it, play with it, pull on it, and maybe lick it for good luck before you got enough of it. I had a half-naked man in my cottage, and that was a serious no-no before the Awakening.

"This isn't what it looks like," I said softly as my mother's eyes flashed with disapproval.

"This wasn't what they meant by 'serve him,'

Magdalena," she fumed.

"He was in the garden with me, pulling bulbs for the greenhouse, when the storm hit. We came here because we were wet and covered in dirt. We didn't do anything inappropriate; you can ask him."

"I didn't sleep with your daughter, she's not even my type," he offered casually, which caused my stomach to hit the floor, along with my pride.

"Not your type?" I asked as I lifted a brow and looked at him.

His eyes flashed a silent warning, but I chose to ignore it. "I'm just waiting for my clothes to get clean, now that the storm seems to be passing," was his reply.

I chewed on my bottom lip and wondered why him saying that had bothered me at all. Hadn't I just told myself that men like him didn't go for girls like me? I moved away from him, allowing my mother and sister inside and out of the rain. Luna moved to my mother and rubbed her head against her ankle in hello.

Did she fail to note that while he may be half-naked, I was dressed? Okay, so I was in clothes that were easy to put on, which she'd probably mistaken for pajamas, since let's face it, yoga pants are often mistaken for them.

I moved into the kitchen again, skipping the tea and going straight for Grandma's stash of wine that was kept chilled in the little cellar drawer. I pulled out a bottle, deftly uncorked it, and chugged. It was so good, and yeah, maybe I should have used a glass, but it wasn't a delicate glass kind of day. It was an *I-need-the-entire-bottle-to-myself* day.

I listened from the kitchen as my mother spoke to Lucian, and did the last thing I expected her to do. She invited him to dinner.

"No, I insist. Besides, the coven thinks that Magdalena got off too easy and they won't leave her alone unless she makes amends to you. She was a half decent cook when she left home, I'm sure she hasn't worsened over time."

"What the hell?" I asked as I stuck my head around the corner and glared at my mother.

"It's the least you can do for him, and besides, considering how I just found you it's expected for him to at least try to court you."

"This isn't the medieval times, and besides, when did it become illegal to be a good neighbor? He was covered in dirt and mud, and there's a storm outside, in case you missed that part. I let him shower. I didn't clean him with my freaking tongue, for heaven's sake!"

"Magdalena," she warned. "Even had I not found you in a compromising situation, you'd still be making up for what you did last night."

"Fine," I said, frustrated with my mother. I gave up; besides, it wasn't like I'd had time to tell her about the slinky little black outfit he wanted me to wear, or that if I didn't follow his orders, I'd be locked in his office with him. She had no idea what an ass he really was.

"Fine," she agreed with a worried frown before she turned towards the door, and then, as if she was remembering that there was a half-naked man inside the cottage, she stopped, turned around, and moved her stubborn ass to the couch. Just what I needed: A lovely chaperone. I loved my mother, but she could seriously be stubborn.

I tilted my head and remembered what he'd said. He'd placed the dirty clothing he'd been in into the 'hello-it's-a-blackout' washing machine, which meant he hadn't planned on changing anytime soon. What else could a sexy, hello-hormones-I-see-you're-all-functioning-because-he's-in-nothing-but-a-towel man be planning to do while he waited?

Okay, so in my head it was playing out in brutal and graphic Technicolor what we *could* be doing. I shook my head, dispelling the visceral images.

I chanced a peek over in his general direction and ended up staring right into his inky depths. His eyes said, *"Fix it. Get rid of them."*

My eyes smiled and said, *"You fucking fix it,"* and then they said, *"Tell me, exactly how long do you think the washing machine has left? Considering there's no power to run it, I'm guessing you figured it would give you just enough time to seduce me and then head home strutting like a peacock?"* I crossed my arms over my chest and shook my head, but mostly at my own stupidity for not realizing it earlier.

He smiled and I felt a violent shiver that I had to forcefully stop myself from exposing to him. His eyes seemed to reply, *"I don't strut. I conquer, I ruin, I claim. Violently. But I do not strut. I claim ownership, little girl."*

"I can't be owned," I blurted, no longer willing to have a silent battle with someone who obviously had the upper hand. For now.

"Never said you could be," he said softly and bowed his head before he turned and left the cottage...in a towel. I was jealous of that towel, so freaking jealous. I'd burn that bitch when it came back.

I moved to the window, unable to help it. Kendra joined me, and our heads tilted at the exact same time. A groan left our lips, at exactly the same time. We sighed like little school girls and then laughed at our reaction.

"Magdalena, do I need to explain to you how important

is to remain chaste during this time?" my mom said, pulling my eyes away from the ripped back, and sinewy muscles that was walking away.

"No, I know the rules. I've done what was asked, but I don't understand why you expect me to cook for that man," I replied hastily. I didn't. Not at all.

"Because this family needs his support as much as this town does. He's offered to take the store off our hands, which would give us enough money to get by while I figure out another way to bring in a steady income."

"You're not selling that store," I argued. "Why did you close it? Cassidy doesn't know anything about tonics, let alone spells. I'm surprised she hasn't done some serious harm to people!"

"Your father took the recipes," she replied softly. "I didn't have the energy to fight with him to get them back, or deal with it at the time. I did what I had to do to survive, Magdalena. Just as you did, but now that you're back, we will figure something out together."

Gut…kicked. I was an asshole.

"We can salvage the store, though; we don't need the old recipes, and we don't even have to make spells. Those shouldn't be for sale anyway; most of the other covens don't charge for them, according to Google. I took botany, learned how to make fragrances, soaps, shampoos, and so much more. I can make tea that does what most of the relaxation spells do, and those were the biggest sellers in the shop. Remember? Tasted like frog's ass, and everyone hated the taste, but they still bought it," I babbled with a nervous laugh.

"I've already started the paperwork," my mom replied her eyes full of tears.

"So rip it up," I said vehemently. "He'll understand."

"He's a businessman, Magdalena. Not a saint. I already accepted the first payment so I would be able to host the opening celebration."

"Then I'll get it back, somehow," I assured her.

My mom shook her head, but she knew it was pointless to argue when I got my mind fixed on something. She, like my grandmother, knew when to just nod and smile and entertain my crazy ideas.

"About dinner, I do hope you haven't given up on cooking since you've been gone?" Kendra injected into the conversation.

"I didn't starve to death while I was away, did I?" Insert 'smartass' here.

"Top Ramen and cups of noodles don't count," she said with a soft smile.

"I remember how to cook, but I'm sure he's used to a lot better than what I can cook in this kitchen."

"You'll use the kitchen in the main house; it's heavily warded," Mom said as she stood and stifled a yawn.

"Is there something I should know?" I asked with a worried frown.

"We've had a few girls go missing in the last week. We don't know if it is just pre-Awakening jitters, or if something else is going on. We're playing it safe, sticking close to the coven. There's been chatter from other covens about suspicious things happening, and problems for the Guild witches as well. Until we have concrete evidence that those girls left of their own free will, we'll continue to play it safe."

I blinked at my mom and started to speak, but shut my mouth and shook my head. Who had gone missing? How had no one even mentioned it to me? The message from the coven I'd gotten before I'd left for home had been short and straight to the point.

"I was so worried, I wanted to come for you myself, Magdalena. The elders warned you of the problems arising with the Awakening coming, I'm sure," she stated with absolute certainty.

"No, they didn't. It was just a basic message. Nothing else. No warning of any trouble," I replied with in a calm tone, which surprised me because I wasn't feeling calm at all.

"It's not something we want to broadcast," Kendra said reassuringly as she laid her hand on my shoulder, feeling my inner turmoil.

Being twins had hidden benefits; feelings, understanding of how or why the other did certain things, and our own secret little code. Unlike others, I could feel my sister. As if a piece of her lived inside of me and vice versa. Mom said it was because we were identical, and closer than most of the twins of the human world. I'd missed feeling her and knowing she was close if I needed her. She was the only one I didn't have to explain things to, because she felt them with me.

"Witches don't leave home, not this close to the Awakening," I said.

"*You* did," my mother spoke calmly, her tone carrying an underlying bitterness that she did little to hide. She'd seemed okay with me leaving, but maybe I'd only assumed it. Maybe I'd only heard what I had wanted to from her before I left.

"I didn't leave right before the Awakening. I was wrong to leave, but none of the colleges here offered what I needed to take and now it looks like maybe leaving wasn't such a bad thing. I plan to save the shop, even if I have to flirt with the devil himself to get it back."

CHAPTER
twelve

I walked into Club Chaos just before 5 P.M. It wasn't full, but it was still early and I knew it would be packed soon enough. The music was loud, something I didn't really miss from my last job at a nightclub. Don't get me wrong, I loved music, and I loved it loud, but there was only so much a person could handle while trying to take orders. I'd made a list last night, one that had been as long as my arm, with things I needed to get done. Most were important things, none of which included playing servant to Lucian.

I'd gone to his house last night, right after the power had come back on and I'd finished washing his clothes. My mother's nagging about making sure he came to dinner spurred me out the door and on the path to his home. However, I really intended to ask him about the store. I knocked, which had taken me a bit to actually get the courage to do, and heard the echo of my knocks reverberate in the entryway.

I stood there, feeling silly as a woman's silky voice asked Lucian if she should get the door. I could hear their voices coming from inside and off to the left, probably a sitting room, as he urged her to, "just ignore it, and she'll go away." Me, I was the one who he wanted to go away. Talk about the king of mixed signals.

I'd made it halfway home, my mind in an angry haze, before I'd realized I'd still been holding his clothes. The clothes which I had taken the time to wash for him. Freaking jerk. I spun around, walked back to his porch, and dropped them in the mud.

Asshole.

Now I had to face him, and my anger had cooled, but my pride hadn't.

My eyes moved to the bar, where quite a few people were ordering drinks while others searched for a place to sit. I saw a few familiar faces, but none that were from the coven, just a few of the locals, mixed in with unfamiliar faces from out of town.

I started towards the bar, and was stopped before I'd even made it a full three steps into the club. The guy who stopped me was huge; he had blue-black hair and blue eyes the color of the sky after a good rain. His arms were ripped, and tattoos seemed to grace every visible part of his body. He was tall, reaching at least six feet in height. His jaw was wide, with a six o'clock shadow that he wore well, and full lips that were drawn into a sexy smirk.

"Boss wants to see you in his office," he announced. "You didn't listen to him the other night when he told you what to wear. You should've listened, little lady. He doesn't take too kindly to people not listening."

"I bet he's used to everyone listening to him, and being

the one in control?" I asked with a smirk of my own.

"Always. He's always in control, and most people don't disobey him. He's quick to punish the ones who don't listen. Disobeying the boss? It's like playing with fire, Miss Fitz."

"It's Fitzgerald," I corrected him.

"Whatever, Fitz," he replied smoothly without bothering to use the correction I'd offered up.

I smiled and bit my bottom lip as I narrowed my eyes on him. He wasn't the guy who was normally stationed at the door. Man-bun hadn't been outside tonight. I crossed my arms over my chest and gave him an even wider smile.

"I'm not his employee, so he can get over it. He'll also never be *my* boss, so his orders? Don't really get followed by me. I'm not planning to stick around any longer than I have to; it's a punishment. What's he going to do, spank me?" I offered as I lifted an eyebrow and waited.

"Maybe; you look like you could use one," he said as his tongue came out to lick his lips as his eyes trailed down my frame.

I moved past him, heading to the rear of the club and towards the stairs that led up to Lucian's office. The music was sensual, and a few people were already on the dance floor, swaying to the beat. My eyes moved over the room as I moved through it, and then wandered further up until I spotted Lucian, watching me from the other side of the wall-to-wall window in his office that was no longer one-way glass.

I almost stopped, almost. I sure as hell wasn't about to let him see that he had any effect on me. Not after last night's debacle. He was stunning in a charcoal gray suit, with a light blue tie, and I was willing to bet the suit was just as, if not more expensive than the one he'd worn to the opening celebration.

If nothing else, the man had damn good taste in clothes.

I tore my eyes from his and continued through the hall, up the stairs and down another hall as I made my way to him. As I stopped in front of his door, I collected my scattered thoughts and took a deep, calming breath.

I needed what confidence I could get. I'd felt out of place since returning home, but today I'd spent my time on myself. Getting back to where I was comfortable in my own skin. Coming back, everything I'd learned since I'd arrived had hit me harder than I'd initially realized. I didn't have time to be weak; I wasn't that girl anymore.

I knocked on the door and opened it without waiting for him to answer. I moved into the room, and quickly regretted it as I found him at his desk, leaning against it, waiting for me. There was a woman in the room; her hair was as black as a raven's wing, and she had a beautiful pixie face. Startling eyes the color of freshly grown moss in the forest looked at me, and then just as quickly looked away. I felt dismissed, and it rubbed.

She moved towards Lucian, her hand running up his chest as his eyes remained locked on me.

"Leave us," he ordered and she pouted.

"I waited for you to return," she said softly as she continued to stroke his chest with her perfectly manicured, dainty hands.

"Get out," he said harshly, his eyes finally leaving mine and looking down at her.

She was gorgeous. Her hair was held away from her face with hair pins that sparkled with jewels. Her dress was expensive, and clung to her body like a second skin. Her breasts were large, probably fake since they seemed larger than was safe for her tiny frame. Her full mouth slanted into a frown as her eyes moved from him to me. The look she gave me could have chilled the sun. What was it with these women hanging out in Lucian's office? He seemed to have an endless supply of beautiful women at his disposal.

She gave him one more look of desperation as I watched, and then stomped angrily from the room. I waited for the door to slam, but it didn't. She'd left it open, and the fact hadn't gone unnoticed by Lucian.

His eyes slid over my body slowly, heating each inch as they moved over it. I didn't move, didn't respond. I held it together, and pretended not to be battling a violent storm inside of me. I replayed his words from the other side of his door last night. Anger is an emotion to be used, not wielded. You have to control it. If not, you make the news as some deranged lunatic. I'm not deranged; the jury is still out on the lunatic part, however.

I looked good, and I knew it. I was dressed in a navy blue eyelet dress with a deep V-neck, showing just enough cleavage to draw the eye, without looking desperate. The skirt just barely reached mid-thigh. I'd paired it with soft black suede boots that stopped just above my knee, and had four-inch heels. Not the best shoes for waiting tables, but they were sexy. I felt sexy, and that's what counted.

I'd taken time with my jewelry, things I'd made myself. A black crystal pendant that hung from a sterling silver chain and had runes etched into the surface for protection. Matching earrings dangled from my ears, along with my quartz charm bracelet.

My hair was up in a bouffant bun, which kept it chic, and out of my face since it tended to heat up in a nightclub whether you were dancing or working. My make-up was light, because sweating it out while busting my ass was never a good thing. Light mascara, soft cheek blush with a soft colored lip gloss that stained my lips a soft mauve color. I didn't look sleek, push-me-into-bed-sexy, but I looked good.

His eyes spoke volumes. I didn't bother trying to read what they actually said, but he gave me a half hooded look that said I'd look better naked, and I gave him one that said I knew it, I just didn't care to flaunt it or do so with him.

"You disobeyed me, Lena; that's not the uniform you were given," he said as I ignored whatever he was saying in those eyes.

"No, it's not. Sorry, but what they gave me? It didn't cover enough."

He laughed, and his eyes softened. "I did give you instructions. In the future, I expect them to be followed to the very last detail. Tonight it's going to be busy, or you'd be staying here with me for the punishment I promised you."

"In the future, I don't plan to work for you. So following orders won't be an issue," I said as I remained just inside the door. I had an exit route planned, just in case.

He smiled, and it wasn't friendly. I narrowed my eyes at him, as if I could read his mind through his inky eyes. I was about to ask what was expected of me tonight, when a man walked in and bumped right into me.

I didn't expect it, and I was shoved forward in his haste, and almost landed face-first on the floor, but instead landed in Lucian's arms. I hadn't even seen him move, and yet my face was pressed against his chest, and his arms were around me. I felt off-balance being this close to him, and my nose was greedily inhaling his masculine scent.

"Shit, didn't see her, boss," a deep, rich voice said from behind us.

I pushed away from Lucian, which didn't go unnoticed as I placed my hands against his chest to manage it gracefully. Electricity rushed through me from the innocent touch, and my eyes lifted to his before I remembered I wanted distance from him; a small gasp left my lips unchecked. Like, a football field between us would be good. His arms dropped as he watched me move across the room.

His eyes never left me as I added a few steps more, and then another for my own safety. I'd heard his inhale, and had known that he, too, had been sniffing me. The only perfume I wore was the plumeria soap I'd made a few weeks back.

"Am I interrupting?" the guy asked.

"No," I said.

"Yes," Lucian snapped.

"Sorry," the guy muttered as I moved my eyes to his. He was decent-looking, with a jagged scar that ran across his face. It would probably make most people look away, but it didn't have that effect on me. His eyes were giving me a onceover, and I knew instinctively that he was waiting for me to cringe, or look away from the scar, as probably most others had done. Instead I took him in.

He had light blonde hair, and his skin was golden. His eyes were a soft shade of chocolate brown, with scattered golden specks. His mouth was full, and scarred, and yet the scar did little to take away from how handsome he really was. He wore a white dress shirt, with the sleeves rolled up, exposing yet more scars that covered his arms in crisscross patterns, as if someone had used a whip on him at some point in his life. His hands were calloused from work, and his muscles that were exposed from the loosened buttons of his shirt showed enough flesh that I could see his chest had somehow been spared of whatever fate his arms and face had encountered.

I raised my eyes back to his face and he smiled, probably because I hadn't looked the least bit repulsed. Jimmy Kendell was from the reservation just on the outskirts of town and a friend of mine from school. He'd been splattered with hot grease and bore the scars of it for many years. Cassidy and her friends, who we'd called the bitch squad, had called him crispy, and other horrifying names, but I didn't think they detracted too much from his beautiful reddish brown skin and we found equally annoying ways to retaliate against the bitch squad's attacks.

"Need something, Bane?" Lucian asked.

"Bartender didn't show up, but there's a guy down there who says he knows how to mix the drinks. Owns a club in Spokane, and he's available now," Bane said as he finally tore his eyes from mine.

"Tell him he's hired for the night. Tell him the rules of the club, and take Magdalena with you. Let Linda know Lena will be helping with whatever she needs tonight," Lucian said as his eyes turned to me and I looked away. "Lena's not to go into the other levels to serve, though, make sure Linda knows that."

I kept my eyes downcast, looking at anything except Lucian. He walked past us, and Bane smiled at me. *Other levels?* My curiosity was piqued.

"We've been dismissed," he prompted with a smile that made me smile as well. "He does that often, little lady. Follow me; I'll take you down to Linda and get the new bartender set up. Make sure he knows the drinks before we give him control of the bar."

I followed the wide shoulders of Bane down the stairs and back into the club. Linda was a tiny woman, maybe a little over five feet, with fire engine red hair, and flashing blue eyes that held a smile that matched the one on her delicate lips. She had a pixie cut, with a heart shaped face, and a voice that carried over the music.

"Hey, this is Magdalena, she's all yours tonight. Treat her good, Linda," Bane shouted over the music and gave me a wink before he turned to head to the bar.

"It's going to get crazy in here tonight, please tell me you've at least you've worked in a bar before?" Linda looked over my dress and then gave me a dubious look. "I was sure you'd gotten the club uniform?"

"I did, but I don't plan to work here a moment longer than I need to. No offense, but it's a little short, and shows just a little too much...everything," I said grudgingly.

She smiled and threw back her head with a full belly laugh. "Told him we needed to fix that damn uniform. Men, they don't listen worth a shit, right? So the boss told me that this is a punishment for you, but for me it's a blessing. We fired three girls in the last week. So I'm really hoping you have an idea of what's needed?"

"I've done this before, mind you not in a club this size. Not sure if you wanted more from me?"

"Nope, getting orders in and out is what I need. It's Friday, we only serve one special, and a few types of appetizers. People don't come here for the food, though, they come here to let loose, which can be an issue. Men get grabby, but Lucian and his boys don't allow anyone to get carried away and they're pretty good at keeping the riffraff out. Any questions?" she asked as she gave me a dazzling smile that reached her eyes.

"What's tonight's special?' I asked as I accepted an apron and quickly tied it on before accepting a notepad for orders and a round drink tray.

"It's called Sex in the Driveway; white rum, pear schnapps, and blue curacao. You should get the guy at the bar to make you one so that you can taste it. Do not drink it all, you don't look like you could hold your liquor well, skinny thing that you are," she smirked. "The slim girls usually can't," she mumbled with a wink. "I need you sober, and on your toes tonight."

"Got it," I said as I moved to do as she had instructed. Normally you needed to taste something before you could sell it well, that much I knew from the other jobs. It was hard to sell something you couldn't explain.

I stopped at the bar and drummed my fingers impatiently on the cool surface as I watched Bane go over the menu with the bartender. He had a nice ass, from what I could see. Long hair, a little shorter than Lucian's, and from the back it looked good. A guilty flush stole over my cheeks as he turned and wrecked me with silver eyes that made my mouth open and close. He had dark hair, and wore a tee that said *I bite.*

I swallowed the nervous laughter that tried to escape as he made his way to where I stood.

"Need help?" he asked as his silver gaze slid over me and came back to mine with banked heat in the melted platinum beauty. "Or you plan on just staring a bit longer? I don't mind it, take your time."

"I'm sorry," I stammered quickly. "I'm being rude," I explained. "I need Sex in the Driveway."

"I'm more than willing to help you out with that," he

teased with laughter in his sexy eyes. "Please don't say it's the drink, and that you really want me."

I laughed, and shook my head. What the hell was wrong with me? I hadn't seen this many hot guys in one place in like…Ever. Now, I couldn't even freaking talk. I was all schoolgirl giggles.

"The special, so I can sell it tonight," I said and watched as his hand moved to his heart and he emphatically shook his head.

"Say it isn't so," he grumbled good-naturedly as he winked and started pulling out liquor bottles. Bane watched him and gave me a curious look before turning to look up at where Lucian watched us all with a scowl on his face. "Why is it the pretty ones are always taken?" the bartender asked as his eyes moved between Bane, myself, and Lucian.

"I'm not with him," I said hurriedly.

"I just had the strangest case of déjà vu," he replied softly with a cocky grin lifting his full lips.

He pushed the drink over to me after slipping the straws in and I pushed them aside as I took a small sip, and then pushed it back towards him. Bane grabbed it and tossed the straws out while he held the bartender's gaze.

"Vlad, Lucian will want to see you after the club closes for the night. Not sure why you're here, but I'm pretty sure it's not because you thought you'd be welcome," Bane said with a chilling look. I looked at Bane, then Lucian, and back to where Vlad stood, wondering what the strange turn in Bane's demeanor was. One minute he'd been thrilled with the help, and the next he turned cold against the guy. Bane looked like he was considering tossing the guy out on his ass, even though it was apparent they needed his help behind the bar.

"Vlad? Did your parents not like you?" I asked, as I smiled and scrunched up my nose.

"It's an old name, kinda like yours, Magdalena," Vlad replied as he moved back to where the bottles were positioned lining the wall, and started making himself acquainted with them. "Names meant something once upon a time, passed through families like jewels with pride."

"Mine was passed down," I mumbled; it *was* an old name. So old you rarely came across it these days.

I saw a group seating themselves at one of the many tables and moved over to take their drink order. It was Dexter and Kat and I groaned as they turned and watched me move in their direction.

Okay, so it was a little embarrassing to be taking orders when I should have been included with the ones who were drinking. I knew it was supposed to be, so I let the emotions flow through me and pushed them down as I smiled.

"What can I get for you guys?" I asked.

They looked uncomfortable but eventually they ordered.

"Hey," Kat said as I turned to head to the bar to fill the orders. "Can I talk to you, maybe later tonight?"

"For?" I asked, wanting to know why she wanted to talk since she hadn't returned any of my calls.

"Look, I know we've been dodging you since you got back, and we want to make it up to you," she said softly as she frowned, as if she thought I'd tell her where to stick it.

Maybe I should have, but it wasn't me. I wasn't that kind of person and I hadn't taken it personally, but I did deserve an explanation. I told her as much and headed back to the bar to get the drinks, feeling a little light on my feet as I did so. It almost felt normal to be back serving cocktails.

Lucian was at the bar, his back to it, with a hooded look as he watched me make my way to him. He leveled those midnight eyes on me and my lady parts took notice, even though I urged them to behave. This guy wasn't for me, never would be.

Grandpa used simple logic when it came to dating. If the branch was too high, you didn't jump for it. Either it bent, or you were stuck jumping in the air looking like an idiot while you tried to reach it. Lucian was that branch, and I wasn't about to start jumping.

"Pick up the pace," he barked when I stopped in front of him and I turned my own heated gaze in his direction.

"I'm doing fine," I replied flippantly.

"You took ten minutes to take an order."

"And you came down from your lofty observation post to tell me that?" I asked as I handed the order off to Vlad without missing his smirk.

Lucian's eyes moved over me, and I shivered from the heat banked in their inky depths. I looked right at him and smiled. "You could have just shouted it down; you do own the place."

"I don't shout, Lena."

"Maybe you should. Let go, live a little," I suggested with a soft smile, which only seemed to piss him off more. Something was up his ass, and it bothered me.

I was about to comment on it when I felt Kendra, and my eyes moved to the crowd that was entering the club. Kendra was with her friends, and I had to remind myself that I'd been gone a while.

She was graceful, unlike me. Her smile was second nature, where I had to remind myself to do it, and often.

My sister exuded confidence; where I had it, she owned it. She controlled it and made it work for her, which drew men to her. Her hair was pulled back, sleek, not a single hair out of place; unlike my quick updo, she'd spent time taming hers. Her make-up was done perfectly, her skin soft and smooth without blemishes.

There'd been no standing in front of the mirror for five minutes and slipping on just a little to highlight her features; she'd used make-up that made her eyes pop, and her lips matched the crimson dress that fit her like a second skin. It hugged her curves, defining them to every lustful eye that watched as she moved into the club.

I turned to find Lucian studying me as I'd studied her. Unlike the others in the club, his eyes had remained on me. I smiled and looked over his shoulder to where Vlad had my drinks ready to go. I reached over the bar and grabbed the tray when the lights went out, and neon lights flooded the place.

A hand curled around my arm and I turned and looked at Lucian, who continued to watch me, until a brighter light started up the wall, highlighting the runes that covered the clubs high ceiling. Lucian's hand slipped and then he was moving away from me.

I swallowed a smidge of regret at the loss as I watched him move in the direction of those who had just come in, including my sister. His men followed him as well. I blinked at the way they moved, as if time and space held no meaning. My eyes strained to follow them, and couldn't.

They disappeared right before they reached my sister and her friends. I was so busy blinking, waiting for my eyes to adjust, or do something, that I jumped when Vlad fingers gently tried to shut my mouth which was obviously hanging open.

"Did you *see* that?" I asked in a hushed whisper of shock, mixed with what the hell was in that drink he gave me? Acid? I looked at him accusingly.

"See what?" he asked as he watched me closely.

"Lucian just disappeared, like vanished. Poof, he's gone. Not there anymore…"

"He's right there," he nodded to the left, and I turned my head and he was. Right in the spot he'd been in before, leaning all sexy as fuck against the bar.

"What the hell was in that drink you gave me?" I whispered as my heart raced.

"Nothing," he said as his eyes moved to Lucian's, and then back at me.

I grabbed the tray and moved through the growing crowd, placing distance between myself and Lucian. I know what I'd just seen; all of his men just moved in an impossible way, which I'd just witnessed. Or I was pretty sure I had.

I made it to the table where Kat and Dexter were sitting, and placed the drinks on the table. Something was off; I could feel it. The moment I saw Lucian move as he did, something inside of me poked its head out and screamed danger. As witches, we're told to listen to that little voice inside, the one most people so stupidly ignored.

I couldn't hear a word Kat or Dexter said to me as my eyes continued to watch Lucian. As if he would move again, and I'd catch him. His eyes consumed, commanded, and made normally bright girls turn into idiots. Point in case, me.

I moved to another table, so busy staring at Lucian that I bumped into Cassidy and the bitch squad from high school without meaning to.

"Bitch," Cassidy snapped as her drink spilled in her lap.

My eyes went wide and I set the tray down as I reached for cocktail napkins to clean her silk dress. "I'm sorry," I said absently.

"You did it on purpose!" she screamed and picked up Natalie's drink, and splashed in in my face. I wiped the fruity drink from my face and glared at her.

"I didn't do it on purpose. I said I'm sorry. Can I get you another, or do you plan to throw that in my face too?" I growled.

"Why don't you just leave town? Nobody wants you or your loser ass family here anyway," she purred, venom dripping from every word. "Just run away like you always do, bitch."

"We were here first, Cassidy. I belong here. You want to move? No one is stopping you," I retorted.

"You think you're so special, Magdalena, but you're not. You'll see," she continued.

"You really need some new lines, Cassidy. You've used them all before."

"You think you can just come back here and take whatever you want; you can't. My mother will see to it that you're given exactly who you deserve," she snapped.

"Who *I* deserve? Tell me, Cass, how can your mother manage that one? Money isn't supposed to hold sway with the elders, let alone the ancestors. She can't decide my fate either; she's not that high up on the council. No one but the ancestors can decide who we end up with anyway; not you, not me."

"I've already proved I have the power to take from you," she seethed.

"Because you took Todd?" I asked pointedly, my heart

thudding in my chest as anger seethed from my pores. "You probably saved me from making a huge mistake. Hate to say it, Cass, but I actually need to thank you for that one."

"And our dad?" she smiled icily.

I paused, and blinked. Holy fucking shit balls. *She* was *my sister*…Oh hell no. Not accepting it. I took a deep breath and filed that one in the folder in my brain and labeled it 'Oh to the fucking hell no she isn't,' and glared.

"He made a choice," I snapped, hating that she was burrowing under my skin to piss me off.

"Yes, he chose us," she smiled.

"He chose money," I replied easily. "That's not a win, and I know how you love to keep tally of who wins between us. Grow up, get a fucking life, Cassidy, and leave me alone. High school is over; we're adults now."

I moved from the table before she could dig deeper, and pushed past Lucian who I hadn't even realized had been behind me. I needed distance between myself and that vindictive bitch before I ended up doing something stupid. I felt my sister before I saw her, knowing she was sensing my emotions through the bond, and heading to the bar to intercept me.

"Shit, double my pleasure, there's two of you beauties," Vlad laughed.

"Kendra," I said as my sister joined us.

"What the hell just pissed you off?" she asked with a frown.

"I'm fine," I sighed as I looked her over. "You look stunning tonight."

"Shut it, and spill. I felt it, the overwhelming urge to club a baby seal? I almost slapped Todd it was so strong. Something or someone pissed you off."

"Cassidy was just explaining how I should get lost," I mumbled and handed the next order to Vlad, who looked a little too interested in the conversation.

"Don't listen to her, she's just bitter," Kendra said softly as she placed her hand on my cheek.

"She was just being her peachy self and tallying up her wins, ya know, being the sweet Cassidy we all love," I growled and frowned at the sound of it.

Okay, I was more pissed off about what she'd said than I realized. The fact that she thought she was better than us was surprising too. Still, after all this time and knowing she wasn't part of the original coven, she and her mother fought tooth and nail to take it over because they thought they were above us.

"She's just jealous, you know that," she replied with a worried frown. "She's trying to get a rise out of you. Don't let her win, Lena."

"That's the problem, Kendra. It's not a freaking game anymore. It's like she's still in high school."

"Cassidy never left high school. She's still the self-absorbed pretty little rich girl she's always been. You have what she can't buy, though, and that feeds her anger and jealousy."

"I know that, but if you haven't noticed, her mother is firmly planted in the elders' circle. Since when does an outsider dish out punishments? Her mother's been doing it since I was in high school. She may not have the bloodline, but she has power," I mumbled.

"She must have bought a seat on the council; our mother earned hers," she retorted with a wicked smile.

Lucian was at the end of the bar, watching me. Kat and Dexter moved in behind us. I gave them a small smile and looked around the club, which had filled up. The music was pumping out of the speakers, seductive and alluring with the slow tempo of the song that played.

I knew I should be taking more drink orders, but I needed a moment. If it was even possible after my encounter with Cassidy, I needed to find my inner Zen place. I blamed her mother's money. It had probably ruined any chance of her being remotely human.

"Hey, this needs to go out to that table," Vlad said, briefly motioning to a table before handing me a tray with a few drinks on it. I smiled politely and accepted the drink tray, turned around, and the music stopped. I moved forward a few steps, and stopped cold as a familiar voice sounded from the stage.

"This one is dedicated to my *sisters*," Joshua's voice said, and I felt my stomach drop. The tray smashed to the floor, and all blood left my face.

"*No*," I whispered horrified by the familiar voice.

"Joshua!" Kendra screamed and the entire club went silent as the witches around us paused, and finally caught on to what had just happened.

"No, Kendra," I warned as I swung around, dodging glass to get to her. I pushed her back as she moved forward. "He's dead; Joshua is buried. That…whatever that is, isn't our brother." There wasn't any way that could be Joshua. "I need you to keep her here," I pleaded to Dexter and Kat, and watched for anyone heading away from the stage through the large crowd.

She fought against the emotions; her overwhelming urge to run to Joshua pushed through me. I moved through the crowd.

I paused as he turned to look at me. A perfect replica of my dead brother. Tears blinded me, but I knew better. I'd buried my brother. He started moving through the crowd towards the doors, and I ran to block his exit.

"What are you?" I screamed when I got close enough to the imposter.

"Lena," he greeted genially, his ice blue eyes narrowing on me. "Don't you know your own brother when you see him?"

"I buried my brother," I growled. Magic? It could be, but glamouring an image was beyond anything we could do. "You're not my brother," I continued, keeping it talking while I moved closer.

"He said you'd be a hard one to convince," he chided with a half-cocked smile. I fucking loved that smile. My brother did it often while he'd taught me how to work on his car. "And here I thought you'd be the easy one. What, with how much time you two spent together."

Tactics. He was using things I loved about my brother against me. I swallowed as I got closer to him. "You're not my brother."

I wanted him to admit it.

Needed whatever it was to show itself.

Its *true* self.

I went down, swiped out my booted foot in a roundhouse kick. Caught off guard, he went down to the floor. The entire room was watching us.

"My brother taught me that; if you were him, you'd have been ready for it."

He jumped up fluidly; his eyes narrowed as he watched me closely. "Nice move," he growled as he reached into his pocket and produced a knife. He flipped the blade open and held his arms wide. "I know a few too, sis," he taunted with the same smile.

"I'm not your sister." I turned sideways as he sliced through the air. I repeated it, dodging his moves. I didn't have a weapon, which wasn't a good thing. Not that I would know what the hell to do with one anyway.

I kicked his arm, not caring that I was showing the entire club that I was wearing thigh-highs with a sexy little garter. The knife went sailing through the air and the guy jumped at me. I turned just in time for him to bear hug me from behind. Stupid. I couldn't elbow him, so I started to drop my weight, forcing him to loosen the hold he had on me; it gave me enough room to maneuver my arm around the back of his neck. I bent over, pulling his neck with me and using my balance to flip him over my back. The move caught him off guard, easily flipping him over until he landed on the floor in front of me. A defensive move Joshua had also taught me.

"He taught me that too," I growled as I moved to kick him, only for him to vanish before my foot could make contact. "Where did he go?" I demanded of the onlookers around me. Many of those were from our coven, and they'd just watched me fighting my dead brother.

"You made him leave!" Kendra sobbed as she folded herself into Dexter's arms. I felt each sob, knew the pain of the loss she felt. "I wish you'd never come back! He was here, and you made him leave!"

Gut, punch, fuck. That one hurt.

I moved to the doors slowly, and opened them; the moment I did, something erupted in the parking lot. I watched it, as if in slow motion. I was frozen, unable to do anything other than watch as it exploded.

One minute I was in the doorway, watching shrapnel fly towards me, and the next I was on the floor, with Lucian covering me as I heard metal and other things hit the side of the building, as well as a few people inside the club.

"Lena, breathe," Lucian whispered against my ear.

I didn't want to. I wanted Joshua back; I wanted to be with him. Kendra would be fine without me. I knew she hadn't meant it; I'd felt it. Still hurt. Still felt like something was embedded in my chest.

"Dammit, girl, breathe!" Lucian hissed and I gasped for air.

CHAPTER
thirteen

An hour later, we were sequestered inside Club Chaos. I didn't know what to think, or how to feel. That thing had looked exactly like my brother. Its voice was an exact match to his as well. Kat held Kendra's sobbing form wrapped in her arms and Dexter gently rubbed her back in a comforting motion.

I was numb and unfeeling, mostly because I didn't know what to feel. Those from our coven had been escorted by Lucian's employees to a secure room, and, luckily, there was a small bar towards the back of the room. The other patrons and employees who didn't belong to the coven had been sent to another room, which we hadn't even known was there until a door opened up in the wall, and people were herded into it.

My mind was racing; a bomb had gone off. Lucian had somehow saved me from the blast, and was being worked on less than a foot away from me. I had a few cuts and abrasions from the blast; however, Lucian had taken the worst of it. His back had small pieces of metal that had cut through his shirt and embedded in his skin. He'd gotten injured protecting me.

I didn't have time to respond; I'd thought I was dead. Lucian had somehow shielded me with his massive body and saved my life. How had he moved so quickly? It seemed impossible, unless he'd been closer than I thought while I'd been fighting against that thing.

I was calling him a thing; that thing that looked so much like my brother. He'd even smelled like my Joshua. I hadn't said a word since, because I knew if I did, I'd fall apart. I was keeping it together. Barely. It could have been a Bogey, or a Boggart, but why one of them would be here, impersonating my brother at this particular time was a mystery. A Fae could easily glamour on a Joshua suit, but again, why?

It had known enough about Joshua to dress and smell like he had. His blue eyes had even sparkled with the same mischief that Joshua's were often filled with. His ivory skin was the same creamy color that made those eyes more vibrant than they really were. Sharp cheekbones... it was all the same. He even had the same crook in his nose, which was from a break that happened when we were kids.

My eyes moved back to Lucian, who watched me silently without making a single noise as yet another piece of metal was dug from his back and made a clink as it was dropped into a glass. Linda worked with deft precision, her eyes only meeting mine when she felt my heavy stare.

It took a strong stomach to remove metal from flesh, and she didn't seem upset or squeamish at all. She looked like she had done it before, which seemed off to me. No one should ever feel okay with digging metal out of flesh. Or anything else for that matter.

Lucian's dark indigo eyes remained intense as he continued to watch me, as if he thought at any moment I'd have a mental breakdown. I offered him a small smile before I turned to Vlad, who was also watching me with a worried look.

"I need a drink, please," I whispered, not trusting my voice to not crack with the emotions I felt.

The entire room was silent; many people watched me, or Kendra, maybe wondering why one of us couldn't stop crying, while the other was almost catatonic. I understood it; it wasn't everyday something walked in looking like your dead brother.

"Pick your poison," he said gently.

"Macallan, top shelf, Vlad, two fingers, make it neat," Lucian directed, his eyes closing briefly before he turned them on the bartender. "For both of us," he finished.

"Fifty-five, or younger?" he asked as his eyes moved to me, and then Lucian.

"Fifty-five," Lucian answered and moved his eyes back to mine. "If she can handle it," his tonality made it a statement instead of a question.

"I can handle it," I whispered, barely audible to my own ears.

I watched as Vlad retrieved the gorgeous bottle, which was shaped to take you back to the old world, when it was a luxury to have and own fine whisky. The moment he pulled the crystal decanter out and removed the ornate cap, my nose was filled with the fragrance of smoky spices. I watched as he carefully poured the dark amber liquid, then pushed the glass in my direction.

I lifted it, swirled the whisky and brought it up to my

nose to inhale the fragrant beauty of the fifty-five-year-old scotch. I wasn't big on different types of whiskies, but I knew this was an expensive drink, and highly sought after by those with means to obtain the more extravagant things in life.

I took a sip, and swirled it in my mouth. I enjoyed the burn; the slight taste of citrus was a surprise, but it tasted far better than I expected. Not something I'd pay for; however, it was a rather cool experience in light of everything.

I took another sip and turned to watch as the elders were brought in, with my mother following behind them. Why had they come to us instead of bringing us to the safety of the abbey? I watched as my mom looked for me, and then quickly searched through the crowd for Kendra.

The moment she found us both, relief softened her features. She moved towards Kendra, and I followed. I'd just reached them when Kendra threw herself into Mom's arms and started relaying what had happened.

I remained silent until the last of Kendra's emotional explanation had played out. Tears filled our mother's eyes, and I choked back my own emotions.

"Joshua can't be alive," my mother said softly to Kendra. "They sent your brother's body home to us."

"It could be him! Just because the Army said it was him, doesn't mean that they didn't make a mistake!" Kendra sobbed.

"We buried Joshua," I whispered.

"You can't know that! Nobody can say it for sure."

"We buried Joshua," I repeated more firmly. "I know it was his body we buried, Kendra."

"You need to stop, you saw him! It was Joshua!"

"It wasn't Joshua, dammit, Kendra, I know it wasn't

Josh because I opened that casket, and I saw what was left of him. Grandmother even did the spell to be sure it was him! We made damn sure it was Joshua in that casket!"

The entire room gasped, and I didn't care.

"Magdalena, he was killed by a bomb," Mom whispered, sadness coloring her words at understanding exactly what I'd seen in that casket.

"I know, trust me, I know. We had to be sure, so I did what I had to and begged Grandma to do the spell for me. The results of the spell were conclusive, and it's never wrong. It was Joshua's body in that casket. He's dead. Whatever that thing was, it wasn't our brother, Kendra. We buried him, the real one. No mistake was made, there's no doubting it. Joshua *is* dead."

Kendra started up again but mother stopped her. "She's right, do not argue it. We were lost in grief. That is not the problem now, Kendra. We need to figure out what is posing as Joshua, and…"

"Fiona, tell them," Grandmother interrupted softly as she placed a gentle wrinkled hand on Mom's shoulder. "They need to know. You knew eventually that they'd have to be told. Now is the time."

A chill ran up my spine as I turned to my mother and narrowed my eyes. "Tell us what?"

What could she possibly tell us now that would get us any closer to figuring out what that thing was?

"Mother," Kendra asked as she sat beside my mom.

"I was eighteen when I became eligible for the Awakening ceremony. My match was chosen by the ancestors at the Harvest ceremony. He was a strong man, powerful. His name was Drake, and he was from the original coven. Nine months later I gave birth to beautiful twin boys, and I rejoiced."

I turned white. Twins?

"Just as any mother would, I loved my sons. They were beautiful babies, but as Benjamin and Joshua got older, we noticed a change in Benjamin. At two, he was casting magic, far more magic than a child should be able to do before an Awakening ceremony; but then, his tantrums took a dangerous turn. He would fly into fits of rage over Joshua playing with his toys. We had a puppy that was given to both boys and we found the poor thing cut up, with nearly nothing left of it. At first, I made up reasons for why things kept happening. At three, I found Joshua with a bag over his head, and tiny cuts all over his body. I realized that it was no longer safe, and I had to choose between letting Joshua live or continuing to deny the darkness I could see growing inside of Benjamin. I took Benjamin to the seer in the woods, and she quickly saw what I had been denying. Benjamin was born of the darkness, and Joshua of the light. I took Joshua to the neighbors, and went back home to spend the night alone with Benjamin before I had to send him away. Darkness cannot live in the light, and Benjamin would have killed Joshua eventually. Any child who is born with darkness is given to the Guild, as they are better equipped to deal with it. This coven is no different than the others; we do not allow darkness to grow within our ranks. I did what I had to do. I removed all evidence of him from our lives; pictures, toys, anything that could prove he existed was erased."

"How do you know he wouldn't change? He was three!" I seethed. "You threw him away, how could you? What about us?" I indicated myself and Kendra. "What if it had been us, would you throw me away too, mother?" I demanded.

"I took you and your sister to the same seer who lives in the woods. When you were three, we took you back to the seer and she said you were pure light, brighter than any she'd seen before you. You and Kendra were inseparable, unlike Josh and Ben; they didn't bond. They fought over everything. Benjamin was not a happy child. He was sullen, and dark. He was born wrong."

"And you just took the word of some nutcase witch in the woods who claims to be a seer? Do you have any idea how crazy that sounds?" I asked.

"The witch serves us. She's the seer of the dark and the light. She's blind, and yet she sees better because of it," my grandmother said as she watched me. "Some children are born with a darkness that will kill the light just so they can remain in the shadows. It isn't their fault; it's just how they are born. This coven was built to keep light magic," she continued as she placed a hand on my shoulder. "Your mother's choice wasn't easy; she gave up one child to save the other."

"Did she? Because it seems to me he's back, and he's a little bent on the whole 'being kicked to the motherfucking curb,' thing. I highly doubt he's here for a family reunion."

"Magdalena," my grandma warned.

"It's the truth. I couldn't imagine learning that I'd been abandoned because of what you assumed *I* was. Just because you can sense the darkness doesn't mean you have to accept it. He could have been taught to fight it."

"He was born with it. You can't stop it from growing if they're not old enough to fight it. He was becoming powerful; so much more than Joshua was or any other child for that matter."

I stopped talking, because I knew it couldn't have been

easy, and I was jumping to a total stranger's defense. I was being harsh, but I felt for him. I could understand why he was angry. I could see that she'd believed she needed to protect her son, both of them, and to do that, she'd made a sacrifice that no mother should have to make.

"I'm sorry," I said softly, but as she stood to hug me, I stepped back. I wasn't sure why, or what I was doing. This information changed everything for me. Every memory growing up took on a new meaning. All of the coven's fears of Kendra and I. They had good reason to be afraid for us, and what we would become as we grew into adults. "You should have told us."

"I wanted to, but I wanted you to enjoy this time. It's your time now, not a time for us to be worried about something you can't change."

"And if it's him taking the others? The missing witches?" I asked, and knew she hadn't added it up yet. "He knows who he belonged to; he knows Kendra and I are his sisters. That wasn't a guess; he came here for a reason."

"Maybe curiosity brought him here?" my mother said with a hopeful look in her eyes that I couldn't stand to see.

"I'm sure curiosity made him pull a dagger on me too."

"He tried to hurt you?" she gasped and covered a sob with her hand.

"He didn't hurt me, but he did set off a bomb. So if you're asking if he is capable of murder, my guess would be yes." I rubbed my forehead as I tried to replay everything. "Which Guild was he sent to?"

"I don't know, Drake took him away before the coven could and I never saw either of them again," she said and pulled herself together. "It's my mess, Lena, not yours."

"It's not only yours. We are family, we stick together. If we make a mess, we clean it up together. Is there anything else you left out?" I was tired, sore, and upset.

The reason why Benjamin looked, talked, and smelled like my brother, was because he was. I'd offhandedly rejected him without even knowing it. Wrapping my brain around Joshua being my half-brother was going to have to wait for another day. I was numb; I didn't want to feel, or hear the answers. I wanted to forget today had ever happened. The moment Helen started adding her input, I wanted to scream.

"Fiona, this is quite the mess you've gotten this coven into," Helen's condescending voice was loud enough that the entire room could hear.

"Helen," my grandmother said, her tone carrying a warning.

"Sara, I may not be from one of the original bloodlines, but at least I don't have any skeletons hiding in my closet."

"He wasn't supposed to learn of us."

Everyone looked at my mother, and Helen's next words broke my heart.

"Well he did, and now our children are missing because of yours!"

"Helen, shut your freaking stuck-up, got to be in everyone's fucking business, mouth!" I yelled. Lightning cracked outside, followed almost simultaneously by thunder. "You have no right! None at all," I continued, feeling the storm coming through me. "You heard what she said; you want someone to blame? Blame the coven," I seethed, and the entire room gasped. "They told her what to do, and they're the ones who allowed Drake to take the baby instead of doing it themselves. She did her job; she gave away her child. Ask the coven how the hell he figured it out. If I had to make a guess, I'd guess his father told him."

"You do not…"

Lighting crashed against something solid, close enough to the club that the power blinked, and went dark; at the second crash, it came back and I was inches from Helen.

"I have every right. She's my mother, *mine*. You don't get to point fingers and judge her because something went wrong that was out of her control. The moment Drake took that baby away with the coven's blessing, her part was done. You want to judge her? Get in line. When it's your turn, you better have fucking facts that can back your mouth up. We do not judge, we accept. We are one; when one is in trouble, many heed the call to stand beside them. Isn't that what you all preach to us, or did buying your way onto the elders' council give you the right to skip being held to the same standard?"

The entire room must have been holding their breath. I wasn't sure where that had come from, but I'd felt a powerful snap inside of me, and before I could stop myself, I'd shouted at Helen. Emotional overload, I realized; the mind stops processing and starts expelling things when it's trying to compartmentalize. Like learning you have a brother, and finding out that life wasn't black and white.

I remembered my grandfather had told me things like that; that the mind can suppress events. If it can't accept it, it fails to acknowledge it. He'd also told me that sometimes sacrifices had to be made for the greater good and that before I became judge and jury, I needed to stop and see if my mind could process it, or if it rejected it. If it didn't accept it, I couldn't judge.

You couldn't judge something you didn't understand.

I looked at my mother and realized something she didn't say, probably something she never verbalized. She didn't only bury one son when we'd buried Joshua, she'd buried them both. Her mutterings in her sleep replayed through my mind, and I felt tears well in my eyes. She'd buried them both, because Joshua had kept Benjamin clean and pure for her. Fate wasn't cruel; sometimes she was a nasty bitch.

I looked around the room, finding Kendra watching me; her anger had already diminished, and her mind was working overtime. She wanted to see if our other brother was as bad as they said, and ask him if he was behind the missing girls.

"Kat, Dexter, make sure she doesn't leave unless she's with my mother or my grandmother," I said, ignoring the others who were intently listening to the elders as they tried to formulate a plan.

I moved past Lucian, pushed open the outer door and walked into the main club. There were holes in the walls, which were letting in the last few rays of daylight.

"Where do you think you're going?" Lucian's voice stopped me.

I turned around and looked at his dress shirt which was covered in patches of his blood.

"I'm going to go out and see if I just lost another brother in that explosion, and if he's outside and by some miracle still alive, I'm going to ask him what he wants."

"Okay, lead the way," he said.

"I don't need you to come with me."

"If he's not here to make friends, he's here to do harm. He set off a fucking bomb and trashed my club. I'd like to know why."

"Fine, but you can wait until I'm done. I need to ask

him a few things, and if he can vanish as he did inside the club, I don't want him getting spooked."

"Fine," he agreed with his eyes devouring me.

"Stop looking at me like that."

"Like what?" he asked smoothly, his eyes sliding down my ruined dress, which was ripped from the explosion, and covered in both of our blood.

"Like you want to eat me," I grumbled and the look I gave him should have made it clear that it wasn't a good idea to tease me right now.

"I don't want to eat you; I want to taste you before I devour you."

"What's your deal?" I asked as I swung back around to face him.

"No deals; I'm not that guy," he purred as his hand moved slowly and he touched my cheek softly. "Let me guess, you want a prince, someone to sweep you off your feet."

"I don't need to be saved by some prince," I argued. "I had the sweet guy, the one I thought I wanted, but he was just a frog in disguise. I don't need saving, I got my shit handled. Don't stereotype me. I'm not the damsel in distress. I'm the one who thinks the damsel needs to figure it out. She needs to save herself, stop waiting for some asshole wearing glitter to do it for her."

He smiled, but it was all teeth. "You can't even see that you need to be saved. Today, when the bomb went off, you froze. You're weak; you pretend you have it all together because one fucking ounce of emotion and everything you've been holding in will come undone. I see you, Lena. The real you, not the tough exterior you show to everyone else. You've pushed the real you so far inside of you that you don't feel anything. You feel too much, care too much. Let it go; for once in your life stop trying to hold it all in, and let it fucking go."

"You're wrong." I turned and headed to the door. "I know my weaknesses." He was quickly becoming one. His touch? Set me ablaze with emotions I couldn't even begin to understand. One night in bed with him? I'd be ruined. I knew it, and so did he.

Not going to happen. He could remain a free agent and flirt with the others. I wasn't interested in spending one night with him; I wouldn't survive it. There were men you could sleep with and walk away from, like the tattoo artist. No attachment. No sweet goodbyes in the morning. Lucian? He would ruin, wreck, and destroy a girl's sensibility. He'd pound out walls, and destroy her foundation. He was a walking, talking, sexy as fuck wrecking ball.

I pushed the door open and froze at the destruction. I wasn't sure if the coven had been able to get in through the front or if they'd come in another way. There were two other roads that lead to the club, and as I scanned the ruined cars in the parking lot, my heart dropped until I spotted baby, parked right in the middle of all the ruined cars. *Untouched.*

Impossible. The air in front of the car shifted and I gasped as Benjamin materialized, and I felt the subtle touch of magic that displaced the air as he used it. Other than a few cuts, he didn't look hurt. He watched me closely, as if he was suspicious of me. I didn't blame him; I would have been suspicious of me too. He lifted a lit cigarette to his lips, inhaled deeply, and exhaled smoke slowly, his eyes never leaving mine as I watched him.

I stepped away from the club, but Lucian grabbed my arm and pulled me back. His eyes locked onto Benjamin.

"If he can apparate at will, you shouldn't go out there. That is not a typical warlock trait."

"I need to do this so that Kendra doesn't. He has answers, and I want them. I also need to know if he is behind the missing girls. The coven will try to kill him if they think it's him. I need to be sure before I lose another brother."

I pulled my arm away from Lucian and moved slowly to the car; lightning erupted from the sky; and would have hit me, if Benjamin hadn't been faster. He disappeared, and we reappeared at the car.

"Testing me, *sister*?" he sneered. He dropped his cigarette on the ground and I looked down, as I struggled to gain control of my body.

"What did you just do?" I whispered as I placed a hand on the car for balance.

"Saved your ass," he mumbled as he looked me over slowly. "You're as pretty as he said you were. You got a pair of steel balls, too. He left that out."

"Who?" I asked cautiously.

"Josh," he grunted, not bothering to elaborate anything other than Joshua's name.

"Why are you here?" I asked.

"I have my reasons," he evaded, his blue eyes probing mine.

"You know who I am, Benjamin."

"That's not my name. I'm subject B. Bred to kill." His voice dripped with sarcasm.

"You came here for answers, to see why she kept one but not the other?" I guessed.

"I don't give a shit what she did."

"And you found two sisters, and you want to know why us? Why did she keep both of us but not you?"

"I said I don't give a shit."

"I do, I want to know why."

"You don't care about me; you want him back. I see it in your eyes," he snarled as he towered over me, trying to scare me.

I reached up to cup his cheek, and he flinched away from it. I held my hand perfectly still, and waited for him to see that I didn't plan to harm him. The moment he relaxed, I placed my palm on his cheek. His skin wasn't as soft as Joshua's, and was cold as well. I brought my other hand up and repeated the motion on the other side, my eyes locked with his as I touched him.

"You're not wrong. I do want Joshua back. You, you're a surprise to me. Before today, I didn't know you existed," I whispered brokenly as tears choked my words. "I miss him; he was my anchor. You met him; what did you think?" I asked, and flinched as he moved his face close to mine.

I was prepared to pull away, but he placed a chaste kiss on my eyebrow, my temple, and then my forehead and I went wide-eyed. That was something only Joshua had ever done. He smiled and winked at me as he pulled back.

"He's not really gone."

"What?" I whispered shakily.

He turned and looked at the crowd coming out of the building. I wanted them to disappear. I wanted him to answer me. His eyes scanned the crowd until I knew he'd found Kendra and my mother and just like that, he turned cold and his features twisted into a mask of anger.

"That's her, isn't it?" his tone was frigid, but I could see that it was his defense against the pain he felt.

"She didn't have a choice," I defended my mother.

"Everyone has a choice, Lenny. Every choice has consequences," he replied as he turned his eyes back to mine. They were cold, lifeless, and void of emotion. "He wasn't supposed to die. It was supposed to be me. He was weak, filled with hope that I could be saved. Don't follow his path; some people can't be saved."

"The girls, the ones that are missing?" I whispered, unsure I wanted his answer.

"I didn't come here for myself," he said. "I don't want to be here. I didn't take any girls; look closer to your own fucked up world. Darkness is coming for you, or I wouldn't be here. They can't save you from what's coming; only you can. Stop trusting what you see and hear, and start looking deeper. Prepare yourself for what's coming, because no one is safe from it."

He disappeared again, but this time, I'd felt his lips touch my forehead and his voice ghosted through my mind.

"You should have stayed hidden, sweet sister, for monsters are everywhere."

"Benjamin?" I whispered.

He was gone, and his last words replayed through my head. Monsters? What the hell was going on? How had he vanished, and how had I heard him? Telepathy? Was that another of his abilities?

CHAPTER
fourteen

I lay on the sofa, glad to escape the coven for a little while and just be alone in the silence of the cottage. Candles bathed the small room, casting shadows on the walls. I'd grudgingly listened as the coven and the elders carried on and on about how dangerous the 'stranger' was. I'd listened numbly as Kendra sobbed, big gut-wrenching sobs. I'd been looked at and judged by those who thought me heartless for holding it together.

That's what I was doing; I was holding my shit together, just barely. I slowly stood up and began to move into the other room, numb, partly in shock, partly in denial. It would have been so much easier if he'd been Fae or one of the other speculated creatures. Nope, it was a secret brother. Secrets always had a way of coming back to bite you.

My mother fell apart after we left Club Chaos and

we'd brought her back to the more familiar surroundings of the main house. It had gutted me to see her in such a state. I'd held her rocking form until she'd quieted down, and I'd somehow managed not to fall apart with her.

Seeing Benjamin leaning against Josh's car had been hard, mostly because I'd wanted to run to him, throw my arms around him and welcome him home. Only one problem. I'd wanted to welcome Josh, not Ben.

I pulled off my sweater and dropped it on the couch, jumping as a knock sounded at the front door. My heart leapt in my throat as I considered who could be on the other side of it. It was probably Mom, needing someone to comfort her. I was mentally drained and had nothing left to give. I could feel the cracks getting larger and spreading like spider veins inside of me. I moved slowly, unlocked the door and pulled it open. My eyes focused on a massive chest, before slowly moving up.

Midnight eyes met and locked with mine.

"I wanted to make sure you were all right." His hand moved before I could stop him. He touched my cheek gently until I pulled away from the warmth his fingers offered.

"I'm fine." My voice was soft and I didn't trust it not to break and give him the truth of my fragile state of emotion.

"It's my understanding that when a woman says that she's fine, she's usually actually feeling the opposite of fine."

He moved inside without invitation as I watched him. "I was actually just going to bed," I lied.

"Liar; you should work on that," Lucian smirked as he sat in the chair, and I returned to the couch.

"Work on what, lying?" I asked.

"If you insist on doing it, yes," he countered with a soft smile as he leaned forward with his elbows resting casually on his knees as he studied me.

I snorted, which wasn't very ladylike, but after my day, I didn't care. "Really, I'm fine."

"Because that particular phrase bothers me," he replied. "It's a smokescreen, a fucking placebo that allows you to hide what you really feel from yourself and those around you. You seem to use that word 'fine' a lot; everything is not fine. That pain you hide, it shows in your eyes when you think no one else is looking," he replied easily, his eyes probing mine for a reaction. "Just like your first time, it wasn't fine. It was a letdown. You couldn't have enjoyed emotionless sex in the back of a car. You need to eradicate that word from your vocabulary."

"What's your deal? Why do you even care? And what's wrong with deeming something fine? People do it all the time."

"You need someone who isn't afraid to be rough with you. You need someone who can erase the connection between the word fine and sex from your mind, and stop the word from ever crossing your mind when you think of sex. Words like 'fucking destroyed,' 'cock-rocking,' and 'never the fucking same again,' should be there instead."

"Because fucking you wouldn't be fine? Here's the thing: who are you to teach me? Maybe I like things just the way they are," I argued.

He smiled and it sent a shiver rushing down my spine. *Change the subject!*

"How did you get to me so quickly tonight? You weren't even close to me when the bomb went off."

"I was right beside you," he said smoothly, his eyes locked with mine, almost daring me to contradict him.

Did he think I was stupid, or simpleminded? "Bullshit; maybe *you* should practice lying. I'm not the only one who sucks at it."

"I was beside you, Magdalena."

"No. You were not beside me. When you're close to me, my body reacts, and it didn't react."

"It reacts?" he asked with a half-cocked smile. "Tell me, Lena, how does it react to me?"

"Violently. As in, I get violent with the need to put you in your place." Perhaps violent with lust, but he didn't need to know that.

"And why is that?" he asked.

"I don't know. I do know that you weren't close to me, but you somehow saved me. So thanks for that. What I really want to know is why you, someone who owns luxury clubs up and down the West Coast; is so interested in this town. You bought something that belongs to my family, why?"

"I'm a businessman," he said casually as he sat back in the chair.

"So you bought it because taking someone's shop that has been in their family for generations is just good business?" I watched his face close off all emotion. Good, I'd hit a nerve.

"Your mother approached me and made me an offer." His voice was quiet, forcing me to strain to hear him. "I didn't ask for it, but I'm also not going to just hand it back to you. I didn't get to where I am by buying investments just to give them back without making some sort of profit."

I understood his logic, even though it wasn't what I wanted to hear; it was the truth, and he was, if anything, a businessman. I stood up, fully intending to kick him out, but his presence gave me comfort, which it shouldn't.

"I'm going to make some tea, care for some?" I asked.

"Anything stronger?" he asked, and I understood. It had been a long night. His club had taken damage, although not as much as one would think it should have sustained with a bomb exploding so closely to it.

"I think I still have wine, or a bit of Grandpa's whisky," I offered.

"Whisky for me," he said as he got up and followed me to the kitchen. I felt an electrical pulse as he got closer to me, and lifted my eyes to his, which seemed to consume me. The man sent out vibes that seemed to reach into my system and find the nerve endings. My breathing grew shallow, and my heart beat faster.

No, he hadn't been close to me at the club, or I would have felt this same physical reaction I was having to him now back at the club when the bomb went off. Being close to Lucian was like standing outside in a massive storm. He was the proverbial eye of the storm. The part that lulls you into a false sense of safety as the storm circles around, knowing at any given moment, the eyewall will break free and destroy you. My body quivered with silent anticipation at his nearness, and I moved away from him, as if putting distance between us would help; it didn't.

I gave him my back as I walked into the small kitchen, and bent down to remove one of the floorboards, revealing the old cellar. He'd probably never seen anything like it, not in his Richie-Rich life. I grabbed the wine and an old bottle of scotch, and set them aside on the floor before replacing the board.

"This cottage must be older than I thought it was," he acknowledged. "You don't see many of the old time cellars anymore."

"My great, great grandfather built this place before

they built the main house," I mumbled as I opened up the small fridge and reached into the tiny freezer to retrieve an ice tray. "You prefer it neat or on the rocks?" I asked.

"Neat," he answered softly as he stood leaning against the doorway. He dominated the room; as if it wasn't small enough, it now looked even smaller.

I reached into the cupboard, retrieved two cups, and poured the drinks before turning to hand him his. He was no longer in the doorway, he was behind me. I hadn't even heard him move, not until he set his drink back on the tiny counter, took mine from my hand, and placed it beside his.

"We should go back to the front room," I offered, hating that my mind was going to places it had no damn business going to. Not with this man.

"Should we," he asked without making it a question. He touched my bare shoulder where an angry bruise had formed. I closed my eyes as the sensation of his touch sent me into overdrive. My breathing became rigid, almost as stiff as my body. His mouth lowered and he placed a soft kiss on the exposed skin, before he pulled away and looked at me with those sinful eyes.

"We should," I whispered.

He smiled and leaned his mouth closer to mine. The heady scent of whisky was on his lips, and I wanted to taste what he'd indulged in. I moved closer, unsure if I should cross this line, or run from it. I licked my lips as he moved in, his intoxicating scent sending me over the edge of no return as I kissed him.

His kiss was hard, demanding. His hands reached for my hips, lifting me up until I was pressed against the erection his slacks concealed. I moaned as he rubbed his need against mine. The kiss grew hungrier, and my back was pressed against the wall, hard. I'm not sure how the wall didn't cave under the pressure of our combined weight. My hands tangled in his hair, holding him to me until he reached for them with one of his and held them in a viselike grip above my head. I was helpless. Trapped and unable to do anything unless he wanted me to. His mouth devoured any coherent thoughts, and his cock was rock hard as it pushed against the thin lace of the panties I wore.

I was almost thankful for the thin barrier between us, but I felt the fabric as it ripped; the sound was loud in the small space of the kitchen. Fingers replaced his bulge, and I pushed myself against the pressure. I was on fire, and he was the match that had created the inferno I was becoming.

I moaned as he pushed one long finger inside; his own moan was swallowed by our kiss as he pulled his finger out, and shoved it inside of me with force. I felt a storm growing inside of me, out of control and unlike anything I'd ever experienced before. My body was tight, stiff with the need to experience this man. I wasn't even sure how he was managing to pin me there while both of his hands were busy elsewhere. I didn't care, either.

"Bloody hell, you're wet," he growled as he pulled his mouth away from mine. "You're already so fucking close to exploding, aren't you, sweet witch?"

"Lucian," I muttered, unsure what was happening. It was visceral, this connection. I wasn't just wet; I was soaking wet. My nipples were hard, needing to be touched by him. I wasn't sure why he stopped, but he released my hands and pulled his fingers clear, sucking the wetness of my arousal from them as his eyes held mine captured, helpless to do anything else but watch him as he did so.

"I need to fuck you," he whispered through a thick, guttural tone that made my body tremble.

"I…" I paused. "I can't," I replied after a moment of silent battle inside my own head. "I can't until after the Awakening."

"I don't breed witches, ever," he said in a tone that set off warning bells.

"I can't do this," I whispered, moving across the room. I wanted to, I wanted nothing more than to strip naked and let him have his way. I couldn't, though. There was too much at stake with the Awakening coming up, and one screw-up could be enough for the ancestors to dismiss me from coming into my powers. I leaned against the fragile counter and fought the urge to turn around and offer him what he wanted.

My body trembled with pent-up need. I could hear and feel him right behind me, waiting for me to decide. I wasn't willing to risk my powers being weaker than my peers when my curse was lifted at the Awakening; I was already running the risk of being a weakling if the elders' theories were right. He was a welcome distraction from everything that was happening.

I turned and he was gone. I moved out of the kitchen, looking around the empty room and blinked. The door was open, and Lucian was gone. I felt angry tears well in my eyes, and wiped them away. I moved to the door and closed it before turning back to the small kitchen to down the whisky and grab the cup of wine.

I moved into the bathroom, placed the wine on the small wash tray, and leaned over to turn the water on. I undressed and climbed into the tub, letting the water wash away the stress of the day, and I finally relaxed. I wasn't going to cry about it; it wouldn't change anything, and I'd probably come undone if I did. He was right; one crack in the dam and everything would come out.

Tonight had been hell, and I wanted to forget it, but I couldn't do that. I wanted to take what he offered, but if I had, I was sure it wouldn't end there. I'd allowed my walls to be shaken, just as I had when I watched Benjamin as he moved towards the doors of Club Chaos. He looked so much like Josh, I'd wanted to be able to believe that there had been a mistake, just as much as Kendra had, but I couldn't. I had known the truth, and we were too close to the Awakening to be taking chances. I hadn't been willing to lose her if I'd been wrong, so I'd forced myself to face the reality that it wasn't Joshua we were looking at. For half a moment, though, I'd let my walls slip a little, and thought maybe I was wrong.

After I'd soaked, I changed into a pink nightie and moved through the cottage, turning off the lights and blowing out candles. I patted Luna's head as she made her entrance, sensing it was bedtime.

"Good girl," I mumbled as I pulled off the comforter and pulled back the soft cotton sheets. I'd opened one of the windows for her before I'd left for the club, knowing she'd spend most of her time outside. She'd adapted to country life pretty well, and the best part had been she'd sensed the need to stay close to the house since the last debacle.

Cats were smart, and picked up on their owners' fears. I settled onto the bed, and she snuggled in beside me.

"He's impossible," I whispered to the cat. "And I can't seem to stop kissing him."

She licked her paw, already bored with me, and closed her eyes.

"Jerk, I listen to you," I grumbled.

She meowed and perked her head up as she looked around the room.

"Well, forget it now," I continued. "The moment's gone. You totally suck as a best friend, you know that, right?"

She looked at me like I was crazy, because maybe I was. I was talking about my love life to a cat, but hey, at least she didn't judge me. I laid my head back on the pillow and closed my eyes.

I was dreaming of sinful things. Lucian was with me, and had me pinned to a bed, one that wasn't mine, a much older one. An antique table with an old-fashioned porcelain tea service was laid out, complete with half eaten scones and almost-empty tea cups. The windows of the room were thick stained glass, the ornate headboard and footboard had a tall wooden post at each end, and rope had been wound around the headboard posts, which held my hands securely above my head.

"Stop," I whispered as I watched him bring the knife up and gently held the tip against my stomach.

"Scream for me, witch. Beg me to stop," he growled as his mouth replaced the knife and he rained soft kisses across my stomach.

"No," I replied, and blinked. He had a knife, and I was tied to his bed; why would I beg? Why was I bound?

"You'll beg me, sooner or later; you always do," he whispered as his mouth fanned hot breath down my belly as he moved it to my pelvic bone and darted his tongue out, creating an array of sensations. His tongue dipped into the crevice, and I lifted my hips. He laughed, the sound vibrated against my flesh as his eyes met mine, hunger bare in the dark blue depths. He placed his mouth on the soft flesh and sucked; the noise we made together was deafening in the small room.

My hair was drenched in sweat; my skin was on fire for him. The things his mouth was doing were unbelievable, and the moment his fingers entered me, I felt as if I would shatter.

"Not yet," he purred as he removed his mouth and his fingers. His hand smoothed over my flesh; his fingers touched the soft mound of one breast, and then the other before he moved up to clamp his hot mouth over one nipple. The feel of his cock as it found my soft flesh and glided over it was unreal.

Pressure on my sensitive places mixed with the storm already building inside of me. Lightning crashed outside, and he smiled against my breast before his teeth grazed the nipple, pulling a moan from me as pain mixed with pleasure. His cock continued to slide against my core, and moisture was forming, giving him the extra lather to use me.

My hips bucked against him, but his weight held me prisoner as his hungry mouth continued to suck, nip, and bite my soft flesh. It was a torturous mix of sensations. Every time my body prepared to go over the edge, he stopped, waiting it out, and would start his assault again. He kissed my neck, rolling one nipple between his thumb and forefinger. His other hand moved down, placing his cock at my entrance, and inserted it, but only enough that it stretched my body.

"One thrust, and I'll own you," he whispered huskily. "You have no idea how badly I want to hear you scream for it. Do you know what happens now?" he asked, and before I could answer, his mouth claimed mine.

It was unorthodox to be in this position with him. I couldn't think past his mouth, past the pressure his body was creating as it rocked into mine, only to pull out as I tried to take more of him. I wasn't adjusting to the fullness he created. He knew it; I attempted to move, and he withdrew from me.

"Lucian," I moaned.

"Beg for it," he growled as he pulled his mouth away and looked over my body. "Tell me what I want to hear, and maybe I'll let you enjoy your last few minutes on this earth."

"Go to hell," I snapped, my mind coming back to what was happening.

"Been there; it's not as bad as they say," he whispered as his fingers entered my body, causing me to twist as pain erupted without warning.

I screamed in shocked horror, my eyes filled with tears as he took it from me. His eyes changed to obsidian. His demeanor changed, and his mouth lowered to lick against my flesh. He continued to push his fingers inside of me, his mouth soothing the ache until he pulled them out covered in blood. He used the blood to write on my flesh—death runes. I watched him as he continued to write, stopping periodically for his mouth to resume its slow, sensual assault.

He pulled his mouth away, and replaced it with his heavy, thick cock. He slapped it against my flesh, and lowered his mouth to claim mine. "Maybe in the next life, you'll be more of a challenge, my little witch. I do hate it when you come back weak. However, your body always gives me enjoyment."

His naked body hovered over mine and his cock pushed inside, further than it had before. As I cried out, he used the surprise of my response to shove a cloth against my mouth, filling it to smother my cries. Another inch, and then another. I remained still, watching him as pain shot through my body as he filled me. Without warning, he pulled out and moved from the bed. I watched him numbly as he moved to the dresser, where a basin of water waited.

"I didn't love you in this life," he whispered with his head down, his face away from me. "You did love me, though, didn't you?"

I couldn't answer, but I struggled against the ropes, hoping to find release before he returned to finish me off.

"Your coven is searching for you, but they won't find you with any life left in your corpse. What they will find is your naked body, covered in my runes, and beautifully broken. I must admit, out of all of your reincarnations, this one has been the easiest to find. The coven, though, poor bastards, they don't understand what is happening. They've all been cursed to relive your past lives in dreams. It helps me, you know, watching them struggle after they turn you against me. I enjoy their pain, but never yours, witch. Yours haunts me until I find you again."

I screamed through the gag, my eyes growing wide as I inhaled the sickly sweet scent of whatever he'd saturated the cloth with. I turned my head, looking to the ropes that held me. Runes I hadn't noticed before covered the walls. A mirror faced me, and I took in my naked body. Black hair and a wide, scared pair of emerald eyes looked back at me. I turned as he moved towards me, and kicked him the moment he was close enough.

"There's the fighter I love, a little too late," he purred as he ran his finger over my cheek. "You're already dying; the gag was soaked in a mixture of hemlock and white baneberry. It's a slow death, as it will sedate you and your heart will seize and beat no more. Funny, you didn't beg me or confess your undying love for me. You always have before, right before you try to seduce and then kill me."

His mouth touched my cheek, placing a soft kiss against it. His fingers travelled lower, and he watched as the poison took control of my system. I struggled to remember the curse, to remember what I was supposed to do. We'd planned this, and yet I couldn't remember.

"Magdalena," he shouted. "Get up!"

"Not yet, I have to remember," I whispered.

"Get up, now, Lena, get the fuck up!" he shouted; only this time he sounded like Joshua.

"I must remember, before it's too late to curse him," I mumbled.

"Wake up!"

I sat up, my eyes wide as the dream changed. *Joshua.* I looked around the room. I was drenched in sweat, my body one touch away from being on fire. It was so bad that I could smell it. I rubbed my eyes with the back of my hands and paused.

"Fire," I whispered as I rolled and stumbled out of bed and moved through the room, not stopping to change into something more substantial than a simple nightie.

I pushed open the front door of the cottage and my blood turned to ice running through my veins. I numbly took a step towards the main house as some of the windows in the lower level shattered, allowing black smoke to billow from the house.

"No!"

CHAPTER
fifteen

The brain is a funny thing. It doesn't comprehend the magnitude of what the eyes see when it first begins to compute the image. I'd like to say I moved quickly, but I didn't. I stood on the porch, unsure of what to do. My response time should have been fast, but it just wasn't. I watched as flames licked the side of the house, seemingly following the trail of the smoke. I moved closer, forcing my brain to function.

Someone was screaming close to me, hysterically. It took me a moment to understand that it was me, and that screaming wasn't going to help my family. By the time my mind reacted, I was running to the front of the house. The smoke was thick, the front window slightly warped from the heat of the fire that was within. I had a moment to react when the window began to make a horrifying sound.

I turned to run to the back, even as the glass exploded, sending molten shards flying against my skin. The pain didn't register, only that my house was on fire, and my family was still trapped inside the inferno. I tried to look through the remaining windows as I made my way to the back door, watching the top floor as window after window exploded, covering me and anything below it in shards of fiery, burning glass.

The back door was already open when I got to it. I paused for barely a moment as I looked at the flames that danced hypnotically on the walls, curling the wallpaper my grandparents installed during the crazy wallpaper phase. It sizzled, popped loudly, and began to melt under the blazing heat.

My eyes burned as I made my way into the house, screaming for my mother and Kendra. I covered my mouth as I inhaled the acrid smoke, coughing violently as I searched. I touched doors before throwing them open; my skin was slick with soot and sweat from the flames that seemed to focus more on the walls than any of the furnishings in each room I passed through.

I started crawling on the floor as the smoke got thicker, and made my way up the stairs. I tried to focus on the doorways, and pushed them open as I came to each one. I wasn't sure which room my grandmother had these days, and I wasn't going to leave anyone behind.

My lungs were on fire, and each time I moved to the next door, my movements began to slow as my body turned sluggish, until I finally decided to rest my head, to gather my strength before moving on.

I am not sure how long I lay on that floor, or if I knew that I wasn't leaving it. I remembered that I needed to get up, but couldn't. I couldn't breathe, or move. I closed my eyes to keep them from burning more than they already were, and felt something connect with my leg. Hands touched my exposed flesh, and I heard someone swear violently, and then I was up, closer to the smoke.

I couldn't force my eyes to open, or get my mind to grasp onto what was happening. Something solid and wet was smoothed against my face and then whoever had found me started moving quickly through the house. The cool night air washed over me as we exited the burning house. I tried, but couldn't open my eyes.

"Breathe for me, Lena," Lucian's voice was urging, gentle. "Damn you, don't do this," he growled as his mouth touched against mine as if to give me CPR. I coughed, violently. His mouth didn't move, but it remained close to mine until my eyes started to crack open. "Don't open them yet," he warned. "Bane, we need water, now. Tell the others that her sister and mother are still inside."

I started to struggle against his hold, but he held me in his lap on the ground as he poured water over my face, and I cried out as it burned.

"You are covered in ashes and soot, you'll be lucky if you're not burned to hell, Lena. What the fuck were you thinking?" he demanded as he pulled the water away for a moment, allowing me to catch a breath.

"My family," I uttered hoarsely.

"That what, you wanted to be entombed in the fucking fire with them? You have no magic to speak of yet. None that would help you live through that," he snapped.

Why was he so angry? He had no right to judge my actions. I'd run into a burning house, I got that, and I would do it again if I had to. Anger was making my mind come back online, and I snapped my burning eyes open and looked right at him.

"My family is in there! They're all I have left," I rasped, even though I'd tried to push any strength I had left, into the words.

"My men are inside looking. I'm taking you to my place," he announced as he started to pick me up.

"No, you're not, not until I know they're safe," I mumbled as I turned my head, which seemed to hurt more than it should. Had I ended up burned? The pain was god awful, and the taste of smoke lingered in my mouth and lungs. I coughed again, and wiped my mouth off with the back of my hand, watching as it came away covered in a black tacky substance.

"The moment you know that they are alive, I'm taking you to my house to heal your burns," he growled and allowed me to move onto the cool grass, which was a blessing. I watched in silence as the house continued to burn, watching the strangeness of the flames as they continued to dance in a multitude of colors. As I continued watching, skulls were visible in the flames, and I blinked to ensure it wasn't my mind playing tricks on me; it wasn't.

"Someone tried to kill us," I mumbled as I fought to stand up, and failed. Lucian was there, helping me up, as my legs seemed too weak to support my weight. "Look at the flames," I whispered in shock. "It's a spell."

"It's a fire," he replied firmly, his eyes moving from me, to the flames.

"Can't you see them?" I asked, watching as terrifying creatures and skeletal figures moved within the flames.

"See what, Lena?" he asked as he pulled me closer until I yelped in pain. He loosened his grip, and as I watched, Bane brought towels over to Lucian, who wrapped them around me gently.

"There are skeletons in the fire, reaching out for me," I whispered. I could see them, beckoning to me, seducing me back into the death that awaited me inside the fire. "See?" I said as I pointed at one that had extended out further than the others as yet another window exploded. "He's telling me to come to him."

"Bane, take Lena to the cottage; she can watch from the porch," Lucian directed as he maneuvered me into Bane's extended arms and moved away from me, closer to the burning house.

"Don't get too close," I warned, my voice cracking as one of Lucian's men emerged from the fire carrying a lifeless Kendra. The air left my lungs at the sight of her and I struggled against Bane and dropped to my knees. Even from this distance, I could smell the smoke that clung to her body, as if it was refusing to release her from the death it offered so seductively.

I made my way to her with Bane's help, not because he was being helpful, but because I was getting to my sister with or without his help. I fell to the ground, oblivious of the pain as I shook her, refusing to believe she was gone.

Angry tears slipped from my eyes as I watched one of the men start CPR on her, as another carried my mother from the fire.

"Anyone else in there?" Lucian asked, and the man gave him a sharp jut of his chin, indicating no one else was inside.

"My grandmother?" I whispered.

"There's no one alive inside that house," he muttered as he placed my mom on the grass with smoke clinging to his shirt, and touched her cheek. "She's not as bad off as the young one."

I turned to look at Kendra, who was lifeless, and still not breathing. I lay on the grass beside her and kissed her cheek, whispering to her, begging her to not leave me here alone.

"Please," I whispered out loud. "I can't be without you." Being apart from her had been the hardest part of being away, and living without her wasn't something I ever wanted to experience. I closed my eyes, refusing to believe that she was gone; I could feel her. Why could I feel her if she was beside me, dead?

I heard a gasp, then violent coughing. I opened my eyes and found her staring at me, even as she tried to gasp for clean air to fill her lungs. I exhaled a shaky breath that I hadn't realized I'd been holding, and an almost hysterical sob rocked through me as I reached up to touch her cheek.

"We need to move them away from the fire, and Bane, call the coven. The fire will go out now. It has failed to do what it was created to; it was only here for them."

I was helped back up to my feet by Lucian, who refused to budge when I asked to be able to stop at the cottage.

"Someone tried to kill you tonight, Lena. Until I or the coven decides its safe, you will remain with me," he ordered. "I'll send someone back for your things later, right now you need to have your wounds cleaned, and your sister needs sleep to recover."

I couldn't argue with him, because someone had done exactly what he'd said they had. I needed to rest, regroup, and regain my wits. Someone had gone out of their way to hurt my family. I felt safe enough with Lucian that I was willing to forego coven protocol and allow him to take the lead. Besides, he'd told his man to call them and let them know what had happened.

I was rushed through his house, unable to take in any detail other than it was extravagantly decorated, with lush furniture that put our old shabby ones to shame. I liked the older furnishings. The antiques long forgotten, that told of another world.

His bedroom was luxurious, with deep masculine shades of blacks and blues, which reminded me of his eyes. The bed was a solid oak four-poster bed that was larger than most, and had cream silk draped around the posts. The duvet was black, with glittering crystals edging the trim, creating the illusion of shimmering diamonds. A fire burned in the fireplace next to the bed, which made me shiver with the heat I already felt. I turned to look at him, only to find him watching me as I took in his bedroom.

"Why am I in your bedroom?" I asked softly, my voice scratchy from the fire still.

"How do you know it's mine?" he asked, his eyes lowering to my burned nightie, which was also filthy.

I swallowed and took a step closer to him, wincing as pain filled every nerve in my body. "It's dark, like you."

"How do you know I'm dark, Lena?" he whispered as his hand slowly lifted and he pushed a few strands of hair away from my face.

"Is there another room I can sleep in?" I asked, dodging his question.

"You need to soak in a tub. You can't wait for your mother and sister to finish using the others, so you'll use mine. Bane is fetching the healing salts, as well as the petals from the flowers we use to heal burns. You can sit and relax while I prepare it."

I swallowed again. Lucian was going to run me a bath, in his bedroom. The man who'd almost had his way with me in the kitchen of the cottage, had infiltrated my dreams and seduced and tormented my body until it had been on the edge of insanity, was now taking care of me.

I wasn't sure how I should feel about it, but I was

grateful that we weren't dead. He'd saved me twice tonight, as well as my family. Something was happening to the coven, someone was targeting us and I planned to figure out why. First, I had to heal. The adrenaline was fading, and with it, came the unbelievable pain from the burns I'd incurred while trying to be heroic, and utterly failing.

I sat in a soft wing-backed chair while Lucian and Bane moved around the room, until Lucian stopped in front of me and offered me his hand. I accepted and winced as pain sliced through me. It was horrible; the simplest movements made me stagger.

I walked into the bathroom with Lucian, who closed the door, isolating us both inside the room. I paused, and turned to look at him as tears trailed down my cheeks, burning everything they touched as they rolled off my face. It wasn't because I was crying; it was because everything burned, including my eyes.

"I can do this myself," I mumbled.

"You'd pass out before you got into the water; burns hurt more than any cut could. Don't worry, Lena, I have no plans of seducing you while you recover. I'm a very patient man." He produced a pair of scissors from one of the many drawers in the wall-to-wall vanity.

"I can do it," I insisted. I didn't want to be naked with him, but I also knew I didn't have the strength to remove my clothing. Talking hurt, everything hurt. Who knew just how many muscles it took to speak, and how many of them were connected to tissues that actually moved when you spoke?

"I'll leave your panties on, but you're getting into the water," he urged.

"Fine," I caved and did my best to turn around so that

he could cut from the back instead of the front. I felt him carefully moving my hair, and placing it gently over my shoulder, and then the sound of him cutting through the fabric filled the room. I hadn't seen my burns, but as I looked down, I could see the angry marks on my legs, already swelling from where they'd been burned. Black fabric was stuck in some of the damaged tissue, and I closed my eyes and silently prayed that the coven would be here soon, so that they could heal my family and me.

"Hold still, Magdalena," he whispered when the blade of the scissors touched my back, and I winced. I could feel his fingers as he tried to place a barrier between my flesh and the cold steel. His touch sent my already blazing flesh to flames. My nipples hardened as the cool air touched them as he freed them from my top.

I had planned to use my hair to shield them, but he carefully pulled it up and put it into a high ponytail. His ability to do this with such ease made me question just how many women he'd been around. He hadn't tugged at it, or missed a single hair. When he was done, he moved around me, and, without taking his eyes from mine, helped me into the warm water that was filled with fragrant petals. His eyes never strayed to my exposed breasts, which I was too sore to cover.

The moment I was in the water, I moaned and closed my eyes. Heaven had to feel like this. The pain numbed, the salt from the leyline eased the burns. Salt from the lines was a type of salve for witches. They were filled with healing properties. It burned now, but it would ease almost any wound if applied correctly as fast as possible after the incident. The scent of the flowers was intoxicating, and I inhaled, ridding my senses of the toxic, sulfurous smell of the fire. I was so relieved that I hadn't even heard him move, or return with a sponge.

"This is going to sting," he warned. "It's got to be done. If we can get the salt deep enough, we can stop any scarring."

"I'm not worried about scars," I whispered as my lashes fluttered open. "Scars tell a story. Everyone has them, even if they're not visible. I have enough inside that it won't matter what's on the outside."

"I'm washing you, so either way, princess, it's going to happen."

"I'm not a princess," I whispered as I turned to look at him.

He chuckled, and shook his head as he reached into the water and pulled out my arm, which pushed against my breasts. I sat up further, watching his eyes as they slipped to my exposed flesh, and then rose to meet mine with smoldering heat that would have made the fire tonight jealous.

"Here," I said, as I moved my arm to the edge of the bath so he could tend to it. "I'm not burned everywhere," I whispered as I silently thought a prayer that I hadn't been burned in other places.

"You don't like to be touched, do you?" he observed.

"It's not that I don't like to be touched," I admitted.

"You don't like to be touched by me?" he mumbled as his eyes assessed the damage to my arm before he pulled me up until I was standing in front of him.

"What the hell?" I asked as I stood before him, almost fully naked.

"I almost fucked you tonight, so don't pretend you don't want me. I'm not a little boy, and you're most definitely not a little girl. You're not a damsel in distress, but you are burned and you need my help. In order to do that, I need to touch you. Stop acting like a child, and take what I'm offering you. I don't normally help people, and I certainly don't make a habit out of it."

"Then why do you keep helping me?" I asked, lifting my eyes to hold his. "Why are you here helping the coven? Based on what I've seen, you've been helping us a lot."

He sighed and shook his head as he removed his shirt and kicked off his shoes. I watched in shock as he continued to strip until nothing was left, and by nothing, I mean Adonis had just stripped down naked in front of me and exposed the massive package I'd already known he was carrying, and unlike him, I didn't keep my eyes to myself. Who the hell could? He was huge, and it wasn't even hard yet. I wanted to instinctively cover my entrance; because there was no way in hell that thing was fitting. I had a healthy sense of self-preservation, and right now, it was screaming for me to slowly back away from the monster between his legs.

His body was ripped; muscles were perfectly sculpted in lines that I wanted to trace with my fingers. His body was sleek, each line carved to draw the eye and hold it. His runes were slightly duller than they'd been before, but even I could see the ancient symbols for what they were. Mortals couldn't normally see a witch or warlock's glyphs, but I was sure my tongue could. It itched to trace the patterns as well as the piercing in his nipple, and shamelessly so.

His own eyes returned my rudeness, and he lowered them until, just above my pubic bone, he found the small pentagram with Latin words in tiny script placed around it. I wondered if he knew what it was; a devil's trap. It was a symbol to ward off demons who would try to take possession of a witch's body. Of course, we hadn't had any demons around the coven in decades, but I'd felt the need to get it. Along with that, I had small outlines of birds that flew in a pattern up my ribcage; it had been my gift to myself when I'd gotten my first paycheck. A symbol of the freedom I'd taken for myself. It also was in memory of Joshua, and said in elegant calligraphy, 'Your wings were ready but my heart was not.'

Joshua had once read me a poem. It was about a bird sitting on a tree, never afraid of the branches breaking, because her trust was not in the tree that had grown the branch, but in her own wings that would carry her if she needed it. She had been born with the means to save herself, and always would. That poem had remained in my heart and soul, especially after he'd left us.

"You have a devil's trap," he said as his hand moved to the smooth skin and traced the pattern. "Perfectly placed," he finished hoarsely as his eyes slipped further, to the sheer material that was now hiding nothing.

He started with the sponge on my belly and worked around my breasts, ignoring the fact that both of our mingled breathing was growing slower and ragged from what he was doing. My nipples hardened, and it hurt, yet I ignored it, turning my head as his hands slid over one with the sponge, and then the other. He quickly finished the bath, and brought me a large T-shirt.

I waited for him to turn around as I dried off, pulled off my panties that were soaked, and slipped on the shirt which was so long that it went to my knees.

"Where am I sleeping?" I asked, needing to find a bed and hide beneath the covers.

"With me," he replied, giving me a sardonic smile.

CHAPTER
sixteen

Lucian showed me to a room that just happened to adjoin his and returned to his own room to change. It wasn't as masculine as his room. It was decorated in soft, delicate shades of lilac and cream. The bed was bigger than my own, but then again, the cottage didn't have enough room to fit anything larger than a full-size mattress.

Lightning cracked outside the window, followed by a loud clap of thunder. My mind replayed what had happened during the bath, and the realization set in that I was with him, in his house, wearing nothing more than his *White Zombie* band T-shirt, and it percolated a bit. My brain was also trying to wrap itself around the idea that we'd almost died tonight, twice.

I didn't know what to feel, or who to blame, but in my mind, I was silently screaming. My body still trembled, the adrenaline slowly escaping as the reality of the events sank in. These kinds of things just didn't happen to us. We maintained our world, kept it hidden from outsiders so that these types of things didn't occur.

I felt him before I saw him, that electrical buzz that slid over me, electrocuting my senses. The masculine scent he gave off was just an added bonus. I stood in place, rooted to the spot for fear of being in the same room with him and a bed. Dangerous combination, considering we almost hadn't even needed a bed earlier tonight.

I turned and looked at him; his chest was still bare. He'd slipped on a pair of sweatpants, which I was sure were for my benefit. Other than that thin trail of fuzz that led into the light gray sweatpants, he had very little body hair. His form was rock hard, with sleek muscles that looked as if they had been sculpted by the finest artist.

I licked my lips as I took in the bulge, painfully aware that he was hard, and I was more interested than I should be. He could wipe tonight away from my mind, quiet the questions that had been playing on an internal loop. So many questions, yet no answers were forthcoming.

He passed me, and I remained where I was, my eyes still locked where his secret package had been. What the hell was wrong with me? I wasn't this girl, a girl obsessed over a man just because he was hot as hell; I liked substance. I went after Todd because he had a great mind. He wasn't the hottest guy in the coven, but he was smart. Really smart. He'd had a soft side to him, one that told me he'd be a good father someday, and I'd wanted him.

"There's no bathroom in this room, just the master suite in my room. You'll have to walk through mine to reach it. There is another bathroom down the hall from these rooms. Your sister and mother have been healed, and have already turned in for the night. If you need anything, just ask," he said as he pulled down the covers and indicated with a slight nod of his head for me to get under them.

I moved slowly, my burns still aching as I moved towards the bed. I was almost to it when a knock sounded on the door, and Lucian quietly opened it and I whispered thanks to whoever had been on the other side.

"Lay down," he said as he shut the door, locked it, and moved back to the bed. "This is a cream we use to speed the healing of the burns." I tried to catch the fragrance of what might have been used in the cream, seeing that my mother had sold lots of different creams and salves for healing. Well, until my father stole the recipes and Lucian bought her shop, that is.

I sat on the bed carefully and extended my hand, but he ignored it. "Pull the shirt up so I can tend to the burns on your thighs," he ordered.

"I can do it," I assured him, my eyes taking in the angry red welts where the heat had damaged the flesh. I'd barely acknowledged the burns until I'd been in his huge, elegant tub. Now, I felt them even though I knew the salt from the leyline was working to fix the deep tissue that had been affected. "I'm not helpless," I whispered as I looked up and found him smiling.

"I will do it, and you'll answer my questions while I do, understand?" he said in a voice that sent needles into my brain.

I swallowed and nodded, my eyes growing heavy as I watched him sit beside me on the bed. My hand absently reached up and traced the line of his sleek muscles. I felt his body tense, and his breathing was a tinge heavier at my touch.

"Do you remember anything from your last life?" he

whispered, and I lifted my eyes to look up at him.

"No," I replied, and wondered why I felt a need to answer his question. My brain ached, but it was minimal. "I remember nothing."

"Who is after you, Magdalena?" he asked, his eyes locked with mine.

"I don't know," I admitted, my eyes working to move away from his, as if it was some kind of spell or enchantment I saw in their inky depths.

His fingers dipped into the cream, and his other hand lifted the shirt. "Lie back, and don't move, Lena. You'll feel no pain, do you understand me?" he whispered, his voice filled with meaning.

I lay back, and watched his eyes as they lowered to my flesh. His fingers worked like the most skilled pianist, working the keys of my flesh as it created a storm inside of me, as well as outside the single window of the room. The lightning was getting closer, stronger. Or maybe it was me that was. My breath hitched in my lungs, got stuck as his fingers moved closer to the throbbing ache that had taken up residence between my legs.

I wanted to close my eyes, get lost in the multitude of sensations his hands created. I felt weighted down, as if moving would be impossible. My arms rested at my sides as he moved my legs apart and sat between them. Why he needed to be that close, I didn't know, or care. I liked him there, close to me, close to the ache he created.

"Lucian," I whispered, watching as his eyes snapped back to mine, as if my words surprised him.

"Who are you?" he asked, his eyes narrowed as his hands continued to apply the salve, sending messages to the nerves which seemed to be attached to each other, all leading to the ones in my belly that created a sensation of need.

"I'm Magdalena, second daughter to the house of Fitzgerald," I mumbled.

"Do you have a dark side, sweet girl?" he murmured and I felt his fingers move inches away from my naked sex.

"Yes," I whispered through a hoarse voice I didn't recognize.

"Do you want me?" he asked.

No! "Yes," I replied. His mouth curved into a knowing smile, his eyes remained locked on my flesh. I felt the chilling air over my exposed core, and moved my hands to cover it, much to his surprise.

I pulled at the shirt, watching as he set the little jar down swiftly and captured my hands. His eyes lifted to mine and I felt my cheeks blossoming with heat. I chewed on my bottom lip, trying to fight whatever the hell was going on. He was peppering me with questions, and what I wanted to say didn't come out, instead, only the truth did.

"You're afraid of me," he noted as his lips lowered and he brushed a kiss on the inside of one thigh, and then the other.

"Yes," I replied. I was absolutely terrified of how easily I responded to him, ten times more so than I had with any other.

"Afraid of what you feel around me?" he continued, his hot mouth skimming the flesh, his eyes holding mine prisoner.

"Very," I replied, wishing my mouth would close, and stop answering him. A moan tore from my throat as his fingers skimmed over my exposed heat. "What are you doing to me?" I asked in a small voice, and he smiled with a wolfish grin.

"Not what I really want to be doing with you," he mumbled. "I can control your body with my lips, Magdalena. Imagine what I could do to you with the rest of my body," his voice was mesmerizing as his fingers once again slipped through the damp folds.

My body moved, and I knew it had little to do with whatever he'd done, and more to do with my desire to have him inside of me. I wanted the ache to stop, and knew without having to be told that he'd fill the void I'd always felt, and quiet my mind. I moaned loudly as he dipped the end of one finger inside and pulled it out, licking it clean as I watched him.

"You taste like I need to fuck you," he muttered, rising up until he was on his knees between my legs. My eyes locked on the massive bulge his sweatpants failed to conceal. After what I saw in the bathroom, I was pretty sure he wouldn't fit and if by some miracle he did, he'd probably rip me in half.

"Why are you doing this?" I whispered.

"Because you're too afraid to take what you need, and I'm a bastard," he growled. "I need the chaos that I see growing inside of you. I need to take you, ravage you over and over again. I want to hear the loudness of the pleasure I can give you as it escapes from your pretty lips. I want to feel the scratches on my skin that you'd leave as I enter your tight body. I want to watch as the storm heightens, as I make you mine."

I moaned even though he wasn't touching me. His words penetrated me harder than he ever could. My body responded, wetness filled my core as my nipples hardened beneath the soft cotton of the T-shirt. He knew it, too. His eyes feasted on my flesh, his hand lifted to skim lightly over my puckered nipple.

Our bodies could be skin on skin, and I'd still want him closer. It terrified me. I think it made him afraid as well. This reaction we had to each other wasn't normal; it was like two storm fronts meeting and colliding, out of control.

"Do you know who I am?" he asked softly as he lifted the shirt, exposing the taut peaks of my nipples to his greedy gaze.

"Lucian," I whimpered as his fingers pinched my nipple hard.

"You're so fucking beautiful," he growled, as if he didn't like the idea that he thought I was beautiful at all. "I should end this infatuation I have with you," he whispered as his head dipped and his teeth nipped at my nipple, stealing a mixed cry of pain and pleasure from my lips. He smiled against my flesh, and his mouth moved up to claim my lips as his heavy erection rested against my stomach. He kissed me hard, hard enough that I was sure our souls were briefly connected. His hand slipped down, cupping my heat. "You should run from me, sweet witch. I'm a one-way ride to the dark side, and there's no return ticket home. Not that I'd let you go once I had you, anyway," his seductive tone sent a chill through me.

"I ache," I admitted, and watched as his lips curved into a dangerous smile.

"I know, and there's nothing you will do about it. You won't pleasure yourself, or allow another man to touch what is mine, do you understand me?" He growled forcefully. "You are mine until I decide what to do with you."

"I am yours," I repeated, with the meaning of the words slamming into my brain immediately after. I blinked and shook my head even as his mouth lowered to mine, his cocky smile sure that he'd won.

"Say it again, my little witch," he ordered as his mouth prevented mine from doing as he'd demanded. His hungry mouth scorched mine, sending a wave of primal desire and heat searing through my body. The moment he ended the kiss, he sat back, waiting for me to follow his request.

"I am *not* yours," I cried out through clenched teeth, with a glare that took a lot of effort to perfect. "I don't know what you are doing to me, but it stops now."

He smiled, and shook his head. "You're stronger than I thought," he said softly with a wild look in his eyes as something darker passed behind them. "You're going to be fun to break," he whispered as he lowered his head yet again, but this time I turned away from his mouth. That thing was dangerous.

He laughed coldly and held his hand against my chin, turning my face back to his with enough pressure that it was painful. "You should have stayed away when you had the chance; it's too late now," he whispered against my ear. "I've decided to have you, and you can lie to yourself, but your body will always tell you the truth. You want me as much as I want you; watching you fight it will be entertaining, sweet girl." He released me, sat back until he was on the edge of the bed. His eyes swirled with black fire, and I gasped at their beauty. "Now, when I say so, you'll remember everything about tonight except for the last five minutes. You will understand that I used a truth spell on you, to see if you were involved in the attacks if you remember this at all, otherwise, you'll remember me being gentle to you, and tending to your injuries."

"How many times have you done this to me?" I

whispered angrily. How the hell *could* he do this to me? How many times had he?

"Forget what I told you to, now," he said, and I blinked, struggling to remind myself not to forget.

"Lucian," I whispered, blinking as his hand trailed down my arm; the soothing cream was thick in his palm as he applied it.

"How's the pain?" he asked, his eyes lifting to hold mine.

"It's fine," I replied. "Did I pass out?" I continued, watching as his lips twitched as if he struggled to hold back a smile.

CHAPTER
seventeen

To judge from the notions expounded by theologians, one must conclude that God created most men simply with a view to crowd hell. ~Marquis de Sade

~Lucian

I paced the room, my eyes drifting back to the connecting door and the woman who slept on the other side. How the fuck? No one was immune to my compulsion, no one. Yet this little wisp of a witch resisted it twice now. It made me want inside her mind even more.

I wanted to see what was in there, to know her weaknesses and learn her faults. I wanted to do a lot of things to Lena, most of which would make the sexy little witch cringe and blush to her roots. Her pussy…Seeing it with nothing between it and myself had almost undone my resolve. The taste of her, fucking hell, I'd wanted to bury my face in it, and listen to her scream as she came unraveled on my tongue.

Bathing her had been a fucking horror show. She hadn't even understood how badly she was burned, or that her flesh had disappeared in places, revealing the damaged muscles of her succulent thighs. Probably better that way; she'd been as oblivious to the life-threatening burns as she was to my efforts to heal her. She'd inhaled enough smoke that I'd feared we would lose her. Instead, she'd disregarded it, and turned her concern to her family. Luckily, she'd be healed by the time she woke up. Thanks to the salve and the salt from the leyline.

Mortals were weak, dragged down by those they loved. Love itself was a fucking disease. It's one I myself will never suffer again. I let myself weaken when I thought I was in love, only to be betrayed and cursed. Never again.

My cock jerked, hard as steel, and begged to be buried in Lena's soft, inviting flesh. I laughed soundlessly, hating that I was hard over something that I shouldn't be lusting after. I would have liked nothing more than to fuck the little imp until she never forgets me or my name for the rest of her days.

I grabbed my cock, yanked it once and imagined her lips, her soft lush mouth that probably couldn't open wide enough to take it. She could be taught, if I had the time. I don't. I could possibly make enough time to ravish her, fuck her senseless, and then do what I came here to do: Kill them all. I tired of the game, though, so only a few would live this time. Each one would be carefully selected; the weak. The weak were easy targets for when she's born again. I grunted, wishing it was that fucking easy.

It was never that easy.

I could easily destroy them all; however, there was always a chance of her being reincarnated into a new coven. That scenario would only make her harder to find when she comes of age.

This last hunt for Katarina had been challenging enough; challenging to the point that I had to use outside help to verify that I had located the correct coven. Normally, she would make an appearance every other generation or so. For some unfathomable reason, her last appearance was over a hundred and twenty years ago, and the coven had hidden itself well since then. I simply did not want to spare the effort to go through the endless searching again.

I opened the door before Bane knocked. His eyes went to my cock and I growled. My eyes turned red as his blue eyes did the same.

"Bringing them here was a bad idea, boss. Should have let them burn. Less to kill later; killing is messy. Messy is fucking time-consuming. I'm tired of burying bodies, and witches altogether. Need to go to the other clubs, find some girls, fuck five or six, maybe twenty, you in?" He absently itched his head where his dark blonde hair was gathered into a bun. He really should cut that shit off or just fucking leave it down.

"No," I growled, my eyes sliding back to the door and the sleeping feminine flesh on the other side. "Pretty sure only one can make my dick happy tonight," I snapped.

"Take her, make her forget it. Then take her again." His reasoning is simple, but then Layton always had been. He had a hunger, one that couldn't be sated. He craved pussy, and a lot of it. His fixation was everything and anything his partners would allow. *Anything.*

"It's not that simple; she's different. Smarter, stronger. I need to know why. I also need to use her to get close to Kendra, who won't give me the fucking time of day. She's different as well, and she was in the group that set off the wards."

"There's that, but there's also someone trying to kill them. We need to figure out why. Her grandmother, she was in the running for high priestess of the coven, and her mother isn't. Like the more powerful magic skipped a generation, which would make the girls powerful," he mused.

"Magic is selective of who gets to wield it; it's possible that both could be powerful, or one. Twins are an oddity within a coven, not even they understand why it happens. This bloodline has two sets; that isn't just a coincidence."

"Again, could be genetics."

"It could be genetics if any of them had it in their lines, but they don't. Therefore, it's not something we should ignore. Unless her brother returned, and isn't really dead," I considered out loud. "I've got Helen on a short leash; unless she can shut her worthless face, she may need to disappear soon."

"She's salivating for the place you promised her: high priestess of the coven."

"Not going to happen, ever. She's cunning, ambitious, and lazy in bed," I growled. Deviant mentioned that she couldn't even suck him off; she gave up. I fucking hate quitters.

"Vlad was in the club, pouring booze like he owned the place. Any particular reason you allowed it to happen?" he asked. His eyes searched for the answer as if it would be written on my fucking face; as if.

"He didn't hide who he was. It is better that we are able to monitor what he sees in the club, instead of him sneaking around on his own. I'd prefer to control what he sees, so that I know what he reports back to the Fae. I like him; respect is earned and he's earned it. His reputation for fairness bothers me. The Fae in general fucking bother me. I don't like that I respect them. We may need them, though; there's something different about this time, and they won't ask too many questions if we need their help. I find them a useful lot, deadly, but useful. There's also the fact that they need us as much as we need them. Back to the matter at hand, I want Dev in position, ready to charm my little witch. If I need a distraction for her, he's it."

"He's already here. Helen has him on her list as one of the sons of a coven elder in Utah. Bloodline originated in Salem," Layton said carefully. "You think they'll go through with the celebrations if they think their girls are in danger?"

"Witches stick to tradition, even if the fucking sky is falling. They think their magic depends on it."

"I think you should fix their house, get them out from under our roof. You already did it at the club."

"No, I can't have these witches thinking anything other than what I want them to. I want to have eyes on this family and this is the best play to do it." I narrowed my eyes on him as a thought struck. "You think I shouldn't fuck her, just say it."

"I don't think you should fuck her."

"Too fucking bad," I growled, my eyes turning to hold his. "My dick has been rock hard since the moment I kissed her. Not even the thought of Elaine and her skills have lessened the effect Lena has had on me. Not to mention I need her, and I want her. No matter if she's my enemy."

"And if she gets pregnant, you'll kill her?" he snapped angrily.

"You seem to have forgotten one of the curses the first little reincarnation gave me was an inability to sire children. It was her first pathetic attempt at protecting her coven from me. It's a new world, Bane; women can prevent pregnancy now. Magdalena Fitzgerald is already on birth control, if the packet in her medicine cabinet can be trusted."

"I thought the point of the Harvest was for them to fuck like rabbits and make a few babies. What if she went off of it?"

"It would seem my little witch is a rebel and has no intentions of making pretty little babies. Perhaps she has a plan in place to play along with the coven and her ancestors. She wouldn't be the first witch to do it in order to obtain her powers and avoid baby spit-up," I grinned, remembering how angry she'd been when she'd told me to go make pretty little heartbreaker babies and get lost. She's got fire, and beautiful chaos inside of her.

"Do we know the plan for the girls who set off the wards?" he asked, his eyes darting in the direction of one of the bitches he referred to that was sleeping inside this house.

"Elaine comes; we'll discuss the plans for the girls later."

~~*

-Magdalena

I didn't sleep as he'd requested, or, rather, demanded in his strange voice. Instead, I kept trying to remember everything I could about tonight. Pieces kept coming to me and I wasn't sure what really happened and what had been an illusion. I snuck a pen out of the bedside drawer and wrote every strange detail that I couldn't quite place on my arms; just in case I forgot. It wasn't until a woman's voice could be heard through the door that I left the bed.

I crept forward, listening to the woman as she bitched at Lucian, her voice rising as she got a good heated steam going.

"That's bullshit, I earned my spot! No stupid little witch is going to replace me in your bed, understand?"

"You forget your place, Elaine."

I lifted a brow at her declaration for her *spot*.

"Fuck that! Who the fuck is she? I'll slice her from ear to ear, and then you'll remember why you love me!"

"I never loved you, ever. I told you that it wasn't possible years ago. She'll die soon enough, but it won't be by your hand."

I clapped my hands over my mouth as images of Lucian standing with a swaddled dead body came rushing back. He was in my room, whispering words to me as he held my throat, preventing air from entering my lungs. No dog. Oh, fuck!

I looked around the room for an exit, realizing my family was in this man's house! Had he set the fire to get us here? It didn't make sense.

"Use me the way you like to. Anything you want, you can even call me her name," she pleaded, and I grimaced.

Desperation was not sexy. Her whiny voice grated on my nerves, and her threats made me wish I had enough magic to curse her with warts.

"Elaine, have some dignity. I told you this was a short-term arrangement, to not get attached."

"Is it *her?* If it is, you can just fucking kill her and be done with it! Or I will, Lucian; it's an easy fix. I'm not going away, and you can't make me!"

I heard scuffling, a window shattered, and as I moved

to the small window in my room, I watched as a small body hit the ground. I slapped my hands over my mouth and trembled. Holy shit! The knob on the door rattled, and I jumped into bed as silently as I could. I pulled the covers up to my neck, and closed my eyes.

I felt the bed give with his weight as he sat beside me calmly, like he hadn't just thrown a woman to her death. What the fuck? His hand slipped to my cheek and his fingers touched it gently. I opened my eyes slowly and turned to look up at him.

His lips touched my forehead as I turned to look at him, keeping my arms that were covered in notes beneath the blankets.

"Hi," I whispered, surprised that my voice was smooth and even.

"Morning, beautiful," he mumbled before his lips hovered over mine before claiming them. "It's not time to wake up yet, I just wanted to make sure you slept free of nightmares."

The only nightmare I was having was him.

CHAPTER
eighteen

He only stayed with me until he thought I was asleep. I waited a few more hours, making sure the house was quiet before I snuck out of the room and slipped out the front door. I ran to the cottage and quickly fed Luna before jumping in the shower and scrubbing the notes off as best I could.

I was careful around the areas that had been burned. The salt bath I took last night—mixed with the cream Lucian used—was amazing, and I wanted the recipe he used for it. The burns looked almost completely healed and barely hurt when I moved.

I stepped from the shower and screamed as I ran smack into Lucian's chest. "What the hell?" I demanded angrily, before I remembered a woman soaring through the air. Yeah, best not to piss him off.

"You snuck out of my house," he said smoothly, his eyes slowly trailing over my wet, naked body.

"I didn't want to wake you, and I needed clean clothes."

"I purchased clothing for you and your family," he countered. I blinked at his words, and faltered for a moment. How did he even know our sizes, let alone accomplish it so quickly?

"I need a towel," I whispered, painfully aware that I was naked, and he wasn't. I felt exposed and vulnerable in front of him like this. I had covered my breasts with my arms, but it did little to hide anything from the heat in his midnight eyes.

"I have those too," he said with a soft smile.

I glared up at him. "You're in my space; you really need to learn about personal boundaries. Now, get out while I get dressed, please?"

He smiled again, but this one said he didn't care much about personal boundaries, and before I could push him out, he captured my hands. "Something changed in you, little witch. You're cold today."

"Because I'm standing here naked?" I growled.

He dropped my hands and turned on his heel, leaving me watching his back as he left the bathroom. I didn't breathe until I heard the front door slam behind him. The entire cottage shook with his departure, or maybe just me. I quickly pulled on panties, a long sleeved shirt, and some black sneakers I'd found in the closet, along with a pair of overalls, and gloves.

I moved out of the bathroom, only to find myself staring at Benjamin, who looked at me cautiously, but with relief, before his smile took on a hard edge of coldness.

My already erratic heart thundered as I looked at him. I wanted to rush to him, throw my arms around him and pretend he was Josh. I wanted to gush over the house catching fire, cry in his strong arms about what I'd gone through; instead, I slowly moved out of the bedroom, and gave him my back as I pulled my hair into a tight ponytail.

"Can I help you?" I whispered as I met his eyes in the reflection of the small mirror. "Perhaps you came to burn down the cottage too?"

"I didn't set the fire, Lenny; when I heard about it, I came to check on you."

"Sure, and you didn't set off the bomb either," I snapped angrily; he had the same 'tell' that Joshua had when he lied: He'd chew his bottom lip after he'd fed me the line of utter shit and then waited to see if I'd believe it.

"Knowing how much you meant to him, I would never hurt you," he said carefully, his arms crossing in a defensive pose as his eyes watched me.

"You mean Joshua, how much I meant to him? I mean nothing to you. You're a stranger." My voice was cold as I turned to look at him. "You made it clear that you didn't come here for us. So why *are* you here? Or tell me this, why does shit start blowing up the moment you show up? Or explain why we end up burned in a fire that was set to the manor and then suddenly I find you here, in my house?"

"You were burned?" he asked, his eyes filled with worry as he looked me over. If he had set the fire, he hadn't meant to hurt us in it.

"I was; I almost died, as well as Kendra, and our mother, too. If you cast the spell, you did a piss-poor job if murder wasn't your intention, *brother*."

"I didn't have a fucking teacher like you did. I didn't have a mother who loved me enough to keep me!" he snapped, and it hurt. I felt it bone-deep.

"So what was your plan or reason for setting the fire?

Why did you want inside the house, and do a shit poor job on the spell? I am pretty sure it takes more than one witch to cast something as powerful as that spell was, asshole. Is there something specific you came here for?"

"I didn't set the fucking fire." He scowled and wagged his finger at me. "You're not sweet and innocent, he lied," he mused angrily. "You also have the darkness inside of you," he growled as he moved closer slowly, his eyes narrowed on me knowingly.

I held my ground, watching him as he stalked around me. "Is that what you think?" I asked carefully. "That I'm like you?"

"You are like me. Darkness can sense others with the same taint. You have it; you stink of it, *sis*."

It was meant to be a slap in the face and we both knew it. "It's nothing, *brother mine*. I got this shit handled, unlike you. I've never used it. No matter how much it tried to make me, I resisted it."

"No one can fight off the darkness alone, not when it sinks its teeth in. You know that. That's why I was thrown away like the garbage. So why keep you, when she didn't even try to save me?"

I smiled sadly at him. "You broke her, Benjamin, believe it or not. She didn't just send you away and move on. She's always been a bit broken and we never knew why. When Joshua died, it was devastating for her, because she didn't just lose him, she lost what little bit she had left of you that day too. It took everything she had just to get the hell out of bed in the morning. You think it was an easy choice for her to send you away? It wasn't. Sad part is, it's what the coven's done since forever; it's what we do when a child is born wrong. It isn't your fault, and it isn't hers. It sure as hell isn't mine. You want a pity party, look elsewhere."

"I could kill you," he snarled.

"Easily, I'm sure. You didn't come here to kill me, though. I don't think you're as bad as you want everyone to think, either. If you were, Joshua wouldn't have told you dick about us. He would have protected us from you and he didn't. I think he saw in you what I do, a lost kid who got a raw deal in life, one who is of our bloodline and family. You may have been raised badly. You, however, you are not full darkness. You accepted it in, sure, but you figured a way to control it."

"What makes you say that?" he asked carefully, a guarded look in his eyes.

"Because if darkness had taken complete control of you, I'd already be dead, and I'm not. I'm not the best at math, but even I can take an educated guess on that one."

"You're playing with fire, witch."

"Why does everyone call me that? My name is Magdalena! Lena, or Lenny to you; yes, I caught that you used the nickname only Joshua called me. So I know you knew him; what I want to know, the only thing I want to know, is what you meant by it should've been you instead of him."

"Got to run, sis," he said with a guarded smile and a haunted look in his eyes. He moved in his creepy way, stopped abruptly in front of me and placed three chaste kisses on my forehead, temple, and cheek before he vanished into thin air.

I threw my hands up at the same moment Lucian threw the door open, burst into the room, and looked around. "You weren't alone."

"I wasn't," I stuttered. "Luna's here with me."

He took in my outfit and lifted a dark brow in question.

"Gardening?"

"I was going to work on the main house."

"I already called someone in to clean it up for your mother, someone who is more qualified."

"Did we ask you to?" I snapped, and then caught myself. "I'm sorry. I'm tired, my mom's house is covered in ash, soot, and debris, and it needs to be fixed so we can move home. I don't like you being so close to my bedroom." I threw in the last to make sure he knew that I knew he'd placed me right next to him on purpose.

I couldn't sleep at all last night. But then again, who could sleep after watching a woman get thrown out of a window? I'd walked by the spot where I had seen her land this morning on my way home, only to discover no glass from the window, and no body. The yard yielded nothing as well, no disturbed dirt from a body being buried. I know what I saw and heard last night and he *had* thrown her from the window. Somehow he'd covered it up without even breaking a sweat. It wasn't an easy task to manage without something being left behind, right?

His eyes watched me as I marched past him. As quick as a snake, he grabbed my arm and pulled me close to him.

"Who was here?" he asked coldly; his jaw tensed, revealing a muscle that hammered with his growing anger.

"Who I allow inside my house isn't your business. I'm a grown woman, not a little kid who needs to report to you."

"You should watch that mouth, it might just get in you into trouble," he growled as he licked his own lips.

"Wouldn't be the first time; doubt it's going to be the last."

"Maybe it needs a purpose, someone to show it what it

can do, and how to use it properly," he mused and before I could think better of it, I licked my own lips and peeked at the python hiding in his pants.

"Let me guess. You're going to offer to teach me? Pass. Now, if you're done I have to get started on the house."

"Last night, you wanted me to fuck you, witch," he stated, and he was right. Not that I would admit it. "Now you're cold, what changed?"

"Nothing," I whispered carefully, my eyes rising to lock with his.

It was a mistake. His eyes searched mine, and I felt a gentle push against my mind, as if he was reading my memories. I felt him hit the walls I'd erected and I smiled, his eyes narrowing at me as I added extra layers around the walls, and felt him pull away.

"Trying to hide something, little witch?" he asked, and I smirked as I glared at him, but kept my mouth closed. I wasn't suicidal, or stupid. I could however, play stupid really well.

"I'm not an architect, and I don't work in construction. I need to get past you, so that I can go work on my mom's house. I don't want to impose on your generosity for any longer than we have to," I replied with just the right amount of saucy sarcasm.

"The coven has forbidden anyone from entering the manor house. It's not been cleared of the spell that caused the damage. Let me be crystal clear about this, because I'm only to say it once: It's not safe for you. Get changed; I have a few things for you to do. Your punishment from the coven isn't over, and I find myself in need of your help," he growled low. His self-assured grin made me want to slap it off his beautiful face.

CHAPTER
nineteen

Club Chaos looked completely different in the morning light. Lucian must have had some of the best damn contractors on the planet. The damage from the explosion the evening before seemed like it had magically been erased. It looked like it had never happened, as if I'd imagined it.

Lucian had given me a list of duties and explained how each duty was to be performed. He also gave me a cart that held a trash can and various cleaners, plastic gloves, and a keycard that only opened certain rooms that he wanted me to clean. I was also given a strict admonition to follow his instructions to the letter. I wasn't a freaking maid, but this chore did fall under the coven's idea of punishment.

I descended to the lower level and found the rooms on my list, then got to work. The rooms were an odd thing to find under a club and looked as if they were used for overnight stays. Each one was set up a little differently as far as adult toys and kinky-as-shit equipment; some things I had to look up on my phone to actually figure out what the hell they were used for. However, each room had a bag of brand-new bedding rather than the freshly laundered bedding as hotels had. With each room I entered, a camera in the corner blinked and followed me as I cleaned.

It wasn't until I entered a room marked 'Boss' that I paused and really looked around. This room was larger than the others, yet this one had a bed, with a length of chain attached to each post. On the table in the middle of the room were a thin, springy rattan cane and a set of black Kegel beads. According to my phone internet search, these Kegel balls evidently had a phone app that went with them, which controlled the vibration level via Bluetooth. I backed away from it, moved to the glass mirrors that made up the walls of the room, and started cleaning them with only a few curious looks back at the beads and the cane.

What the hell was this place? I removed a glove when it ripped against my fingernail and tossed it in the garbage can on the cart before resuming washing the glass. The moment my flesh touched the mirrored surface, it turned into clear glass, and the room beyond it was revealed.

Soft grey couches were situated against the walls of the room, which had a raised stage in the center of it. A wicked looking X was affixed to one of the walls and had chains similar to the ones attached to the bed in the room I stood in. These ones dangled from each point of the cross. I swallowed as my mind ran wild; a torture room? Oh my God, he was hosting some kind of mutilation club here!

I spun around and was about to run from the room, when I found him leaning against the door. His smile was soft as his eyes moved from me to the table and then to the room beyond the glass.

"You're sick," I snapped without thinking.

He lifted a brow but said nothing. The door behind him closed and clicked as he slowly moved closer, forcing me to back up until I was flush with the glass. "You're a sadist, aren't you? Some kind of freak who gets off on torturing people," I whispered shakily.

"Is that what you think this place is?" he laughed, the sound cold and merciless.

"I have eyes," I snapped.

"It's a sex club, Lena. Not to say that there isn't a bit of torture that happens here, but those who receive it do so willingly. You've been sheltered more than I thought. The sex industry is a lucrative business, one of the highest grossing industries in the world."

"You run a sex club here?" I whispered, horrified. "Does the coven know about it?"

"The elders do. They get a portion of the club's revenue to help maintain the town. I'm not hiding it, if that's what you think."

I took another step back as he moved closer. "I can show you a few things, if you're still curious."

"I'm fine," I swallowed hard, my eyes watching his as a smile flittered across his mouth, as if it was a joke. As if he'd set me up, which he probably had.

"There's that word again."

"I should go," I whispered as I tried to move past him, only for him to block my path. I ran straight into his chest with a dull thud that rattled my brains. "Stop doing that!"

"Doing what?" he asked as he picked me up even though I struggled against him. He moved me to the bed and held me against the mattress.

"This! Stop it," I gritted out as I fought against him to

get back to my feet. I was just about to shout at him that I'd had enough of him when someone laughed close to us. I turned my head looking around him, intending to tell whoever it was that this wasn't what it looked like.

I stopped cold as I watched the woman I'd seen being thrown from Lucian's window last night laugh as she pulled three men with her into the room on the other side of the mirror. Now that I could see her face, I realized she was the lovesick woman in Lucian's office the second time I was there. I felt Lucian tense and rise from the bed to move to the glass. He touched it briefly before he stepped back.

She was in one piece, not buried in some patch of land, as I had assumed she was. At the moment, she was naked as the day she was born, and the men were as well. I watched silently as she went down on her knees and began sucking one off.

"Oh wow," I whispered, horrified that I was witness to it. Lucian was stiff, his back to me as he watched the woman with the men. I now knew what the glass was for. It was some sort of two-way glass; they couldn't see us watching them. The man she was working on grunted as he gripped her hair and pulled her mouth away from his engorged cock before shoving her up onto the stage painfully.

I heard Lucian grumble, but he didn't look away from her beautiful body. She was petite, with slender hips and a swelling bosom curved perfectly, even though her breasts were overlarge for her small frame. Her midnight hair was down and free of the sparkling pins this time, and her green eyes reminded me of a cat. Her skin was porcelain; not a single bruise or blemish marred it. She was too perfect.

I moved closer without realizing it, covering my mouth as one man approached her wielding a wicked looking cane. I heard a sharp crack and watched as it found its mark. On her skin. She cried out and smiled. *She fucking smiled!* I could see the angry red welt where it had touched her and marked her beautiful skin.

Another crack sounded and another welt rose on her skin, this one from a whip, and she purred as if she enjoyed the pain. I couldn't grasp what I was seeing, or what it actually was. One man with dark hair moved behind her, gripping her hips as he pushed his heavy cock inside of her until he was buried in her heat.

I fought to control my breathing, as well as my body. I was growing flushed at what was happening in the room beyond the glass. I felt Lucian's eyes turn to me, and yet I couldn't look away from the show. The blonde man who used the cane a few moments ago was in her mouth, as the third stalked predatorily around the trio with a whip that he would flick out intermittently with a sharp snap and leave another welt on her back. Although most of their sounds were muffled, her noises were loud, even with the cock buried in her throat—and it had to be buried, because it was huge and I couldn't see it, any of it!

I felt my hands as they balled into tight fists as I tried to process the scene, but failed. Lucian moved to me; his hand touching my cheek made me jump out of my skin.

"No!" I cried with wide eyes at the thought of him taking me in there increased the overwhelming fear I was beginning to choke on. "No. Not me, I can't. I won't do that, ever. I've got to go!"

"Lena, stop," his voice cracked in the room, loudly. Ignoring him, I sprinted for the door and tugged on the handle. "You weren't supposed to see that; it was meant for me," he replied angrily.

"I need out of this room," I whispered.

"They locked it, which means you and I are stuck here until they've finished."

My cheeks were crimson; my hands trembling as my eyes unwillingly went back to the show. I wasn't sure what terrified me the most, that I was turned on by it, or that I was an unwilling witness to it.

"You're okay here, no one will do anything to you," he assured me, but my eyes, traitors that they were, were glued to the absolute debauchery happening in the other room. His eyes watched me, and yet it took one hell of an effort for me to remove mine from where she was pleasuring them all now. I wasn't even sure it was humanly possible, but she had all three of them inside of her and she was making noises that indicated she was more than just enjoying it.

"That's…wow," was all I could get out as I finally turned around and faced him, but the look in his eyes didn't make me feel safe, it made me feel hunted.

"You like watching," he commented casually as his eyes narrowed on me, and then lowered to my moist heat that was definitely wet. "That's unexpected."

"I do not," I whispered and yet my brain demanded I turn around so that it could see what was happening now. Two of the men were grunting, and a third must have finished because she was screaming like a banshee. She wasn't screaming any of their names though; she was screaming *his*. "You're being called."

"I'm not interested in her," his voice rumbled softly as he pulled me close to his body, ignoring the fact that I was stiff, so stiff a board would be jealous of my posture. "You, though, you're just full of surprises."

He spun me around in his arms, his arm trapping me there as it pressed against my breasts, his lips pressing against my ear. "You think she's going to say its *fine* when they've finished with her?" he teased huskily, his tongue touching against my pulse as it raced.

"Yes," I whispered unwilling to change my opinion.

"You're wet," he announced, his hand slowly moving down my body until he cupped my sex. "Do you want to take her place? I could arrange it."

"No, definitely not," I replied quickly. *No way in hell!*

"Liar," he whispered as he turned me around and smiled at me. "Sex isn't a vile act, no matter who tries to convince you otherwise. God didn't make a mistake by placing Eve in the garden with Adam; he knew what he was doing. For fuck's sake, he put them in there naked, and they were only human. It was in their nature to take what they needed. They did what came naturally. They fucked and ultimately blamed it on a serpent. How perfectly fucked up is that? I personally believe that they blamed the wrong serpent."

"I'm not sure the bible belongs in a place like this," I replied as I tried to avert my gaze. "I'm pretty sure even the devil would blush here."

"I wouldn't be so sure of that," he mused softly as his eyes moved to the other room. "Do you think you'd like pain?"

"No," I whispered.

"Why not?" he asked softly, his eyes filled with molten heat. "There's a fine line between pain and pleasure; sometimes it can't be separated."

"You gave her pain," I murmured.

"I gave her what she enjoys."

"I don't think she knows what she needs," I whispered.

I was unsure if I meant myself or her, and he'd caught that.

He smiled and picked me up effortlessly, then tossed me unceremoniously onto the bed, hard. I tried to sit up, but he slammed over the top of me, knocking the air from my lungs painfully. His hand cupped my sex, and pinched it, making my hips buck against him as I cried out, and then he rubbed it carefully, making fluids rush to my entrance.

His mouth moved over one breast, finding the nipple and biting it hard through the shirt I wore, then released and rubbed it with his lips as his hot breath fanned it to a painful ache. I was helpless against the sensations that rushed through my body. I was wet, soaking wet. His hand captured both of mine and held them painfully above my head, in a vise like grip. His teeth skimmed over my carotid artery and nipped it, then kissed it. It was intoxicating, and no matter how much I tried to convince myself otherwise, I was enjoying what he was doing to me.

"Your heart is racing, Lena. Do I scare, or excite you?" he whispered hoarsely as his mouth crushed against mine painfully; teeth slammed together, his tongue demanded entrance and took it. He was hard, unyielding as he laid claim to me. As if he had lost control, just as I had while witnessing the act in the other room. His fingers dug into my wrists painfully, making me moan and scream at the same time, which opened my lips further to his enticing, demanding kiss.

I kissed him back, and he groaned as he dug his free hand into my jeans, finding my clit and squeezed it hard. I bucked against it, and cried out as the storm of emotions built inside of me. He released it, and with two fingers entered my body painfully, spreading them until it was pain and pleasure. The jeans ripped, the button and zipper breaking free under the pressure. He smiled against my mouth as he held me there, kissing me, fucking me hard with his fingers as the moans and cries from the other room filled the one we were in. Or maybe it was our own now.

I felt the storm crest, and then I came undone. My entire body trembled and quivered, and wetness coated his fingers, my body clenching against his intrusion. My ears rang from the cries that filled the room, his mouth cutting them off as he kissed me softly through the storm. His fingers continued to move slowly inside of me, his thumb tenderly rubbing against my clitoris. Tears leaked from my eyes as I tried to comprehend what was happening to me.

"I own your first orgasm, Magdalena. Only me," he growled as he pulled away and rolled from the bed. I watched as he left through the now unlocked door. I moved from the bed on shaky legs, and ran.

CHAPTER
twenty

I'd tried to dodge Lucian for the rest of the day, and had somehow managed it. I hated that I'd enjoyed his touch, but mostly, I hated that I'd been turned on by watching the foursome in the other room. I wasn't kinky by nature. Curious would be a better description. What I'd witnessed in that room was so far out of my comfort zone that I might as well have been in Hong Kong trying to speak and understand Chinese.

I'd skipped dinner, and didn't leave the room other than to try and find a bathroom to take care of my personal needs. I just stepped out of the room when I heard soft footsteps behind me and spun around to see my sister and mother coming down the hallway.

"You've been to the house?" I asked, noting that they were dirty with soot.

"The people Lucian hired just finished with the house cleanup and the coven is done with their inspection. It's been cleared, but the damage is more than I thought it would be," my mother said sadly. "The abbey is being prepared for the Awakening ceremony, so Lucian has been kind enough to allow us to stay a few extra days until rooms can be made ready for us there."

"A few days?" I groaned, wondering how I was going to manage to dodge him for that long. The contractors Lucian hired for his club had done an amazing job overnight, perhaps we could hire them to work their magic on the manor house, and move back into it.

"Magdalena, it's a kindness you shouldn't complain about. Besides, the coven wants us here. Well, at least until we know for sure it's safe to go home," my mother hissed quietly, as if she feared the walls had ears and would report my words straight away to the master of the house.

"I'm not complaining, but we have events coming up. Tomorrow is the first mixer to allow us to get to know the men from the other covens better. Kendra has nothing to wear! Neither do I," I lied. I had a few things, but nothing really dressy, or appropriate for the events that would be taking place in the next few days. Lucian had mentioned purchasing clothing for us, but I'd yet to see them, which meant I had no idea if they'd fit, or what to expect.

"We will manage, we always do," Kendra said, her eyes daring me to argue.

"You need to be perfect so that you can carry on the family's bloodline," I teased with a small smile.

"I don't think it will matter to our ancestors if I'm dressed in couture or not. Are you okay?" she asked, noting that I was searching for pretty much any excuse to get away from the house we were currently stuck in, or more to the point, away from him.

"I'm fine," I said, because other than my total embarrassment, I was fine. I just had to figure out a way to continue dodging Lucian until the abbey had room for us or the manor house was fixed. "What did the coven figure out?"

"The fire wasn't an accident," Kendra confirmed, her blue eyes lighting with anger. "Someone tried to kill us; they think it was someone close to us. They also think I'm the one who was targeted. They said it was some sort of alchemy." Something in the way she said alchemy and wouldn't make eye contact with me caught my attention and set off warning bells.

"How is that possible?" I gasped. "Alchemy is only done with the approval of the elders; the slightest mistake is deadly."

"They don't know how or why, but they think the bomb was the work of the same person. It could be that Benjamin is in league with them, but it's highly unlikely; if anyone around here used it, the elders would have sensed it. The spell was pretty complex, and they said this type of magic has unique fingerprints."

Alchemy was bad news. Especially if the coven couldn't trace whoever was creating nasty spells that seemed to be getting entirely too close for comfort. Those weren't the type of things we needed this close to the Awakening.

I looked at my mother as she studied me carefully. Her eyes seemed to see through me, as if she was trying to read my mind.

"Mom?" I asked carefully.

"You took botany, Lena. Classes that could help you learn alchemy," she whispered.

"I took botany to help the business," I said with

a frown. "I took business ethics, too. I took anything I thought would help us with the growth of the business, shit, I even learned how to make soaps and other things to sell in the shop. I haven't had my curse lifted and nothing I learned could help make bombs or supernatural fires. It's not like they have a class on *how to create magical flames* at the community college."

"The coven is just looking into every possible scenario, Lena. Just as you come back to town, things start going boom…" Kendra said softly, her eyes filled with worry. "You've been gone a long time, and they are just being careful. One of the elders has suggested that we try a memory spell, just to be sure. It would get you off the hook," she said quickly.

"Memory spells are usually blood magic, aren't they? Wait, just *who* the heck will be doing the spell?" I growled.

"Me," Lucian said from behind me.

I closed my eyes and shook my head; so much for the dodging. "You really think this is necessary?" I asked, refusing to turn around and deal with the wild storm of emotions that ran through me knowing he was directly behind me, probably from remembering what he'd done to me just a few hours ago.

"We have already agreed for you to do it, that way they can move past you and on to who is really behind these vile acts. There's also the concern that we have girls who were eligible for the Awakening, who have seemingly vanished into thin air." My mother's eyes pleaded with me anxiously to not disagree.

"Thanks for having my back, Mother," I whispered through the pain that sliced through my heart. Most types of blood magic hurt; it was old magic, and hardly ever done in our coven. It could link the participants, create a false bond that wasn't there.

Of course they'd put me together with Lucian, and why wouldn't they? Except for Kendra, no one knew I'd kissed him or that he'd been in my pants, literally. I turned to look at him, only to find him looking at me as if he didn't feel a damn thing.

"I was just going to shower," I said softly, before I expelled a deep shuddering breath. "Guess it can wait since we have to be purified...together," I finished with a cringe.

The preparation for blood magic had to be done carefully, the area quarantined to keep any outside magic from influencing the spell. The elders would be present, erecting a wall around us to keep anyone out while we were vulnerable. It would also give Lucian a fast ride through my past, my horrors, my sorrows, and pretty much everything he had no damn right to see.

"It's not as bad as you've been told," he said with a wicked look in his eyes that was for me alone. "We should go; it takes a while to be purified, and the coven will be here shortly."

I rolled my eyes, and followed behind him, refusing to acknowledge my mother or sister behind us, even when Kendra tried to get my attention. I didn't have anything nice to say. They'd agreed to this, this medieval bullshit ritual that would show him everything about me! Why him? Of anyone they could choose from who knew blood magic, why him?

I knew that there weren't a lot of people who knew how to safely do the ritual, but I was willing to take my chances with someone else. I was willing to do pretty much anything to clear my name that didn't have me going through this particular ritual with him.

We walked down the long, winding stairway at the end of the hall, and moved partway down a darkened hallway. I paused as he placed his palms on the wall and pushed, revealing a set of rooms that I never would have guessed were there.

Inside the room was dark. He whispered a short chant and candles leapt to life. The earthy scent of sage was overpowering and we could hear the sound of running water, as if a spring actually ran through the room. Maybe he had a fountain in here why not? The man had his own sex club, so anything was possible.

He indicated one of the other rooms and I looked in that direction to find a huge bubbling pool, which had steam billowing from it. A curtain was suspended from the ceiling and encircled it for some semblance of privacy.

"Your mother and sister will bless the room. The water will act as the purifier to remove any outside taint. I will cast the spell once we are sure there is no outside influence present."

Dark eyes held mine captive as his sensual mouth curved into a lopsided grin. He was daring me to fight with him about this situation, as if I had any actual say in what was going to happen. This was going to be an awkward situation at best if my mother and sister were going to be in the room while he and I were both naked.

"The sage, what is it for?" I asked, changing the subject to something safer.

"It's to cleanse the air and help open your mind to allow me inside," he said softly, his eyes lowered to the shirt that fit a little too snugly against my breasts.

"The red salt around the pool is to keep evil out, or in?" I asked pointedly with a little smirk of my own. This guy was evil; maybe not in the biblical sense, but the way those eyes peered through me wasn't good.

"Outside," he acknowledged with narrow eyes.

"Do we have to be naked for this?" I questioned, hoping to any God listening that they'd take mercy on me.

They didn't.

"I'm pretty sure no one has ever gotten clean with their clothes on in the bath or shower, Lena," he said absently as he turned to watch my mother and sister, and offer advice as they purified the room. Sage and saffron burned around the edge of the pool in small cauldrons. I watched Kendra as she added a thick line of black and green salt in a circle around the pool. My mother tried to reach the sheer material that surrounded the pool, and when she couldn't reach it, Lucian offered to loosen it, and put it in place for her.

Kendra added purple and white flowers into the water, and I shivered as Mom murmured a spell that seemed to slide over me with each syllable.

"Scared to be alone with me?" Lucian whispered softly.

"Yes," I admitted with a nervous laugh that bubbled up from deep inside of me. "Terrified, actually," I returned with a pointed look.

"You should be, considering the things I want to do to you," he replied easily as he let the words soak in. He reached down, grabbed the bottom of his shirt and swiftly lifted it over his head, revealing sinewy muscles that looked as if he never left the gym. My eyes latched on to the tattoos and runes that my fingers itched to trace.

He stood there, allowing me to take in my fill. He knew he had this effect on me, and he was enjoying it. I stood motionlessly, needing him to continue his little perverted strip tease, but instead he purposely ran his fingers down his chest. It was a slow, deliberate move to make my eyes latch on to the dark tendrils of hair that disappeared into his jeans.

"I've finished the cleansing, Lucian," my mother said as she whispered one more spell to light the candles that now circled the pool. I wanted to scream at her, because it looked like some romantic little lovers' nest instead of a ritual site.

The flowers floated on the water, and the scent of sage and saffron irritated my nose, yet the subtle hint of the lilies and the hyacinth flowers soothed it. The candles glowed, illuminating the room in a beautiful contrast of shadows and light. The sheer material of the tent that surrounded the pool gave it an alluring appeal. I turned to my mother and started to speak, but she shook her head, stopping me.

"We will be just outside the door, Lena. Relax; Lucian won't allow anything to go wrong."

I opened my mouth to explain that everything was already wrong, but shut it as Lucian gave me a warning look. Interesting; he didn't want my mother to know we'd been in a scandalous position just this morning.

Kendra gave me a reassuring hug and patted my back. "You'll be fine, the sooner this is over, the sooner they can start looking for whoever is really responsible," she said comfortingly.

I watched as my only hope slipped out of the room and closed the door firmly behind them. I turned back to Lucian, who was watching me carefully.

"You won't be able to hide anything from me now, little witch," he purred as his thumb flicked the button of his jeans and they slid down his hips.

I swallowed, once, twice, and wondered when they

had relocated the Sahara Desert into my mouth. I shook my head and spun around as his dick was released from the jeans.

"Get undressed," he ordered. The command was just that: an order to get naked in front of him. I nibbled my bottom lip with apprehension and uncertainty. This was the man who'd brought me to climax with his hand earlier, and the same one I'd tried to hide from in shame for the rest of the day, only to end up stuck with him in some archaic ritual.

I carefully pulled my shirt over my head, knowing that I couldn't waste time, not with the coven on their way here. I kicked off the soft leather slippers, and carefully undid the button on my pants. I bent down to remove them and enjoyed the hiss that sounded from behind me as he took in the little thong panties I wore.

I turned and moved slowly towards the pool, where he waited. He just about filled it up. It no longer looked big; it looked small with him in it.

"Turn around," I whispered.

"I've already seen you naked, Lena."

"I really don't care if you have or not, turn around," I ordered and watched as indecision played in his eyes. He wasn't used to being given orders. He was the one who dished them out, and everyone around him jumped to do as he bid, but not me.

"Fine," he said after a few moments of watching me.

Once he turned around, I slipped out of my panties and bra and entered the heated pool. I moved to the other side, away from him, and sank far enough into the water that the flowers covered most of me.

"You can turn around now," I whispered, feeling shy and inadequate. This man probably had been with women who were beyond beautiful, and yet he flirted with me. Maybe it was pity, or maybe he actually liked me; either way, nothing more was going to happen between us.

"You weren't shy at my club," he reminded me as his eyes moved to where my hands crossed over my naked breasts beneath the water. "Witches are normally open about sex, and you are not."

"That's a stereotype if I've ever heard one. That's like saying we all have warts and ride around on brooms," I countered defensively.

"I didn't say it was a bad thing, Lena," he replied smoothly as he moved further into the water, uncaring that the water barely hit his waist, or that I could see his ass. It was a really nice ass. Adonis would be jealous of that man's ass. I bit my lip, and jerked my eyes away from him.

"Is that why you opened the club? So that you could enjoy sex?" I asked carefully, my eyes still on the other side of the room, as if the wall was the most interesting thing in this universe.

"I opened the clubs because I have certain needs, and they can be fulfilled there while making a profit."

"What are you into?" I asked curiously.

"You're not ready for what I am into," he replied closer to me than he'd been, forcing me to turn my head, only to find his lips inches from mine. "You would probably think I was perverted, maybe even deranged if I told you what I like."

"How do you know I would? You don't even know me, so you shouldn't be judging what I would or wouldn't do."

"I like control," he said softly, his obsidian eyes lighting with banked heat as he scanned my face.

"Explain," I urged.

"I like to have total control in the bedroom. The women I have sex with have no problem giving it to me. I become the master, and they become whatever I crave them to be," he said with a guarded look in his eyes.

"You make them slaves?" I countered with a question, my heart racing at his close proximity.

"Some. I like them to feel helpless, dependent on me. I like to make them beg for things, and I enjoy their pain."

I blinked rapidly. What. The. Fuck? Sadist?

"You're a sadist," I whispered.

"I'm whatever I want to be at the moment," he countered as he moved even closer. "Is the water too hot?"

"No, why?" I asked carefully.

"Because your skin is red," he said with a small smirk as he placed his hands against the pool on either side of me, trapping me in the spot I sat in. "Think you could handle doing whatever I wanted you to?" he whispered hoarsely.

"No," I replied honestly. "I'm not into those types of things," I finished breathlessly.

"Is that why you were so fucking wet today? Because you weren't into it at all?" he asked as he pushed away and seated himself across from me.

"It wasn't what I was seeing that was turning me on, Lucian," I whispered watching him from beneath my lashes. "It was you."

"Liar," he laughed softly. "Then why were you hiding from me all day?" he asked as he rested the back of his head his against the side of the pool, and closed his eyes.

CHAPTER
twenty-one

"I wasn't hiding," I lied as my eyes focused on a tendril of water as it slowly moved down his chest.

"Hiding because you want me, or hiding because you're unsure of how you felt today?" he questioned.

"Today shouldn't have happened," I replied softly as I glanced back up at him. He opened his eyes and studied me for a long moment before he spoke.

"You want me, and you were turned on by what you saw. You just can't admit it yet, which is fine; you'll get there. Admitting you want me is the first step down a very dark path. I'm willing to lead you down it, Lena."

"As *if*," I blatantly lied to him as my heart raced, my pupils dilated, and my back arched a sliver. I fought to control the reaction I had to him. "Tell me about the ritual." I changed the subject to something a little safer—okay, a *lot* safer.

He smiled coldly and whatever had been in his eyes slipped back inside of him. He pushed off the edge of the pool and moved towards me. When he was closer, he sat beside me and once again rested his head on the pool's slick side.

"We will exchange words, and I will see into your past. How far I go depends on you. I'm just along for the ride. It is a bit like hypnosis; we will be delving past your conscious mind to your unconscious mind, only, instead of you telling me what you see, I'll be able to see it too. The herbs in the water and flowers should help you focus on particular events."

"Do we stay naked for it?" I asked apprehensively.

"We will be in robes for the ritual itself. The spell is difficult, so precautions will be taken," he whispered as he opened his eyes and turned his head to look at me. "Don't trust me?" he asked after a tense moment had passed.

"I just don't trust anyone when I'm naked and out of it."

"What we did today, Lena, it was consensual," he whispered as his hand slipped through the water and slid over the inside of my thigh.

My breathing hitched, and then got stuck in my lungs as he closed his eyes again and continued rubbing my leg erotically.

"Lucian," I whispered breathlessly.

He moved so quickly that I didn't have time to respond, or even react. His immense body pinned mine to the side of the pool, and his heavy cock rested on my belly. I looked down, noting that it went past my navel, and was incredibly thick. It twitched and my eyes flew up to Lucian's. I opened my mouth, only to have it filled with his hungry, dominating kiss.

I moaned against him as he rubbed himself against my stomach. His hands captured mine as I tried to place them against his chest. His kiss was hungry, intoxicating my senses and lowering any argument I might have had about him being this close to me naked.

One hand held mine locked in a vise grip while the other pulled carefully at my hair, opening my jaw even wider for his kiss until it hurt. My nipples hardened, need filling them with every passing second his mouth remained locked with mine. Moans filled the small room, both his and mine, and I felt him parting my thighs. I willingly helped him, until a knock sounded and he pulled away from me so fast, I barely registered that he had.

We struggled to control our breathing, fought against the overwhelming lust and sexual tension that filled the room. His eyes watched me, as surely as mine watched him as he controlled his labored breathing.

"This isn't finished," he warned as he turned his head and called for the intruder to come inside the room.

That was it! I was going to the abbey and joining the damn thing! This man drove me over the edge of sanity, and straight to the fucking crazy train boarding for the loony bin. I'd never been so sexually frustrated in my entire life.

I watched as one of the elders entered, and Lucian slipped from the pool unabashedly to take the white robe the elder offered him. I followed his cue, watching his back as I slipped into my own robe with a little help from the elder. The silk was soft and cool against my heated flesh, and I felt a shiver as they helped me pull the hood up.

I followed Lucian's broad back through the door we'd entered the hidden room in, and towards another room. On the other side of the entrance was another small room that housed something that almost looked like an altar. In the middle of the room was a wide circular table carved out of redwood and low platforms that looked like kneelers had been carved from stone and were placed intermittently on the floor around the table. Salt had been poured in a ring on the floor surrounding the table and rocks. In the center of the table, a crude pentagram had been carved into the wood. In the middle of the pentagram was a chalice along with a long, ornate ceremonial athame.

I felt Lucian at my side, his finger slowly touching mine for comfort as I started to panic. That simple touch said a million things, yet nothing at all.

"Are you guilty, Lena?" he whispered, even though we were close enough for others to hear him.

"Oh, what exactly am I being accused of? No one has said much of anything about which charges or what they really think I have done," I replied through trembling lips.

"You'll do fine," he smiled reassuringly even though he dodged the question. "Kneel at the table; the salt will keep us protected and grounded from anything that seeks to harm us inside the world created by the spell."

"You didn't say anything about leaving this world," I hissed as I decided which of the kneelers I would rather be at.

"It's going to be okay, Magdalena, I'll protect you," he said with a sexy half-smirk. "I got you; nothing bad will happen when you are with me."

I kneeled on the smooth stones, placed my hands on the altar, and watched as he did the same. I watched silently as he whispered a few words in a strange language, and the candles shot to life with flames too high and too hot for the small room we were inside of. He chanted, softly at first, until everyone started repeating his words.

My heart raced so quickly that it hurt, and I trembled as the power rushed through the room and me. It was immense, making it hard to breathe, almost as if I'd grown claustrophobic instantly. I felt tears as they slid down my cheeks unchecked. The flames flickered against the walls as the only light fixture blew out, sending glass shards onto the floor close to us.

"Is that normal?" I whispered, but Lucian had his eyes closed, chanting with the others in the room. It was surreal, the maddening sounds of an entire room filled with people chanting the same thing over and over. The candles flickered, illuminating the protection runes that covered the walls. I wanted to cover my ears, protect myself, or run away. Maybe do all three.

My hood was pushed back by a gust of wind, and my eyes moved towards the door to see who had entered, only to find it still closed. I turned back to find that Lucian's hood had been pushed back as well, and he no longer chanted with the others. His eyes were locked with mine, and his left hand was palm-up on the altar as he reached for the ceremonial athame with his right. I watched in horrified silenced as he whispered more words and sliced through his palm.

I yipped and started to move away, but those eyes… They held me lost inside their tempting depths, and without breaking the new chant he had started, he told me to remain still. I expelled a steady breath and held my hand out for the blade, accepting it to do as he had done. He repeated the words; I followed his lead in dutifully repeating it verbatim, then sliced through my palm and hissed at the pain. He took the blade from me and placed it on the altar as he picked up the chalice and drank from the red liquid before handing it to me.

Don't let it be blood, don't let it be blood…Wine, yes! I drank deeply, taking more than I should have before I placed it back on the altar, and watched for Lucian to lead me. He relaxed a little before he held his bloody palm out for mine. I hesitated, wanting to do the spell, but not wanting any bond that came from using blood magic—not with this man. After a moment of hesitation, I placed my hand palm-down against his. Blood mixed, the candles erupted, chants became frenzied, and then I'm pretty sure I passed out.

"Breathe, Lena. Let it happen," Lucian's voice cut through my mind, bringing me back to the here and now. Or at least that's what I thought. We'd been in the room with the altar…

I turned to look at a little child, barely more than a toddler. She had long caramel colored hair that was gathered into a high ponytail; stray strands had come undone and circled her cherubic face.

"Joshy!" I cried. I was chasing my brother, who couldn't have been more than five or six years old. I was giggling as he made faces at me, getting me to walk a little more as he took a few large steps away from me. I fell, big alligator tears began to drop from my blue eyes, and he dropped to the ground beside me.

"Don't cry, little Lenny, I got you. You were so big! You did so well. You walked before Kendra, always the first to try everything. I'm so proud of you," he said encouragingly, even though I'd remained on the floor beside him, bawling.

Tears filled my eyes as I watched my brother being tender with the baby I'd been, holding me as I cried. He'd only been a child, yet he had always been there for me as Mom focused on Kendra, who always seemed to take more of her attention.

"It's too far back, Lena. Take me to where we need to be," Lucian said. I turned to find him watching me as I wiped at the tears, unwilling to allow them to fall.

"I don't want to leave him," I admitted.

"He's not real, it's just a memory," he whispered as he placed his hand against my face. "Focus for me."

"Did she do it?" Grandpa asked, his wrinkled face filled with pride as he watched me struggle to get back up.

"Grandpa," I whispered brokenly.

"Of course she did, Papa, she's my sister. Lenny's going to be tough as rocks by the time I teach her everything I know!" Joshua declared with a cheeky grin.

"I know she will be, what with you for a brother and treating her like she's your equal. She ought to be a force to reckon with when she's old enough to date."

"Gah, never! She'll never date. That's gross!"

Grandpa laughed and shook his head. "You say that now, boy, but someday someone's going to steal her heart. When they break it, you'll be there to break their nose for me?" he laughed as Joshua shook his dark head vigorously.

"No one is ever going to break her heart; she's going to be the prettiest girl in the entire world! Even prettier than Momma is."

The memory faded and I exhaled a shuddering breath that seemed to do little to calm the pain I'd felt at watching my brother in a memory I hadn't even known I'd had.

We'd left one memory to another one. This one I couldn't place. I heard a woman's screams rip through the woods around us, and I felt as if the wind had been knocked out of me. We were in a forest, thick with greenery. The screaming was coming closer, getting louder as whoever was screaming moved right towards us.

"Where are we, Lena?" Lucian asked and I shook my head.

"I don't know this place," I whispered as I tried to find anything I could recognize. I could make out smoke over the tops of the trees, high in the sky. The stench of it singed my nose with the subtle reminder of the fire I'd just been in. I moved in a circle. "Can you smell that?" I asked, wondering if he as tuned in to the memory as I was.

"Lena, come to me, now," he ordered sharply, and I did without hesitation, as if he was my anchor to this place.

A woman tore through the bushes, her blonde hair disheveled and her old fashioned corseted dress ripped; that dress made her look like she escaped from a Ren Faire. She tripped and landed hard on the ground; masculine laughter followed her as I moved to help her up.

"You can't interact," Lucian growled as his eyes consumed the woman as if he knew her. "Bloody hell," he growled thickly as he pushed my head against his chest.

A horrified scream ripped from the woman as she jumped to her feet and fled through the brush once more. I tore myself from Lucian, needing to see what it was that she was so terrified of. Her screaming escalated as I moved closer to her, and the smoke grew even thicker as I pushed through the bushes, Lucian hot on my heels.

I skidded to a sudden halt as I broke free from the forest. Bodies littered the ground, pools of blood everywhere. Something had torn these humans into pieces. *Fucking pieces*! I covered my mouth to muffle my own scream of horror as the terrifying sight sank in. Sadistic laughter sounded from the bushes, growing closer with every second.

"You don't belong here!" The woman shouted, looking right at me. I paused. In the last memory, Joshua and Grandpa hadn't noticed me.

"You can see me?" I whispered as I looked over my shoulder to find no one there. Not even Lucian.

"Magdalena, go home! You don't belong here, you must help me, and I need you in your own time! You have to stop this from happening again. Leave now before he senses the ripple! Find the grimoires; they are closer than you think they are. They hold the keys of the past to save the future. Don't let him do this to your people; you must protect them from him. I have failed, but if you are here, it means he is close. Now go, please. He comes."

She took off running, leaving me dumbfounded as I turned to find Lucian with a wide-eyed look on his face, his mouth twisted into an angry frown as I turned to look for the man who was pushing through the bushes, chasing the woman. Lucian growled an angry curse and moved towards me, shoving my face against his chest, smothering me. My lungs burned for air. I could hear sardonic laughter, and the world was beginning to spin around me.

When he finally pulled me from his chest I slapped at him. I caught air into my starved lungs and fell to my knees as I looked around us, trying to judge where I'd taken us to now. I'd wanted to leave the other place, but I wasn't sure who had moved us, me or him.

I was in my bedroom, and Todd and Cassidy were making grotesque noises in my bed. I closed my eyes, not wanting to relive the horror. I knew it was coming, because I was standing just inside my bedroom, watching them with stark pain etched into my face.

"How could you do this to me, to us? I loved you! I wanted to give you the rest of my life, Todd. Her? You're with her?" I screamed as his head turned and his eyes grew large and round. He scrambled from the bed, his dick still hard, bare. He hadn't even cared to use protection. I turned to run but he was faster. His hand bit into my arm, pulling me back as he slammed me against the wall.

"Lena, I can explain!" he rushed, his words breathless from fucking Cassidy. I tried to move, and he pushed me back against the wall as Cassidy laughed, her skirt still up from where she'd lifted it for my fiancé to gain entrance.

"She's waiting, Todd; tell her how you've been fucking me while waiting for her to figure it out. Tell her how you never planned to marry her," she said snidely, and Todd's eyes got even bigger.

"That's not true, Lena, I love you. Only you, baby. It's always ever been you and me. We're always together, remember?" he begged, his eyes widening as he saw the hate that was building inside me.

"Asshole," I whispered, watching the 'me' of the past as she slammed those walls down and became cold. They'd done it in my home, in my bed, as if they'd planned on being caught.

I moved us from the memory without checking to see Lucian's look of pity that would surely be there.

"Ma'am, is your mother home?" the soldier asked, his hat crumbled in his hands as he looked at me with a pitying stare. He was older, hardened by war. Scars adorned his face, his hands, and his neck. Behind him stood a decrepit priest, probably in his late seventies or early eighties. He barely made it up the stairs by himself.

I heard Mom coming and turned to look at her. I wanted to push her away from the door, hide her from what I already knew was coming. This wasn't fucking happening. It couldn't be. I was trembling as it soaked in. My hands were fisted at my sides and I shook my head.

There was only one reason the United States of America's Army showed up on your door with a priest in tow, and that was to tell you that someone had been killed in action. My knees started to buckle, and I backed up. Mom stopped in the doorway, her hands reaching out as she figured it out.

I continued to back away, unwilling to buy it. It was a mistake. It was a god damn fucking mistake! Tears escaped and I wiped at them hard and angry. You don't cry when someone isn't dead, and Joshua wasn't dead! I backed into Kendra and spun around to look at her. Her eyes filled with tears.

"No, no. No! He's not dead, he won't leave me. He promised me. He isn't. It's a mistake, Kendra, it's a mistake. A horrible mistake," my words cracked. My head turned to watch as my mother fell to the floor on her knees. "They're wrong! Josh is coming home, he said so! He's coming home!" I was shouting. My heart was broken, shattered into a million pieces in that one single moment.

"Lena," Kendra broke down; her hands reached for one of mine and I jerked it away hard.

"No, I said no! Joshua is coming home!" I spun around and ran from the manor. I didn't believe it; they had to be wrong. His 'baby' was in the barn, covered for him for when he returned. His projects weren't done, he *wasn't done! I ran to the old church in the woods, where Josh and I used to go to escape housework. It bordered the properties, dilapidated and abandoned and yet still beautiful and calming.*

Inside the church I collapsed, curled into a ball and cursed him. I cursed him for leaving me alone. For lying to me when he told me that everything would be fine. I cursed myself to hell. It's where the darkness first found me. Hopeless, alone, and broken on the ground of the abandoned church.

"Lena," Lucian warned.

I know he sensed it, slithering over my skin. This time it was visible to us as we watched the memory. I chose to ignore him as I watched it take root inside of me.

"I let it in," I admitted. I exhaled a deep breath, one I'd been holding since I'd first felt the darkness. "I know we're not supposed to allow it to enter our minds," I whispered, turning to look at him. He was granite, watching me as if he thought I was evil, or guilty of some terrible crime, maybe. "For months I allowed it to whisper to me, and then I shut it out. I locked it out of my life for good. I beat it."

"Indeed," Lucian said softly. "Why did you let it inside at all?"

"Because it promised to numb the pain," I whispered. I tilted my head, watching as he nodded, but he didn't look convinced.

"And you think you just kicked it out afterwards?" he asked with a frown.

"Indeed," I spit his words back at him.

"Or that's what it wanted you to think," he countered, and I frowned.

"I beat it," I snapped angrily. I didn't wait for him to say more; I moved us to the next memory and flinched.

I stood beside my mother as the funeral droned on. My heart was empty, I was cold. I'd died with my brother. I didn't feel anything, didn't even cry. I watched as the people around me mulled through the line, feeding us the same fucked up line. "He's in a better place now." *What the fuck does that even mean? In a better place, they don't know that, no one does!* "He'd have loved the service, it was beautiful." *The fuck you say! He'd have hated it. Country music playing, his family broken to fucking pieces, what the hell would he have loved about it?* "He'd want you to be happy." *If he wanted that, he should have come home alive. Idiots.*

"You show no emotion," Lucian noted and I nodded.

"I felt hate. I wanted their blood, every last one of them. I wanted to bathe in it, to watch them die as they choked on their words and empty condolences. I know it wasn't me who wanted their blood, but at that point in time, I wasn't ready to feel anything. Being cold and empty was easier. I was weak, I know it," I said softly, watching as Kendra sobbed and I stood as still as a marble statue, and just as cold. "He was my anchor, and he was just gone."

He didn't say anything, just nodded, and we moved into the next vision effortlessly. I groaned.

"That's it, baby, damn. You're so tight, yeah! Move like that, I like that, baby."

I had looked bored. My head had been tilted away from his so that he couldn't see the tears of loathing that I'd cried. He hadn't even realized that I'd been crying. His pants were down to his ankles and we were jammed in the back of his outdated, piece of shit car. He'd pulled my skirt up, and pushed my panties to the side, and easily squeezed his little dick through the small opening. I was miserable; my eyes were open, locked on the back of the seat that my face was smashed into. He was grunting, breathing hard, and asking me if I liked it. My response was a nod, and then I closed my eyes to block him out, to block out what I was allowing him to do to me.

"That wasn't even close to *fine*…" Lucian said beside me as he watched the memory play out. "That was fucking pathetic."

"Maybe he was a virgin too?" I offered lamely; shit, it sounded lame even to my own ears.

"Now you're going to make excuses for that sorry piece of shit?" he asked crossly.

"Wait for it," I said with a grin on my lips.

"Are you coming?" he asked breathlessly, his dick already limp because he'd been done less than five seconds into the actual act. He hadn't even lasted a full minute. "God, baby, tell me you're coming," he begged.

"Mmhm," I whispered already pushing him off of me to cover myself up. "Couldn't you tell?" I asked as I stood up in the crisp air and pulled my skirt down and back into place.

"You didn't tell me," he said with a pointed look. "You want a guy to know, you got to tell him."

"Only once with him?" Lucian asked with a sharp look that boarded on anger and derision.

"Once was enough," I said with an embarrassed frown. He snorted and shook his head.

"Best you ever had, girl?" he asked with a puffed up chest and a cocky grin.

"Best sex I ever had," I replied as I started back to my apartment to wash him off of me.

"Thanks, I don't get many complaints," he assured me with a self-satisfied smile.

"I don't imagine you get many callbacks," I smarted off. "Can't beat perfection…" I amended, trying to put more distance between us, which wasn't working since he

was following me.

"Hey, you going to call me or something?" he asked.

"Or something," I shot over my shoulder as I disappeared around the corner.

"Remind me to remedy your opinion of sex, *soon*," Lucian said offhandedly as we watched the memory fade.

"He was *fine*," I said with a straight face.

I moved us into the next one, and then a few of my wild memories of being away from home before we entered my small apartment.

I was at the table with Luna in my lap, cramming for a big test. Coffee was on in the kitchen, and I'd just downed my third cup. My finger made a circle as the spoon stirred the liquid inside the cup, soft music played through the house as I tried to memorize the chapter I'd been reading.

I sang softly with the music, enjoying the way Luna butted her head into my chest if I went off key. Magazines and a few books lay around the apartment, mostly naughty romance novels I'd checked out from the library.

"See, no books on how to make bombs or kidnap anyone, or set houses on fire," I said softly, as if I was afraid to disrupt the memory.

"You lived in this shithole for three years?" he asked, instead of answering me.

"It's not a shithole, and the rent was cheap. Neighbors kept to themselves, so it worked for me. Plus the landlord reduced my rent in exchange for shampoos and soaps I made in my spare time. I kept to myself after the first couple of months, did what was needed, and then got notified that the Awakening was coming, so I moved home. The rest you already know."

As if it wasn't enough, we began moving into the next memory.

I was outside of the party, staring at the backdoor as Lucian approached me. I watched as he kissed me, and then as my own eyes grew heated with the need for him to do more, so much more. A total stranger, and I'd almost allowed him to distract me from the opening ceremony.

"You enjoyed it," he mused beside me. I turned to see his cocky half-smile back in place.

"I never said otherwise. Still doesn't mean I want to kiss you again," I retorted with a smirk.

"We'll see about that," he said as we both watched a dark figure step out of the bushes after Lucian entered the house a few moments behind me, oblivious to the figure that watched us.

"I don't remember anyone else out there at that time," I said.

"Neither do I," he agreed.

I pushed off the blankets and looked around. I sensed that something was wrong. Horribly so. I sat up, moved Luna off of me and moved towards the front door. Smoke, putrid and thick wafted from the main house towards the cottage. I opened the door, and tried to scream, but nothing came out. My heart hurt with how badly it beat against my chest as I moved towards the house barefoot, half-naked, and uncaring as I tried to find a way inside.

I ran from the front of the house to the back, and rushed inside.

"That proves you didn't set the blaze to your house, nor did you have time to consort with bombers or kidnappers," he said as he turned to look at me. "Now, what do we do about the darkness?" he asked carefully, his eyes narrowed and I had a sinking feeling in the pit of my stomach.

"I beat it; there's nothing to *do* about it."

"Your ancestors will see it inside of you, and you won't be chosen for the Awakening if they do."

"Then I'll deal with it when it happens," I said softly, watching him. He was up to something.

"There are ways to hide it. If you want help, let me know." His twisted smile sent chills racing up my spine.

"Are you going to tell the coven?" I asked with trepidation and fear rushing through me.

"That isn't my baggage to carry around. I'm only here to see if you're innocent. If I'm asked though…"

"If you're asked what? You'll tell them?" I demanded.

"Unless you offer me something in exchange for my silence." The heated look he gave me made my knees weak.

"That's blackmail," I pointed out.

"Yes, it is. Sue me," he laughed.

"Do me a favor, Lucian. Hold your breath while you wait for my answer," I growled with a deadly glare.

CHAPTER
twenty-two

I slept most of the following day, only to be awakened by one of Lucian's men with a letter written in a masculine scrawl and a capital L at the bottom, which formally gave me approval to attend tonight's festivities. I trudged sleepily to his bathroom to ready myself and tried to ignore the idea that I could totally snoop through his room with no witnesses. As if, but I knew that I could.

Lucian had made good on one of his promises, and my clothes had been brought up from the cottage. As I didn't see any new items, I had to assume that Lucian must have been willing to say just about anything to get me to agree to stay at his home. Sorting through my clothes, I realized I didn't have much to wear, not in the traditional sense of glamourous evening wear, so I'd settled on a little navy blue dress that was chic and pretty. It had a deep V-neck, and while it brought attention to the girls, it didn't scream *look at me*. I'd paired it with nude heels to make it look more dress-up than country chick, and added a silver clutch purse for a bonus. My hair was down, reaching my bottom in gentle wavy curls that somehow I'd managed to not screw up. Curling hair and looking perfect wasn't something I could usually manage alone; I just hadn't been born with those skills.

Kendra had, and she leaned closer to the mirror as I applied a luscious shade of cherry red lipstick to my full lips. She was dressed in a longer dress; her own deep V-neck exposed more flesh than I would have been comfortable revealing. Her hair was in an updo, with a few stray strands that had been left out to frame her face. The dress was silver, with dark navy blue embroidery that was woven intricately though the material.

"You look amazing," I said as I turned to look at her.

"You look underdressed," she replied with her nose scrunched up. "Everyone else will be wearing evening wear."

"Then I'll stand out," I announced as I shifted back to the mirror to apply mascara.

"You do know that Mom has enough money saved to buy you clothes for the events," she replied.

"I don't want her to," I snapped, much harsher than I had intended to. "Look, Kendra, Mom needs to save her money to get the store back. It's not going to change anything if I wear what I already own instead of some designer dress that she'd have to donate a kidney to be able to afford. Besides," I continued softly with a gentle smile. "You're the one who needs to look beautiful tonight. You and I both know that you hold the power and the family legacy is up to you to uphold. Which, thankfully for me, lets me off the hook," I laughed as she made a face.

"Jerk; no pressure, right?" she giggled as she checked her make-up and asked if I was ready to go.

"I'm ready, but not sure my stomach is." My nerves seemed to be having a massive battle inside me, and I was feeling a little sick at the idea of yet another party.

"Is there something between you and Lucian?" she asked, catching me off guard.

"Why do you ask?"

"Because I'd have to be blind not to see the way you two look at each other. He's trouble; Grandmother is wary of his presence here."

"I don't plan on doing anything with him. I'm here for the ceremony, Kendra. Besides, he isn't signed up for it and doesn't plan to be. My options are open, same as yours. Have you decided what to do about Todd? If you really want to be with him…" I paused, swallowing past the lump in my throat. "You know there are ways to make it so he would be your selected partner for the Harvest."

"Marry him," she whispered as she shook her head. "He's still in love with you, Lena. I'm not stupid; I called him last night. He doesn't want me when he thinks he can get you back."

"He isn't getting me back, Ken," I said, using the nickname Joshua had given her when he'd dubbed me Lenny. "Not even if we were the last people in this universe and the human race was dependent on us repopulating it. I'd die first," I announced as I smacked my cherry red lips together and watched her through the reflection in the mirror. I hated that he'd upset her, or that the bastard had told her that.

"You know I don't like that name, and that's pretty dramatic, Lenny, even for you." And just like that, she closed off her emotions, and my heart clenched for the sliver of pain I felt coming from her. "He would say your name when we had sex; I'm such an idiot. I thought if I loved him enough, he'd love me back. I've been crushing on him for a long time; you know that. Whatever," she dismissed the subject with a wave of her hand. "Ready?"

I turned to look at her and smiled. "You're not an idiot, Kendra. You expected him to be honest, and Todd can't handle that. He had problems when we were together, but like you, I figured I could change him. The truth is, he doesn't want to be changed."

"You should be pissed at me, scream at me, do something besides be okay with me getting together with him after you left."

"I'm not angry at you," I whispered as I felt the turmoil of her emotions that she failed to hide this time. "Oh, Kendra," I hugged her to me, giving her a tight squeeze. "He's just a stupid boy, and you're my sister. I love you for suggesting I get angry, but I'm not going to. He's simply not worth it, and I kind of want to kick his ass now for upsetting you."

"Well, we could kick his ass, but that might affect our chances at the selection," she whispered through thick tears.

"No crying," I said as I pulled away and rushed to grab a tissue. "You'll mess up your make-up and then we'll be late," I dabbed gently at her eyes and smiled. "Besides, we can't let Cassidy sink her claws into the good guys. I'd be devastated if she got a better match than you did. I think part of the reason I came back was to watch her get jealous when you to get the better partner."

"You're insane," she whispered with a soft frown. "But, I've kind of been looking forward to that too, honestly."

"Good, let's get going. We have heads to turn," I whispered as I grabbed my clutch and guided her towards the door.

✦∿✦∿✦

I'd had three tumblers of scotch, twenty-five mock interviews—or at least that's what they felt like—by men who were both from town and out of town, and one confirmed marriage proposal by a guy who was more freaked out about the coming Harvest than I was—but I was pretty sure he'd been throwing a Hail Mary into the wind to cover up that he was playing for the same side. I'd seen him throwing Dexter some pretty big *come hither* looks.

I was moving towards the small bar when a hand touched my shoulder, and I turned around to see who it was. I stopped short, my eyes taking in the man who'd stopped my progress towards the bar. He was drop dead sexy, with a killer smile that said he knew exactly how hot he was.

"Magdalena Fitzgerald, I assume?" There was a soft hint of an accent in his words.

"You assume correctly. And you would be?" I inquired, my lips tugging in the corners as I fought off a smile. Shit, why didn't we have men who looked like this here?

"Devlin St. James, from the Park City Utah coven," he announced dramatically and gave me a mock bow. "At your service, beautiful." His wicked smile indicated that his services could be anything but chaste.

"And what services do you offer?" I asked, openly flirting as I allowed a smile to twitch at the corner of my mouth.

"I can't tell you yet…first, I need to get you another drink," he announced as he headed towards the bar before turning around to smile at me. "Find us a table, and I'll meet you there."

"You assume I want you to get me a drink?" I replied, my eyes smiling as I tried to keep a straight face.

"I do, because right now Thatcher is trying to work up enough courage to approach you, and he spits when he speaks, so I'm doing you a solid by distracting you and keeping the vultures at bay," he said as he tipped his head to where a red haired guy stood with overly thick glasses watching me.

"Oh good lord," I whispered with a small laugh that I hid behind my hand. "Fine, but you better bring me something that isn't too girly."

"Indeed my fair lady, it will be strong enough that I can get you drunk enough to have my way with you," he grinned as he wiggled his eyebrows.

"Oh, you are a naughty boy," I laughed and moved away to find us a vacant table.

I found one, took a seat, and looked around the room. I'd felt the weight of his stare for most of the night, and knew exactly where he was. Lucian was in a darkened corner of the room where the wall was at his back, and he had a vantage point of the entire room. Once again he was wearing an expensive suit. At this stage of the game, I would have been disappointed if he hadn't been dressed in a bespoke suit of some kind. I'd done my best to ignore the feeling of his eyes, as they seemed to track me down no matter where I was in the room, but it was a hard thing to do when it made my body respond, even when he wasn't close to me. I watched him from beneath my lashes as he smiled wickedly and continued to swirl the two fingers of scotch in his glass.

The way he looked at me was predatory, with a heat that slid over my skin. It made the butterflies take flight in my belly, and my body responded to him every time he was in the same room. The man was sinfully gorgeous, with a bad boy flare that made me want to see just how bad he could be. It pissed me off. He shouldn't be having this effect on me, not on this level.

"Wow, who pissed you off?" Devlin interrupted my thoughts as he sat across from me, unfortunately doing nothing to block my view of Lucian.

"Nobody," I mumbled as I accepted the glass he offered and took a sip. I closed my eyes and gasped with a small giggle as the liquid burned on its way down. "Mmm, that's good," I said softly as I opened my eyes to find Devlin watching me.

"That was sexy," he said as he took another sip, then set his own drink down. "Do you always make that face when you drink? Because I can go back and get the entire bottle and we can find some place more secluded."

"You move fast," I noted, my eyes taking him in.

This guy was hot as hell; his eyes were the color of the scotch that was currently swirling in Lucian's glass. They had flecks of black, which created a beauty that was almost otherworldly. He was tall; even sitting, he engulfed the chair, and I had the strangest urge to peek beneath the table to see if his knees were touching it. His sleeves were rolled up to his elbows; both covered in tattoos that made my bad girl rear her head with curiosity. His hair was longer than most of the guys here, touching his shoulders in strands of deep chocolate to burgundy. Totally a dye job, but who cared? He was panty dripping hotness, and right now, I needed a distraction.

"Only when I find something I want," he said with a half grin that lit his eyes.

"And have you?" I asked, my eyes moving to his tattoos.

"Have I what?" he countered.

"Found something you want." I placed my elbows on the table and lifted my glass to take another drink as my eyes met his over the rim of the glass.

"Let's see, a woman who's hot as fuck, doesn't give a shit about impressing the men here with some ridiculous, overly fancy dress, one who also prefers whisky…I think I have," he stated, his finger tracing the rim of his glass as his eyes held mine.

"I didn't have anything formal to wear," I replied to his words, my eyes holding his. "I'm not rich, and couldn't afford to buy so many different formal dresses for so many events. I sort of dropped it all on the opening and wasn't about to shake my family down for more." I cringed inwardly, waiting for him to move on to the next table.

"That was meant to turn me off, wasn't it?" he asked carefully, his eyes probing me as he narrowed his eyes.

"Yes," I scrunched up my nose. "Sorry, I'm used to warding off men, not selling myself to them."

"Nah, that would make you a hooker, and I'm kind of glad you're not a hooker," he said with a lopsided grin. "I prefer not to pay for sex, but I'm not totally against it if it's with you."

I laughed and it felt good. I smiled wide and shook my head. "I was right about you. You are naughty."

"I'm also not partial to rich bitches that think they're entitled to everything their little heart desires. Same goes for educated women who think they're superior because they have an education while others don't. So trying to scare me away won't work, pretty girl. Now if you tell me you like biting delicate flesh, me and my boys might run away. You don't look like the biting type, though, but then I've been wrong before," he replied easily as he watched me set my glass down and reached for my hand. "May I?" his eyes heated to liquid amber as I accepted and placed my hand in his.

His fingers trailed over the palm of my hand. "You have soft hands," he traced the lines in my hand a bit like a palm reader would, "yet you're not afraid of hard work," he continued, gently tracing the life line in my palm as his finger sent shock waves through my entire body. They weren't as powerful as Lucian's, but they were affecting me. "You haven't had an easy life, but you don't choose to blame others for it. You have pain, but you won't share it or let anyone see it, because you're not willing to…yet. You're strong, but not because you want to be; it's because you have to be." He smiled, his fingers continuing to read my palm as he sent a trembling sensation through my entire body with a single touch. "You also want to skip the whole Harvest ceremony thing, mostly because you want to marry someone sinfully handsome who has great hair."

I laughed, and pulled my palm away from him. "You do have really great hair," I replied as a blush colored my cheeks.

"I do, but yours would look better covered in sweat and spread out across my sheets."

"Is that so?" I whispered as I chewed my bottom lip.

"Indeed," he pushed my glass closer towards me. "So, now we play one hundred questions…and I get to know you better."

"It's supposed to be fifty questions," I countered.

He smiled wickedly. "It's one hundred because I figure if I ask them slow enough, you'll marry me just to shut me up."

I laughed causing eyes to turn in our direction. "You're horrible," I giggled with an amused smile. "Go for it, but I'm not marrying someone I just met."

"Isn't that why we're all here? To listen to the wisdom of the dead who don't know jack about our century, who plan to slap us together like livestock to breed the next generation for your coven?"

I laughed again and shook my head. "You don't agree with tradition?"

"I don't think the dead should be allowed to dictate to the living or decide who we end up with for the Harvest, I'm the kind of guy who prefers picking his own fuck buddy."

"There's always a way out of it," I paused and looked him steadily in the eye. "You could always just randomly marry one of the girls, and be excluded from the entire process."

"Oh sure, and be the reason the divorce rate spikes? I think it's high enough without us adding to it. Don't you agree?" he asked as he sat back and slung his arm behind his chair in a laid back position. As if he didn't care what anyone else thought of him; it was refreshing.

"Yes, I can agree with that, but then I'm just one of many who aren't entitled to question those who came before us."

"Tell me this, Magdalena. Are all of the women in your line this hot and open-minded, or did you break the mold when you fought your way into this world?" he asked smoothly, his eyes lowering slightly to the neckline of my dress.

I swallowed at the heat in his eyes. "I come from a long line of highly sought-after witches, so I guess being from my bloodline has its perks. I think women should think for themselves, and about being hot, there's prettier girls here tonight."

"Anything you want to ask me?" he said after he nodded at my answer.

"Where did your coven originate; was it Park City?" I asked curiously.

"Salem. However, mine headed west a long time after yours passed through and paved the way for us to do so. Instead of coming to where your coven was, ours moved south down to Texas, where we remained in the shadows, much as your coven did."

"Texas." Well, it explained his perfect tan and rough hands. He obviously wasn't afraid of hard work. "How did you end up in Utah?"

"Aww, that's two questions and it's my turn," he said with a soft smile. "Tell me, are you looking to get married before the Awakening and skip this entire charade, or are you seriously planning to allow a bunch of dead people to choose for you?" There was almost a hint of a dare in his eyes as he took a sip from his drink.

"Are you asking me to marry you?" I countered and he shook his head again as he smiled against the drink.

"Ah, you're dodging the question, naughty girl," he whispered with enough heat in his eyes to melt my insides.

"I'm not sure what I'll do, but I do know that I'll do whatever is needed to unlock my powers and take my place in the coven."

"Good answer," he replied easily.

"Now answer *my* question; did you ask me to marry

you?" I watched as his eyes narrowed with heat.

"Only if you plan to say yes, because if you say no, you'll break my heart," he countered.

I laughed.

"Tell me; are all the guys in your coven as limp as their powers currently are?"

"Excuse me?" I coughed and covered my mouth with my hand to keep from spitting whisky all over him.

"Do all of the men here have their balls as restrained as their magic currently is?"

"Why do you think that?" I laughed as my eyes grew large at his bluntness.

"Because you're single, and they seem unaware of it. It makes me think that they're fucking idiots. You're hot, smart, and you come from a long line of highly respected witches. You're also sexy as fuck, and probably a wildcat in bed, which guys talk about. You go after the wild ones if you have the balls to do so, and no one has. So, either they're limp or you're playing hard to get, but you seem pretty down to earth to me."

"It's not that simple," I said softly as heat fused my cheeks. "I've been gone a long time."

"Witches, we tend to stay together," he tapped his glass thoughtfully with a long finger. "I couldn't imagine you'd leave home. There's protection in numbers."

I winced and frowned. "I was going to get married," I swallowed hard and took a deep breath. "He cheated on me, and then my brother was killed in Afghanistan. I guess too many things piled up, because I left town shortly after we buried him."

It was his turn to wince. "Someone cheated on you when you'd agreed to marry him? Was he fucking insane, or gay and he cheated on you with a guy?" he snapped, his eyes narrowed as he awaited my response.

"Neither, but I did run. It's unconventional, and frowned on in my coven…and pretty much all covens."

"Look, I like you," he said softly. "Smart, sexy, and seriously funny, plus, you drink whisky instead of some fruity girl drink." His quiet laugh made my lips twitch in response. "The only thing better than that would be me knowing that you were a fucking knockout between the sheets, which, if you allow, I'd like to figure that one out for myself," he smiled flirtatiously. "You're a serious catch and who cares what happened in the past, that's why it's called the past, because we're here, in the present, Magdalena. I may not be from the best bloodline, but I promise if you elope with me, you'll never go hungry, and I will make you happy. I'll also probably never let you leave my bed, but I do promise to run to the fridge to keep you well-fed so I can continually ravish you."

"I couldn't tell you if I'm good in bed because I'm not as open about sex as most witches are. My experience with sex is pretty limited, and eating in bed isn't something I do."

"Oh, tell me it isn't so! No one around here's been itching to get into those pretty panties?" he whispered as he leaned over the table and his hands grasped my knees beneath it. I jumped, and pulled my legs together, or tried to; he held them firmly as he parted them. "Again with the limp dicks, what the fuck you guys raising up here, monks? I'd have worn you down until you'd agreed, and then kept going until your senses were well and truly defeated, then I would have rocked your fucking world."

"It's not their fault," I laughed as heat shot through me. "I didn't follow the coven's thinking, and I was saving it for something special."

"Was, but you're not anymore."

"No, I gave it up and got a severe let down for my first time, and then I just stopped trying, I guess. I'm not a virgin, and I'm really not open to discussing it with someone I just met ten minutes ago."

Something caught his eye and he nodded, so I turned to see what it was. Lucian was the only one behind us, and he wasn't even looking in our direction. I followed his eyes to where he watched Cassidy as she flicked her hair and smiled at him. She was dressed beautifully tonight. His eyes lingered on her before slowly moving to me, and I felt a tug and twisting in my belly as jealousy spiked. I reminded myself that I had no right to be and turned back to Devlin.

"I need to figure out where I'm staying tonight, Magdalena, but I'd love to see you again, soon," he announced as he pulled a card from the pocket of his slacks. "My digits—and I want yours."

"And if I say no?" I teased with a smile.

"This town is pretty small; I'm sure I could find you," he said with a smirk on his sexy lips. "I'd really like to get to know you better, so do me a favor and give me your number so it can happen. I promise I won't disappoint you."

I scrunched up my nose as I pulled a pen and tore a piece of paper off of a receipt that I'd had in my purse, then jotted down my number, before sliding his card in my purse.

"Wait, no address? How am I supposed to sneak into your bedroom and ravish you if I don't know where you sleep?" he asked with a wicked grin on his face that lit up his eyes.

"Who says I'd allow you into my bedroom to ravish

me?" I stood up and watched as he held his hand over his heart.

"That hurt, but I like that you play hard to get. Don't worry, Magdalena, you can run all you want; I enjoy the chase. Tell me, princess, do you run fast?"

"No, normally if you see me running, you should probably turn your ass around and start running too. The only way I ever run is if something scary is chasing me," I replied easily, with a straight face that pulled a laugh from deep in his chest. His laughter was as contagious as his smile, and soon I was laughing with him.

"God, I love your sense of humor," he picked up my info and slid it into his pocket. "I have to run, but it was very nice meeting you, and I can't wait to see you again."

I moved from the table, shaking my head as I made my way to the terrace at the back of the restaurant that overlooked the deep ravine. I needed the cool night air to relieve the heat from being in the overcrowded room. Before I reached the doors, feminine laughter pulled my eyes to where Lucian stood with Cassidy, who was smiling as she rubbed her hands down her lithe frame invitingly.

I rolled my eyes as a stark, painful slice of jealousy punched me in the stomach. I had no business being jealous. It wasn't as if we'd been together, or were even dating. I was a free agent, and that meant he was as well. I chose to ignore them, and pushed open the doors and enjoyed the cool night air as it met my overheated skin.

CHAPTER
twenty-three

I leaned against the railing, my eyes searching the dark depths of the ravine as I enjoyed the break from the party. I told myself I didn't care that Cassidy was moving in on Lucian; the two of them probably belonged together. I did, however, hate the jealousy that seemed to heat me from the inside as I basked in the chilly night's air.

I closed my eyes and dropped my face into my hands as I exhaled a deep breath, and then I felt him. That raw, powerful current of energy that was always present when he was near. I didn't turn around, didn't open my eyes until I felt his hands on my hips, curving around my ass until I was forced to turn in his general direction.

I shouldn't have turned around; it would have been safer to leave him exploring my curves. His eyes were angry; his body tensed as he lifted me up, cradling my ass as he sat me on the railing. It forced me to cling to him, as the fear of falling washed through me.

"Lucian!" I hissed as he spread my legs and pressed his erection against my thin panties.

"Did you enjoy flirting with him?" he growled as he held me there, teetering between him and certain death.

"Actually, I did," I admitted.

He laughed cruelly, his hands tightened on my ass and I whimpered as pain rippled through me, along with scorching heat where his cock pressed against me. It was both thrilling and terrifying, a combination I'd never experienced before.

"Don't drop me," I whispered as I leaned closer towards him.

"I'd never let you fall," he assured me, yet his eyes were darker than normal, and his fingers bit into my flesh.

"Enjoying Cassidy's company?" I wondered why I would choose to ask something so stupid while he held my life in his hands. One single push and I'd be dead. No one would ever know what had happened, either.

"Jealous?" he whispered as he lifted his head and looked at me.

"Hardly," I countered as a shiver ran down my spine from the heat I saw in his eyes. "You're free to be with whomever you want, as am I." I was surprised with how even my tone was.

The wind picked up and he held me tighter as my hair flew in my face. I felt a familiar rush of power as it sent a mixture of heat and fear into my spine. The sexual heat and tension between us was thick enough to cut with a knife.

"I hear stalking is illegal," I mumbled as I narrowed my eyes on him and nibbled at my bottom lip.

"Hunting isn't," he replied easily, his voice cold and

filled with a raw trace of emotion that I couldn't place.

"You don't have a license to hunt me," I whispered as I licked my lips nervously. "Besides, I'm out of season," I was feeling a little cockier than I should, considering he held my life in his perfectly manicured hands.

Tonight his suit was midnight blue, fitted to perfection to accentuate each sleek muscle that his body had. A black silk tie rested against the crisp white dress shirt he wore beneath his suit. He was dark, easily blending in with the shadows.

"You think I need one to hunt you?" he challenged as his fingers moved from my ass to where our bodies touched. I held on tighter, the fear of falling fading away as his fingers slid over my bare thighs.

"Put me down," I pleaded as the knowledge that he had me at his mercy sank in. I tried to wrap my legs around him, but I couldn't, and he laughed softly as he watched me struggle. He had me right where he wanted me; exposed and at his mercy as I teetered over certain death perched on the railing. My lips trembled as my heart beat painfully against my ribcage, and worst of all, I was turned on.

"What's the matter, Lena? Don't you trust me?" his voice was low and seemed to mock me a little as he wrapped one hand around the small of my back, the other moving to the heat between my legs.

"Lucian," I whispered huskily, which was all the encouragement he needed. His fingers parted my panties, pushing them out of his way.

"I warned you that you were mine, didn't I?" he growled as his fingers slid between the wet flesh. The friction caused my back to jerk, as he held on to me securely. "You're mine, Lena, only mine." The tone of his voice, mixed with the growl that resonated deep from inside of his chest, sent a thrill down my spine.

"You can't claim me. That's not how this works, and no offense, but I don't plan to marry you. Therefore, you don't own me. No one does," I whispered through the thickness in my mouth as he parted my flesh and teased my naked core.

"You need another lesson in who owns this body?" His fingers pushed into me, and I cried out at the fullness. "So fucking wet for me," he whispered hoarsely, his mouth pushed against my neck and kissed the frantic vein that beat wildly at what he was doing to me.

I felt my body latch onto his fingers, clamping around them as he moved them in and out of me. My body was trying to pull him in, take more from him. My hips rocked, and spread, offering him everything it had, freely. My head lolled back, and his lips and tongue pushed hard against the vein as he growled hungrily.

"The moment the Harvest is over," he said as he pulled away from me. "You're mine. I won't share you with anyone else. I plan to own you the moment you are free of these fucking events, and I plan to make you into a quivering, screaming mess. I'll show you exactly what it means to be owned by me."

"And what if I conceive a child during the Harvest?" I whispered, and yes, maybe I was trying to get him to offer for me exclusively, which I would probably kick myself in the ass for later.

"You won't," he said in a matter-of-fact tone, as if he could predict the future. Heck, I couldn't; the insert inside the birth control packet said it had a ninety-two percent success rate. Eight percent was still pretty big a chance as far as I was concerned, and asking my partner for the

Harvest to wear a love glove would probably be frowned on considering the entire point was to *get* pregnant.

He pulled me away from the railing and slammed me against the wall without extracting his fingers. It pushed them painfully deep, and more moisture pooled between my legs which he used as he continued to hold me pinned to the wall with one hand securely under my ass as his fingers brought me closer to climax.

I whispered his name as his mouth pressed against mine, the orgasm just out of my reach. I wiggled my hips, trying to extract it myself, only to feel and hear his laughter as he continued to kiss me.

"Not yet, my hungry little witch, the next time you come will be when I decide you've earned it," his voice rumbled as he pulled away from me and allowed me to slide down the wall to my feet.

Both of our breathing was labored, and I felt the proof of his denial as moisture moved down my leg, unhindered by the thin lace panties I'd worn tonight. I struggled to regain my composure, and when I finally did, he was walking away from me as if nothing had happened!

"Lucian," I bit out through gritted teeth.

He glanced back to look at me as something dark and possessive passed over his face. I stood proudly and adjusted my panties and dress to how they were supposed to be as he watched.

"I think I hate you," I growled as my body ached from being left in such a state.

His mouth twisted into a cruel smile as he tilted his head and shook it softly. "You hate that you want me. You hate that for once in your life, something you want terrifies you. You're used to playing it safe, and *fine*," he turned back around and strode towards me as I moved back a few steps. "You chose Todd because he is and will always be fucking weak and you knew he'd be safe. You chose the other asshole because he was even weaker than Todd, even though he at least was driven by a need to fuck. I'm not safe, and I'm sure as fuck not weak. You can't control what you feel, and it terrifies you. Good. You shouldn't feel safe with me. You should be fucking terrified. I taste your excitement and the way you crave the filthy things I do to you, and it turns me on. You don't hate me," he said, and shoved me against the wall with one hand as his other reached down, pulled up the hem of my dress, and effortlessly ripped the panties from my body. I cried out as he brought them up and held them against his nose, smelling the proof of his words. "You hate that I slipped past all those fucking walls you erected to protect yourself from being vulnerable. You hate that I'm inside your mind," he growled as he deposited my panties in the pocket of his slacks and slid a finger back inside me as his thumb pressed against my clitoris. "You hate that you want me as much as I want you, admit it, and I'll give you what your body craves," he demanded.

"No," I whispered as a traitorous moan escaped.

"Beg for me to make you come, right here, right now," he growled as he increased the pressure of his finger bent inside of me. His other hand released my chest and pinched my nipple, hard. I yipped even as I bucked my hips to get more. His eyes held mine; the contact was intense, as if he could see into the depths of my soul. "I crave the taste of your flesh and I'm pretty sure, sweet girl, if you could read my thoughts right now, you'd be fucking traumatized," he mumbled hoarsely as he pulled his finger out, leaving my body bereft of his touch. His heat left me just as quickly, sending a shiver through my body.

"You're an asshole," I hissed as I once again struggled to fix my clothing, only to feel a chill on my delicate flesh as I was reminded by the crisp night air that he'd stolen my panties. "Give them back."

He laughed; his eyes lowered to where my pussy was drenched from his touch. "I don't think so; they belong to me now. A reminder of what belongs to me, and how wet it gets at the idea of me owning it."

"This is ridiculous! You just stole my panties!" I hissed in a hushed tone, not wanting anyone to know he had them. Heat flushed my cheeks as anger raced through me. Who steals someone's panties?

"You're even more beautiful when you're angry, Lena. All that delicate flesh, I bet it looks beautiful when it's bound and receiving pain."

"You are sick! Give me back my…" I spun around as voices neared our location. "Lucian…be reasonable, please?" I whispered as I turned around to find nothing but air where he'd just stood. Gah!

It would be okay; I knew where he slept.

Twenty minutes. That's how long I lasted at the party wearing no panties. Each moment was a reminder that he had my panties in his freaking pocket! His hand would drift to them if I so much as looked in his direction. I'd downed another drink before I found Kendra and noted she was deep in conversation with a man who had to be from out of town.

It wasn't unheard of to bring in more guys when a coven's ratio between male and female was off, but this year we seemed to have a lot more. The coven had invited an increasing number of powerful lines into the fold, a precaution and strategic move that would bring more power to our side should the need arise.

My eyes scanned the room and I found Todd at the far end across from me. His eyes moved between Lucian and me, and then back to mine with a hatred in them that I didn't think he was even capable of. Lucian noticed it as well, and instead of moving closer to me, he pulled out my panties right there in the middle of the room and brought them to his nose with a look that claimed ownership. Todd noted what he held, and his eyes turned to me filled with accusation. His face turned hard, and something sinister flashed in his gaze as he smiled at me.

I swallowed and shook my head as I turned and headed to find Dexter. He never drank alcohol and was a safe ride home, or, back to Lucian's house anyway. I so needed my own house back, since he was dictating what I could and couldn't do, and so far, the coven had decided to add salt to the wound and leave us under Lucian's *safe and secure residence and watchful eye*, as they'd put it.

Thankfully my grandmother was still working to get us moved to the Abbey until the house was ready for us to go home. I found Dexter in the corner, and his eyes snapped at me as I approached him.

"Can you give me a ride home?" I asked, and he groaned.

"Thank you, God! Yes, I can. There's a guy chasing me around here, driving me batshit cray-cray. He's been giving me some serious vibes, and I'm not sure he cares that I don't *sway* that way. Let's go, quickly before he spots me again. He isn't taking no for an answer, and Cassidy is looking for you. Something about you being a slut and taking her guy."

"Her guy?" I asked as the familiar jolt of pain lanced through me. Had Lucian agreed to be with Cassidy? He'd acknowledged that I had to attend the Harvest, and had even said I was his *after* it. Could he have agreed to be hers, and marry her? "Wait, is Claude crushing on you? He was asking me some pretty good questions, but he stared at you the entire time, *rude*."

"She's had eyes all over Lucian long before you got back. He's been ignoring it, but her mother is pushing for any reason to make it happen. You know Helen. She takes what she thinks she's entitled to have, and seems not to give a fuck about the little inconvenient truth that she isn't god, and the only way her daughter and Lucian would be paired during the Harvest would be if they married before the Awakening ceremony. Thanks for the heads up about that guy, by the way," he said in one single breath.

"You think he's going to agree to it? Cassidy must think it's a sure thing if she's calling him her guy. Yeah, I probably should have given you warning but it's not as if I thought he'd invite you into the men's room for a little meat pounding."

"*Meat* pounding? Fuck, that sounds painful," he winced, his eyes darting around the room for his admirer. "Did you hear that Helen announced that she wants to be included in the choices for next high priestesses of the coven?"

"She'd never get it; she's not descended from one of the original bloodlines." I felt a little sick at the thought of that psycho bitch in that position of power in the coven. The high priestess was supposed to be a nurturer, not some power hungry control freak with her bitch pants on too tight.

"No, but she is an elder, the first chosen outside of the bloodlines. She's making her way to the top rather quickly, too."

"It will never happen, right?" I asked and watched as he shrugged as he held the car door open for me.

"There's a lot of shit changing pretty rapidly around here. I wouldn't cross her off the list. She's one determined bitch; materialistic and motivated by greed, too. However, the coven isn't doing well moneywise, and she's been bringing in money, which is badly needed. She might be what we need, Lena," he said as he pulled out of the parking lot.

"She'll ruin us all if she is allowed to, but there's something off about her, too. I just haven't been able to figure it out."

I looked out the window to the little side mirror and caught Lucian hidden in the shadows, watching me leave. I'm not sure how I knew it was him, other than I was sure I could hear him growling inside my head. He wasn't happy that I'd escaped his panty sniffing theatrics, but I'd had enough fun for one night.

CHAPTER twenty-four

I like not fair terms and a villain's mind. – **William Shakespeare**

I moved through the house, enjoying the silence after the bustle of the party. I'd lived alone for three years and sometimes enjoyed the solitude it provided. At other times it had been stifling, and tedious. I'd grown up in a loud house, filled with laughter and love, but that had ceased when Joshua left. The silence had been a reminder that our family was incomplete. Now, being in Lucian's fancy house with the luxuries it offered, and alone? Priceless.

I turned the music on in the bedroom, opened the door to Lucian's room that connected with mine, and made my way to the shower. The intense masculine scent of him was everywhere, and I closed my eyes and inhaled his addictive, enticing aroma. Normally, I thought men used entirely too much cologne, but Lucian didn't. He smelled like sex, mixed with sin, wrapped up in a hot package of masculine hotness. It was downright addictive.

I showered quickly, letting Adele and Christina Perry's sultry voices wash over me. I exited the shower, fully expecting to find Lucian waiting for me, but luckily he still must have been at the party which was probably going strong even though the hour was growing late.

The towels in his bathroom were ridiculously soft, so I took my time drying off before I slipped on a pair of black shorts, a light pink camisole, and my Tieks. I made my way to the room I was using, grabbed a thin zip-up sweater and moved through the house silently as I made my way to the door, slipping away from the house to go feed Luna.

I unlocked the cottage door and pushed it open, hearing her gentle purring as she jumped from the couch and sauntered towards me. I made quick work of the litter box and fed her before sitting down to give her some much needed TLC. Perhaps I should bring her to Lucian's house where it would be easier to care for her. This whole thing of being strong-armed to stay at Lucian's home was Lucian's and the coven's idea anyway. I was pretty sure I'd be safe at the cottage, protected by the wards and salt.

I was seated on the couch when I heard the first scream. It sounded like Todd, screaming from outside the cottage. I set Luna down and moved towards the door. I tried to figure out which direction the scream had come from when another one sounded from the woods.

"Todd?" I shouted, moving slowly down the stairs of the porch as a chill crept up my spine.

Silence.

I walked in the direction of the woods, pulling the sweater around me for warmth as I made my way to the edge of the woods that led further into the mountains that surrounded us.

"Lena!" he shouted, and I didn't hesitate, I ran towards his voice. He'd sounded hurt, and even though I didn't carry a weapon, two people could usually scare off predators in the woods better than one.

I broke through the thicket, my heart beating rapidly as I found Todd standing in the clearing with a strange look on his face. As I got closer to him, his eyes rose to mine and I paused. He looked terrified, and sweat beaded his brow, his skin was sallow, and ashen.

"Lena, go back," he pleaded, his hand moving to his jacket. "Damn you, run!"

"Todd, what's the…" I stopped as he pulled a gun from his jacket and aimed it at me.

✳~✳~✳

~Lucian

I studied Kendra, her emotions so different from Lena's. She was an open book; Lena was the opposite. Where Kendra went out of her way to meet men, Lena held them at arm's length, afraid to let them get close to her. Where Lena hid her pain from others, Kendra used it, knowing it bought her sympathy. Kendra also appeared to care what others thought of her, where Lena didn't. Lena was a breath of fresh air, and Kendra was stale air, mixed with too much fucking make-up—Lena didn't the need cosmetics to be beautiful.

They were almost polar opposites.

"Lucian, Lena left her house. Spyder is setting out to see if he can track her in the woods."

I looked at Devlin, and his amber eyes moved to Kendra.

"Fuck me, twins?" he asked, his smile twisting into a

tight grin.

"Lena left the house?" I asked, ignoring his eagerness to learn more about Lena. That idea was driving me bugfuck crazy. Watching him flirt with her had brought out a bitterness that was foreign to me. I didn't get jealous, period. Yet when he'd touched her, I wanted to rip his arms from their sockets.

"The watch said she headed to the cottage, and then ran out the door towards the woods," he returned softly, his eyes moving back to me. "What's she done to get your attention anyway?"

I smiled coldly, but didn't get a chance to respond before a scream tore through the room. My eyes darted to Kendra, who was clutching the side of her stomach and screaming in obvious pain. I started to move towards her, but stopped as others rushed to her side.

"Kendra," her mother whispered, her eyes wide with uncertainty as Kendra lifted her hand, as if she was seeing something, which obviously wasn't there.

"It's not me; it's Lena," she whispered, horrified by whatever she was feeling. "I think she's dying."

I vanished, not giving a shit if anyone else felt the disturbance in the air.

She's not dying—not yet at least.

$\ast \sim \ast \sim \ast$

-Magdalena

I brought my hand away from my side, covered in blood. My ears rang from the sound of gunfire. He'd fucking shot me! "Todd," I whispered as he held the gun back up, fighting against something only he could see.

The wound wasn't deep, and if I was right, the bullet either grazed me, or it was a through and through; nothing important was hit. It felt like I was dying, though. I didn't have time to stop and examine it.

"Run, damn you! Run, don't make me do this."

"You don't have to do this," I watched warily as he came closer to me, luckily the gun was now aimed at the ground.

"You don't understand. I can't control it, Lena. You aren't listening to me, run! Now!" he screamed as he strode towards me.

I wasn't fast enough; my side ached but I'd been able to determine that it wasn't as bad as it felt, even if my thin sweater and shorts were covered in blood. Sure, he'd shot at me, but he'd yanked his own arm away at the last second, causing the bullet to veer from its original target. Flesh wounds were better than dead, but something wasn't right with him.

I had just turned to run when he tackled me, hard. My body hit the ground beneath his with a hard thump that knocked the air from my lungs. His hands captured mine as he dropped the gun beside my head so that he could hold me down.

"Todd," I cried as his knees spread my legs apart wide, and with one hand he reached around to the back pocket of his jeans and pulled out a knife.

"Why didn't you fucking run?" he demanded as his mouth smashed against mine. His kiss was hard, brutal, and yet I could feel him trying to pull himself away. I felt the nick of the knife as he cut through my shorts, exposing my skin to him. He paused, looked me in the eyes and said the last thing I had ever expected him to say: "Kill me, Lena. It's the only way to stop it from killing you."

"Kill you? Just stop," I cried with trembling lips. His hand came up and grabbed my hair, slamming my head against the hard ground painfully. Stars erupted in my eyes and ringing began in my ears as tears leaked from my eyes, or maybe it was blood. I struggled against him but he was so much stronger than I was. He straddled my waist as he began to work his pants, exposing his hard dick. His legs held mine down, until he forced himself between my legs, and I begged him to stop.

I looked up at him, watching as tears slid down his cheeks as he readied himself to rape me. He wasn't willing; something was wrong. I couldn't think, my head was woozy, my vision was blurry as I tried to comprehend what was about to happen.

"Todd, stop this," I whimpered. "Please," I begged, but his eyes slid to mine, and what I saw in them would haunt me for the rest of my life. He was going to rape me, even if he didn't want to; as if something was forcing him to do it.

"Kill me," he begged as he positioned himself into a better angle to get inside of me.

My hand fumbled for the gun, and I knew he knew I had it. He didn't try to take it away; instead he pushed himself inside me roughly and painfully as he took from me what I'd never willingly given him. He pushed until I was sobbing and struggling against him; my unprepared body ached with every thrust. He brought the knife up as if he would drive it through my heart. I lifted the gun, and shot him.

Taking a life is never easy, even if the other person is the vilest creature on the planet. Todd wasn't, but he'd given up fighting whatever had control of him. He'd planned to finish the job. He had, in no uncertain terms, told me it was either him or me who was dying, and he'd tried to give me a chance to save myself.

His body landed on me, and I sobbed as I struggled to fight my way out from underneath him. I was half naked, with blood covering my body, and I hurt, physically and mentally. I looked at the boy I'd once loved and dropped the gun I'd used to take his life.

A sob ripped from me as I tried to get to my feet. I heard scuffling, and then voices. I turned to find Lucian and another tall man with messy black hair and icy blue eyes running towards me. Lucian flinched as he took in the carnage. I was covered in blood, numb, and there was no denying that I'd been raped.

Todd had gained entrance into my body, and I'd been unable to stop him. He'd tried to hold back, but something darker had taken control of him. The gun I'd killed him with was next to his body, probably one belonging to his father that we'd taken out for target practice a time or two.

"Damn," the man beside Lucian swore, and Lucian moved into action, pulling his coat off and covering me as he lifted me in his arms and, without a single word, headed to his house.

He said nothing, just held my trembling form tightly as he marched towards his expansive house. The moment we got there, cars were already showing up, and Kendra was beside us quickly.

"Is she shot?" she demanded, "I felt it!"

"She'll live, Kendra, Lena's a fighter."

He ignored her other questions as he continued to move through the house. My family followed us up the stairs and into his room.

He sat me down on a small bench before turning on the shower. His eyes kept looking me over, probably waiting for me to become hysterical. I felt numb, as if I was watching it happen to someone else. I was trembling; my heart ached as I considered the consequences of what I'd just done, and what had happened to me.

My teeth began to chatter a little and I struggled to pull myself together. "Perhaps this sex thing just isn't in the cards for me," I rasped softly. Lucian's eyes widened for a moment and I thought I saw a hint of a smile.

"I told you, you just haven't had the right kind of sex yet," he murmured. Good, he didn't pity me. I hated pity.

Lucian turned, removed the coat and gently unzipped and removed the sweater and camisole that were covered in blood. He moved with me into the shower, uncaring that he was ruining his expensive suit. After checking the water's temperature, he soaped up a soft cloth and began washing me carefully; avoiding the wounds from the bullet, and where Todd had cut me with the knife as he'd removed my shorts and panties. His fingers gently traced the wounds and rinsed them with water.

He didn't ask me if I was alright, and I was grateful. I didn't want to speak, because I didn't trust myself not to become hysterical. I needed the silence to figure out what the hell had just happened, and to accept it. I needed to compartmentalize it, and push it behind the wall of emotions I wasn't willing to deal with yet. Eventually that wall was going to crack, and then I'd have to face it all at once.

He carefully washed my hair, and I watched as blood rinsed down the drain along with shampoo bubbles. I wasn't sure who had bled more, or whose blood was being washed away.

When Lucian finished, he guided me out of the shower and began drying me off. He pulled open a drawer and retrieved something as I gazed blankly at the wall. I could feel him examining my wounds and slathering a cream on them that smelled like the cream he used the other night when I was burned so badly. I sighed with a bit of relief; it had healed the burns efficiently, and it had taken the pain away. He cut off lengths of gauze and medical tape and covered the area where the bullet had grazed me, then wrapped a soft towel around me.

He didn't need to ask questions about the rape. He'd seen what had happened, or more to the point he'd seen the evidence of it. He didn't push, or ask me to open up about how I felt; only an idiot would ask that, seeing as I'd just killed someone. Someone I'd once cared a great deal about, on top of that.

He maneuvered me to his bed, where my family was waiting, and helped me onto the bed before he pulled the covers up, lay down beside me, and held me close. I closed my eyes, shutting out everything but the feel of Lucian as he gave me warmth and the sense of protection I needed to sleep.

No one said anything. I was pretty sure it was because Lucian was warning them with one of his patented glares that makes you shrivel up inside before you have the urge to run for your life. I heard feet shuffling through the room and out the door.

"Thank you," I whispered.

"Sleep, Lena. I've got you," he whispered back, placing a soft kiss at the thundering pulse on my neck. "Nothing can touch you here; you're safe."

I slept dreamlessly, escaping the nightmare of reality.

CHAPTER
twenty-five

~Lucian

I'd just made it through the woods when the shot was fired. Her hand clung to the gun long after the body had landed on top of her. No sound had escaped from her, no emotion. I'd stood in shock, and I knew Spyder was just as shocked. We waited for the barest of moments to see who prevailed as their bodies collapsed on the ground. She'd pushed him off of herself, revealing that their bodies had been connected and the proof of his rape.

Where most girls would have been hysterical, Lena was clinical, cold, and detached. She'd been covered in his blood; her hair had been colored red with it. She struggled to her feet, half naked, her face bruised; even with the blood covering her silken flesh, the bruises were visible.

We'd waited in silence for what felt like an eternity for her to scream, or, fuck, something. I'd expected screaming…anything would have been better than the look of detachment that she leveled me with. Dead eyes, as if she'd shot herself instead of her rapist. I'd run to her, watching her tremble as the adrenaline that had briefly taken hold of her slowly escaped her system now that the danger had passed. Lips trembled, hands shook, and she had remained still until I got close, when her eyes had snapped up, meeting mine.

She didn't want comfort, didn't want words. I'd wrapped her in my suit jacket, covering her partially naked body as she'd wrapped her arms around my neck and buried her face in the crook of my neck. She allowed that small bit of comfort, her silent release of the breath she'd been holding fanned my skin and showed her relief that it was over. I swallowed down the growl; the urge to reanimate him, to kill him again, shot through me.

I whispered comforting words to her, something I hadn't done to a woman in a very long time. I'd passed her family without a second thought, moving towards the bathroom. I'd set her down once we were inside, peeling her bloodied clothing from her body as I took in the abuse she'd endured. She was a fighter; even though she hadn't been the stronger one in that confrontation, she'd won the battle. Her body was proof.

She was compartmentalizing. Pushing it from her mind, pretending it had never happened. Her emotions were raw, sizzling and igniting the fire in her eyes. She held it at bay, as if it was a nightmare and she would wake at any moment. Her body trembled against mine, my suit ruined as she leaned against me for comfort; me, not her family. She didn't ask for them; instead she'd clung to me as a lifeline.

With the softest of voices, she said the last thing I expected through teeth that had begun to chatter a little. "Perhaps this sex thing just isn't in the cards for me."

I stared at her, watching as she waited for me to respond. There was steel in this woman, a strength I never would have dreamed she'd possess. Blue eyes stared back, life and emotion flowing back into them as she watched me.

"I told you, you just haven't had the right kind of sex yet." I wanted to be careful in my teasing, because as soon as she had recovered from this and the Harvest nonsense, I would show her exactly what the right kind of sex was.

Once I was sure she was clean, I walked her from the shower, covering her with a towel as I dried her skin. Words weren't needed here; she knew I had her, she knew she was safe, and she knew I wouldn't ask if she was okay.

She wasn't. She'd been fucking *raped*. I'd been too late, forcing myself to remain at the party to give her space. No one was fine after a rape, and she didn't need to be asked that stupid question. Why humans asked it after violence had occurred was beyond me. Her little show of fire a bit ago that replaced the deadness I'd seen in the woods surprised me, and I'd felt a rush of relief push through me as she slowly came back from what had happened. Most women didn't for weeks after being raped, if ever.

From one of the drawers, I retrieved some gauze and medical tape, as well as the cream Bane brought me the other night. The cream was a sham; it had a nice fragrance, but did nothing. I ran my fingers over the worst of her wounds; partially finishing the job I began in the shower.

I didn't want to heal her too much, as to draw suspicion to what I could do, just enough to take away the worst of the pain and prevent scarring, as I had with her burns the other night. Better she think it was the fucking cream than me that healed her. I smoothed a length of gauze and medical tape over the wound to complete the camouflage.

After stripping off my wet clothes and slipping on a robe, I didn't take her to her own room; instead, I guided her to mine, tucking her beneath the silken covers, my eyes mentally noting each mark, each bruise. She'd fought him. My fierce little warrior had fought him off, and even though she hadn't won, she'd prevailed against his strength. She'd lived.

Spyder had remained behind with the body and his mental voice drifted across my mind. *"It was an Asmodeus demon. Chicken shit fled as soon as the boy died; his body reeked of the possession once the demon had left it. Bad news is, it wasn't one we know."*

The Asmodeus demon must have taken control of the boy some days ago, possessed his body, and claimed ownership of it. They'd then gone after her, which meant only one possible thing. Demons had come to play at Haven Crest. The big question was, why? Todd and Cassidy's tryst in Lena's home and in her own bed made sense now. He wasn't just weak; he was pathetic enough to be possessed by a very nasty creature whose earmarks were lust and violence.

It could be Asmodeus demons who were responsible for the rash of young women disappearing lately, or it could be her brother who was responsible. It was something we needed to look closer at, seeing as whoever it was, was fucking around in my business. Young witches had a variety of uses, be they alive, dying, or even freshly deceased.

I could sense her emotions although I had missed what he'd said to her. Normally I'd try to read her mind, but with Lena, I couldn't. She'd perfected her walls, and with each new day she woke, she reinforced them.

Once I had her tucked securely in my bed, protected in my arms, I heard a whispered, "Thank you," her voice raw from screaming for help that hadn't come in time.

"Sleep, Lena, I've got you," I replied, holding her tighter. Before I knew what I'd done, I kissed her pulse that ticked wildly. "Nothing can touch you here, you're safe," I watched as she closed her eyes and her breathing grew even with sleep.

~~*

~Magdalena

I awoke alone, stretched out on a huge bed that was as soft as silk. My eyes snapped open, and I looked around the room. I was in Lucian's bed, my body still naked and battered from last night. I sat up slowly, pulling the covers up with me to hide my nakedness. I ached; even sitting up hurt too much.

I moved sluggishly, taking inventory of all the aches I felt, or could see. There were a lot more than I had initially thought last night. Between my legs, the soft flesh was sore, painfully so. Bruises covered my inner thighs, and after peeling away the gauze and tape, I saw that the bullet wound was nothing more than a thin angry red line, and not deep. The side where Todd had cut me had scabbed over as the skin began to heal. As it had after the fire, the cream did an amazing job of healing. The burns should have taken weeks to heal, and I knew that somehow Lucian was using something more than the cream to speed up the healing process.

I looked at myself in the mirror, noting I had bruises on my lips and my chin, as well as the side of my face, where swelling made it look worse than it actually was. I'd felt no pain when I'd fallen asleep, dulled by the adrenaline, no doubt. Today I hurt like hell, and moving took a huge effort on my part.

I slipped into the shower, noting that someone had left a change of clothing for me. Taking extreme care with my aches, I cleaned up, then briskly toweled off and slipped into the sweat pants; a floral pattern of roses covered them, so most likely my mother had left it. The shirt was baggy, so I tucked it into the sweats and slipped on the zip-up jacket that matched the sweats. I tied my hair up into a high ponytail, which made me wince in pain from the large bumps and cuts on the back of my head. He'd smashed my head against the ground, and yet he'd begged me to kill him, to stop him from hurting me. It didn't make sense.

It still seemed unreal, as if I'd watched it happen to someone else instead of living it. I wasn't ready to deal with what happened. I knew distinctly that I hadn't been the only victim. Todd had been fighting something off, even as he'd attacked my body. Strangely enough, I didn't feel violated, nor did I blame myself for what had happened. I had heard it was a common thing that victims did after being raped.

I entered the kitchen, ignoring the fact that the noisy room went silent the moment I entered it. Lucian was there with the man who'd been with him last night, the only two who knew exactly what had happened. My grandmother and family were there, along with several elders from the coven who looked at me with pity. I didn't fucking need pity.

"Magdalena, are you alright?" my mother asked as I poured coffee and turned to look at them better. It was time to deal with this, and sometimes a good offense was better than always being on the defense.

"No, I'm not. Neither is Todd, and what happened was awful, but I need you to understand that I am not the only victim here. I was attacked, so don't ask me if I am fine, because right now I can't give you that answer. I felt something in Todd; he didn't want to do what he did. Someone was controlling him; he practically begged me to kill him. That's what we should focus on."

"I felt everything that happened to you," Kendra said softly, her eyes filling with tears. She was speaking about the rape, and I wasn't willing to go there. Not yet.

"Learn to turn it off, Kendra," I replied crisply. Probably more because I was embarrassed by what she'd felt. My body being violated violently; I hadn't wanted that for her. No one should ever feel something like that, ever.

Sometimes, with the bond Kendra and I shared, it was hard to separate from each other. I felt her, as if she was an extended part of me, as she did with me. I hadn't been able to close the bond during the attack, which meant she knew every vile detail of what had happened to me, as if had happened to her.

"What happened to you...it's," one of the elders started to say, her gentle gray eyes watching me carefully.

"It shouldn't have happened. It sucked. I'm dealing with it in my own way, and I'll thank you all to not treat me like a piece of fine china. I won't shatter. I do, however, need you to know that Todd saved me. He deserves to be buried with honor for his sacrifice. Without it, you'd be getting ready to perform my burial instead of his."

"He tried to harm someone from one of the original families; he will not be buried with the honor of the ancestors," another elder replied carefully.

"You're not hearing me. Todd didn't have a choice; it wasn't him. Something had control of his body, somehow. I don't understand it exactly, but from the moment I stepped into that clearing to the moment he died, he'd begged me to take his life to save my own. Does that sound like someone who wanted to do what he did? He knew I'd picked up the gun and yet he didn't stop me from killing him, and he could have, easily. Todd allowed me to win, and that right there should alert us to the real problem. I felt something else inside of him, something dark and evil. Focus on that instead of the things that can't be changed, like what happened to me. You can't change what's been done, but we can prevent it from happening to anyone else."

No one said anything. They just looked at me as if I'd gone off the deep end. I set the cup of coffee down on the counter and fought for control of my emotions. The electrical pulse in the room that alerted me to Lucian gave me strength. Why it did, I wasn't sure. Every time I'd awoken last night crying, he'd held me through it, whispering soft words against my ear until I'd fallen asleep. He didn't have to do it, but he had. He'd been my comfort through the storm as I struggled to fight through the nightmares.

"Listen, I know the laws. I know if a person is used by possession or compelled to do something, it can be forgiven because they weren't in control of their own actions. He deserves this. He fought it long enough to be sure I won. For that, he deserves respect."

"Dark magic, as you described, would have caused a ripple; we'd have felt it, Magdalena," my grandmother whispered, her blue eyes locking with mine.

"Are you sure about that?" I asked. "You didn't feel Benjamin, and he's dark. He was outside the manor house right after the fire; did any of the elders who arrived during and after the fire *feel* him then?"

"This is true, we did not feel him," Grandmother said as she wrung her hands in worry. "But if what you say is true, it means someone is powerful enough to prevent us from sensing their presence. We must start the Awakening immediately. We are more powerful when our full potential is standing with us."

"This is all quite shocking; however, I don't think we should make hasty decisions. If we start the Awakening early, it could create a ripple effect in the generations to come. The timing has always been chosen because magic always flows strongest at Beltane and Samhain, and the postulants would get more of a boost of power by holding the ceremony at one of those two times. Preferably Samhain, as the veil between worlds is easier to cross. It takes less magic to call the ancestors to us, which leaves more to protect those who are receiving their powers."

"We should tell Helen," the other elder said, stopping the silver haired woman before she could expound more about the potential effect on future generations.

"We are under attack; we must start the preparations. This cannot continue to go on, and you know why, Nancy. It could be connected to the past, and the same reason the records of what happened to the generations who came before us were so spotty," Grandma said, her eyes closing briefly before she looked at the others.

"What are you talking about?" I asked as a chill ran up my spine.

"You shouldn't discuss coven business so openly!" one elder hissed, his eyes moving around the room carefully.

Grandmother nodded to the other elder and spoke. "Call the assembly, Nancy. We must bring this new information before the high priestess immediately. We must ensure that we protect the children from whatever is hunting them, quickly."

Kendra wasn't interested in the elders; instead, her eyes took in each visible bruise, and she winced, reliving each one of them. I closed my emotions off, knowing she would feel it the moment I shut her out. Her eyes went wide with surprise, and I looked at her. I'd only done it a few times before, completely closing myself off to her. I turned on my heel and left the room, heading to the cottage to make sure Luna was safe since I hadn't shut the door when I'd heard Todd's screams last night.

"Magdalena, you will attend the assembly. Your marks will show the others that the need for haste is not something that can be put off," my grandmother said, stopping me in my tracks.

"You want to show off my bruises?" I asked, incredulous that she'd even suggest it. "So that all women can be terrified that they could be next or because you think the other elders will refuse the idea of moving up the Awakening?" My mouth was moving of its own volition before I could stop it.

"Because you are proof of the need to rush the Awakening, and to break with tradition," Nancy explained, as if I was a daft child.

"No, thank you," I whispered. "I'd rather not stand in front of the entire coven as a battered, broken example.

I'm battered, but I'm never broken. You'll figure it out without me."

I didn't wait to see if they agreed. I left with my emotions barely in check. I needed a quiet place to be alone, without Kendra's prying eyes watching my every move. She'd stand in for me at the meeting, it was why they'd let me go. She knew every dirty detail.

CHAPTER
twenty-six

I knew my mom worried that I might implode or crack when the eventual reality of what happened hit me. Kendra was afraid of the silence she felt, hating that I was refusing to talk about it. Lucian was giving me time to process, as if he thought I actually would. Kendra was relentless, so I had been sending her on meaningless tasks, and each time she'd finished, she would end up right back in the room with me.

"You need to talk to me," she demanded quietly once she'd figured out that I was purposely sending her out on unnecessary errands.

"No."

"So, what, Lena? What's the fucking plan, shut it off and just not feel anything, just like you did when Joshua died, because that ended so fucking well. You need to open up and talk about it; I already know everything, so just talk to me!" Kendra said as she paced the length of the room.

"I don't need a therapist right now, Kendra," I mumbled as I grabbed the pillow and lay on my side, watching her endless pacing.

"You took a life; you need to cry or shout, or, shit, Lena…Do something besides sit there and pretend it didn't happen to you, because it did!" she ordered.

"I don't need to scream, or cry, or anything, Kendra. I'm exhausted, and I just need to sleep for a little while."

"Fine!" she growled as she kicked off her shoes and crawled into bed, curving her body next to mine as she wrapped her arms around me. We'd done this a lot as children, sometimes as teenagers, but never as adults.

It felt good, and eventually I closed my eyes.

"He raped you," she whispered. "That has to be hard to deal with."

I opened my eyes and felt the panic building inside of me.

"He did, but it wasn't Todd. I don't blame him for it, I blame whoever made him do it," I muttered as I turned to face her. "I can feel your mind, Kendra," I admitted, hating the way her brain was itching to blame herself. "He loved us both, and he never would have willingly taken my choice from me, or forced himself on me. You have to know that. Todd did a lot of stupid shit, but he wasn't mean to me, ever. He saved me, he watched me grab the gun and he told me to do it. Don't let what someone forced him to do change how you felt for him."

"How can you be so calm and accepting of the fact that you were *raped*?"

"Because screaming and crying won't change the fact that I was, Kendra. Fuck, listen to yourself. You want me to scream?" I asked, my voice already rising. "You want me to cry? What the fuck will it change? Will it take it away? Will it make me forget that someone forced Todd to fucking rape me? What the fuck is it going to do? Make me better!?" I was crying, I was yelling, and I felt worse for it. "Nothing will ever take it away! Nothing can change it, and I am dealing with it! I'm not falling apart. Someone *wanted* to hurt me. I won't give them fucking control! I won't let them have that power over me, ever!"

The door opened, and Lucian, my mother, and Spyder, the guy who'd been present last night, all rushed in at my raised voice.

"Lena, I didn't mean to…I didn't mean to upset you," she whispered as I pulled the covers over my head and shut out the world. "I just want you to deal with it; you've been brutalized. You can't just turn it off; it's going to eat at you until you fall apart."

"Get out," I whispered. "I am not you. Quit trying to make me feel or behave like someone I'm not," I emphasized my words with more strength than I felt. "Just leave me alone for a while, all right?"

I didn't blame my sister, but I hated that she'd made me visualize it again. I was watching Todd on top of me, pushing inside of me; Todd's hands smashing my head into the ground, hard. It was all there, on instant replay inside of my head. His look of shock as the bullet hit him, and his blood splattering everywhere, and Todd's body falling on mine, and me, having to push his dead weight off and out of myself.

I was trembling. I heard the scuffling of feet as they left the room and then a slight pressure on the bed. I didn't need to peel off the blankets to know who it was; I could smell him. Feel the sizzle of power that I knew was his.

He didn't try to move the covers. Instead, he sat

silently on the bed as I let the emotions wash over me before forcing them back into the dark box, which I pushed back behind the wall inside my head. That was a box I didn't plan on opening anytime soon.

Eventually, I pulled the covers off my head and looked at him. His eyes were closed, and he was breathing evenly as if he'd fallen asleep beside me. I looked at his long lashes, darker and longer than I'd ever seen on a guy. They almost matched the darkness of his eyes when they were open, and at the moment, I wanted to see his eyes open. I wanted him to press me with some sort of sexual innuendo as he had been doing. I hated that almost everyone was handling me with kid gloves, and acting like I was a delicate thing that needed to be coddled. Then there was Kendra, who was badgering me to act in a way that just wasn't in my nature.

I moved closer to him, unwillingly drawn to his welcoming warmth. My cheek touched his chest, and I let the calm and security I felt in his presence wash over me. I closed my eyes, and drifted towards sleep knowing that whatever was out there trying to get me, couldn't. Not when I had Lucian this close.

I felt protected.

I shouldn't feel this comfortable with a guy I hardly knew, but something told me that with him near, I was safe. Safe from everything except for him, that is. I didn't care, though. I was exhausted, mentally and physically. I flinched as his arm moved, and wrapped around me as he pulled my body closer to his, holding me close.

"Sleep, Lena," he whispered, his eyes opening a sliver. "Spyder will keep everyone away from your room for now. I'll hold you through the storm."

"I'm still not a damsel," I whispered against his chest.

"Distress is a state of mind, and my mind is strong enough to make it through this. I just need time to figure out how."

"I know, Lena, you're a fighter. You won, but winning comes with consequences. You took a life; it will leave a mark on you. No matter the reason it happened, it happened. You don't feel like a victim because you refuse to be one; it makes you stronger than most of the people in this world."

"It doesn't make them weak," I whispered. "Being a victim doesn't mean they wanted to be one. It just means it happened. I don't feel like a victim; I mean, I know I am, but it feels like it happened to someone else, not me. I was raped, and yet I don't feel like I was; I guess it helps knowing he didn't want to do what he did. He didn't enjoy it, forcing himself inside of me. He hated it. You have no idea how much knowing that helps me process this. Maybe because he was a victim as well, or maybe because I took his life and I know it can't happen to me again, not the same way."

"Or maybe because you're refusing to believe that it happened to you, as Kendra said. She's worried about you, they all are. You bottle everything inside, and eventually even the strongest walls tumble to the ground."

"You think I should talk about it?" I asked, unsure why I felt comfortable talking to him and not my sister.

"I think you just did," he murmured against my ear and I turned to look at him.

"How do you do that?" I asked, and watched as his lips curved into a smile as his eyes searched my face.

"Do what?" he questioned.

"Make me so comfortable, as if I've known you forever instead of the short time that I actually have."

Something dark entered his eyes but when I blinked,

it was gone. He shook his head and pulled me tighter against himself, and closed his eyes.

"Anyone ever told you that you talk too much?" he laughed against my neck. "Go to sleep, little fighter," he finished, and I felt my eyes finally give in to the weight that had been pulling them down, and slept cradled in his warm embrace.

CHAPTER
twenty-seven

The assembly had been postponed for a few days to allow me time to heal, as if they thought I'd attend it if I had more time to cope with what had happened. After a week had gone by without me changing my mind, they decided to finally move forward without me. When it came time for the meeting, Kendra agreed to stand in on my behalf, leaving me free from the prying eyes and having to relay my story to the entire coven that would have been in attendance.

With time on my hands, I'd decided to pull weeds from the garden, knowing it was therapeutic in its own way. I had just managed to clean out five rows of weeds when I felt the shift in the weather; it went from cloudy to beautiful blue skies in less than a minute. I stood up, looking around for the cause of the sudden change.

"Magdalena, it calms you to garden," a soft voice said.

I turned to find her, the high priestess of the coven.

Tabitha was beautiful and ageless. She had golden blonde hair that cascaded to her hips in soft curls. Her almond shaped eyes perfectly fit her oval shaped face and were the color of freshly fallen snow.

"It's always calmed me," I replied. My grungy, dirty hands weren't something I wanted to offer her but she deserved respect. I bowed my head and gave her a quick, awkward curtsy. "I should wash up."

"There's no need for that."

"Can I get you something?" I asked as my eyes darted from the cottage to her. She deserved to be given more than I could offer her, but it wasn't as if I could invite her into the main house, which didn't even have power restored yet.

"I'd like to see what happened to you, and know why you asked your sister to beg for Todd to be buried with the honor and approval of the coven."

"Tabitha, he gave his life for mine. He could have easily killed me, but he didn't. I understand that no one wants to believe that he was being controlled by someone else, but I felt it. It was evil, violent and it was absolutely in charge of him. He shot at me, and yet he fought it so that I didn't end up with a new hole in my stomach. When he raped me, and even before that, he begged me to take his life to stop him from hurting me. He fought whatever it was *for* me. He didn't have to, but he did, and that means something. I wasn't the only victim. He was used as a weapon against me. Todd didn't have a chance of escaping from them, and he knew it. He watched me pick up the gun while he fought against the spell, and he let me win. He loved me enough to make the sacrifice; you don't need to see it to understand that."

"I need to 'see' to argue your case," she murmured

softly as she reached up and pulled a twig from my hair. "Some choose not to honor your wishes because we all know that at one point, you loved and cared for that boy. They believe you're making excuses for his behavior and if I am to take your side, I wish to see the event through your eyes to understand what really happened."

"You don't believe me?" I asked cautiously.

"I have not felt the presence of darkness," she answered softly with no accusation in her tone. "It's alarming that you have and I have not, Magdalena. If it's present, then not only are we all in danger; we must consider moving up the Awakening. In the old days, demons would be attracted by the power increase around the time of an Awakening. It's been a very long time since a coven was attacked by a demon and many have forgotten the evil they bring. When I was little, the old ones spoke of such things. They referred to demons sent by the gods of hell, ones who sought out witches for their powers. Darkness used to be accepted; however, with the dangers that surround us on a daily basis, it was safer to expel those who harbored the darkness in their souls. Demons are attracted to darkness and want to exploit it. Once the darkness was removed from the covens, the demons hunted us less and less until eventually they stopped. That's why I asked the coven to expel your brother."

My pulse ticked with anger at her words but I managed to hide it, or so I thought.

"You don't understand," she stated. "Demons would come again if darkness was allowed to grow inside the coven. We are ill-equipped to fight them, and allowing the past to happen again would be devastating for the coven."

"Demons," I repeated, because we'd all been given a crash course on the coven's history, or what was left of it.

The coven had abandoned pretty much everything each time they moved west.

"Demons are deadly to witches, Magdalena. We won't take the chance of encountering them. They covet our powers, and the only way to take a witch's power, is to take her soul. Without a soul, you can't be reborn to the coven."

"We can be reborn?" I asked, noting the way she'd said it. As in, we could come back.

"Only the more powerful ones, or those cursed by darkness before death. My grandmother told me the story of one of our ancestors; she was cursed to be reborn. She was a little hazy about most of the details of the story, only that she was a very powerful witch. It was rumored that she was cursed because of something she had done long ago to a very powerful demon."

"I heard a little bit about her, that story is part of the catechism."

"Yes, I made it part of the catechism; her story is not one that is shared often. My grandmother taught me the story so that I could share it with others before my time on this earth was finished."

"You're dying," I whispered with wide eyes.

"Not today, but every priestess can sense her time drawing near. Mine won't be for a little while longer; however, you should know her story can and does repeat itself because of the one who cursed her."

"What does her story have to do with me?" I questioned.

"Because it used to reoccur every sixty years or so, and with the events happening lately, I think it's begun again."

"You think I'm being targeted by the same monster

that killed one of our ancestors?"

"If I didn't sense the darkness, it could spell trouble for the coven, Magdalena. It worries me, though, that this is the second attempt on your life, and that of your family's bloodline."

"That's only an assumption. No disrespect, but you didn't sense my brother here, either. He has darkness inside of him, and yet he's somehow learned to hide it," I divulged.

"You're correct about his darkness. I felt the shift in the balance when he arrived, but he carries no malice strong enough to do harm to others."

"If you felt him, why didn't you warn us?" I asked, aghast that she'd known.

"Because those are your mother's scars to heal," she replied with a soft smile. "My job is to protect and teach the coven, not necessarily to meddle in their affairs. I guide, and lead. Only you can choose which path you follow; I can only lead you to the fork in the road, Magdalena."

"Oh," was all I could say.

"If you'd like to change into something more comfortable, I'll wait," she announced as I opened the door to the cottage.

"Please," I said as a blush stole across my cheeks. "My grandmother would have heart failure if she knew you'd seen me like this."

"It matters little to me if you're covered in dirt, Magdalena. I find gardening comforting as well, and with everything you've been through, I was pleased to find you doing something to occupy your mind. I know that he raped you…"

"He didn't rape me," I interrupted. "Todd was a victim as well, and once you see it, you'll understand. I don't consider it the same because I don't feel like I was raped. I feel like I was violated, but it wasn't by Todd. He loved me, even if we had our differences."

"You're not like most women I've known. Witches don't value chastity, and yet you do. I was told by your grandmother that you had chosen to remain pure until your wedding to the boy."

"I wanted it to be special, I guess, to mean something more than just sex. Todd agreed; he thought it was something that we would share on our wedding night."

"Many assume he took it by force after you rejected his advances at the opening ceremony celebration," she mused.

"I wasn't a virgin when he…when it happened," I stammered.

She smiled and shook her head. "I see; maybe there is hope for you, after all."

"Hope?" I asked feeling the blood rush from my face. She thought I was hopeless? Not good.

"I was joking, Magdalena. Go change, I'll start some tea. This can take a little while," she announced.

I grabbed a camisole of soft pink satin and pair of comfortable black slacks, and moved into the bathroom. I washed up quickly and pulled my hair into a high ponytail before slipping the clothes on and heading to the small, comfortable front room.

"To do this, you have to let me past those walls you've erected," she announced, surprising me.

"I have no walls…"

She smiled and shook her head.

"I'm fully aware of what you have done to protect yourself from feeling emotions you don't want. I don't blame you for doing it, but for me to push through them would prevent you from replacing them anytime soon. I assume you plan to erect them after we've finished."

"I'm not sure how to take them down," I admitted.

"You have to want to take them down," she replied.

"I don't want them down; if they're down, I have to feel everything."

"I'll keep the pain at bay, if you'll let me," she said sadly. "I wish you'd have remained here after your brother's funeral; I'd have loved to have gotten to know you as I have the others."

"I couldn't, I just needed time…"

"You needed to heal, but that's what we're for; we heal together. It's how we bond and grow together. I could have helped you through the pain, taught you how to use it for good. Every emotion has a place inside the magical trifecta. The Fae feed from it, but witches, we use it to strengthen spells, to tether bonds and strengthen wards."

"I didn't know that," I said, watching while the candles ignited around the room as the tea kettle floated by my head and poured tea perfectly into the small mugs on the coffee table. Spoons stirred inside the cup with the flick of her finger and sugar cubes danced in the air and plopped right into the cups.

"You missed a lot of things while you were off studying herbs," she smiled mischievously. "I know you have a mother, but I am your mother as well, in a sense. It's my job to watch over you. That includes my flock that leaves home before they've been awoken to the powers that protect them."

"Let's do this," I said, and then winced at how bitter I sounded. "Do I have to see it again?" I asked.

"No, I'm just going to look through your mind to find the memory; you won't see anything, you just have to allow me in."

"I don't understand why I had to endure a blood ritual if you can easily sort through my memories. You could have done this and excluded me as a suspect in the house fire," I stated, watching as she smiled and nodded gently. Enduring Lucian sorting through my past? It was seriously embarrassing. It was like handing a total stranger your diary and watching as he read through every entry.

"I could have. I meditated on it for some time before deciding to stay out of it. First off, most of the coven doesn't know I can do this outside of blood magic." Her eyes had a mischievous glint in them. "A girl has to have some secrets, you know. The bigger reason is as I said before: my job is to protect and teach the coven, not meddle, and that did fall under the category of meddling. In this situation, I need to see so I can protect the coven and guide them in the best direction. Now sit there and relax." She lowered herself gracefully on to the carpeting and patted the space in front of herself.

I sat cross-legged on the floor across from her and accepted her hands as she offered them. She was silent, but I could feel her magic already filling the room as she prepared to use it to enter my memories.

"You'll feel me poking around a little, but remember, I'm only looking for what transpired during the attack," she said with a quick tightening of her hands on mine for comfort. Her hands left mine and carefully touched my cheeks. I felt the shock of her magic as she delved into my mind, but she didn't get far. "Walls, Magdalena, I need them down. Trust me," she whispered.

I imagined them crumbling down, exposing the pain that I'd tried so hard to escape from. Tears filled my eyes as the first ugly slice of pain tore through me and then just like that, it was gone. I opened my eyes to find hers filled with the same tears that I'd just had in my own eyes.

"I can see why you hide from it," she whispered sadly, but seemed to be handling it all the same. That was more than I could say for myself.

I felt her tugging at my mind, pulling and pushing memories until she discovered the freshest wound. I felt her pushing through it, heard her gasp inside my memories as the violence exploded, and the moment I felt her pulling out, I replaced the walls and pushed her from my mind with enough force that the candles extinguished and the room went dark as a single bolt of lightning hit the ground outside, followed by a booming crash of thunder that was too close for comfort.

"How did you do that?" she demanded.

"Do what?" I asked as I whirled through the emotions, pushing them away so I wouldn't feel any of it.

"You pushed me out," she said as she lifted her hands and the candles leapt to life again. "You expelled me from your memories. No one has ever done that to me."

"I'd have felt them, again," I said uncomfortably. "I was protecting myself," I admitted.

"Todd wasn't spelled by magic, Magdalena," she whispered as she got to her feet.

"Bullshit, I know what I saw!" I argued.

"It wasn't magic; it was a possession. He was possessed by a demon," she replied shakily. "We have to move the Awakening up, and call the other covens to aid us. If they have found us, no one is safe, no one."

"Demons, but you said…"

"I must go; I'm not safe," she whispered, and with a rush of wind, she vanished. I swallowed and looked around the room.

Todd had been possessed, which meant I was raped by a demon, but why me? Why him? I felt the blood leaving my face as reality set in. Demons were hunting me, playing with me. I pushed out to feel Kendra, and felt her inner panic. She was with Mom and Grandmother still, and Tabitha had reached them already.

I heard a chant begin in my mind and before I could stop myself, I started chanting the ancient words to call forth the other covens. Hundreds of voices began chanting, and then thousands. Hell had come to Haven Crest, and no one was safe here, no one.

CHAPTER
twenty-eight

I sat on the couch, numb, and unmoving. Netflix was offering suggestions for movies and shows, loading them as I stared blankly at the TV. A partially melted pint of Cherry Garcia waited for me on the coffee table, and Luna slept peacefully in my lap, unaware of the nightmare that was brewing.

The door opened and I jumped, scaring Luna, who hissed and darted from the couch and out the door. Lucian stood in the doorway, his face angry as he looked around the room. He moved into the room with long strides and stood in front of me, taking in the ice cream and Netflix randomizer, not to mention my disheveled state.

"You were supposed to be at that meeting, not here at the cottage, and certainly not alone," he pointed out, and I gave him a blank stare.

"I told you more than once that I wasn't going. I didn't need to be present to be an example of what could happen if they didn't do the right thing. I also wanted some solitude, so I did some gardening."

"There's a situation," he said softly. "Some facts have been brought to light, and you shouldn't be alone right now."

"Demons are coming to take me away?" I laughed nervously. His eyes hardened and he pushed aside a pile of clothes I'd placed on the couch to fold. I'd never actually folded any of it, because I'd been too busy imagining a world where demons existed and hunted witches, because my life wasn't complicated enough.

"The Awakening is happening tonight," he said as he sat down and turned to look at me.

"And?" I asked, my eyes meeting his. I knew exactly what he meant; I'd be off limits to him, at least for longer than either of us wanted. There was a cool-down period after the Harvest, to see if conception had occurred. You could either continue sleeping with the same guy or go without sex until you were sure you weren't expecting a child. It was a way of marking which bloodlines had successfully bred during the Harvest.

"Magdalena," he said softly, his eyes narrowing on me as he considered his next words. "I need to know why you were specifically targeted by the demons. Do you have any idea why they'd want to attack you?"

That threw me. Mister Know-It-All was asking me? I laughed and shook my head. I wanted to know the answer to that question as well.

"Maybe because my family is one of the original bloodlines, or maybe he liked my outfit; how am I supposed to know why he did that to me?" I asked with trembling lips. I'd thought it was dark magic, but it hadn't been; it had been a fucking demon. Then again, Tabitha had mentioned that demons were attracted to darkness.

"This isn't a joke," he growled.

"You think I don't know that? I was…he did that to me, not you. I know exactly how serious this is."

"Good. You'll be okay, I'll make sure of it," he said firmly as something passed behind his eyes and he settled back on the couch and turned towards the TV. He crossed his arms and closed his eyes.

"I can take care of myself," I whispered, hating that he'd been the one to save me from the fire and pick me up when my legs were too weak to make it back to the house after the attack. It was becoming a pattern; I was starting to feel like a damsel, and I didn't like it.

"Of course you can." I wasn't sure if he was mocking me or not. "However, you can't save yourself from me," he replied, his eyes heating as they raked over me slowly.

"Why would I need to save myself from you?" I asked softly as my eyes lowered to his sexy lips and I absently chewed on my bottom lip. He hadn't kissed or touched me in a week, and I missed it. I was glad he was giving me space to make sure I was okay, but I didn't want space. I wanted him.

He laughed soundlessly and a chill raced down my spine. His fingers moved in slow motion towards the thin strap of my camisole, and he ripped the strap off, pulling a soft gasp from my lips.

"What the hell?" I demanded as I moved to sit up, only to be pushed back down as a cocky grin formed while heat flooded his eyes.

"I told you that I would have you, Lena," he said hoarsely, his mouth lowering to kiss my shoulder, which sent heat racing through me and caused an inferno in my stomach.

"Lucian, the Awakening is tonight," I replied breathlessly as I subtly reminded him of why this was a bad idea.

"So it is," he continued as his fingers slid inside the soft material and pinched my nipple. His eyes watched me closely for any reaction to his touch. I knew he was testing me, seeing just how damaged I was from the attack. "I actually feel sorry for the fuck that gets paired with you," he growled.

"That's an asshole thing to say. I'm not that bad," I replied harshly, my pride was already dinged, but hearing him say that sent anger pulsating through my already throbbing body. Pretty much no one had looked at me sexually since the attack, and it stung. I felt like a tarnished toy, one that no one wanted because it wasn't new and shiny.

"Because he'll never get to have you," he clarified softly, his fingers pinching the puckered flesh of my nipple, pulling a gasp from my lips. "Not fully; you may fuck him, but you'll be thinking of me, wishing it was me between these sexy thighs. It won't be his face you see when you come, it will be mine."

"And why's that?" I demanded.

"Because you're mine, Lena. You and I both know it. You don't want another man, you want me."

"If that's the case, then why not make me yours now? Why not take the choice away and undo it after the Harvest?" I watched him close down and frowned. "I may want you, Lucian, but I have no choice in this matter and, really, neither do you," I mumbled. "Besides, I'm not yours. You don't own me. It's my Awakening; it's my time to gain my powers. It's important to me that I do it correctly."

"What happens if you're not selected? There is always that chance," he said harshly. "What will you do then?" He waited until I shrugged and then whispered, "I never said I that I own you; I said you're mine."

"I don't know much about the ritual itself, but I know that no Fitzgerald has ever missed being selected at their Awakening, and I don't plan to be the first. Especially with demons moving into town," I replied with pride. If a fight was coming, I planned to get revenge for what I'd been put through.

"Demons are deadly," he mused as he continued to stroke my nipple distractingly.

"That's mine," I announced when the ache between my legs became painful.

"Is it?" he asked innocently, his breath fanning my neck before his lips lowered and pressed a kiss to my racing pulse. "I don't care too much for traditions, but I do know once the Harvest is through, you will be mine in every sense of the word. I plan to do bad things to you, until you're begging me for more."

"Is there anything you *do* care about?" I asked, hating the fact that a simple touch, or pretty much anything to do with him turned me on.

"That's a loaded question," he mumbled as he sat up and looked at me. "Find something that isn't ripped; the coven is requesting a headcount of all witches."

"Well, it *wasn't* ripped," I murmured as I reached up and pulled him down until our mouths were inches apart. "Until you ripped it," I finished breathlessly.

"I like your clothing on the floor more than I care for them on you, little witch," he said before his mouth touched mine softly, and his teeth nipped at my bottom lip, pulling the flesh before he released it and dipped his tongue into my mouth. It wasn't demanding, but it still curled my toes and made heat flood my core.

I struggled to hold him against me. The sound of the fabric ripping more only intensified my need to get him closer to me. His mouth left mine and I cried out at the loss of its heat, only to suck in air as his teeth clamped against my nipple and sucked the heated peak while his teeth grazed the flesh. His hand moved down, cupping the ache between my legs and pressing against it.

Our breathing was labored, mingling together in the electrical field that the connection of our bodies charged. His touch locked me into a luscious fog of intoxication, fueled by lust and need. I pulled his hair, needing the heat of his hungry mouth against mine. He allowed it, his tongue drawn by the invitation of my tongue.

His mouth never left mine; his hand stroked my pussy, slick with the wetness he'd created. I felt the material of my slacks give way, felt the rush of soothing cold air as it fanned my naked flesh, and then it was on fire as his fingers slid between the folds, creating a violent reaction that tore through my body from head to toe. My legs fell open, exposing the mess he'd made to his greedy eyes.

He didn't speak; instead he added his thumb to the mix of fingers strumming my soaking wet, heated flesh that seemed to only respond to him in this way. He pulled his body away and I shied away from his heated eyes. I felt a rush of panic at the idea of him not wanting me because of the attack. I'm not sure where it came from, but it did and I didn't want to see him look at me with anything but the heat he usually held, in his eyes. His eyes watched me as I began to close myself down, trying to cover my exposed flesh against his greedy eyes, unwilling to watch them change.

"Don't do that," he demanded. His hands spread my legs as I tried to place them together, hiding the mess and reaction that he'd created with just his kiss. "Show it to me, witch," he demanded, as if I had a choice. His hands pulled my legs apart and those midnight blue eyes feasted on my wet pussy. "I'm going to get what I want from you, sweet girl. You see, I always get what I want and right now, that's you. In a day, or a year, you will be mine. I can wait until you're ready. What happened to you, it didn't touch your beauty, or tarnish you in any way. I want you the same as I did before it happened. Don't think to shut me out because of what happened to you; I won't let you. Now stop thinking, and kiss me," he demanded as he claimed my lips hungrily.

He broke the kiss after a moment, and I growled from the loss of contact. The moment he moved from me I felt barren, chilled by the loss of his heat. He towered over me, his face hidden in the shadows of the room, and yet I felt the heat of his eyes as he took in my disheveled form. Once again he'd ripped the panties I wore, and my slacks were on the floor, tattered and torn in a useless heap of material.

"Go change, Lena," he growled, his hands delving into his jeans as he fixed his erection that strained against the material. I heard something slam against the house, and my mind fought to escape that haze of lust. The next explosion shook the cottage violently, and I sat up, but Lucian was faster. He picked me up and moved in the direction of the bedroom, placing me on the bed as he pulled the blanket up and wrapped me in it.

He turned to look over his shoulder, and Spyder entered with a hard look on his face. His eyes scanned my blanket-clad body before moving back to Lucian.

"We've got unwanted company," he announced.

"Find them," Lucian said as his eyes held mine. "And take care of it."

"Good, was getting fucking boring around here anyway," he said, ignoring my wide-eyed owl look. "Incoming," he growled and disappeared.

What. The. Fuck.

The entire cottage shook and the windows heaved from impact.

"This thing between us, Lena, it isn't finished. Understand me?" he growled as he helped me up from the bed and pulled out clothes from my closet.

I couldn't think past the noise outside; it sounded like a war zone. The only thing missing was bomb sirens going off. I flinched as he moved to me, pushing a bra and panties into my hands. I noted that they were anything but sexy, as well the clothes he gave me. He pushed more into a bag and I smiled as I realized what he was doing. He was sending me to the harvest with anything I owned that wasn't sexy.

The cottage shook again and he paused, his eyes scanning me with heat mixed with uncertainty.

"No pretty babies; you belong to me," he growled and smiled. "Remember that when they try to tell you how important it is to reproduce bloodlines."

CHAPTER
twenty-nine

Lucian had walked me out the front door of the cottage, shielding me from anything that might be outside, slipped me into a sleek black car, and drove me straight to the abbey and the protection of the coven. Before I could get out of the car, he'd pulled me back and kissed me hard, so hard that even hours later, I could still feel the pressure of his lips against mine. With my head still reeling from the kiss, he'd walked me to the massive main door of the abbey and left the moment I was inside, safe from whatever had been outside of the cottage.

As soon as the door closed with a bit of an ominous boom, I'd been grabbed by the arm by Helen and dragged to a small anteroom where other elders of the coven waited. For close to an hour, I was grilled about everything that had happened when Todd attacked and raped me. I almost felt like I was on trial for something I didn't do and Helen had appointed herself my judge and jury, and I was sure she would have loved to have been my executioner if they would have let her. The moment the others had left the room, she threatened me to stay away from Lucian. Apparently she was still planning to set him up with her daughter...but considering there were only a few hours before the Awakening began, I didn't see Cassidy and Lucian tying any knots together.

It was the only way to be excused from the Harvest selection, and Lucian didn't seem like he was all that into her, considering his obsession with frustrating me to the edge of sanity. At least, that's what I kept telling myself. I could be wrong. He could be planning to do a quick and dirty handfasting, which was the same as marriage to the coven.

Now, I waited with the rest of the postulants in the small library and idly examined the ancient pictures and portraits that lined the walls. I also took note of the old books of spells and incantations that previous generations must have been using well before the abbey had been built. It was telling, because unlike what we'd been taught... The elders had more information available than they'd led us to believe.

"Ladies," Samantha, one of the elders, chirped as she whirled into the library wearing an outfit that looked straight out of the set of *Little House on the Prairie*. The bell skirt was outdated and even had a lace apron which she was currently wiping her hands on. Her gray-streaked dark hair was swept up in a topknot and she had little curls framing her face, giving her an overall schoolmarm look. I smiled at Kendra, who was trying to smother a giggle with the back of her hand.

"I'm to teach you all about what you should expect

during the Awakening, and time is limited. I need you to pay attention, because you'll only be told once."

I felt a chill race down my spine as worry flittered across Samantha's brow. Her eyes moved to me and Kendra, and she quickly looked away. Like the others, she didn't look at me too long, as if she didn't know what to say to me, or maybe it was because they thought I would snap if they did. Whatever, what happened had happened. It wasn't my fault or Todd's; only the demon who had taken control of Todd was to blame.

"Normally you'd have longer to learn about the changes that are going to happen to you. I wish I had the luxury of giving you that time, but I don't."

"I'm sure we don't need to know more than we already do," Cassidy smarted off, and I looked at her, really looked at her. Shortly after I arrived, Kendra had informed me that Cassidy had stood up for me at the assembly. She'd defended me against Todd's mother when she'd accused me of murdering her son before we'd learned that he'd been possessed by a demon. The thought of Cassidy standing up for someone not of her clique was mindboggling, although at the moment, I couldn't see any trace of the kind of person that might have had a little humanity tucked away in there. Right now, she was the same old self-serving, bitchy Cassidy.

"Is that what you all think?" Samantha demanded, her eyes moving around the room as many of the girls shifted uncomfortably.

"Everyone is afraid, but admitting that we are is a weakness," I mumbled. "It's not that we don't want to learn, it's because change isn't easy. Growth isn't easy, though, it's painful. The pain is what will remind us of what is needed to become the Awakened witches of the next generation. Change isn't easy, either. It's supposed to take effort on our part, because the struggle that makes us into the people we become will always remind us of how we achieved it."

The entire room looked at me as if I'd grown another head. I realized I was repeating my mother's words as if by rote, her logical reasoning for why change was needed and why it was never easy to do so. It was supposed to be hard and scary. It was that way so you remembered it.

"Thank you, Magdalena," Samantha said as her eyes skimmed over me and finally looked right at me. "There is nothing to fear from the changes that are coming. This Awakening is being rushed for good reason. We've been sheltered from the monsters of the past, which, I've said to the council many times before, is a mistake. Knowledge is power, ladies. These monsters want to destroy us. With your curse lifted, we're stronger. Together we can face whatever is coming," she said with a soft smile that didn't seem to reach her eyes.

Once everyone had quieted down she hurriedly launched into an overview that was hard to hear because her voice was soft as she spoke so fast. "We will start with the Awakening. We will take you to the rooms where the rites will take place. In the antechamber, we will have you change into ceremonial robes. Just the robes, everything else comes off; you won't need anything, and if you bring anything from the outside into the ceremony, it could taint the ritual." She looked pointedly at all of us to make sure we got the message that nothing meant *nothing*. "From there you will go to the main chamber, where the fire pit will already have a nice sized fire going and the ceremonial cauldron should already be at a rolling boil. You will assemble around it as the ceremony begins. Salt will be laid behind you, sealing you into the circle, and torches around the circle will be lit," she explained as she wiped her hands nervously on her apron and continued.

"The coven will begin to chant the spell to bring the ancestors forth for the selection. You may see some elders moving around you as herbs and salts are added to the fire and cauldron for the rite. This part of the ceremony can be intense for some as senses and the inner eye is opened. Once the spell has been cast, each of you will receive four runes that have been carved into different crystals. The Rings rune is carved into moldavite, a traditional Gender rune carved into jet, the Harvest rune is carved into selenite, and the Eye is carved into azurite. After receiving the crystals, the elders will assist you in moving a little closer to the fire and kneeling as the protection barrier slips into place just before the ancestors appear. Now, during past Awakening ceremonies, it has never been clear as to which ancestors have been seen, just that they do become visible and they will select those who are worthy of having their curse lifted, so there be no doubt in your mind if you have been chosen or not. As they are roaming amongst you, the elders will give you each a mortar and pestle to grind your runes; a bit of your blood will be added to the ground mix to channel the power of the runes and stones through you. The ancestors usually make their selections then, when the third eye is open and they can see to the depth of your soul. Once you've been selected, the elders will chant the incantation that will remove the curse that binds your powers. After you've had a small respite, our friends from out of town will join us and we will begin the Harvest Ceremony. The ancestors will pair you up with the person they feel will make the strongest match, then a spell will be cast to bind the union for the duration of the Harvest. The dead will then be released to go back into the veil, and you will be bathed and prepared to enter the chambers of those who you have been paired with. This preparation will protect you as well as your partner as you..."

"Fuck," Cassidy said and her girls giggled brainlessly.

"Mate, produce the next generation, who will preserve and carry on our heritage and bloodlines," Samantha said with red cheeks. "After that, you'll be sequestered in the abbey while you learn to respect and use your new powers. It's a time to bond together, and learn to use and wield your powers for the good of the coven."

"So we won't have powers right away?" Kendra asked.

"It takes time to learn to use them correctly." She smiled tightly, and nodded at Aurora, who had raised her hand.

"So what's the point in lifting our curse if we can't do shit?" Aurora asked, and Cassidy made a grunting noise of approval, which had Aurora beaming with a cocky smile.

"The point is that we can draw from your powers once the coven is tethered and bound together. When a new witch is awakened to the powers of their soul, that magic is pooled into the coven's bonds. Each one of you will add something to the magic this coven already has. Think of it as a cauldron that is already half full. Each one of you will add a cup of power to it, making it full again."

"What if we're not selected?" I asked.

"Anyone not selected would return to the abbey and wait to be excused to go home," she said softly.

"I get that, but what happens then?"

"You'll wait until the next Awakening, but it's highly unlikely that if one wasn't selected during their first Awakening, that the person would be selected in a second attempt," she whispered with a frown. "But it isn't unheard of, either."

"Will Lena be excluded because she was raped? You know, the whole not having sex within the month leading up to the Awakening rule thingy," Cassidy asked, and my stomach dropped.

Every one turned to look at me, and it took everything I had to remain emotionless as I stared at Samantha, and waited for her to answer the damn question.

"What happened to Magdalena was horrible, and certainly not what anyone should consider sex. The ancestors choose from bloodlines. Cassidy, the question you should be asking is if you will be chosen. Your lines are watered down, to say the least, and power isn't something that can be purchased."

Ouch.

"I think money can pretty much buy anything, or anyone," Cassidy countered smugly. "I wasn't asking to be rude, but she could be pregnant; she was after all, raped, right?" Her eyes moved to mine with smugness.

"Actually, he didn't finish before…" *I killed him.*

"Before what?" she pried. "Before you killed him?"

"Enough, Cassidy! This is not something to be shared with the room. If you have questions for Magdalena, ask her at a more appropriate time," Samantha interrupted.

I felt sick to my stomach, because the question brought up the images I'd refused to see for the last few days. I stood up and left the room, moving towards the entrance of the abbey to feel the cool, fresh air. The moment I touched the door, Tabitha stopped me; her hands on my shoulders were calming, her words comforting as she whispered something in a mixture of English and Latin.

"Better?" she asked after a moment.

"Where the hell did you come from?" I asked, looking around the bustling room.

"I felt the discomfort. I told you, Magdalena, we're connected. All of us, even Cassidy."

"I'd rather be connected to a skunk than that bitch," I retorted, and winced. I'd no sooner said it than regretted saying to the high priestess. "Sorry."

"You're not," she said softly. "Just because you're connected doesn't mean you have to like her. What she did in the library was callous, and meant to hurt you. She lashed out because knows the selection can't be bought and things she can't manipulate and control frighten her. She's a spoiled child, one whose mother indulges her entirely too much. Not to mention, the one man she decided to have, hasn't paid her any attention since a certain witch rolled back into town. He's only had eyes for you, and that has added a good deal of salt to her wounded pride. Helen has dropped hints on many occasions that he was courting her daughter, and Cassidy would be the key to bringing wealth back into the community."

"Perhaps that's why I've always been told that one should never assume or indulge in idle gossip," I mumbled.

"You like him, Lucian, yes?" she continued.

"He's not on my radar for the Harvest," I admitted.

"Because you think he is better than you? I will admit, he's a mystery, that one. I've heard that his mate was killed by a monster, which is why he refuses to attend a Harvest. He isn't an easy one to read, either. I understand his birth coven is scattered, however, he does descend from a pure bloodline that originated out of Aberdeen. The coven that we believe the Blackstone line belonged to took a different route to get to the New World; however, it appears that his coven wasn't able to withstand the creatures who hunt witches, as ours was."

"He's from Aberdeen?" I asked, my curiosity piqued at knowing more about him.

"He has not said as much, but when anyone new approaches the coven, we dig into their background and our records to be certain it is safe to allow them near. In the early 1600s, there was a very powerful family with the surname Blackstone, of English descent, and rumored to have been a very powerful bloodline, one with enough power to match our own. They were granted land outside of Aberdeen by the Queen of Scotland herself. If it's true, that he is descended from that bloodline, he would be a very powerful mate."

I blinked, and whistled low. "No wonder why Helen is trying to land him."

"Exactly, but he isn't interested in her daughter anymore, not since the moment he laid eyes on you," she said with an impish grin that made her eyes brighter. "I personally wouldn't wish that spoiled child on any man," she laughed.

"Someone is going to end up stuck with her," I mumbled, my mind considering how far Helen might have her claws in Lucian, and I'd been right about her trying to force a match. No wonder Helen was being such a bitch to me; I'd ruined her plans for a powerful match before the Awakening for her spoiled little brat.

"Yes, but it won't be Lucian. He's not interested in being among the men who will join us in the Harvest, not even tempted by the call of the blood of the original line which has brought in a large selection of males hoping to be chosen to mate with one of the women."

"I thought that they were here because the ratio was

off, and we needed the extra studs?" Studs? I frowned.

"Studs indeed, Magdalena," she laughed. "We did have a ratio issue, as you so delicately put it. Too many flowers and not enough bees to pollinate them." She smiled and shook her head. "I do enjoy our chats, but in all seriousness, they're here because there is an abundance of girls being awakened from the original bloodlines, which is a rarity for so many to be coming of age at the same time, let alone awakened. Speaking of awakening, you're missing out on the questions and answers about the ceremony. Cassidy is smiling right now, thinking she won. Don't let her win; you're stronger, and just as easily as you can build walls in your head, you can build walls around her instead."

CHAPTER
thirty
The Awakening

I watched through my lashes as Lucian and his men poured thick black salt behind where we assembled around the fire pit shrouded in ceremonial robes and nothing else. Between the salt, postulants and fire, we must have looked like a gigantic target from above. The whole thing seemed off to me, that Lucian and his men were here, as no one was welcome at the Awakening ceremony unless they were an already awakened witch of the coven, or a postulant.

When I spotted him, Kendra leaned close to me and whispered that he and his men were here for our protection against any demons who might be attracted to the power that this ceremony would generate. Evidently, Helen had also been making it abundantly clear to anyone who might be listening, that it was she who had brought them here for our protection, with a donation from her, of course.

I watched silently as torches were lit and placed

outside the circle, one at each point to signify the elements of nature. Quartz crystals for protection had been woven into the fire pit and amber, coral, and petrified wood pieces were added to the fire, creating colorful flames as spells were whispered to intensify the incantation carved into the crystals. The scents of sage, lemon grass, hibiscus, sandalwood, and vanilla tickled my nose as these elements were added to the giant cauldron that bubbled merrily in the center of the fire. A few of Lucian's men monitored each torch, but he wasn't watching them, or ensuring they were performing their duties correctly; his eyes were on me.

I could feel the heat from the torches and from the fire, and even nervousness contributed to the sweat that dripped down the back of my neck. He knew as well as I did, that there would be no chance between us. Not with the events already in motion. There were no do-overs; I was locked into my fate, one that had been a tradition for the coven for centuries.

That dismal knowledge sat like a boulder on my chest, especially with the heat of Lucian's eyes weighing on me. I wanted to grab him, a strip of rope, and handfast the sick twisted freak right here and now, no matter what kind of kinky fuckery he was into. Just skip the entire Harvest and be somewhere, lost in those midnight eyes of his. I swallowed past the lump in my throat and turned to find Kendra staring at me curiously.

"Are you okay?" she whispered softy, as not to be heard or disrupt the ceremony.

"I'm fine," I lied as more sweat beaded at the base of my neck. I felt the heat, mixed with the knowledge that this was it. I was going to get my powers; however, I was also about to be mated and it wasn't by him, and that just sucked. At best, I'd be stuck with the same man for a few weeks until the moon phase passed and then I'd be allowed to have whatever sexual partner I wanted. Unless I ended up pregnant, which luckily I'd taken steps to avoid.

"You are *not* fine," she hissed. "Magdalena, your emotions are all over the place."

"Something's not right," I whispered. Something wasn't, I could feel my body pulsating, and it was all pushing to one place…my vagina.

"It's the Awakening, and the Harvest spells because both events are together. You're supposed to feel like that," she said with a worried look. "Horny, while on fire," she smiled. "You missed that part because of Cassidy's bullshit."

"What?" I hissed. Fucking great! I was on fire, burning up with an emotion I couldn't fathom. It felt like fire ants were biting me everywhere! I felt as if my skin was on fire, and moisture was pooling between my legs, and I kept fucking looking at Lucian, because he could make it stop. My hands trembled, and I fisted them against my sides to hide the violent reaction I was having. Everyone else was standing around, and I was shaking. They looked calm, collected, I was a freaking mess! "I'm dying," I mumbled.

"Some experience it on a massive level, others tend to handle it…" she paused, looking at me carefully. "…better."

Awesome-sauce! I was handling it like shit!

My eyes found Lucian's; heat banked in their depths, as if he could sense my brutal arousal, and itched to fix it. I itched for him to do so, quickly.

Another set of quartz crystals was being placed

around the ground, surrounding the wide salt circle, and I wanted to run away. Someone else dropped a handful of sea salt into the cauldron; a few clear quartz crystals were placed into the mixture as well, and then chanting began from the singular witch who stirred the contents of the cauldron. With each herb that was added, the fire inside of me burned hotter.

"I'm going to pass out," I announced as sweat beaded on my brow line.

"Lena, are you okay?" Kat whispered and I turned to look at her. My hair was saturated, sweat was actually running down the side of my face and neck, and I felt sick.

I felt a hand touch my shoulder, and without turning to see who it was, I knew it was Tabitha.

"Breathe, Magdalena, you're going to be just fine," she whispered, and a cooling breeze moved around me, causing the hooded robe I wore to catch air. It felt amazing. "You are showing signs of much power, indeed. Those who harbor the most, unfortunately also suffer the most."

I felt Kendra tense beside me, and felt the jealousy stir inside of her. Our entire lives, I'd allowed her to think I had never felt my powers, not after the few incidents where I'd been in trouble for using it. As firstborn, she was the favored one to be more powerful, but she seemed to be weathering the Awakening spells just fine. Or more to the point, the pre-Awakening, or pre-Harvest, or whatever they wanted to call it; we hadn't even gotten through the protection spells!

"Tonight we welcome the newest members of the coven; tonight, we awaken the next generation of our bloodlines," one of the male elders announced as someone else passed out runes that were a mossy green color and had three connecting rings carved in them, symbolizing the connection of the new witches among the coven. Next were the shiny black Y-engraved runes for women and ones with arrows for men, then the iridescent white Harvest runes, blessing for a fruitful union. Last but not least, the vivid blue veil runes with an eye carved beautifully into the smooth surface were placed in our palms, to allow the dead to know who among us could be selected for both rituals.

Flames erupted and the popping noise as the protection barrier slipped into place around us caused more than a few of us to jump. Nervous laughter filled the circle, and one by one we were moved closer to the edge of the circle and asked to kneel and place our stones in front of us.

I felt a chill racing through the circle and as we watched, flickering silhouettes began to take form within the circle, until five figures materialized where small circles had been carved into the earth. At first, the figures were diaphanous, but as they remained frozen in place, they began to take on color and life.

The first one to move was more than beautiful, she was gorgeous, with raven colored hair and green, jewel like eyes. She held her hand out to a redhead, and then a brunette, who held hers to a blonde, who looked up at a man with black hair and light blue eyes who was still forming. He smiled at her, and she waited patiently as he continued to take solid form. He finally moved, and bluebells grew from the ground wherever they stepped as they moved from their circles.

They bowed to the elders, and each one set off, inspecting the young women and men who formed the circle. I watched the new arrivals as they slowly took in each of the postulants as the elders moved around us, placing mortar and pestles in front of us. The elders then moved through our groups, using a small blade to slice through the tip of our left index finger so that we could place a few droplets of our blood into the bowls, along with the runes, and crush them as we were being inspected by the dead.

The crushing of the runes wasn't quiet, but it was a welcome distraction from the dead who would nod in a certain postulant's direction as they watched us work. I lifted my head as the raven haired woman moved towards me, her eyes on the bowl. When she looked at me, it was as if she couldn't even see me. I looked around and then back at her as I watched her reach down into the mortar I'd stopped working so she touched the blood. She brought it up to her nose and turned her face to Kendra with a smile. *Weird.*

I ignored it and went back to smashing the crystals into my blood to finish the mixture. When it was done, I sat back on my knees and watched as the dead continued to examine the others. They were looking at them, whereas when they were looking at me, they looked through me, as if they couldn't see me.

My heart raced with the uncertainty of emotions that swirled through me. They had to have seen me; it wasn't like I was invisible, right?

I looked at Lucian, who was no longer staring at me, but at one of the witches who had been brought back from the dead for the Awakening, the raven haired one. She was beautiful, though, and I didn't blame him for staring at her. She was dressed in a black satin dress that hugged her form. Jewels were set in a makeshift crown with long golden chains that flowed intricately though her hair and created a necklace with a crescent moon that hung to her waist. Her hair flowed invitingly to her slim hips, and her lips were painted crimson red. She was perfect, nothing was out of place. Being dead hadn't been hard on her, obviously. She looked happy, which was a lot better than I looked right now.

Something dark passed over Lucian's features and the woman lifted her eyes and looked around the circle as if she'd felt him. It was physically impossible, since he was outside the circle, on the other side of the barrier. Those sinful midnight blue eyes moved from hers to mine, and back. I felt a tightening of nerves and maybe a little jealousy as he sought hers again. Today was really starting to suck, but at least the fire that had been racing through my body had been momentarily put out.

One after another, the blood in the mortars was tasted and hands were held out to help the postulants from the ground to join the circle of those who were being selected to be awakened. I watched as more and more were moved into the growing circle, until only a few of us on the far side remained.

I smiled as the man walked towards me, but much like the others, he looked through me and then around. He kneeled down and tilted his head, as if trying to see something. I felt my heart begin to hammer against my ribcage as he reached down to sample the blood. I turned to look at Kendra, who was being helped from the ground and moved into the circle.

The man moved his hand, pushing it through my chest which sent pain mingled with an iciness that felt as if I was being torn apart. He pulled it back and slowly got up, looking around before he moved to the next girl.

What the actual fuck! That shit had hurt like hell!

Wait, had he just…I felt angry tears burning my eyes

as it dawned on me. I hadn't been selected…I looked at my mother who stood with her mouth open; my grandmother had a frown on her face as she tried to puzzle out what had happened.

"What happened," I whispered brokenly. "I…don't understand."

Tears dropped and I rubbed at them with the back of my hand. I didn't understand it! I'd followed the laws, I'd been good! Why couldn't they see me? I stood up, moving before anyone could stop me, and I pushed past the onlookers as the chanting began to break the curse for the selected postulants.

I barely held it together as I stopped at the antechamber to change back into my clothes and headed towards the library to wait.

A sob ripped from my lungs as I opened the heavy doors, moved inside, and fell to my knees with heavy sobs escaping me. It wasn't my fault. I hadn't asked to be raped, I'd followed the rules. I'd fought off the darkness; I'd turned down Lucian, and for what? They couldn't even see me! It was like I didn't even exist to them.

I heard the music begin for the Harvest celebration, so I pulled myself up from the floor and forced my feet to move to the giant horsehair sofa, where I curled into a ball. This wasn't happening. I'd be the oldest un-Awakened witch in history. I didn't have a choice in the matter anymore. There would be no harvest, no learning how and what to do to help the coven with Kendra, because she'd be sequestered in the abbey, and I wouldn't be allowed to participate in their lessons.

It wasn't fair, none of it. Cassidy had been chosen, for fuck's sake, and I hadn't missed Helen's smug look as I'd pushed through the crowd to escape the looks of the people who slowly figured out I'd just been skipped for the Awakening and everything it entailed. I was fucked.

I wasn't waiting until the next one, screw that. I didn't need magic to help the coven. I had botany, which meant I had to get the store back because I had no backup plan for life. I could grow plants like nobody's business, and I was damn good at creating tonics and other concoctions. Mom would help me, and I could live at the cottage. I could make money, enough to live off of. I closed my eyes, ignoring the chants and laughter that filtered up from the ceremonial rooms.

I was going to be fine. I would make it through this. Somehow, I had to.

I wasn't a quitter.

CHAPTER
thirty-one

I numbly moved through the abbey without seeing or hearing as the events continued without me. I moved through the rooms, looking for signs of life. Apparently everyone but me was at the Harvest Ceremony.

The common room was empty when I entered it and grabbed my bag, not wanting to be anywhere close to here when the excited people returned—or Cassidy, with her sure to be smug face. I left the room, tossing my bag over my shoulder as the gut-wrenching emotions filtered through me. It was as if I was living a nightmare, and there was no waking up from it. I hadn't seriously considered that I wouldn't be selected to get my powers.

It sucked; I was the first one in the Fitzgerald line to be excluded on their first Awakening. Considering my age, I should have been a shoe-in! I groaned as chanting began from outside the abbey, my heart twisting as I felt the excitement from Kendra as they began the portion of the Harvest that would pair off couples. I swallowed the pain and stopped in the middle of the room, considering my options.

The weird burning and tingling I had felt earlier during the ceremony was back. Fuck, the spell for the Harvest was ramping up again and racing through my body, lighting up bits and pieces of me that had no business being lit up right now. It just wasn't an option. I moved without knowing where I was going until I stood in the parking lot of the abbey, and realized I didn't have my car here; Lucian had dropped me off. As if tonight didn't suck enough already? I was about to go back inside when I spotted Kendra's car, and laughed.

Maybe there was hope that the entire night wasn't ruined. I opened the door and pulled down the visor as I shoved my bag into the passenger seat. The keys fell into my palm with a satisfying jingle. She was predictable. I plugged my phone into her cassette tape adapter, found Theory of a Deadman and hit play on *Hate My Life*, then pulled out of the parking lot and onto the road.

I got home, and realized I'd already made up my mind without considering the consequences. I was going to Lucian's club, and I was taking what I wanted, whether he agreed or not. He owed me that much after all of his dirty words and slow seduction.

I quickly showered and made sure to use the plumeria shampoo and body wash I'd made in Pacific City, and then stared at my reflection. My eyes were puffy from crying, and I looked worn out. I shook my head and moved into the room, opening the closet to find the little black dress I'd purchased three years ago, but never had the balls to wear.

It was sexy, short, and with a pair of thigh highs and heels, it would say exactly what I wanted and needed. It had a deep V-neck that exposed cleavage, and also made it impossible to wear a bra with the darn thing. I slipped on a pair of black heels that strapped at the ankle and gave me just enough height while allowing me to walk without breaking my neck in the process.

I applied a thin application of make-up and some cherry red lipstick to make my tired appearance look cheerful, and headed towards the door. I didn't stop to think about it; thinking hurt right now, thinking was overrated.

I paused as I heard my phone go off, pulled it from the little clutch I held, and looked at Kendra's name and picture as it flashed across the screen. My heart clenched, and while I was happy that she'd been chosen, I felt empty and cold at the knowledge that I hadn't been. The elders had said it was a possibility that one of us would have more power, but this was stupid. The next Awakening wouldn't be for five more years, which would make me the oldest witch to ever be selected, if I even was!

I set my phone on the coffee table, opened the front door, and locked it as I left and made my way to where I'd parked Joshua's car. I slid into the driver's seat and headed towards the club. My body was burning and buzzing, my mind on autopilot as I drove through town and made my way to the middle of nowhere, where his club waited for me, bright as a beacon in the darkness.

As I pulled in, I started to second-guess myself. If he wasn't alone, what was my plan? He'd been there when I wasn't selected, so was he waiting for me? Or had he already made plans with someone else? My eyes scanned the couples that were scattered between the cars in the parking lot and noted that Mister Man-bun wasn't at his normal spot guarding the doors tonight.

I slipped from the car, ignoring the couples locked in compromising positions that didn't seem to care about the public displays of heavy petting. I slipped behind a group of women who were all dressed up a little bit too fancy considering it was a sex club, but what the hell did I know? Maybe there was a dress code? I didn't spot one posted when I worked here so I really hoped there wasn't.

Once inside, they headed to the doors that led into the lower levels and I passed through a set of doors, which I knew from being here and cleaning the rooms below, led into the actual sex club. The women didn't stop, even though I paused as I noted couples barely dressed, and some completely naked.

The next room was just plain fucking weird. Some men and a few women were walking around with their partners on leashes, and some had tails! Not real tails, but my mind wanted to know exactly how they stayed in place, until I figured it out. Then I wished I wasn't so freakishly curious. As I passed a man, he held out his hand and showed me a leash. Oh hell no, I wasn't an animal to be walked around…and oh my God, was she drinking from a dog's dish…Exit! Exit! Exit! I left the group, unwilling to see anymore.

The next room was actually labeled 'Sir's Playground' and that piqued my curiosity. On stage was a woman, tied up and being whipped. I looked around at the people who watched her, and noted that many of them were fully clothed, while skimpily dressed waitresses took or delivered orders. It was as if it was a show for entertainment, which I guess was exactly what it was.

I couldn't look away as the whip cracked loudly and

the woman on stage begged for another. Was she fucking insane? I cringed as he gave her what she wanted. A few more lashes and he moved behind her, entering her quickly as the crowd applauded.

Okay, maybe I was the insane one because I didn't understand why they'd applaud her counting or begging for more. I left the room with a rash of questions that I never planned to ask a living soul.

In the next room were a threesome and a couple of… five…somes? It was hard to tell in the dimly lit room, and while I did stop because my brain tried to figure it out, I remained in the shadows, hidden as I watched them. Okay, so this was kind of hot, in a kinky-how-the-hell-are-they-fitting-the-puzzle-pieces-together kind of way.

Someone touched my breast and I jumped, my eyes flying to the woman who smiled at me. She moved closer and I went flush against the wall.

"She's beautiful, Kyle, and un-collared," the woman purred as her hand continued to fondle my breast. I looked down, watching as she stroked me and then looked up at the couple. Kyle was tall, and built like a guy who forgot there was life outside the gym.

"Mmm, look at those lips, they beg to be filled," he agreed.

I blinked. "I'm flattered, but I came here for one man and one man alone."

"And who's the lucky man?" the woman asked as she continued petting me, as if I was a strange cat she'd picked up.

"Lucian," I said, and her hand dropped and they turned abruptly and left me standing there, alone. Weird.

This whole place was weird, but that reaction to his name? It must be what it's like to be standing in a meth lab and announcing you're D.E.A. I left the room, heading down the long hallway to the set of rooms that I'd cleaned, knowing that the one he'd brought me to climax in was his. There was only one boss in this place, and it was Lucian.

I rounded a corner and watched as a woman entered the room, leaving the door open just wide enough that I could see inside. I hesitated at the door, wondering what I would do if he rejected me tonight. I'd been through an emotional rollercoaster since getting home, but he'd been a constant distraction. Another rejection tonight wasn't a possibility. He owed me a lesson, and I planned on having him teach it to me tonight.

Squaring my shoulders and pulling my courage around me, I pushed open the door, and walked in behind the woman who had just gone in.

"Get out," I growled, looking her right in the eyes, my face hard and dead serious.

"Excuse me?" she asked, as I took in her topless outfit.

"I said get out; he's mine tonight," I repeated moving towards her, hoping to the Gods I looked threatening.

"Lena," Lucian's voice said my name with something cold in his tone.

"Don't you fucking 'Lena' me," I growled and leveled him with a threatening look. "You promised to teach me that sex wasn't just *fine*, and it's time to pay up."

His eyes heated and his lips twitched. "Is that so?"

"It is, so she needs to get lost because I'm just not into sharing you tonight," I replied.

"This is Leslie, a serving girl," he said, and I narrowed my eyes.

"I bet she is, and just what exactly does she serve?" I retorted.

"I serve drinks, my lady," she whispered meekly and I turned to look at her. Yep, she was holding a tray and I groaned. I guess the uniforms here could be skimpier than the one I had been given.

"Of course you do," I grumbled. I seriously should have just stayed in a ball and cried myself to sleep on that sofa instead of coming here.

"Would you like a shot, or something?" she asked and the sound of Lucian's laughter brought tears to my eyes.

"Can I have a do-over?" I asked, and she looked at me.

"Go, Leslie," Lucian said as he held my gaze. "Lena," he whispered as he stood, but I moved away from him.

"This was a stupid idea," I whispered, and shook my head as he moved closer. "I should go."

"You should stay," he eyed me speculatively. "Not to poke at what is obviously a sensitive subject for you, however, I am curious. Did you find out why you weren't selected?" I shook my head miserably.

"They don't tell you why," I replied as I wiped away the tears. "In the end it really doesn't matter anyway. Once the Awakening has begun, the situation isn't in our hands. It's in the ancestors'."

"And you came to me," he replied as his eyes took in the short skirt and fuck-me heels, and heat filled them as they moved back up to mine. "I'm flattered."

"Make me forget how miserable tonight has been," I whispered as I moved closer to him, slowly reaching for his shirt as I tipped my head back to watch his face for direction as I began to unbutton it.

"If I do, there's no changing what will happen," he replied in a husky voice.

"What do you mean, what will happen?" I kissed his

stomach as I found his flesh. I heard his sharp intake of breath as my tongue darted out to trace his well-defined abs.

"There would be no going back." his words were measured, carefully. "You'd be mine," he growled as he captured my hands and picked me up, forcing my legs to wrap around him. "No other man would touch you, *ever*. There would be no comparison to see if anyone can teach you more."

"Fine," I whispered as I kissed him hungrily.

CHAPTER
thirty-two

He began to move us towards the door and, guessing where he wanted to go, I began struggling to get loose and heard his laughter. He set me down, watching as I righted my dress and turned to look at him. I wasn't going out there. I wanted him here, in the privacy of this room without anyone else. I'd had enough of prying eyes and judgmental looks to last a lifetime this past week. If I was going to do this with Lucian, I wanted him to be the only witness if I freaked out. He must have realized the train of my thoughts as his eyebrow quirked up and a slow smile spread across his features.

"Last chance, witch," he said carefully. "The moment I close this door, there's no changing your mind; you will be mine and mine alone." His face turned hard, and something vulnerable filled his eyes before he could conceal it.

I moved to the door and briefly hesitated as I placed my hand on it. Not because I wanted to leave, but because I still had a bit of self-preservation, which was rearing its ugly head, warning me that I was playing with fire. His seductive gaze promised me that if I chose to stay, he'd alter my world and everything I thought I knew about it. He'd promised to teach me things that most would shrink away from, or at least sane people would. I knew he was kinky—for Christ's sake he ran a fucking sex club, and he did it well. I'd tasted only a small sampling of his darker side and, instead of being scared, I was curiously drawn to it. I wanted him. I closed the door, sealing my fate willingly. Whatever drew us together was undeniable and I didn't want to live without discovering the pleasure he could give me. I turned to look at him and found him watching me with a guarded look, as if he'd expected me to leave instead of staying with him.

"You should have listened to those who told you to stay away from me, little girl," he whispered as he ran his hands through his hair and his eyes filled with desire, knowing he had me at his mercy.

"And why's that?" I asked with a spark of sass in my tone that told him I wasn't afraid of him or what was sure to be a sexual awakening that I wasn't going to forget.

"Because I'm going to turn you inside out. I'm going to do very bad things to you that will be imprinted on your psyche for the rest of your life," he replied as he slowly moved to the chair, turning it towards the glass wall that I already knew was double-paneled glass. "Come here," he ordered and I obeyed, moving slowly as I watched him take a seat in the chair. Once I was in front of him, he twirled his finger.

"What the hell does that mean?" I quipped, not

understanding what his finger motion meant. I wasn't playing dog games with him, if that was what it meant. Considering I'd witnessed a woman drinking out of a dog bowl earlier, anything was possible.

"Show me what belongs to me," he replied, his eyes slowly moving over my outfit. I spun around quickly as relief washed through me and he smiled. "Slowly, Lena," he amended in a thick voice.

I spun around slowly, making sure it was sexy and with enough swagger to entice him, and once I faced him again, the naked desire in his eyes was filled with enough heat to melt the glass behind us. I started to move towards him and he held up his hand with a wicked smile.

"Turn around and touch the window, sweet girl," he said and my eyes grew large and round as a saucer. I looked from the window, to him, and then back at the window with unease. "I didn't ask if you wanted to, I said *do* it," his voice was soft, yet rang with authority.

I swallowed and looked at him again, finding his eyes hooded with desire as he watched me. Oh, hell. I knew what was going on in the other room, so it wasn't as if the debauchery would be a surprise. I exhaled and did as he asked, watching as the room came into focus. The room was far more crowded than I expected, some of the guests were lost in ecstasy, while others turned as the window exposed us.

"Come to me," he said, and as I moved close enough for him to grab, he did, turning me until I was facing the room. I watched the revelers curiously as they noted what the window revealed, and many more were turning to watch us. "See anyone you want to fuck?" he asked, and I shook my head.

"No," I replied without hesitation. I had who I wanted;

I was sitting in his lap. "I have what I want the most," I whispered, turning to look at him.

He smiled, but it didn't reach his eyes.

"And tomorrow if you discovered I'm a fucking monster, are you still going to want me?" he asked and I paused, knowing he was asking for a reason. There was a hidden meaning to his question, and I wasn't sure what it was.

"That depends," I replied, watching him closely.

"Depends on what, Lena?" he continued carefully as his eyes took on that guarded look. If I didn't know any better, I'd say someone hurt this man. Badly. It wasn't the one he'd lost long ago. No, someone had fucked him over, and hurt him somehow.

"On if you grow two heads, because you're mouthy enough with one," I joked, needing to hear him laugh.

He smirked and shook his head.

"I'm not a nice guy," he said seriously.

"I didn't ask you to be nice," I countered.

"That's probably a good thing, because I have no intention of being nice tonight," he said as he pulled my legs apart and my eyes moved back to the people in the room who watched us. "Look at them," he whispered as he pulled me back, kissing my neck. "They want to see what this skimpy little dress is hiding; should we show them?"

They were getting closer, as if drawn to us by some unseen lure. I felt his hand as he pulled the dress's bodice to the side, exposing one breast. A man moved closer, kneeling in front of the window and stroking his cock as his eyes remained between my legs.

"He wants you, my pretty little witch," he growled. "Should I kill him?"

I blinked at his words. Kill him? He couldn't be serious; the guy was just doing what everyone else was. He just didn't seem to care who knew he was turned on by what he was watching unfold between myself and Lucian.

"Why?" I asked turning my eyes to Lucian. "Maybe it's not me who he wants, but you."

Lucian laughed and shook his head. "Look at the couple in the back right corner."

There was a woman and a man; the woman's eyes were latched on to my naked breast that Lucian fondled absently, while the man worked her from behind, watching me as well. He didn't seem to be paying attention to the woman who he was fucking, but he was definitely paying attention to me.

"He's fucking her, wishing she was you. She wishes she was you." His voice was smooth and even. His fingers moved to my nipple, pinching it as he rolled it between his fingers. His other hand slipped beneath my panties which caused the guy who was kneeled in front of us to lose it. "It's you he wants, Lena," he murmured as I arched into him. "One touch of your pussy and he wouldn't be able to hold it back."

"I thought you said that I was yours alone; this feels more like you want to share me, with them," I whimpered.

"You are mine. This is me showing them what they will never have, showing off what belongs to me," his voice was rough, like gravel.

I wasn't listening; I was lost in his touch. Fuck the other people. I wanted him buried inside of me. I ached to be his, to be taught what I knew only he could show me. I spread my legs further, ignoring the ripping of fabric as he removed the thin panties with a simple tug on the delicate lace and exposed my willing pussy to the entire room, showing them exactly how wet I was for the man behind me. He was showing them who owned me, and I couldn't have cared less, because in this moment, I was his to claim.

The couple moved faster, their motions hurried as they watched his finger slide through the chaos between my legs. I moaned, uncaring if they heard it. It was bold because I knew without a doubt that no one would touch me but him. He rubbed my clit slowly. His other hand left my breast to expose the other as he placed soft kisses on my shoulder. His finger pushed inside, slowly dipping inside my opening.

He continued to slide into my body with his fingers; his other hand left my breast to hold my pussy open, exposing my most intimate place to the crowd who watched us intently. He added another finger, forcing me to move my hips to accommodate him, but that wasn't enough. He released my pussy and lifted my leg, moving it until it was draped over the arm of the chair. He did the same with the other one, making it impossible to do anything but take his fingers even deeper as the people on the other side of the window watched.

I was soaking wet, turned on by the others as they fucked in frenzied movements as we watched each other take pleasure. He withdrew his fingers, pulled me tighter against his chest, and slid my bottom into a better position. When he reentered my dripping pussy, it was with three fingers and it hurt as it forced my body to stretch.

I groaned and rocked my hips, trying to accept him, as he pushed me apart. His other hand moved back to hold me open, and he pressed in deeper than before; I cried out as the friction started to unravel the tight coil in my belly.

"You want to come with them watching you, don't

you, sweet girl?" he asked, driving his fingers in faster as he moved them in a steady rhythm. Moisture flooded my pussy and he used it to his advantage. "Fuck, you're on fire. So fucking wet for me; you want me to fuck you," he growled as he bit my earlobe and I felt it all the way to where his fingers pounded into me.

I could feel my body grasping him, even as it burned from being stretched to the limit. He undid me. Made me bolder than I ever thought I was; in his arms, I became someone else. "You like me owning this sweet flesh, exposing it to them as I stretch it for what you really want…Such a good girl," he whispered when I arched my back, allowing him to go deeper. I needed him to rub my clit, or hell, even just touch it and I knew I'd erupt like a freaking volcano, but I also knew that he was aware of just how close I was to coming. My body was tightening around his fingers, inviting him to do whatever he wanted. He growled against my ear and I felt him smiling against my flesh as he withdrew from my pussy, showing the room the mess he'd created.

It was fucking hot, watching their eyes glaze over with lust, knowing it was my flesh that they wanted. Needed. It was a powerful feeling. I understood why the woman on the stage enjoyed the spotlight, but I didn't crave it. I wanted the man who made me feel this way. He continued to glide his fingers through the slippery wetness, much to the titillation of the crowd who were enjoying his slow torture of my aching pussy.

"You haven't picked anyone out to fuck, Lena, choose," he taunted, breaking through the haze of bliss I was getting lost in.

"I did, Lucian, I chose you," I replied, watching as a man moved to the window and flipped me off, or I assumed it was me he was flipping his middle finger at. "What the hell is his problem?"

"That wasn't for you," he clipped as he picked me up and set me on my wobbly feet abruptly. I watched as the guy started pounding on the window, his hands covered in blood which caused a panic in the other room. I moved to the window, watching as he continued. "Lena," Lucian growled in warning. "Move away from him." I continued watching as the man drew strange symbols in the blood that was smeared across the glass.

He was screaming something and I moved even closer, trying to read his lips since I couldn't hear him. He was frenzied, and upset about something. I watched as he used his head to pound the window, which caused me to jump as Lucian grabbed my shoulder and turned me towards him. I looked at him and then back to the guy, but he was gone yet the symbols he'd written in his blood remained as evidence of his presence.

"You shouldn't have had to see that," he offered at my mystified look.

"Where'd he go?" I asked.

"Don't ask," he said as he moved me towards the small counter, which had a wine refrigerator under it. He removed a bottle and opened it while I watched him curiously as he ignored me. He pulled down two glasses from the cabinet, poured the wine, and handed one to me before he looked absently at the room beyond.

Lucian must have called someone to take the guy away, I was sure of it. How he did it I hadn't puzzled out yet; I only knew that somehow he had. One of the waitresses was cleaning the blood, and as she did, the people moved back into the room. I watched Lucian, noting that whatever the symbols had been, they'd disturbed him, which wasn't something I ever thought I would see.

"You know him," I said, and Lucian set his glass down and leveled me with a cold look that was meant to make me shut up. "Don't worry, Lucian. I know you didn't get to where you are by being generous or making friends. You buy his family business too?"

His face changed, softened, and he shook his head. "The world's a cruel place, Magdalena, but then, you know that better than most people."

"I'm wet," I said as I felt cool air as it blew up through a nearby vent. I wanted to go back to what Lucian was doing to me before the asshole ruined my fun. "This vent, it feels good." I smiled and his mouth twitched. "You suck at giving lessons. Next time, leave the crazies outside the sex club."

"I don't suck at giving lessons, Lena, yours haven't even begun," he announced as he nodded at my glass of wine. "Finish that while I go take care of business, and don't let anyone into this room."

"Not even the serving girl?" I asked, and he laughed. "I'll bet she could totally teach me about *fine* things, like where you hide the *fine* wine."

"Not even her," he mumbled absently as he moved towards the door and turned to look at me. "Lena, when you leave here tomorrow, you will have a new definition of *fine*."

"I guess I better work on a new word for it then?"

"I'll be back; I expect you to be naked and in bed when I return."

"Bossy ass; maybe I want you to unwrap me?" I countered with a saucy look.

"You plan on ever wearing that dress again?" he asked as he opened the door, and I opened my mouth, thought better of it, and closed it. "Then take it off, because the way I want to remove it won't end with it being one piece when I remove it from your sexy-as-fuck body."

CHAPTER
thirty-three

I got into bed as Lucian directed. That much I was willing to do; however, I couldn't bring myself to strip down to my birthday suit with all those people in the room on the other side of the window. I felt vulnerable without Lucian, unprotected. Somehow, letting Lucian fondle me and show off my bits to the crowd seemed all right as long as he was there. I wasn't sure if it was from the burn of the Harvest spell, or if it was just him lowering my inhibitions and letting him do what he wanted. My eyes moved to the couple, who were back in their corner and watching me closely, as if they'd assumed I was going to give them another show. She'd changed positions, and my eyes moved to where their bodies joined. His fingers slowly rubbed her clitoris and even though I knew I should, I didn't look away from them. There was something erotic about watching it happen, the way her hips swayed as they moved to a slow beat.

I jumped as the door opened and Lucian walked in, his eyes moved over me and then to the room beyond the glass. They paused on Elaine before moving on as he walked to the window and touched it. I expelled a breath I hadn't realized I'd been holding as the clear glass changed to a mirrored surface. I felt relief with being granted privacy from the crowd of voyeurs. It also allowed me to ignore the fact that his ex was in that room too.

"You're not naked; I'm guessing you're not as attached to the dress as I'd assumed. Pity, you look so fuck-able in it."

"It's cold in here without you," I fibbed. It wasn't cold; as a matter of fact, the spell was making every part of me burn and some places were throbbing uncomfortably. He moved to the chair and gave me a somewhat amused, knowing smile.

"It's about to get really hot, Lena; now fucking strip," he ordered as he turned the chair around and sat in it as his eyes dared me to disobey him.

"Make me," I replied, unsure why I wanted him to undress me himself, but I did. I moved from the bed as he stood up, his eyes noting every minuscule move I made. He was the hunter, and I was his prey. I moved around the bed, using it to keep away from him.

"You don't know how much I want to fuck you, little witch, or how badly I want to hear you scream, or you wouldn't be taunting me," he rumbled huskily.

"Is that supposed to scare me?" I laughed and darted away from him as he moved around the bed. "You use intimidation a lot, don't you?" I continued, recklessly. "You know you can't scare me."

"Is that so?" he asked as something moved behind his

eyes and his smile was predatory. I moved right before he lunged, but not fast enough. One minute I thought I had the upper hand, and the next I was pressed against the wall with my hands pinned tightly above my head, and my legs wrapped around his waist. His eyes smiled, even though his lips didn't. "Caught you," he growled before he allowed me to slide down his body, making sure I noticed how hard he was already as he pressed his erection against my belly.

"So you did," I whispered as I chewed at my bottom lip. "What happens now?" I asked as the coil he'd created in my belly tightened.

"Now I claim what's mine." He lowered his mouth to my neck and kissed my rapidly beating pulse softly. "Scared of me now, witch?"

"Terrified," I whispered breathlessly as I felt his hands moving to the hem of my dress.

"You should be," he replied as he lifted the dress, revealing my nakedness to his greedy eyes. "By the time I'm finished with you, there's going to be nothing but a quivering mess left." He pushed me against the wall and kissed me. As his hungry mouth devoured mine, he picked me up and carried me to the bed, pulling his mouth away from mine, and tossed me on it. "Take the shoes off," he demanded, and I sat up, removing them and the stockings, feeling a rush of uncertainty at what I was about to do.

This man was wild, bossy, and an outright asshole when he wanted to be. He admitted that he wasn't a nice guy, and didn't care about much of anything. He could have any girl in this place, and he wanted me. That made me pause, knowing his ex was in the other room, beautiful as a porcelain doll; and he wanted me, why?

"Stop that," he growled as he took in my face, which

probably had turned into a frown. "Stop thinking for tonight, Lena, just forget tonight. You can't change what happened."

He thought I was thinking about the Awakening. He thought my frown was about that, and not being selected. I should have let him assume that was the problem, but I didn't. "Why me? You could have anyone in this place, and yet you want me."

"Because, Lena, no one has the same light in their eyes. A little bit of sunshine mixed with a whole lot of hurricane. Most of those women out there? They don't give a shit about anyone but themselves, but you do. You're a fucking flower in a war zone, one that grows brightly even in the midst of chaos and destruction. You're different than the others; you're a fighter. You shine from the inside out, and that isn't something that can be bought or faked."

Tears filled my eyes and I shook my head, refusing to let them fall. "I'm not all shiny," I argued.

"No?" he asked as he began removing his shirt. "I'm surrounded by beautiful people every fucking day and so many are nothing but shallow, empty, pathetic creatures. You're the second woman in my life that I've ever truly cared about, and I fucking hate that I do care, Lena. I shouldn't care about you, because I work damn hard at remaining detached from those around me. Yet you walk in here with that sexy-as-fuck dress, and everyone else pales under the beauty that escapes from inside you. And you kicked out the serving girl, because you want someone as fucked up and twisted as me to teach you how to get fucked." He snorted. "How fucked up is that?"

"I think you need glasses," I laughed.

"Maybe you need glasses," he retorted as he undid

his pants and my eyes latched on to his massive cock as it bounced free from the confinement of his slacks.

"Nope, the eyes work a little too well," I smirked. I swallowed as I took it in, noting that it still hung to the right, even when hard. "I don't think that's ever fitting inside of me. That thing is huge." I blanched as my thoughts came out of my mouth unfiltered.

"It's going to fit," he replied with a cocky smile as he moved onto the bed and pushed me down abruptly, using his eyes to keep me there once he had. "*Everywhere*," he grunted, making sure I understood what he meant by everywhere.

"You sure about that?" I whispered, losing my bravado and feeling the heat begin to swirl inside of me, like a vortex. "I'm thinking we might have a problem getting him in."

"Positive. I need for you to let me know if you're on birth control?" he continued as he spread my legs apart, taking in the wetness his heated gaze created as his eyes inspected me.

"Yes," I whispered. "I told you; no pretty babies."

"That you did, I also seem to remember you telling me to go have pretty babies," he smirked as if he had some inside joke only he knew about as he lowered his mouth and kissed the inside of my thigh before doing the same to the other.

"No babies," I whimpered as I let my legs fall apart, as I felt him smile against my thigh. "What about diseases?" I asked, hoping it didn't ruin the mood, but the man ran a sex club. It was a valid question.

He laughed huskily as his eye went alight with laughter. "Trust me; I can't give or catch anything. I'm protected from STDs; think of it like a supernatural STD repellent."

"Good to know," I replied as his mouth touched my flesh again, making me forget about anything but what he was doing.

"Good, because I want nothing between us when I make you mine." He nipped my thigh, pulling a surprised shriek from me. "Play with your pussy, Lena," he commanded, and without a second thought, I moved my hand to rub myself in the place where I wanted him. My fingers moved through the slickness he'd created and my eyes moved to his as heat accumulated in his midnight eyes. His hand came up and captured mine, pushing it hard against my pussy, pulling a moan from my parted lips. His eyes moved to where our hands worked my swollen flesh, and then lifted to mine as I watched his. "Bloody hell, woman, I'm not sure I can wait to fuck your sweet flesh."

"Then don't," I whispered, and watched as he smiled.

"If tattoo asshole was feeling what I am at the idea of filling this sweet flesh, it's no wonder he didn't last more than a fucking minute. I actually feel sorry for that prick. I'm pretty sure your body would tempt a fucking saint to become a sinner."

"You talk too much," I replied, and he grunted. He pushed my hand away and pushed his fingers deep inside of me, filling me until I thought I would explode.

"Use them; I need you wet and stretched to fit me inside you," he ordered. He moved up closer to me, which sent his fingers deeper, a calculated move that was meant to make me feel them more. "Move your hips, fuck my fingers for me, Lena, show me what you plan to do to my cock when I claim your pussy," his eyes watched what I was doing with a hungry intensity and I followed his lead, crying out as I watched him pull them out before pushing them back in harder. Muscles I didn't even know I had burned with his invasion.

His mouth found mine, and his teeth grazed my lip before he caught the bottom one and latched on. Pain shot through me, heading straight to where his fingers worked my pussy. He released it, only to do it again until I was riding his fingers in a feverish hurry. "That's it, good girl. Come for me, Lena, show me how much this pussy wants to get fucked by me," he encouraged and lowered his head to nip at my nipple, sucking the puckered flesh between his teeth.

I exploded, back arching off the bed, whispering curses as my body detonated and shattered as he continued to move his hand and his thumb kept moving in a circular pattern against my soft nub.

"Bloody hell, you're so fucking tight. Such a greedy little thing," he crooned as he continued to fuck me with his fingers, allowing the orgasm to continue until I was trembling and crying out his name.

The moment the tremors subsided, I expected him to get on top, but nothing was that easy with Lucian. He smiled as he watched me gain my sight back and I whispered his name.

"Ready to be taught what a sick, twisted freak I really am, sweet girl?" he growled with a smirk that sent a shiver down my spine.

I nodded, watching as he moved up the bed until his cock was close enough to kiss, and stopped. His eyes watched me as he pushed it against my lips, forcing me to open and take him into my mouth. The moment I had him there, straining my jaw to take him further, his hand wrapped around my throat, gently applying pressure as he withdrew from my mouth. His eyes were locked with mine, which I figured was his way of judging if I could handle what he was doing. When I didn't pull away, he grew rougher, applying more pressure as his cock pushed deeper between my lips. I moaned and tried to open my jaw further, but it was painful, the thick cock too much for my mouth. It burned, and I wasn't getting enough air into my lungs, and we both knew it. Instead of withdrawing, he pushed in further as more pressure was applied against my throat.

I couldn't breathe. My life was in his hands. His eyes grew hooded as they watched mine, enjoying the moment I figured out just how fucked I was, if he decided to increase the pressure. He pushed in deeper, and his hand tightened. I brought my hands up to his, and his grip tightened until I thought my neck would snap.

I moved my hand to my own sex, which drew his eyes to what I was doing to myself. His hand released the pressure and he pulled out enough that I was able to gasp for air. His eyes moved to mine, and he waited. For what, I had no idea.

When he didn't move, I moved my head to take him again. That made his eyes grow large with surprise, and he paused, as if he couldn't believe I was into it. I wasn't, but with my hand working my own growing need, and his eyes on mine, I was. His fingers touched my neck and he grinned as he applied a slight pressure, enough that we both knew he was in full control.

His other hand moved away and slapped my pussy hard, which tore a moan from me that was smothered as his hips surged forward, using my distraction to his advantage. The slap had sent a jolt of pain straight to my center, which he rubbed into pleasure as he watched me try to take even more of him.

There wasn't skill in my movements, just a desperate need to please him as he had me. He smirked as he moved my hair away from where it had fallen into my face as I'd been brazenly sucking his cock. He pushed in and then withdrew. I brought my hand up to my throat as he watched, and something cold briefly lurked in his eyes.

"Did I hurt you?"

"A little," I replied.

"It turned you on, though, knowing I held your life in my hands."

"Yes," I replied.

He smirked and nodded as he moved between my legs. He didn't ask permission, or if I was ready, before he started devouring my flesh. I watched him for a moment, until he held his hand out; the wine bottle that had been forgotten on the counter sailed through the air and into his hand. He poured a few drops on my sex and my eyes grew wide as I watched him lick and savor it while his eyes locked with mine. He poured some in my belly button next, and slurped the liquid noisily which made me laugh. He continued to move, until he was mouth to mouth with me, but he didn't kiss me, instead he pushed his finger into the tip of the bottle and brought it to my lips, tracing them with the wine as I watched his reaction to what he was doing to me.

He kissed me as he released the bottle, sending it sailing back to where it came from. His kiss was hard, demanding, and I gave in to it, knowing that he was claiming ownership. His finger stroked my flesh, as the other hand held my chin. When he released me, I watched him move between my legs.

He sat there, looking at my body as he rubbed his cock

against my opening, teasing me. Every once in a while, he'd slap my naked flesh with it, and watch as I responded to the pain. Or, he'd use his hand to slap my pussy, which he'd then kiss until it was pleasure. He did this for a while, occasionally pushing the tip of his cock into my opening, only to pull out to continue his brand of play with me. When he finally adjusted my legs, I felt fear creeping up my spine as he readied to claim me.

"This is going to hurt, because you're too tight. There's no way to make this easier for you, not that I want to make it easier; watching your pain is fucking intoxicating," he said as he leaned over and kissed me gently, as if he couldn't get enough of my lips. "I want to hear you scream as I fucking destroy this tight pussy," he admitted. "I really hope you aren't expecting me to be gentle, because I have no plans of doing so. I plan to fuck you so hard that you'll feel it for days, and every time this pussy aches, you'll know exactly who you belong to. Every time you move, you'll think of me. You'll get wet just thinking about it. Your pussy is going to be red and sore, and the moment it starts to forget that it's been owned, I'll remind it."

"Lucian," I growled as he positioned me, bringing my legs up to his waist, and encouraging me to wrap them around his lower back, which tilted my ass and would give him deep access once he was in. I pushed myself against his cock, which was aimed and resting against my opening. "Just shut up and—ah!"

I screamed as he surged forward and my body shuddered violently from his entire cock being suddenly buried inside of me. My body burned, and I arched and struggled to get away from the intrusion. His cock split me in two and tears slipped from my eyes as I shrieked and struggled to pull myself together through the pain. There had been no warning, and his entry into my body was violent. I'd felt the muscles pulse and burn to the nerve endings as he'd pushed inside. Even as he remained still, his muscles bulged with the restraint it was taking him to hold still as my body adjusted to his size.

I fought to get away from it. That thing was a fucking monster, and my body was rejecting it violently. It wasn't until I cried and shook my head, trying to get him to stop this that his hand slipped to my clitoris and began working a maelstrom of sensations and I paused in my struggle to get away. "That was *not* good," I whispered even as I began to rock my hips to work him inside. He remained still, even though I knew it was taking one hell of an effort on his part.

Once I'd gained some semblance of my mind back, he finally began to move. He moved slowly at first, his eyes watching mine as pain mingled with the sweet whisper of pleasure. My body continued to struggle to expel his massive cock from it, even as the pleasure took hold and I rocked my hips with each thrust, needing more of him. He continued picking up speed until I was helpless to do anything but accept what he was doing. I started matching each thrust of his with one of my own, until my body was lost in the dance of pleasure. Eventually, I stopped moving and just felt him. The way he controlled each thrust…each one calculated as he pushed against the pleasure zone deep inside of me. I could no longer tell where he ended and I began. It didn't matter. He was creating a tempest inside of me that was growing out of control.

He bent over me, stealing my lips as a groan slipped from his own, and sent him deeper into my body. I bucked wildly even as I cried from the beautiful storm that threatened to devastate my world. His teeth clamped hard against my lip, pulling it without releasing it as he hammered his cock into my flesh. He enjoyed hearing my whimpers of pain even as it was turned into pleasure from where he was annihilating my slick flesh.

I'd never considered that I might like pain with pleasure; it wasn't supposed to be an intoxicating combination, but with him, it simply was. He enjoyed giving pain while dishing out pleasure as well, and I found myself wanting it, needing it. It was beautiful and explosive. His cock was destroying me, just as he promised he would. It stretched me, filled me, and I needed more.

He didn't stop fucking me, but his hands and mouth added more pain to the pleasure. Teeth grazed flesh, nipped, his hands pinched, slapped, and rubbed until the combination was too much. I exploded around his cock, screaming violently as he continued to fuck me hard. Stars and lights erupted behind my lids, even as he demanded I open my eyes to look at him.

I did as he commanded, his own hooded eyes locked with mine as he rocked his hips, continuing the earth shattering orgasms as if he held control to extend it. Muscles clamped and struggled against each violent thrust, until his muscles bunched and his stomach tightened and he threw his own head back and let loose a guttural roar as he drained his cock deep inside of me.

He wasn't finished there; once he'd taken me, it became an obsession. He flipped me over and took me from behind, using my legs as leverage, holding them apart to reach places he'd been unable to get to in the other position. He sucked my pink flesh, kissing it before he fucked it again and again, until I was nothing but a moaning, crying mess of pleasure.

When I'd thought he'd had enough, he took more. When I thought I couldn't handle anymore, he proved me wrong until we collapsed on the bed together. He wasn't finished, though; he was already growing hard inside of me again. The man was insatiable, and put an entirely new spin on addiction. I was hooked, and never once asked him to stop, not even when I grew sore and swelled around his cock from the abuse it was dishing out.

"Fucking owned," he growled.

I grinned at him as I felt something inside of me falling into place. My stomach burned painfully and I moaned as heat swarmed my insides. I shivered as he started to move inside of me, holding my legs apart for more.

I whispered his name, knowing something was wrong. It was as if something inside of me was unlocking, and then a rush of power shot through me, forcing my body to jerk in pain. I closed my eyes against the pain and focused on the pleasure. As I let him continue, my body moved with his in unison, like perfect matches that had been forced together.

After taking me over the edge a few more times, I closed my eyes, but needed something to drink before I allowed myself to sleep. I was pretty sure he'd wrung every drop of moisture from my body. I sat up as he moved off of me and my eyes locked on the window that was no longer a mirror, but transparent, with full view of the now overfilled room that watched us. I could hear and see them, and at the front of the pack was Elaine, with a snide smile on her face. Her hand was pressed against the window, her eyes gloating as the people began to clap at what they'd just witnessed…*us*.

"Oh my God," I whispered as I looked at the faces of

those who continued to applaud Lucian.

"Spyder," Lucian growled, and the man seemed to come out of nowhere and slipped his hand over the window, closing it off. "Lena," Lucian said, his eyes taking in my ashen color.

"This was supposed to be between us, not them," I replied through a sob as the reality of it hit me. I hadn't given the okay to be watched, because I didn't want to be part of a sideshow. I felt violated. What happened last week didn't make me feel nearly as violated as her cruel act did. A tear slipped from my eye and I turned to look at him. "Did you know?"

I was already up and dressing. His eyes turned cold as he watched me withdraw from him. His silence was deafening, and gave me the answer I needed. He may not have been the one to allow it to happen, but he had to have known we were being watched.

"I didn't know she did that, Lena. I was a little fucking busy, with you!" he snapped and I turned on him with an angry glare.

"That bitch had no right to show them that!" I screamed pointing my finger at the glass, and it shattered.

I stood there, looking at the tiny pieces of glass as they dropped to the floor. I looked at my finger and shook my head. Lucian gripped my wrist painfully and I gasped at the Celtic symbol for a new beginning that was raised on the inside of my wrist. "Impossible," I whimpered. It was the brand for newly awakened witches, still in the first year of receiving their powers. It was the mark that signified the start of our new beginning as we took our place in the coven.

"Guess you're not the only one who was tricked or had their rights violated tonight, witch," he sneered. "I told you and the coven I wasn't interested in participating in any of the Harvest events. Or did they plan from the beginning to send you to me to get impregnated to keep my business in town? Are you even on fucking birth control, or did you just say that to convince me you wouldn't get pregnant? Was it all an act? Nothing but lies?"

I was trembling with anger. "You saw it, Lucian, you know damn well I wasn't selected and I was here with you instead of being at the Harvest..." Had he really just suggested I was part of some fucking plan to steal his fucking sperm? I didn't want it! I didn't want to be pregnant. "Fuck you, Lucian. Fuck you for thinking I could do something so low..."

"Leave," he said, interrupting me as he moved away from me and began to dress.

"Screw you, asshole," I snapped as everything built up inside of me. I couldn't believe after something so beautiful had happened, that he'd be so fucking stupid to think I'd steal a child. Shit, Helen would, but me? Never. That was low, and it was screwed up for him to even say something like that. Not to mention he'd said it in front of a room full of strangers.

"No, I just screwed you, Lena," he murmured as he ran his fingers through his hair.

"Too bad it was just *fine,* asshole," I sputtered as I pulled my dress on, watching as fire lit in his eyes as I said the word he'd promised to eradicate from my vocabulary. I didn't bother with my shoes, just grabbed them and my purse from where I'd dropped them earlier and pulled out my keys as I ignored the fact we had a fucking audience, or that he followed me as I marched angrily through his stupid club.

People stopped to watch us as we moved through the

rooms tensely, and I hoped that some of them hadn't been there for my absolute humiliation at the hands of his ex-bitch. I didn't stop until I was outside and moving towards the car. The leyline stopped me as I felt another rush of power jolt through me. I turned to find Lucian watching me, dressed in nothing but his stupid perfect jeans. I felt hot tears forming in my eyes and I spun around and moved towards the car. I made it halfway before a drunken guy intercepted me and pushed me against the car. His hand tore at my dress, and before I had a chance to respond, Lucian had him on the ground and was driving his fist into the guy's face.

"Lucian!" I cried as I tried to save the asshole from becoming a fixture in the pavement. "Stop," I continued until his eyes turned on me with a coldness I'd never seen before. I backed away, shook myself out of it, and unlocked the door as fast as my shaking hands could turn the key, then slipped into baby. I slammed the door and slid the seatbelt on, turned the key in the ignition, then fired up the engine and floored it, refusing to look back.

I'd been right; I should've just crawled into a fucking ball and cried myself to sleep. Instead, I'd been passed over for the Awakening, and somehow, I'd ended up with powers. Something was really wrong. I wiped angrily at tears as the faces of the leering lookie-loos moved through my mind.

Sex with Lucian had been everything I wanted it to be, and then what should have been a private thing had ended up being a show for his entire fucking club, and he'd seen nothing wrong with it. Hell, maybe he planned it to be exactly that, his show. The bartender had mentioned that Lucian did that kind of stuff, but I'd been too eager to do what I'd been holding off on, and maybe I deserved this.

I wasn't a fucking prude, but showing someone's intimate moment without their permission was wrong. So why the fuck hadn't he been angry? Or been more shocked at being the star of the fucking show? Everything we'd said had been broadcasted to those outside the glass. I shook my head, shoved in a CD and pushed on the gas pedal. It was done and over, and the pain inside of me was growing still; I needed to focus on it instead of something I couldn't fix. I turned off the highway onto the road that led to the abbey and towards my family and the people who might have the answers.

CHAPTER
thirty-four

I pulled into the abbey a mess of emotion. My brain had shut off, while my body was still sore and needing more of what Lucian had done to it. It hadn't been enough; I was already aching for the next round, and the burning and throbbing had started up again. I was such an idiot. Discovering that our time together had been turned into an exhibit at the same time I found out I had my powers after all was more than I could handle, and honestly, it freaked me out more than I ever believed I could be. It hurt. He hadn't even been upset, and he should have been. Who cared if the asshole ran a sex club, I wasn't one of the girls who'd signed up to be on stage, and that's exactly where I had ended up tonight.

The abbey was lit up brightly, and I slowly made my way to the door, hating that I didn't have panties on, and I was pretty sure I could smell sex oozing from my pores. My hair was a mess, and every step towards the abbey hurt like hell. I was raw, swollen and he definitely made sure I would be. He'd been right; with every step I took I was reminded of being with him. It sucked.

I tried to push the door open, only to find it locked. I used the cast iron knocker and waited; when the door opened, I moved inside, holding my stomach as I came face to face with Helen who blocked me from getting any further than the threshold. I almost groaned, but concealed it.

"I need help," I announced, showing her my wrist.

"You little slut," she snarled, venom dripped from each word.

"Excuse me?" I asked, but her eyes raked over me with hatred, and there was no denying I'd been fucked: my legs were red in places from where his hands had held me apart, and some areas were already bruising. I reeked of his scent, which personally I enjoyed most of the time, except for right now; right now I was mad.

"You're just like your mother," she continued, her disdain for my family abundantly clear to hear in her tone.

I was about to respond when my mother entered the room, her eyes wild with relief as she looked me over. Then Kendra moved into the room, her eyes narrowed on my dress, and she smiled as she put it all together.

"Mom," I whispered showing her my wrist, which made her eyes grow wide with fear. I felt my insides turn tightly as I watched the color drain from her face.

"Oh, Lena," she whispered as she shook her head. "No…"

"What? It's good, I have my powers," I replied as more people entered the room. I noted that some still looked rumpled from their own Harvest celebration, but the elders looked at me as if something was wrong with *me*. Shouldn't they be happy for me?

"She wasn't selected by the ancestors, which means she's dark!" Helen shouted, as if she was afraid the people in the next county wouldn't hear her.

"What?" I asked, and watched as my grandmother shook her head with tears in her eyes. "What the hell does that mean?" I demanded.

"It means you do have powers, child, but in this coven, those who have come into their powers without being selected and blessed by the ancestors, did so because they were dark," she whispered as she started to move closer to me and stopped. "It means we can't help you until we know what you are, for sure."

"I'm family," I whispered as nausea swirled through me, mixed with pain. "I'm a Fitzgerald for Christ's sake! I belong here," I hissed as what was unfolding started to make sense. "I'm not dark! I'm good; this has to be a mistake."

I'd been awakened outside of the ceremony, without being selected by one of the ancestors. My powers weren't dark, but there was no actual way to prove that to anyone. Helen knew it, and she was already gloating over her victory, I could see it in her eyes. Kendra shook her head as I looked at her.

"This has to be a mistake, mother. The ancestors made a fucking mistake. Someone made a mistake, she's our blood!" she cried. "She's my sister."

"It's the law of the coven!" Helen continued with a gleeful look in her eyes. "She's an abomination; it explains why the demon was attracted to her before she was even awakened to her powers. She's not welcome here."

I glared at her. My father touched her shoulder and she jerked it away.

"Helen, she's my daughter." His eyes moved from Helen's face to mine.

"If any choose to follow her, they have to leave the coven, and reject its protection and any right to belong to it. That is the law that protects the coven. We cannot allow darkness inside this abbey; we must protect it!" she said cruelly as her eyes moved to mine, triumph shining in them.

"I am a Fitzgerald, one of the original bloodlines to this coven, Helen. It's not I who doesn't belong here, it's you."

"You need to learn to hold your poisonous tongue, child," she sneered. I was still in the doorway, so when her magic slammed into me, it pushed me from inside the abbey and slammed me outside. She should have stopped there.

She didn't.

In front of all those who poured out of the abbey and watched us, she lifted her hand and immediately, I couldn't move, as it felt as if daggers were slashing at me all over my body. I glared at her and screamed with all of the emotion that had been building up, and the entire forest shook as I let my power out. It was stupid, seeing that I had no idea how to control it. Lightning cracked, flashed, and zigzagged to the ground, dangerously close to us; thunder boomed and rolled, shaking me and those who were witness to what was happening. The wind turned angry, my hair whipped around in it violently, and a few trees snapped in half, crashing to the ground. I pushed my hair away from my face as the wind died down, and listened as the world righted itself as Helen stared at me in surprise.

"She's not safe! She needs to be restrained and stripped

of her magic! She's a dark witch!" she howled.

"That's not your call," my mother said with pride shining in her eyes. "It hasn't been proven that she's dark, either."

"I am the one in charge!" Helen snapped, her eyes were wild as she turned them on me. I heard cars pulling up behind me, and I ignored them as I faced the coven and my family. "Cassidy!" she hissed, and I sensed her daughter as she moved to the front of the coven and held her hand up, as if she expected her magic to be more powerful than mine. I felt them working together to apply pressure to my organs and something snapped. Me.

I lifted my hand and shouted the Latin words to bring her daughter to me, unsure of how I knew them, or why I was doing it. I watched as her toes dug into the ground and her arms moved like a bird trying to take flight as she started sliding to where I stood, her eyes wild at being unable to prevent it. Helen was frantic and I could sense she was terrified of me. The moment Cassidy was in front of me, I smiled.

"You want to see what real power feels like, *sis*?" I whispered before I grabbed her and kissed her. Her eyes bugged out, and the comical look was fucking priceless. I didn't care that she was a girl, my half-sister, or that everyone was watching us; I kissed her hard, open mouthed, until she was helpless to do anything except kiss me back.

My hands held her head between them, and I kissed her with everything I had, watching as her eyes widened as she felt the power that pulsed inside of me. I released her and she screamed as her jaw opened and closed at what I'd done, her eyes filled with panic and outrage.

"That's what being a descendent from one of the

original bloodlines feels like, something you and your mother will never experience," I snapped as I released her and turned to find my mother watching me with a horrified expression on her face.

I'd crossed a line, and I knew it. But I hadn't hurt anyone, and they'd tried to hurt me. Even alone and without a coven, I was justified in my defense.

"What is the coven's decision?" I asked, watching my grandmother and the other elders who stood by her. I felt Lucian watching me. I didn't know when he'd arrived, or how much he had seen. Why he was here, I didn't know, nor did I care. What had happened between us was a mistake, one I didn't plan to ever make again.

"Until it can be brought before the high priestess, we must agree with Helen and denounce you for now," Maria said softly. "You came into your powers without being selected, and it's very suspicious. Magdalena, it's very dangerous that you have obtained them in such a way. Only a few have ever had their curse lifted without being selected and blessed by the ancestors and those who have, drew their powers from the darkness and broke the curse themselves. I am not saying that's what you did; however, this coven will not allow darkness inside. This is a very dangerous time for the coven. We must adhere to the laws, and let the high priestess decide."

Helen smiled as my stomach sank.

"There are demons out here," I whispered more to myself. "I'll be alone," I said as I looked at them. "I'll be an Awakened witch, alone. There's no one to help me out here," I watched as my mother looked helplessly at my grandmother, her head shaking silently as they made eye contact. "Mom," I said, needing to know I wasn't alone.

"Go to the cottage, Lena, and wait for the decision to

be made," my grandmother said softly but firmly. Regret shone in her eyes.

"You fucking sheep!" I snapped and the trees cracked around us. The wind picked up, howling as my emotions churned. "You are throwing me away as you did Benjamin, Mother! I'm not bad! I'm your daughter." Tears slid down my cheeks as I shook my head in denial. "I didn't ask for this; I accepted being passed over by the ancestors. Why am I being punished now? I am not dark; I'm still your daughter!" A couple of trees uprooted; power flickered and went out, and a few windows from the front of the abbey exploded in response to my pain and fury. The world felt my emotions, and they all knew it. I was using more magic than I'd ever witnessed, even by an entire coven performing a ritual together, and it scared the hell out of me.

"Lena, baby," Mom whispered as a sob ripped from her lungs.

"Screw you, screw all of you." My whispered words were barely audible from the pain of rejection I was feeling. "I shouldn't have come home." I turned to walk away, only to find Lucian watching me silently. Fuck him too; I didn't need any of them. I'd be fine on my own; I had to be. When it came down to it, I could either be the lake who easily dried up in a drought, or I could be the fucking ocean and destroy anything that tried to hurt me. I walked towards the car, hating that anything I did was wrong. No matter how much I tried, I screwed up everything I touched.

I slid into the driver's seat and slammed the car into gear, tearing out of the abbey without a backwards glance. I had no fucking idea how I was going to ward off demons, or if I even could. I had to, because I wasn't giving up. I'd come too far to do that.

The moment I got home I raided the cellar of the manor house for salt, pouring thick layers around the cottage. I whispered a protection spell and sat on the top step of the front porch, still dressed in the slinky black dress, with make-up running down my face from the pain of my mother's startled look, and then her rejection.

"Magdalena," Kendra's voice whispered through my mind. *"Stay safe; we will figure this out."*

I didn't answer her. Instead, I closed off my emotions and watched as the sleek dark sports car that Lucian owned pulled into the driveway. His door opened and he slid out of the vehicle and looked at me, his face an unreadable mask. I stood up, using the little bit of remaining salt to cover the step I had been sitting on and moved inside the house, ignoring him.

He pounded on the door and I leaned against it, applying my slight weight there to bar his entrance, as if it would stop him. I listened to him swear, and when he called me a liar, I swung the door open and tried to slap him, but he was quicker. His hand caught my wrist and he held it.

"I didn't fucking lie to you, asshole. This isn't some game to me. It's my life! I just got kicked out of the coven, and now I'm stuck here with no protection, and demons are all over the place hunting witches. You think I want this?" I cried as he watched me. "Had I known I'd be awakened I would have remained in the abbey. It's not like your cock is powerful enough to bring my powers online, jerk! It just happened. Now I'm alone." My voice dropped to a whisper as I yanked my wrist from his steely grip, uncaring that it hurt like hell. "Go ahead, Lucian, destroy what's left of me. I'm waiting," I hissed coldly.

"Lena, you're not alone," he said, and I laughed.

"Yes, yes I am," I said as I moved behind the door and closed it, listening as his footsteps retreated down the porch a few moments later. I slid down the door, hugging my knees to my chest as tears flowed and the pain in my stomach grew. Eventually I crawled into a ball and slept, unaware that my carefully constructed world was disintegrating around me, and that nothing would ever be the same again.

Lucian

I slammed my fist into the plaster; the entire house trembled from the impact. I pulled it back, watching as the skin healed over the exposed bones. Tonight had been a fucking clusterfuck, one that I'd never forget. One I never wanted to forget, either.

She'd been everything I wanted, and so fucking perfect. I hadn't been able to get enough of her; even now, my cock was hard and needing more. The connection I felt to her defied laws, and it shook my perfectly controlled world just as I had done the same to hers. Right up until she'd noticed the transfixed audience, a few seconds after I had. Normally I'd have sensed them, but I was lost to the pleasure she was giving while receiving. She'd been fucking wild with it, untamable in her lust. I had seen the results of the Harvest spell plenty of times and I had never seen anything like what I witnessed tonight.

My motherfucking match, she'd demanded more the first time I tried to move away from her. She challenged me and grabbed my dick, and started forcing it down her little throat, uncaring that it didn't fit. She'd taken more than half of it into her mouth and throat, and no one had ever managed that feat. Then what did she do? She motherfucking swallowed it! She'd placed my hand on her throat, which had been the hottest thing I'd experienced in my very long life. I knew she wasn't into it, but she'd done it, for me! She'd wanted to please me instead of the others who wanted me to please them, and endured the pain just to be with me. I'd known she was going to be different, but never in a million years had I expected the innocent little witch to be my perfect match between the sheets. Right up until Elaine fucking ruined it. Lena's eyes had been accusing, and she withdrew from me, denouncing me and everything we'd done.

I had shown her my need to give pain with pleasure, and she'd enjoyed it. She'd given me just as much pleasure as I'd given her. With Lena, nothing was muted; I'd exploded and felt everything. I'd been shocked as her body drained me, so shocked by the magnitude of the release, I was immediately hard enough to fuck her again and again until she was exactly what I told her she would be: nothing but a squirming, coming, quivering mess.

And then I'd fucked her again because I'd been a selfish prick with the need to find the release only her body could give me. I'd listened to the sounds of her pleasure as it had turned to pain and pleasure, as her sweet pussy grew sore from my cock. She never complained, just took it like a good girl, and even started me up again when I was drained.

Fucking Elaine was one of the few who knew the secret to turning the glass from that side and had abused my trust by tripping it and allowing everyone to watch my time with Lena, something she'd be punished for. Stupid bitch couldn't accept the fact that I would never take her back to my bed after she lured my men into her little scene.

She knew Lena would be pissed at me, so she recklessly went forward with her little revenge. I could even see the snide little smirk she wore when Lena figured it out, but she wasn't stupid; I'd never once made a sound the entire time I was fucking Elaine, and I moaned and shouted with every release Lena gave me like some sort of fucking animal. I made noises. Hell, I fucking came, which Elaine knew she couldn't make me do though she'd tried. She would have been jealous, and watching me with Lena, I knew she was floored. I saw it in her eyes right before she'd concealed it.

"You're losing sight of what is at stake here," Spyder growled as he joined me on the balcony, his body tense with the need to fuck or fight. "They have their powers."

"I know," I replied, turning to look at him. "I'm done playing. Damn, that girl. She was something else tonight, wild. She shook my world, man, fucking rocked it." I didn't keep secrets from Spyder, and I wasn't about to start. He'd been with me from the beginning.

"You also kissed her," he retorted. "That's against your own rules, Lucian, and I know you adhere to them to the fucking letter. I watched you with her, and I understand the attraction, don't get me wrong; good pussy is hard to find. Doesn't change what we're here to do."

"No, it doesn't," I mumbled as I turned to stare at the dark cottage, which was being surrounded by demons who all sought to get to the little witch inside. They wouldn't get past the salt I'd placed around the ring she'd laid down just before I arrived, or the runes that marked each side of the cottage.

"She's been rejected by her coven because they assume she is a dark witch. She's vulnerable, and could be of help in finding Katarina. I fucked things up with her tonight. I accused her of shit I knew she wasn't a part of. Her powers came in and I was caught off guard, so I reacted badly. Said things that hurt her. In light of what we'd just done, I was a prick to her; she'll keep her distance for a while. I do, however; plan to bring her back and to our side soon. You weren't at the abbey tonight, but Lena is powerful," I said as I turned to look at him. "I watched her control the wind, which is something only a few witches that belong to the more powerful bloodlines can do, and even then it's only a little flutter of wind. Lena blew fucking trees down. She uprooted them in her anger at being rejected; lightning struck and she was fucking glorious to watch. If I can make her mine, Katarina wouldn't know what hit her and we can finally put an end to this."

"You're so sure she's not Katarina, but what if that's the plan? What if she is and you're falling right into a fucking trap."

"And what will she do? Fuck me to death? She can't hurt me; curse me, yes but the runes will take care of it. That's all she has the power to do, and most are easily undone. When it's time, she'll come to me, and it will end. Besides, they've just been awakened and you know we normally do not find her before she's received her powers."

"You tire of the games," he said leaning against the rail. "I know I've said it many times, but this time seems different. You haven't even asked what I found in the woods when I captured the demons."

"I know what you found," I growled pushing my fingers through my hair. "You found Lucifer's watchdogs."

"I did," he replied, not surprised that I already knew. I knew who the fuck it was when I sensed them outside the cottage. "I also learned he's put a price on Magdalena's head, because your attention to her hasn't gone unnoticed by the prince of darkness. Tonight's activities drew in a less-than-saintly crowd, and he was there when Elaine turned the mirror and allowed everyone to watch you claim ownership of your pretty little new toy, which was quite the show. Others are going to want her now, especially since you claimed her and did so publicly. While most wouldn't touch anything you laid claim to, some are going to want her as a fucking trophy."

"It wasn't meant to be that way," I snapped. My hands crushed the wooden rail and I kicked it, watching as the wood hit the ground below. "Triple the price on Lena's head that way those soulless fucks bring her to me. Make it known she's to be unharmed, and untouched. If one fucking hair is harmed, they'll pay for it in spades as I wipe their existence from this plane."

"And what will you do when they drop her at your feet?" he asked, laughing as I smiled coldly.

"Claim what's rightfully mine. She willingly chose to become mine tonight, and she'll do it again," I whispered, listening as he hissed.

"What?" he asked, shaking his head.

"I gave her a choice, to leave or stay. She stayed, she's rightfully mine. Even if she didn't understand it, she agreed. Lena is innocent, uneducated of the ways of the world we live in. It had to be done; you think Lucifer didn't plan to try for her soul? I took that card away from him, and I'll keep snatching it from his grasp. Besides, she's the first woman I've thoroughly enjoyed fucking in centuries; you think I'm giving that up?"

He snorted, but dropped the subject.

"You want them gone?" he asked, his eyes taking in the swarm of un-hosted demons that she wouldn't be able to see without enhanced sight.

"Indeed; let's send Lucifer a message he won't forget. Obviously he needs a reminder of who the fuck I am and why you don't cross my path."

"Every time you two fight, people die, Lucian. Let's hope not too many innocent people get killed in the crossfire."

"He's after something that belongs to me; it's not something I'll ignore. Call the men to us; to secure peace one has to prepare for war. Bring in hellhounds, give them Lena's scent; they'll protect her when I cannot."

"Unless she senses them, and destroys them," he argued, his eyes moving to the demon that toed the salt, and watching as fire consumed him painfully. "You're already protecting her."

"You doubted that I would after watching me with her tonight?" I questioned. "No one woman has ever given me what she did, and I don't care if I have to throw her over my shoulder and keep her locked away; the moment she agreed to be mine, it was sealed. She's different than anyone I've ever met. She's a puzzle. Nothing about her makes sense. She wasn't selected by the ancestors, and yet she took what was rightfully hers regardless of tradition. How many witches have ever done that? Not even Katarina could manage that one. Lena defies logic; what should break her only makes her stronger. Imagine it, Spyder, an awakened witch who has no bond or loyalty to a coven. She's a fucking unicorn."

"It's a new world, as you reminded me. Maybe they are evolving as well?"

"Witches cling to tradition; they think it makes them stronger. Did you see *her* at the selection?" I asked, turning my head without looking directly at him.

"I saw her, the original witch, blessing the selection. Did you notice that they looked *through* Lena, as if they couldn't see her, or if she was invisible to them?"

"I noticed that too. As if she wasn't there. It's just another piece of the puzzle. I just need to figure where it fits," I whispered, considering it odd that not a single one of the coven exhibited any trace of Katarina. I'd watched them, studied them, and tested every fucking one of them, even Lena, and nothing.

Either she was getting better at hiding, or someone was helping her this time. A few times it had been easy to find her, but the last time, she'd laughed as she died, as if she knew something I didn't. As if dying had been her plan.

Most of the time, I'd find her soon after the Awakening, which meant I should be out hunting for her now. Ending the fucking game before it could begin. With the witches locked up inside the abbey, though, it would be a little difficult. Sooner or later, they'd have to come out. I jumped from the porch, landing lightly on the ground and looked up at Spyder, who smiled at me.

"Going somewhere without me?" he asked as he jumped to the ground, already pulling his daggers out. "You force this mask on us; it's the least you could do to let us be ourselves when the need arises."

"I'm going to watch my little witch sleep, to see what she dreams of this night," I replied, giving him an evil grin, already smelling her wetness as I walked through the demons that couldn't sense my presence. Lucifer wanted to fuck around, I'd fuck back, and this time, I'd give no fucking mercy and there would be no lube. "Slice them into fucking pieces, send what's left to Lucifer, and do it quietly. She sleeps, and I need her well rested."

"As you wish, but tonight we need to hunt for Katarina," he said, already slicing into two demons that got too close. "Lucian, I'll kill her if it means protecting what we've tried to guard for centuries. I know you deserve whatever happiness you can get from her pretty lips, lord knows after watching her with you, I wouldn't mind a little piece of her myself, but the fact remains, if that thing gets out, there will be nowhere safe from the ruin and devastation left behind from the evil that will be released."

"I'd kill her myself if for one second I thought she was the key to ending this."

CHAPTER
thirty-five

~Magdalena

There was no worse feeling in the world than knowing I was alone. I felt the emptiness deep in my soul. The silence. Three days had passed since the Awakening, three long days of silence with only Luna to keep me company. If I hadn't come back, it wouldn't have been such a slap in the face. Living alone was something I could handle; knowing I was cut off hurt.

I moved through the small grocery store, putting things in the cart absently. I had to focus on keeping the power inside of me around the town's people. Feeling the buzzing in my ears constantly reminded me that I needed to contain it. My head hurt, my body ached in ways it shouldn't, and there was a pain in my stomach that seemed to be getting worse. Occasionally, I had listened in on what Kendra was up to, and noted that they were all still under the Harvest spell, but I didn't have the convenience of a partner to help take the edge off.

Lucian had been silent since he'd left me three days ago. I'd locked myself in the house, listening to music, watching Netflix, anything to keep my mind from what was happening to me. I was always horny, as if he'd awoken a monster who couldn't think of anything else but his cock and figuring out how to get it. I didn't need it; I fucking craved it, more than food, more than air. It was pathetic, considering he'd actually had the balls to think I'd wanted his pretty babies.

The cash register was loud; each code she punched in grated on my nerves. The fact that I was being followed by Lucian's guy grated even more. I slipped my card in the device and punched in my pin, only to watch the cashier shake her head.

"Have another card? This one was declined."

"What?" I whispered as I ran it through again, and punched in the pin.

"Still declined," she said with a frown.

I pulled out the emergency card that each coven member carried and slipped it through. "The first card should have money on it," I replied, knowing I had at least a few hundred dollars left.

"I'm sorry; it's not allowing the transaction to go through. Do you have cash?" she asked as I eyed the food and I was fairly sure my head was going to erupt. "This card declined too, so unless you have cash..."

"Of course it did," I whispered as I continued eyeing the food. I dug through my purse, and found twenty three cents. I tossed the change in the jar on the counter and started out of the store. How fucking embarrassing. I took one last longing look at the groceries and then to where Lucian's guy, 'Man-bun' as I'd dubbed him, was leaning against a car across the street and thumbing through an edition of Cosmopolitan he must have picked up. "I'm sorry; I can put it all back, Becky," I whispered.

"No, we pay Kevin to do it," she replied with a frown. "I haven't seen your mom or sister in days, Magdalena, everything alright? I know the store closed down; money must be tight."

"Fine," I said awkwardly, "everything is fine."

I walked out, my stomach growling with hunger, my emotions swirling inside of me as pain tried to rip me apart. Life was just freaking amazingly fine. I'd put off going to the store until I'd had no choice, and now, I had no food, no nothing. I slipped into baby and headed home, ignoring the sleek car that followed me to the road and then disappeared as the driveway split in different directions.

I stopped off at the manor house and dug through the cellar before moving on to the kitchen. I only found a can of string beans and two cans of creamed corn. The food from the cupboards had been removed, along with anything that the fire had damaged.

Back at the cottage, I called the bank, and listened as they ticked off charges for transaction fees and apparently my student loan payment had been pulled along with a payment that shouldn't have been pulled due to a computer glitch, and then everything else continued to accumulate until I'd earned a negative balance. The loan officer I spoke to about my student loan apologized profusely, and said it might be eight to ten days for the charges to be reversed. I called the company that managed the MasterCard from the coven, and found out my account had been frozen by

Helen herself. That bitch was on a serious power trip, go figure.

I turned off the TV, and wondered how desperate I'd have to be before the cans of vegetables looked appetizing. I left the cans on the coffee table and moved through the house numbly, until I decided it might be a good idea to see if there might be anything edible in the garden.

The garden was destroyed, almost as much as my life was. Something had gotten into it, and dug holes that had killed a lot of the plants. Winter was coming, and the coven…Wait, *I* needed herbs. I went through the motions, picking, replanting the annual plants, and dropping things into a basket as I tried to ignore the heavy gaze I felt with every move I made.

By the next day, the cans of vegetables were empty. The herbs I'd picked had died overnight, and I'd discovered by accident that I could 'see' through Kendra. It had to be from the Awakening, a boost to the connection we shared, or, knowing my luck, it was some freakish accident that would kick me in the ass. I peeked through Kendra's eyes, watching as she rode some guy, and groaned. How much Harvesting were we supposed to do? It was getting tedious watching my sister with her guy, who was actually getting better at making her scream, when I was so horny I thought I was going to die. She'd tried talking to me a few times, but I'd closed her down before she could. I wondered if she could see how shitty I was doing through my eyes, if I allowed her to get through. In retrospect, I should have let her know what was happening so perhaps my mother or grandmother might help, but stubborn pride got in the way. I really didn't want to face another rejection from them.

Five days later, I was becoming delusional. I'd begun

to dream about Lucian watching me sleep, and hearing monsters around me that couldn't possibly be there, hissing and cursing as they tried to get in. It was probably because I was living off of the scant berries that could be found in the forest. To make things worse, I'd fallen asleep with my phone one night, only to find it on the floor with a cracked screen. It made it hard to identify plants, or what was safe to eat from the surrounding forest.

Nine days after the Awakening ceremony, I was desperate. I stood on the front porch as my eyes scanned the huge house that Lucian owned and I knew there was plenty of food there. I was going to go insane without food, and my body was aching, craved him painfully. Like he was a drug, and I needed a fix. Without thinking, I moved towards the house, but the moment the door opened and Elaine walked out with a wicked smile, I paused. Lucian walked out behind her, pulling his shirt on as he swung his arms around as if he was arguing with her.

I stood rooted to the spot, my stomach clenching with hunger and need as well as a new spasm of jealousy. I knew the pain was a byproduct of the Harvest spell that was still driving my body to what it needed the most: to be fucked. I turned towards my house, hating that she was with him, but mad enough at the sight of them together, to ignore the pain. Apparently my presence didn't go unnoticed, and as if I wasn't having enough shit go wrong, the bitch screamed my name.

"Lena, is it?" she taunted and I turned to look past her to where Lucian stood. His eyes looked me over slowly, hunger banked in them, visible even from where I stood, and I wondered if I looked as bad as I felt. I felt weak, starved, and my body didn't care. It wanted him.

I flipped her off, mostly because talking took effort,

and I couldn't be bothered. I started back towards the cottage, dismissing them both. Screw them; I had enough on my plate, or more to the point, I needed to deal with my shit to get food *on* my plate.

"Stupid child, you think you can just take what doesn't belong to you? He's mine!"

"Have him!" I yelled and the wind whipped my hair violently as I turned to face her. "Keep him, I don't fucking care!" My words came out as a whispered hiss, which was weak.

"Lena," Lucian growled, and heat erupted inside of me as my name left his lips.

I tried to go back to the cottage, but it was as if something took control over my body, and before I could stop myself, I was striding towards him. My clothes were in the way, and I was taking them off as other people came out of his house and stood on his porch to get a better view of what was going on, and I didn't fucking care. My shoes left my feet, my shirt was lifted and tossed to the ground and I started removing my shorts, and he smiled as I growled like some wild thing who was hunting her prey. I didn't care that we had an audience, didn't care if they watched as I took what I wanted. Nothing mattered except getting him naked, and getting him inside of me.

I knew everyone was watching us. I heard gasping and comments as I stripped down to nothing but my tiny lace panties and bra, and slammed him against the wall of the entryway hard. I enjoyed the sound of his head hitting the door as I slammed against him. My lips found his and I moaned from deep in my throat. He kissed me back; even as I pulled away, ripping his shirt from his body, needing him naked and ready for what I needed him to give me. I tried to move back, but his hands buried in my hair, pulling my mouth back to his. I worked his jeans, and he growled as the people around us catcalled and made comments. I was too distracted to hear. I was fucking starving, and he was about to be devoured.

"I hate you!" I hissed as I pulled my mouth away to get air, crushing it against his before he could reply. He laughed against my mouth, reaching for my jaw as he pulled it away, even as his other hand pushed the door open and he walked us through the doorway.

"Good," he growled. "I hate you, too, little witch," he smirked as he slammed the door behind us when we entered the house, the small window embedded in the door shattering with the force of him slamming it.

I ripped at his pants, enjoying the sound of tearing fabric as it gave under the pressure and the sting of my skin as he tore my panties off without a thought. He pushed the glasses, silverware, and china off the dining room table with his arm, and slammed me against it. He lifted my legs as he entered my body hard, painfully, and so fucking deliciously. I arched my back, spreading for more, even as I screamed for him to move faster. I didn't need soft; I needed hard, and right now. The table cracked as he slammed his hands down beside my head, and then we were falling. The sound was blissful, and his body pounded into mine even as we fell to the floor. He picked me up, still inside of me as he moved me against the wall.

"Fucking witch," he grunted as he pinned me to the wall, driving his cock into me without mercy as he held my legs apart, giving him full access and control.

"Screw you!" I yelled, raking my nails across his flesh as he claimed my mouth. I reached for his hair, yanking it and enjoying his growl as I gave him a taste of his own medicine. I felt the drywall give way with how hard he was fucking me. Something shattered and crashed against the floor, and then he was moving me to the couch in the front room.

He slammed me down on it, his hands pulled my legs apart and his mouth swooped down between my legs, lapping at the wetness. His fingers pushed inside and I jerked as he started to move them, his mouth nibbling at my clitoris. I pulled his hair hard, watching as his eyes grew hard in turn and filled with liquid fire. He dropped his hold on one leg and withdrew his fingers from my body, reaching for my hips.

He lay on the sofa as he pulled me over himself and his hands tangled in my hair to pull my head down and control my hungry mouth, forcing his cock down my throat—and I took it. I groaned around it as I took more than he'd tried to feed me, my nails dug into his thighs, and he yelped in surprise as I took all of him.

I wasn't even sure how it was possible, but I did it and looked up at him victoriously as my lips touched the base, and I let my teeth skim his delicate flesh as I pulled away from him. His eyes watched in wonder as I did it a few more times.

I slammed him back against the couch when he tried to move away, slid him into my body, and began riding him hard. The couch protested, cracked loudly and we landed on the floor with a mixture of grunts and moans. I was trembling, but so was he. It was violent, like electricity hitting water, and I wanted more. I wiggled my hips, daring him to take control, and he growled as he bared his teeth and I detonated around his cock. The windows shattered as I screamed with my release and wind rushed through the room, flinging the paintings off the walls as it filled my hair and cooled my skin.

He allowed me to have control for a moment, but then he picked me up, pushed me off his cock and flipped me over until I was on my stomach with something poking against the soft flesh of my belly. He grabbed me by the hair as he moved in behind my ass, his cock pushed against my wet pussy, and then he plunged inside without mercy, riding me hard from behind. Fingers in my hair, he pulled it as his other hand smacked my ass; pain shot to my center and threatened to shatter me. He pulled me back against him, releasing my hair as he grabbed my hips and lifted my ass as he drove into my pussy excruciatingly. More glass shattered around us as another orgasm violently tore through me. Crashing noises sounded outside, but I ignored it as I felt his hand gripping my throat and forcing me to my knees. Still gripping my throat, the fingers of his other hand pinched my nipple until I screamed.

He released it and my neck as he yanked my body flush against his frame. He slapped my pussy as he pulled his cock out and flipped me over, taking in the marks on my body.

"So fucking beautiful," he growled as he shoved my legs apart and slammed into me, filling me. I climaxed again, watching as his muscles strained beneath his own impending release that he was withholding from me. It didn't last long; I used my body to clamp down hungrily on his cock, tightening the muscles until his eyes grew heavy, his head rolled back, and his body released inside of mine.

We collapsed on the floor, on broken things. My eyes closed and I smiled. Our breathing was labored, his front room and dining room were destroyed, and I laughed, and then started crying as he sat up and looked down at me.

"Lena," he whispered, but I ignored him as I stood up,

and walked around the broken glass. I opened the door, not giving a shit that I was naked, or that the evidence from our rough sex was visible to everyone who waited outside.

"Jesus, where the fuck do I sign up for some of that?" someone said, but I ignored them, turning to walk my very naked ass back to the cottage.

"Did that just happen?" another voice said, and then asked, "How the fuck did that just happen?"

"Lena," Lucian's voice was angry, and I listened without listening as he snapped orders. "Lena, stop!" he shouted, and I finally looked back, tears filled my eyes as a victorious smile quirked at my lips. He was still naked; his cock bounced with each step he took towards me, and he wasn't done. He was hard, ready. Good.

"I need a witch like that, shit, you guys seeing this?" another voice said, but their words were muffled as they returned to the house.

"Lena," Lucian shouted as I slammed the front door in his face upon returning home, and he kicked it; it threatened to disintegrate when he proceeded to pound on it. Finally, he tried the knob and, finding it unlocked, he opened it and moved with frightening speed to the bedroom, where I was already bending over the bed as I tried to move the covers to crawl into it.

He entered me, and I cried out in bliss. He lifted my body, forcing my face into the mattress as he spread my legs painfully apart, pushing my body to its limits.

I wasn't sure how much time passed, but when I woke, I was alone again.

I sat up, taking in the bruises from his hands, his cock, and his teeth. I'd been in heat, or the witch's version of it. My stomach growled loudly, reminding me that I was starving, and I had no way to fix it. I moved my fingers to my pussy, taking in the inflamed and sore mound and felt the electrical buzz that was Lucian as he filled the room. His eyes locked on to my swollen flesh and I smiled up at him, needing a distraction from the gnawing pangs of hunger in my stomach. When he didn't move towards me, I ignored him, pushing my finger inside, and moaning loudly as I began to move with purpose.

"That's mine," he growled as he grasped my hands, holding them above my head as he used a pair of stockings from my nightstand drawer to tie my hands to the headboard of my small bed. I watched him, not wanting it to end. I needed him, needed the contact of our bodies. When he touched me, the pain I felt in my stomach eased and dissipated. He used another pair to secure my feet, lifting them until they were apart and tied to the footboard. I was open for him, and he knew it.

"You missed me, Lena, admit it."

"Fuck you," I snarled, whining and wincing as his hand slapped my exposed pussy hard. Then he kissed it, and I whimpered and rocked my hips. "I need you."

"I know," he said against my heated flesh. He pulled back, slapping it again. "That's for locking me out and ignoring me when I was at your front door." His mouth kissed and sucked, and I moaned loudly. His hand slapped my tender flesh again. "That's for making me wait for what's mine." He moved until he was kneeling between my legs, his cock pushing slowly inside my body.

"Hard, asshole," I demanded and he smiled as he reached for the drawer of the nightstand, pushing his cock deep into my pussy as he leaned over me to get into it. I watched him as he pulled out another pair of stockings and pushed them into my mouth, making it impossible to tell him what I wanted.

"You'll get it how I want to give it, Lena, and it'll be slow this time. Because I want you to *feel* me," he growled as he pulled out, and pushed back in slowly. "Feel that? How your sweet pussy is stretching to accept me perfectly? Feel how your body clenches my cock, sucking it as it accepts what I give it. You were made for me, my sexy little witch. Your body knows who owns it, who destroys it." He pulled out, lowering his mouth to kiss it and then my thighs as he slowly touched and ran his fingers in slow, small circles where my skin was red and already bruising.

"I missed this sweet flesh. Ever since you left my bed at the club, I've thought of little else than wrecking you again. I missed the sexy little noises you make when you come for me," he whispered as he moved up to suck on my nipples.

I felt his heavy cock resting against my stomach. I groaned, needing to feel him inside of me. I didn't want slow and soft, because he was right: it made me feel him. I wanted mindless fucking, like we had when we'd destroyed his living and dining rooms. I moaned as he sucked on my pulse at the curve of my neck.

"You hate me, and that's okay. I can live with it," he whispered, pinching my nipples as he slid back inside my body, taking me slowly. Tears slid from my eyes as he watched me. "You hate that you can't *really* hate me; trust me, I know the feeling. I hate that I want you, too, Lena, but I love what you feel like when I'm inside of you. This," he said pushing into me and pulling out slowly, "this is something not even I can deny. You undo me, make me weak. I need this from you, and you need it from me."

"Screw you," was my muffled reply. He smiled and

slapped my pussy as he slowly drove himself inside me. His movements were precise, each thrust meant to seduce and tease. Slowly, he created sensations with his fingers, his touches and slow kisses. He knew exactly what he was doing to me, and he had no intention of doing what I wanted him to. Mindless fucking was easy. It wasn't messy. This slow seduction was brutal because it pushed past my walls. I felt him, inside of me. Lucian was forcing me to feel my body's reaction to his. Each penetration into my body was another inch he moved into my soul. Breaking his way past the barriers and crumbling my defenses.

"Keep it up and this flesh is going to be sore for weeks," he growled as he slowly traced his fingers over my body before finding my clitoris and rubbing it. "You need to be taught who you belong to. Tell me now. Who do you belong to?" he asked, his eyes resting on my mouth with a twisted grin. "Guess it might take a while to get the lesson across, but I'm up for the challenge. That's it," he said as I closed my eyes and rocked my body against his as an orgasm ripped through me. "Good girl."

CHAPTER
thirty-six

And though she be but little, she is fierce. – **William Shakespeare**

~Lucian

I moved around her cottage, noting the lack of things. Food fit for humans, for starters. Her fridge was devoid of anything; not even a stick of butter remained. I noted a bag of dry cat food and a few cans in her garbage and that was it. I fished through her garbage for anything else she might have eaten in the past week other than green beans and creamed corn. Who the fuck eats that shit with nothing else? I moved into the bedroom, slapping her naked ass hard.

"Lena, what happened to all of your food?" Selfish prick that I was, I needed her fed. Fucking consumed energy. She needed energy, because I needed to fuck her again. She rocked my fucking world; stripping her body bare in the front yard as she'd marched up the front porch and took what she wanted fucking destroyed me. Nothing in my entire existence had ever affected me like that, but she did.

She mumbled weakly, and I paused. My ears listened to her heart, and it was weak. I pushed her over onto her side and my cock was up. Hard, ready to pound her welcoming flesh; I couldn't get enough of her. It felt good knowing I could fuck her until I was sated. Normally, women begged for me to stop before I was ready to, not her, though. She took everything I could give her so far, no holding back. With Lena, I achieved, I dominated, and *we* exploded, in that order. Lena was wild last night, and it had rocked my world, *she'd* rocked my world.

"Lena, what happened to all of your food?" I repeated, touching her swollen flesh and wincing.

I'd taken her hard, soft, then harder. When I was sure she'd had enough, she took more. I let it happen, greedy fuck that I was, I wanted it as much as her. She scared the demons off from around the house with how loudly she was coming; assholes probably assumed some priest was in here doing an exorcism. She opened her eyes, and I flinched from what I failed to see last night. She was fucking wrecked, and it had little to do with what I did to her.

"Get up," I ordered, watching as her eyes closed weakly. "Bloody hell," I snapped angrily, picking her naked body up and moving through the cottage and out of it swiftly. We just went to war with our bodies, and she was ill-prepared, fucking starved for nourishment, and she never complained once. Didn't stop, either, she gave it right back to me, tit for fucking tat.

I moved into the main house, not giving a shit that my men stood around, dicks in their hands as they tried to divert their eyes from the wreckage from last night. Some looked impressed, and a few seemed confused. As if they weren't sure where to start fixing what we destroyed by fucking.

"Layton, you forget to tell me something?" I snapped; my anger was palpable, pulsing through me.

"Did I?" he countered, eyes sliding down the sexy-as-fuck, albeit unconscious body in my arms. "Is she dead?"

"No, but she's close. When's the last time she went shopping for food, or you saw her eat?" I demanded, and his eyes grew large and rounded as he started to curse.

"She went to the store days ago, I think she might have had some trouble at the register and she left with nothing. Figured she was eating inside, you told me to keep my eyes to myself, let her have privacy. Didn't want me eye-fucking her, so I stayed outside the grocery store and never went inside the cottage," he admitted.

"Stupid fuck; she's starved and I just drove her harder than I have with anyone on stage at the club," I growled, and listened as they made noises of surprise. Yeah, my girl, she's a fucking rock star in the sheets. She could make a porn queen look lame in bed. Lena didn't growl in bed, she fucking roared like a monster, like me.

"You didn't notice that she wasn't fucking back?" Devlin asked, his eyes glued to her figure, and I growled low, threatening. *Mine.*

"She did, all fucking day and night long. She took what I gave, and then she took more." I let that sink into their heads; listened as they whistled, and pride swelled my chest. They know exactly what I am, and what I can do, and she'd kept up with me. I fucked hard, she fucked harder. "Get food, now," I ordered, stepping over what was left of the furniture she and I fucking destroyed. She didn't do wild sex; she went to war when she fucked. She wasn't weak anymore, held back by limitations of being human, she was a fucking hurricane.

I moved her to my room and covered her up, then ran my fingers through my hair at my own stupidity. She moaned, and I had to force myself not to crawl between her thighs. She was mid Harvest, and she'd tried to suppress that urge to ride it out on her own. I should have been there, should have fucking realized it. Instead, I'd been hunting for Katarina with Spyder, enjoying the thrill of finding the clues that might lead to her...and found nothing. Meanwhile, Lena had been alone, hungry, and dealing with an almost unbearable urge to fuck, if my memory of that spell was correct.

I leaned over the bed, feeling her pale face. Her skin was slick with sweat, but I was fairly positive that was from fucking for hours. She whimpered, and her eyes opened to look around and she groaned as she held her stomach. She wasn't going to be able to hold anything down, and it was driving me bugfuck crazy knowing it was on me. I'd never taken a partner to the brink of death, never. I have rules, and I hold myself to a standard. I always check vitals, make sure girls are healthy, fed, ready to be taken on an adventure of sexual awareness they won't ever forget, but Lena...Fuck, with her, it was like I was fucking greenhorn fumbling around in the dark. She made me forget things, turned me into someone who fucking cared.

I moved around the bed, considering my options. She was fading fast; the bouts of vigorous sex tapped her already stressed-out body. Her pulse was already slowing, and she was spiraling towards the drain. There were a lot of things I could heal, but it would take time and I needed to fix this fast. Fuck! Women who are starved to death don't fuck like that; they sure as hell don't initiate it.

I knew where I could go for a fix that would save her, but the idea of asking for help wasn't appealing. I needed to figure out a way around it. I thought about how I should look that would be the most intimidating and a black suit with a crisp white dress shirt and black tie appeared on my frame. I paused for a moment, listening to her breathing as it grew labored, and I exhaled deeply.

I displaced molecules, severed time and space, and re-formed inside Vlad's bar. It was darker than usual as I looked towards the bar, and noted it was packed with Fae, and from the look of it, the increase of Lucifer's foot soldiers on this plane hadn't gone unnoticed. They had one laid out on the bar.

Stakes held him firmly in place while Ryder dripped what I assumed was holy water over the demon's forehead and it screamed and cursed, and I paused, watching them from the shadows. My eyes searched the tables; looking for the kid I knew Vlad had been hanging around with lately. I finally spotted his shaggy, longer brown hair in the crowd and he was with one of the regular fang-bangers, Rebekah, who had dark blond hair flowing down to her ass. The banger had goo-goo eyes for Ryder, who couldn't be bothered to notice she even fucking existed.

I watched as the kid pulled her towards the open doorway in the extended hallway. Vlad's version of a sex club and mine differed, hugely. He looked at the bar, and his eyes slid over Synthia, who didn't seem to notice. Her eyes were only for Ryder.

As far as I was concerned, it was a fucking soap opera in this place; everyone longed to fuck everyone, and it had a simple fix: Throw them all in a room, and let them fuck it out.

Ryder looked around as if he sensed me, and I smiled. No one senses me unless I allow them to. I moved through the shadows, allowing myself to blend in with them. The kid closed the door to the small room, but I was used to it; doors didn't keep me out, and neither did wards.

I watched as he pushed her against a wall, kissing and touching the girl who giggled pathetically. Lovely, the girl was imagining the kid was Ryder, and he was imagining she was Synthia; both were fucking failing with their fantasies. He was limp, she was dry, but both more than willing to fake it for a blood fix, which most of the regulars here are rewarded with. If the vamps fed from them regularly, they had to replace a bit of it. It was simple fucking logic; Vlad was smart, and didn't want bodies piling up. He'd been doing it for a long time.

Rebekah had been hanging around Vlad and his people for well over fifty years, yet she looked no older than twenty because they would give her vampire blood. Rotating the vamps that fed from her kept her from being in thrall to any particular one.

I watched her strip naked and found myself comparing her to Lena—and she was so fucking lacking. Her breasts are larger than Lena's, but it didn't turn me on. I could smell what that the blood she'd been fed couldn't conceal: she was aging. Her organs and her body knew that they're supposed to be older. He could smell it too, his nostrils flared and even as she lowered herself to the floor as she worked his pants, he rolled his eyes.

I smiled. A few years ago, Synthia was his, but he'd fucked up. Deals with devils have a way of fucking you over in the end. He accepted Ryder's deal, guised through Vlad. He lost the one thing he loved the most in the process. Synthia.

I materialized as his turquoise eyes widened, and before he could open his mouth to alert the others, I was already there, one hand at his throat silencing him and placing the other hand on the girl, and watched as her eyes grew vacant, and she fell to the floor, limp, and unseeing.

I grabbed him, not caring if he'd sent a mental telegraph to his maker or if Vlad sensed his fear, and we apparated from the building; no wards were disturbed, no alarms sounded. We materialized back in the room with Lena, and I released his throat and arm, and watched him dispassionately as he hit the ground hard. He's used to sifting, but I don't sift.

"What the fuck!?" he demanded, and I smiled coldly, showing him the darkness inside of me. Ghostly skeletal images pushed and writhed over my skin as my armor formed; souls of the condemned that couldn't escape because I was their judge, executioner, and warden. In my world, execution comes before incarceration.

"You know who I am," I asked, even though it sounded more like a statement. My eyes turned blue, the color of the flames that burned in hell.

"Lucian, right-hand man to Lucifer," he snapped, his legs still not quite willing to hold his weight.

"The girl on the bed," I replied, ignoring his look of panic as he tried to decide his best exit route, which would only end badly for him. "She needs blood."

"And if I say no?" His question was almost belligerent. He had balls. I had to give him that.

"Don't say no, kid. That means this trip ends badly for you."

He looked at me, and I allowed more of the darkness I concealed to become visible. Soulless eyes watched him, the blue hellfire burned brightly, and my armor that contained the souls slipped, purposely. Like tattoos, they slithered over my skin, moving around the runes that held them to me. His mouth popped open, and his fangs retracted, completely unable to look away from the walking nightmare I'd become.

I didn't just collect evil mortal souls, I collected immortals. Immortals gave more power; they fed what I had become with endless power, making me stronger with each new piece I added to my armor. Their powers became mine, and the transfer was quite painful for them.

"Who is she?" he asked, his eyes still glued to the souls undulating on my skin like dancing tattoos. I pushed the armor back below my façade of a body, where I could still pull from their powers and let him feel the electrical intensity of the raw power they fed me.

"She's a witch, one who doesn't deserve to die. Unless you plan to follow her into the next life, I suggest you remedy it. Now," I said evenly, not needing to scare him more than he already was. He was new to being immortal, too weak to become part of my collection.

"Guild?" he asked as his eyes moved to Lena. I felt his lust, strong and powerful as he looked at her naked body. She'd kicked the covers off while I'd been gone.

"No," I replied, wanting nothing more than to hide her nakedness from the kid's lustful eyes. Spyder waited in the shadows in the corner of the room. He'd sensed I'd returned, and that I wasn't alone.

"No; that's all I get? I'm about to give her my fucking blood, you can at least tell me who she is and why she needs it," he replied aggressively. I growled, and the kid started to move, as if he'd stand up and take me on. Spyder moved forward, his eyes cold with death as his own souls escape from his armor. "What the fuck, house of horrors much?" the kid mouthed off, and I smiled.

Kid really did have big balls, which was probably why Vlad kept him around. I moved to the bed, sensing the moment the Fae arrived outside my house. Unlike them, I knew how to keep undesirables out of my house.

"You can either give her your blood willingly, or I can feed it to her as the life drains from you. Choose."

"Lucian, we got company," Devlin said, hellfire burning in his eyes as he entered the room, fixing his gaze on the young vampire. His eyes moved from the kid to Lena, who groaned and curled in on herself as pain rocked through what had to be her stomach.

"Choose; either way, she's getting your blood," I warned, hoping he would choose wisely.

I watched as his fangs slid down and he scraped one over his wrist to slice it open. He slid his other arm under her upper back, carefully avoiding her naked flesh as he forced the lifesaving blood down her throat. I relaxed a hair, watching as color filled her cheeks, even as she latched onto his vein.

"Lucy, you got some 'splaining to do," Ristan's baritone voice was mocking as he materialized into the room. "Time to drop the Fae wards, asshole," he demanded angrily. Fucking soul-seeking demon. The house was warded against Fae and Lucifer's demons. Fucking half-breeds.

CHAPTER
thirty-seven

Everything's fine today, that is our illusion. ~Voltaire.

~Magdalena

"Who the hell is she?" a

deep voice asked, and my eyes blinked open, finding the light blinding. I closed them, and wiped at my mouth where the sharp taste of copper made me gag.

"That's none of your fucking business; the boy wasn't hurt, and I didn't have time to dick around," Lucian's sharp retort brought me awake, and I blinked up as a pair of strange silvery eyes that seemed to swirl loomed over me.

It was an angel, it had to be. He was beautiful in a masculine way; his features were sharp, and well-defined. His black hair fell over his shoulders as he watched me struggle to sit up. The room was full of men, beautiful men. It was official, I'd died.

"Is this heaven?" I whispered, even as my body reacted to the weird vibe that was pulsing through the room.

"Why do you ask?" the guy with silvery eyes asked, his eyes smiling with the question.

"Because if I got to choose what heaven would be, this would be mine," I said as I licked my lips and looked around. Damn, they weren't just hot; they were ethereal, as if they were created just to drive women insane. One had brown-black longish hair and green, tri-colored eyes. He also had thick black tattoos that seemed to pulse and move on his skin. A golden eyed one with shorter black hair looked sort of familiar to me as he studied me, his eyes slowly moving to where I'd uncovered my body in my haste to get up and see what was going on. He smiled as a woman slapped his arm, his eyes immediately moving to her with a look that made my ovaries hurt.

"Fairy," she growled, her azure blue eyes locked with his in silent battle.

"Witch," he growled back with a hungry look in his eyes.

"Stuff it, right where the sun doesn't shine," she countered and the silvery eyed guy who had been sitting on the bed coughed to smother a laugh.

"You two," he said. "Can't take you anywhere," he smiled and winked at me.

I winked back, unsure of why I was winking, but I was pretty sure he had just signed up to be my baby daddy. Or so my ovaries had decreed it. I swallowed as my eyes moved back to the green eyed guy, who watched me with something dangerous etched in his eyes.

"Adam, vibes," silvery eyed guy said, noting my discomfort. I wasn't sure what he meant by vibes, but whatever he'd meant by it, the discomfort in my body eased, even as my eyes moved to Lucian, who stood in the corner near the bed with his back to the wall, watching me as I took in the buffet of hotness that filled the room.

"Magdalena, always a pleasure," Vlad said as he moved into the room; a young man with brown hair and turquoise eyes stayed close to his side. "Lucian, next time, I suggest you ask before you take something that doesn't belong to you. In the meantime, maybe you could answer some questions about…"

"Not here, not now," Lucian said, cutting Vlad off mid-sentence. "Innocent ears and all," he amended, and everyone looked at me, and I looked down at my naked breasts, because that many eyes on me? Too freaking much.

"Are you well, Magdalena?" Vlad asked.

"Kendra?" a woman called softly as she moved into the room.

My eyes lifted to hers and I narrowed them. She wasn't beautiful in the sense of the others in the room, but she had a classic beauty that made her stand out in this crowd. She had red hair, and blue eyes that looked at me as if she knew me.

"That's Magdalena," Vlad offered.

"Kiss my knickers, that's Kendra," she quipped, giving him a stare that dared him to argue with her.

Kiss my knickers?

"Olivia," Lucian nodded cordially to her; her eyes moved to his and she smiled weakly.

"Lucian, it's nice to see you again," she nodded back, though something in her demeanor changed, and she moved closer to the guy with the weird silver eyes. It seemed as though she didn't think running into Lucian was as nice as she'd said it was. "I hope business at the club is well?"

"Always," Lucian said, with a slight bow of his head as his eyes moved to mine.

"Kendra, are you well?" she asked, moving to the bed and reaching for my hand. I pulled it away, moving closer to Lucian, which the entire room seemed to notice.

"My name is Magdalena," I replied, as I reached down and pulled the covers over my body. I wasn't sure why everyone was in the room, or why I was still naked, but at the end of the day, I felt as if they had me at a huge disadvantage.

"You lied to me?" she asked. "At the Guild, you told me you were Kendra Fitzgerald," she whispered and my hackles were up.

"Guild?" I squeaked as I looked around again, noticing things my brain hadn't computed. Like tri-colored eyes. "*Fae*," I whispered. "And *Guild*." I was up, moving towards the door as if the hounds of hell were on my heels.

"Lena," Lucian barked, as the others moved out of the way of the sheet I dragged with me.

"No!" I shouted as I turned around with a fire inside of me. "You brought the fucking Guild here? How could you! We've hidden from them for centuries, and you *bring* them here? And Fae! To my fucking doorstep, you brought them here, to us! You told them who we were?" I seethed angrily.

"No, Lena, you just did that," he replied coldly.

"No...Grrr!" I growled with my teeth clenched as I bared them at him like a wild animal. "You suck! I hate you!"

"You said that last night, right before you ruined most of the lower level riding me," he replied with a cocky smirk.

"And?" I countered as I pointed my finger and poked him in the chest.

"And you're about to do it again," he smiled as a wave of heat swirled through me.

"No! No, no! Just no! Ah," I doubled over as heat tore through me with the words.

"It's going to be okay, Lena, you hating me works out pretty fucking well for me," he said with a wide smile as Spyder groaned from the corner where I hadn't even noticed him before. He fucking blended in; as in, he *was* the shadow in the corner, because the moment he stepped from it, the shadow was gone.

"You guys might want to go downstairs for this," Spyder said, and I ignored it because the heat was burning me inside out.

I dropped the sheet and was moving towards Lucian with purpose, even as the others watched us.

"Bloody fucking hell," the golden eyed guy said as I pushed Lucian onto the bed, not caring one little bit that the others didn't have a chance to leave yet. "Damn," he said as I ripped at Lucian's clothes. The others watched us with wide eyes, and as if they remembered they were here, they all started moving out of the room.

"Oh, oh shit," the platinum blonde said. "Shit, we should…wow, go," she said as she yanked on the green eyed guy's arm, who was watching us with a naked hunger that I wanted to explore. "Adam, move, Ryder, help me," she said, and the moment Lucian's cock was free, the room emptied as if they'd all just vanished.

It was a few hours before I had my fill of Lucian, and even as I pulled the sheet around my body, I wanted more. I was just coherent enough to know better. I could hear the people downstairs.

"Lena," Lucian warned with his naked body still bare as he relaxed next to me. He was hot; even after sex I still couldn't dampen the attraction I felt to him. His tattoos stood brighter than they had the night before, and that stupid perfect nipple ring still tempted me to taste it.

"Don't," I laughed mirthlessly as I struggled to get out of the warm bed. "You undid what we have worked centuries to achieve in one day. Don't 'Lena' me, asshole."

I was halfway down the stairs when he caught up to me. He grabbed my arm and I yanked it from him, my heart racing with the complications of what the Guild being here meant for the entire coven. My grandmother told me on many occasions that the coven wanted to have nothing to do with the Guild; either they would try and get us to join them, or they would alert the Fae and demons to our presence. In trying to be some sort of supernatural police force, they just attracted trouble.

"Let me go!" I snapped, and marched down the rest of the stairs, ignoring his anger which I could feel as I strode through the room. The heat of his stare ate at my nerves as I ignored the curious stares, and dodged plaster, which, as I looked up, I discovered was falling from the ceiling where a crack had split it. Great, I'd ruined his house.

"Dammit, Lena," he whispered as I opened the door and slammed it behind me as I left the house and walked the distance between our properties and into the cottage, before collapsing on my ass as my legs gave out.

∼∼*

I'd ignored them after that, all of them. Luckily someone had dropped off groceries, which meant that someone knew I was broke. It stung; my pride, my heart, and everything hurt. On the second day of my self-induced isolation, I cautiously tried a little magic, tapping the line as I watched the elders teach Kendra through our bond.

I was outside of the cottage, trying to call rocks to me. It began to annoy me when they wouldn't move on command, then anger would grow, mixed with frustration at being unable to use the magic I knew I had inside of me. The angrier I became, the more the rocks on the ground shook Just as I was about to lose my temper, they abruptly lifted from the ground around me, and waited. When I gave the command, they sailed directly at me, resulting in goose eggs and a lot of bruises.

The next day, I'd decided to practice again. I ignored the newcomers who would show up like they were taking shifts or something and seemed to be watching the cottage and me. I wasn't sure what had happened with the demons; if they were still present but keeping their distance, or if they were just invisible unless they had taken control of a host, which was what the elders had taught Kendra. Apparently the ones who hunted us were dark souls; ones who needed a living host if they wanted to spend any amount of time in this world.

I decided that I really didn't want to stay cooped up in the cottage for the rest of the day, so I slipped into shorts and a camisole, and headed towards the garden. I had been at it for some time when a gentleman who had to be in his early fifties kneeled beside me and ignored that he was getting dirty. He didn't speak; he just quietly pulled roots and cleaned them off before placing them in the correct baskets.

Eventually, the platinum haired beauty, the green eyed guy, the girl with red hair, and that guy who was with Vlad the other day were gardening with us. It wasn't a fantasy of mine, either. I watched them carefully as I continued to pull the roots to preserve them for the coming winter, since it looked as if I might be alone through it.

Finally, the older man spoke.

"I understood your coven's need to separate, while a lot of the other elders didn't. Yours didn't want to make warriors of you, and the Guilds did. They wanted to be the law and govern the supernatural creatures they sensed moving out of the shadows. The Guilds wanted to train children for war, and the covens wanted peace," he said as his blue eyes turned to me. "That was your coven's choice, and it should have been respected. Mistakes were made in the beginning, but that was centuries ago. It wasn't your war, or mine in those days. I was the teacher of the children at the Spokane Guild; I taught them how to fight, and how to use the leylines and control the magic within them. Not too long ago, enemies infiltrated the Guild and I was considered a liability. They've changed the Guild. It's a dangerous place now. It took me a long time to see that it wasn't a place I wanted to be a part of anymore. Most of the Guilds now are secretly being run by the enemy who are killing Fae and their own indiscriminately. Those who aren't part of the enemy ranks are still influenced by them and are too proud to see that they fall from within, because they, too, stick to tradition. It's what I call witches' pride. You and I, Lena, we are descended from a proud race."

I looked at him, noting that the platinum blonde watched me with a careful gaze. She trusted me as much as I trusted her. My eyes gravitated to the brands on her arms, which I knew belonged to the Fae. They slithered just beneath her skin, moving seductively.

"Hers aren't real," the tri-colored eyes man teased, his green eyes alight with laughter. "Mine are, if you want to touch them?" he offered, holding his arm out as I looked at his. I lifted my hand, but stopped before I actually touched them. "I don't bite," he said.

"I do," I whispered as I gave him a cool stare before I started to pull more roots.

"I noticed, it was kind of hard to miss," he said with a sexy smirk. "I occasionally attack as well when the hunger…comes," he laughed.

"Don't get Adam started," the blonde said. "He's a relentless flirt."

"As if, Syn, I'm a freaking Casanova," he replied.

"Children," the older guy admonished paternally and they shared a smile before they went back to pulling herbs.

"Need a few corners for them, old timer?" the guy with the weird silvery eyes asked as he moved in closer and looked at the dirt with a smile.

"Nothing I can't handle, demon," he said, and I was gone.

I was up and moving towards the house at a dead run.

"Shit," I heard the old guy say.

"Something I did?" the silvery eyed guy asked.

"Demons; she's from a coven that's been running from them for centuries."

I watched them from the window, my eyes taking in their friendly banter as they finished curing the herbs and preparing the roots to be stored. They looked normal, even from where I stood peeking at them through the curtain. They laughed, and other than a few differences, looked like humans. I watched as the guy with golden eyes arrived and waved his hand, and a table filled with food and everything they needed to finish processing the herbs materialized. I finally recognized him. He was the prince of the Dark Fae. He had been all over the magazines for a while there, but what I couldn't figure out was why a bunch of Fae and a Fae prince were hanging out with witches from the Guild in my garden.

"It's called glamour," a deep voice interrupted my thoughts, and I spun around, pulling the curtain rod with me.

"Get out!" I yelped as I wielded the curtain rod as a weapon, and he held up his hands as if he meant no harm. Yeah, right.

"I'm not the kind of demon that has been preying on your people. I won't hurt you; I don't kill without reason, and I'm not here to hurt your coven." He pointed out the window. "I'm in love with that little angel over there; she is my world. I'm half Horde Fae, Ryder is my brother and he is Horde Fae, not Dark Fae as the press believes. He's with Synthia, and they have the most beautiful children together. Adam over there is the real Dark prince of the Fae and he was raised in the Guild, as was Synthia. Olivia, Adam, Adrian and Synthia were all raised as witches inside the Guild and have known what they truly were for just less than a year now. Synthia was a mere child when Fae, her own brother to be precise, killed her adoptive parents. It called Adam to her, because he was her familiar. That event also made her one of the best Enforcers the Guild had ever seen. Olivia was sent the Spokane Guild when her mother died during childbirth; her father was an Archangel. Adrian, he's the one whose blood healed you, was Synthia's boyfriend at one time, and Adam's best friend, but Ryder made him an offer for power, and he took it. He's a vampire, like Vlad, who I understand you met at one of Lucian's clubs. So you see, we're all misfits," he said. "The thing is, Lena, we've all been mislabeled and misunderstood, and we survived. We're not here to hurt you, or try to figure you out. We're willing to help if you need it."

I watched as Lucian came in through the front door, as if he'd sensed my discomfort, and our eyes locked. He turned to the tall demon-fae, or whatever the hell he was, and growled from deep in his chest.

"You're making her uncomfortable, Ristan," he warned, his eyes turning angry as he lowered his head in a slight tilt.

"I'm just letting her know that she's not alone. We're not here to hurt her," he replied; his strange eyes moved to mine and then he vanished.

"I brought some groceries," Lucian said, nodding to the bag in his hand.

"You've been bringing me food," I whispered as I exhaled. Great, I was a fucking charity case. "Thank you."

"Don't thank me, Lena, I have my own reasons for needing you well-fed," he whispered with a wicked grin on his lips. "How's the pain from ignoring that hunger?"

"It's fine," I growled, but it wasn't. I already needed him again, and it was becoming down right embarrassing.

CHAPTER
thirty-eight

Lucian

I stood on the balcony, watching as the Fae continued to come and go from the property surrounding Lena's cottage; none of them showed signs of giving up anytime soon. She'd kicked me out right after I'd kicked Ristan out, but at least I knew she had food. The thought of her being alone and starving was something that made my insides twist. She'd remained inside that cottage for a couple of days now, locked up to avoid the Fae who persistently waited for her. It had given me time to consider my next move, as well as giving her time to crave what we had between us. I could get sex anywhere, but it wouldn't contain the chemistry that was alive between Lena and I. Perhaps that's why I felt a pull to her.

"Lucy, time to start 'splaining," Ristan said as he sifted in with the Horde King and his pet hellhound, Zahruk, close behind him.

"I don't have to explain her to you," I growled, knowing they weren't leaving until they figured out why so many un-hosted demons were converging on this place. I knew it because I would have done the same thing in their place. Demons are deadly, but the sheer numbers amassing here at the moment was something they wouldn't let go.

"Then explain why her cottage is swarming with demons trying to get in," Ryder amended, his golden eyes locking with mine in silent challenge.

"Ask them, Ryder," I mumbled, noting the lights in the cottage being extinguished as she moved through it, slowly blowing out candles.

"The type of demons swarming this area can't speak without a host, and Gods forbid they take one," he growled. "Something is going on, besides what we can obviously see."

"Magdalena was abandoned by her coven, why?" Ristan asked, changing the subject. I debated how much I should disclose to them about her. As much as I despised admitting to any fault or weakness, I would more than likely need their help this time and unless they fully understood what was at stake, I wouldn't get them on board.

"Because when her magic came online, she wasn't with her coven, nor was she supposed to be awakened. She wasn't selected for the Awakening. When she wasn't selected, she came to me at the Metaline Falls club," I said, smirking with the memory of her nervousness, even as she kicked the serving girl out. "The coven hangs on to their archaic rituals, and they have three steps that are followed to the letter. The first step is being chosen by the ancestors who are ritualistically brought back to choose which witch is ready to handle the power and magic. The second one is attending the ritual of awakening the magic. During that ceremony, they do another ritual that breaks the curse that limits their magic until they are of age and have been selected. Lastly, they go through the Harvest, which is to ensure that the next generation is created from the best bloodlines. Lena wasn't chosen by the dead to receive her powers, but she did. She was in the abbey when they began the ritual to break the curse. She wasn't among those who were selected; the ritual should have failed with her, but she managed to obtain her powers."

"You left out the Harvest, and the part where you fucked her, and she could be carrying your child," Ryder injected.

"I can't create children," I replied, noting his wince as he probably thought about his own children. Unlike him, I didn't want children. This world was a fucked up place, and my enemies were too many to add a child into the equation anyway.

"Is that so?" he asked, his eyes slowly moved to Synthia, watching her in the distance as she laughed at something Adrian said.

"That doesn't bother you, his constant eye-fucking of your woman?" I asked, noting he tensed ever so slightly, giving away that he wasn't immune to it.

"She's done with him, and I keep her well sated," he announced, his eyes glowing with the hunger his breed was known for. Fucking kept them fed; they fucked, a lot. If humans ate as much as the Fae fucked, they would be obese. "Killing him isn't an option; she'd hate me for it."

"Is that a job offer?" I asked, watching as his head

shook a negative answer. "Didn't think so; she's a weakness, one your enemies won't hesitate to use against you."

"Magdalena is yours," he said, giving me his full attention. "Is that why those demons are around her, even now?"

"She's not a weakness, she's just something to pass time with," I answered harshly. "If she knew who I really was, she'd run. If she knew why I was here, she'd fight me. She'd lose, but Lena would try her best until she forced my hand. It's bred into her genetics, through hundreds of years of bloodlines."

"Elaborate," Ryder said.

"To know the ending, you need to understand the beginning. Over ten thousand years ago, another was in charge of holding the seal. Think of the seal as a key, one that unlocks everything. It was created with the best of intentions; however, humans have an apt saying about roads to hell being paved with good intentions. The creation of the seal didn't turn out as expected and it was discovered that it would bring hell, heaven, Faery and every other world into this one. It would be an apocalypse, one so cataclysmic that no would survive.

"The first holder, or rather host of the seal, thought he could find love with a succubus, but she knew what he held within his soul. She used him to bring forth a child. The seal was released from him when he created life, a life she manipulated and twisted to bring forth chaos. Before the seal could realize its true purpose, the Gods were able to reclaim it and restore order. They then took the seal and placed it in a box, although if that box was ever opened, it would create a new seal holder, per se.

"I was selected to be the keeper of the seal and I

brought it with me when left the Underworld. When I first came here, it was to collect the souls of witches, to help power a ritual that would destroy the seal. The seal is too dangerous to exist and I looked for centuries for a way to eradicate it. Now that I had a viable plan to get rid of it once and for all, I just needed to put it into action.

"I located a large coven just outside of Aberdeen, Scotland, one that was strong; the bloodlines were powerful as they descended from the first witch created by Hecate. In the midst of the ignorance and hatred of the time and witch trials that were spawned from it, they stood strong and were a force to be reckoned with. That's when I met her.

"Katarina appeared to be pure of heart, untainted by greed as most of the others in her coven were. Where they wanted power, she just wanted to live and thrive. She was the most intriguing creature I had ever met, and eventually I started courting her. She never took from me, never asked for anything. I admit that I fell in love with her; she was everything to me," I whispered, hating that even now the emotions made a twinge of regret tighten my heart. "I was going to explain what I was to her, bind her to me; make her immortal. I never got the chance. Her coven discovered enough about me to figure out what kind of threat I posed to them and the games began. Over a period of weeks, they turned her against me and she changed. I didn't understand at the time what was going on, the change in her demeanor, how she was almost frightened to be around me and was forcing herself to stay.

"Understandably, I was curious and suspicious of her behavior. Being in love with her didn't change my purpose. I needed the power her coven would provide. I never stopped trying to identify the ones who held enough power that we could reap for our cause. In the end, not even love could stop me from my end goal, but then I had a bigger threat to worry about.

"One night, as I watched them, I found the coven performing a ritual I'd never seen before. As I watched the ritual play out, I realized that the spells had been designed to try and destroy me. They discovered that night the foolishness of their actions as I killed Katarina's brother mid-chant. He was the high priest of the coven and as we interrogated the rest of those who participated in that madness, I discovered what they had learned about me, and what Katarina had been up to. Stringing me along, keeping me occupied while they worked on a way to destroy me.

"As I slaughtered them, I learned that she was at my house, waiting to complete the curses her coven had set in motion; waiting to curse me back to where she'd thought I had come from, and the box containing the seal was well-hidden, but she was a strong witch. I am sure it sensed her power and called to her, or she discovered it through her magic. Doesn't matter how she found it, but she did.

"The moment she opened it, she released it into herself. The seal was never intended for a human host; they're not strong enough. I finally found her as she wandered around the forest that surrounded the meadow we'd once lain in for hours, making love…Her mind was fractured by the seal, and as I began listening to her words, I noted she was cursing me. I think she knew she wouldn't survive the seal's possession, and she was using what little time she had left, trying to complete the coven's curse.

"At the time, I was enraged by her betrayal, devastated at what I knew she had become, and there was nothing I could do to save her. I confronted her, and she admitted that she and her coven were sending me back to hell. The fools had no idea that their silly curses couldn't keep me there, and I made damn sure she knew it. She changed tactics and cursed herself to be reborn until she killed me. I was angry and amended her curse so that I would always be able to find her and the seal. After I killed her, I returned her body to the coven members who still lived, but I'd modified some of the details of the memories of those who bore witness and helped Katarina and her family. Unfortunately, due to their actions, I had to abandon the original plan and try to find a way to destroy the seal under the changed circumstances.

"You have to understand; the seal is sentient. It's not like the relics that you are looking for. It has its own awareness and we discovered, after it passed from the first host, that it has become evil and thrives on destruction and chaos. It wants to be freed. Killing Katarina, I had hoped would be the end of the seal as it could only be sustained by an immortal being.

"I discovered when Katarina reincarnated the first time and came into her powers about sixty years later, that the seal is attached to her soul. It found the one thing within her that was immortal, and clung to it. Every time Katarina is reborn, the seal has the opportunity to awaken and as long as I can find and kill her reincarnation before she comes into her full power, the seal remains dormant. If I fail to find her before she reaches her full powers and the seal awakens, I may not be able to stop them from unleashing hell to our worlds. Up until the last reincarnation, the reincarnations seemed to arrive every fifty or sixty years or so. This makes it very hard to manage as it isn't predictable. Right now, I know she's been reborn again and she was one of the witches that just came into her powers. This is why I am here; I have to find which one she is, and end this."

"So you can kill her, again?" Ryder asked. "You loved her."

"I love her, still," I laughed coldly. "The original was the love of my life. She cursed me, and every time I find her again, she tries to find new ways to try and destroy me. With every reincarnation she gets faster, smarter. After I killed her first reincarnation, the coven moved on me. Fled the country. And when I felt the pull again that told me she had been reborn, I had a bitch of a time finding them again. I finally located them outside Port Royal, Nova Scotia.

"Around this time, I realized the connection to her maturity and coming into her full power as the trigger for the seal. I couldn't risk her coming into her powers before I figured out which one she was or where she was if they ran again, so the idea of the Awakening was, shall we say, 'suggested' to the high priestess. She thought she was protecting the coven from irresponsible young witches that might be unwise and attract monsters; she had no idea that was giving me time to stop a far bigger monster."

"Do you love her every time?" Ristan asked, his eyes narrowing as he considered exactly how fucked up the whole situation was.

"No. There have been a few I grew fond of or cared for; however, I can't really say I have loved any of them," I mumbled absently. They weren't my Katarina. She had been lost to me the moment she'd turned against me. I'd never allowed myself to truly care for them, knowing I would be the one to end their lives and some of their deaths had been downright sadistic, depending on how badly they betrayed me at the end. Betrayal wasn't something I had any tolerance for."

"And yet you continue to kill them, even though you care for them?"

"If you had to choose between Olivia and the entire existence of Faery and any other world connected to yours, what would you choose, Ristan?" I asked without judgement.

"I wouldn't choose," he said, but I knew he already had.

"You choose the many, even if you have to sacrifice what you love," I replied. "I didn't choose to do what I have because it was easy. The seal was my responsibility and it was released while under my watch. Until I can find a way to destroy the seal without accidentally 'turning the key' and releasing the horrors, I will have to keep finding and killing her reincarnations. Another thing to consider is what would happen if another creature figures out what is going on with the seal and got to the reincarnation first. I remember what happened when the succubus twisted the seal; you have no idea the chaos the seal can create, much less the seal trapped in the form of a corruptible human with the power of the witch."

"And the demons around Lena?" he asked.

"They are attracted to power that happens around the time of the Awakening. The coven had a few girls go missing before the Awakening and once the big event happens, the coven holes up in the abbey and the demons can't get to the young witches. After the Harvest is over and they are done breeding, the elders will train the new witches on how to use their powers to defend themselves. With Lena being pushed out of the abbey, they think she's easy prey."

"Are you sure they don't think she's the seal? What

if word got out about the seal being released?" Zahruk rubbed his chin thoughtfully.

"That's doubtful. Until today, only a few outside of my own people know what happened and I trust those few implicitly. I don't believe she is Katarina; she failed all the tests that I use to find her reincarnations and I would have sensed her essence by now, especially with her powers in play. I will have to wait for the witches to be released from the abbey to know for sure which one is the reincarnation. Lena's a welcome distraction from knowing that soon, I'll kill Katarina and disappear from the lives of this coven until I feel the pull again. I am trying to think of ways to keep tabs on the coven, just in case they disappear again. The last time they abandoned their homes, it took quite a bit of time and resources to find them again and I have other responsibilities to see to. I can't wait around for her to be reborn again and I really haven't been able to spare the manpower to leave a spy behind, although I may have to consider it."

"You said you've modified the coven's memories and made suggestions to the high priestess before. Can't you just do it again and prevent them from running?" Ryder was trying to be so reasonable over something he really had no fucking clue about and I chuckled dryly.

"That's part of the problem; I can make suggestions and I can tweak their perception of events, however the strongest ones, over time, will always break the conditioning and when their memories come back, they have trouble determining reality from the implant and invariably, that's when they run."

"I no longer wonder why you are so cold," Ristan said; his eyes drifted to Olivia and I was sure he was considering what he'd do if he lived in my shoes. "I thought Tèrran demons were ruled by Lucifer, what does he think about them coming here, not to mention what happened to the seal?"

"Lucifer doesn't know about the seal and I am sure he is the one sending many of them here," I replied honestly. "He's grasping for things that he shouldn't be and after what he pulled the other night, I think he needs a reminder of who I am."

"I thought you were his right-hand man?" Ryder asked carefully. His keen, golden eyes watched me for a sign, but found none.

"I am not one of his demons and neither are my people. Rumors are easy to spread, but then you already knew that, *Dark Prince*."

"Then who the hell are you?" Ristan asked, his eyes moving to Spyder, who was stepping out of the shadows from my connecting bedroom.

"Pray this world never needs to ask that question, demon," I mumbled as a light turned on inside the cottage.

"The hellhounds have arrived and are patrolling, Lucian; Lena is protected," Spyder said as his eyes moved to Zahruk's, who had inched closer to Ryder.

"Wait, you are controlling hellhounds?" Ristan asked, his eyes growing large.

"Indeed," I replied, turning to look at Ryder. "Don't get in my way on this one," I said.

"You have to kill the woman you love, on an endless loop to protect worlds," he mused, his golden eyes expressing his disbelief while concealing his keen intellect. "That has to take a toll on you. Is there anything else that can be done to remove it?"

"If there was any other way, don't you think I would have taken it by now?" I laughed soundlessly. "Now you know why I am the way I am, but considering the choice, you'd be strong enough to do the same. Had Katarina known what she'd done, she would have taken her own life; unfortunately, after the seal attached itself to her, she was struggling between bouts of insanity and lucidity as she tried to resist it. Katarina was a powerful witch and I had to make the decision for her before the seal could grow any stronger, and with her being human, I didn't know if it would kill her or drive her insane. Killing her was merciful at that point."

"I understand why you do it, Lucian, but I know that the Gods enjoy tricks, they always place a safeguard on things; you just have to figure out how to get past it and unlock the puzzle pieces."

I laughed grimly as Spyder snorted at how simple he made it sound, and Layton moved onto the balcony with his hair freed and wild as it moved down his back in an array of different colors.

"We have a problem; seems someone started trouble inside the abbey. The coven is divided; half want to come for Lena, the other half is moving to kick the first half out of the coven. It's a cluster fuck of witches bickering."

"That's not my problem," I replied.

"It is when Helen was just seen with Lucifer, plotting to kill Lena," he replied, already reaching behind him to redo his hair into that fucking bun. "Told you that bitch was poison—and her daughter? She just agreed to become Lucifer's bride."

"I guess he left out the part of eternal hell as her honeymoon?" I smirked, imaging the little princess in hell; Cassidy wouldn't survive it, but then not many could.

"Lucian, the high priestess's head was the rest of his price for the deal," Layton continued, and I flinched.

"I guess it's time to send Lucifer back to where he belongs," I whispered, enjoying the darkness that swirled inside of me. "Ryder, take your people home. It's not a request. You are not part of this dispute; you have your hands full with your own conflict."

"You think I'm leaving the fate of the worlds up to you?" he countered.

I smiled, letting him see the blue hellfire that swirled behind my eyes. "Don't say I didn't warn you, Ryder."

"I'll take it into consideration, but Synthia won't leave the demons to overrun the humans, so neither can I."

"Women are trouble, but then I'm sure you're aware of it," I replied, watching the cottage as yet another light turned on. She was having problems sleeping, or she was fighting off the need to fuck. "If your woman and her uncle plan on helping Lena with her powers, you may want to try a different tactic; camping in her yard won't get her out; Lena is different. She doesn't move towards people; she moves away from them."

"Synthia won't let her be alone, and she shouldn't be. If what you say is true, that girl's in danger," he argued.

"You think I'd let them get that close to her?" I smiled.

"I think you need more eyes to find the seal, and you'll need our help soon enough," Ryder said before he sifted, taking his men with him.

"Pray that isn't the case, because if I do, this world is heading for something that will change it forever," I mumbled as I turned to look Spyder. "The coven needs to be protected as well, go."

"You know we can't enter the main sanctuary of the abbey," he said, watching me. "Lucian, Lena is the most powerful witch of the coven that we've seen so far. You need to figure out if she's Katarina; maybe you're too close to her to see it, but we do."

"Is that what you think?" I asked carefully, noting he had doubt in his eyes as well. "I think I have spilled enough innocent blood over the centuries; I find myself not willing to spill more. It won't stop us from our other responsibilities, though, nor will we cease the killing of those whose souls are bound for hell for their deeds. The bitch buried in the yard murdered children and deserved to meet her fate. There will always be more like her. If Lena turns out to be Katarina, I will not falter the course. I'll take her someplace where it can be done properly."

CHAPTER
thirty-nine

-Magdalena

Smoke billowed from the village; thick black plumes of it filled the otherwise beautiful sky. My hands were covered in blood, my dress as well. Tears slid down my cheeks as I stumbled over a body, and fell to the ground beside it. I struggled to get back up, my hands slipping over the blood that was mixing with the mud.

"Get up," a woman said; her green eyes watched me carefully. *"Get up now. You need to listen to me."*

"What happened here?" I whispered through the pain in my throat.

"Death came for us," she whispered; her hands smoothed her dress, and bother her hands and dress were covered in blood. I looked back down my own dress,*

noting the blood spatters were an exact match. "I need for you to cast a spell; you have to repeat the words after me. Hurry, there isn't much time!"

"Repeat what?" I asked, watching as she looked around, her own eyes full of unshed tears.

"The curse is blocking you; you have to say the words with me before it's too late."

What? "What curse?" I questioned as I slipped again in the mud, and cried out as my backside landed on a rock.

"That's not important," she muttered as she reached down to help me to my feet. The moment I was on steadier ground, she pulled me with her to a clearing. "Say the spell, it's the only way to save your coven; the curse won't let you remember until he is ready to close the trap, but we can fix that."

"I'm what?" I asked, wiping my hands on the dress as she did the same.

"You did this to yourself," she whispered absently. "We did this."

"Did what?" I asked, wondering where the hell she'd escaped from. As far as I knew, there were no looney bins around Metaline Falls. "You're not making sense."

"Say the words!" she cried. Her eyes welled with blood and a few blood tears slipped down her cheeks.

"That isn't right," I muttered, watching as she shook her head and her eyes gained focus and clarity.

"Undo the curse that claims the mind; remove it from this space and time. Open my mind from the chains that bind, that let me see through space and time. Hear my call to here and now, release the curse that holds me bound. Let me see what he's erased, give me back my mind in this time and place."

I looked at her, and her eyes once again filled with blood, and turned black. I stepped back, but then she was there, her nails digging into my flesh as she screamed for me to repeat the words. It hurt, and her desperation shook me from my stupor.

"Let go!" I screamed and pushed against her.

"Listen to her," another woman said, and then the field was filled with women. All of them were talking at once, and I covered my ears as their voices painfully assaulted me.

"Listen to her, or share our fate," they whispered in hushed tones that made my ears feel like nails were scraping across a chalkboard.

"You must remember, you must free us! He comes for you, he's close. Can't you feel it? The death he brings?" they said in unison as they too, began to bleed from their eyes. "Find the grimoires, and undo the curse, you must! It's the only way we can be set free to rest."

They began chanting, even as more and more people arrived in the field, each joining the chant. They were dead, all of them. I looked around, noting the blue of their lips, and the black veins that rose and fanned out like lacy spider webs through their delicate porcelain skin. They hadn't looked dead to begin with, but with each word they chanted, they began to look more like decaying corpses.

"Say it! We don't have long," the first one said, her eyes watching me with terror. "We've only enough power to do this now, you must! If you fail, everything is lost."

"Fine," I whispered through my terror as I watched one of the women fall to the ground, and nothing but dust remained where she had fallen.

"Undo the curse…that claims the mind; remove it from this…space and time. Open my mind from the chains

that bind, that let me see through space and...time. Hear my call to here and now, release the curse that holds me bound. Let me see what he's erased, give me back my mind in this time and place..."

They all started chanting it and I could feel the magic of the spell working inside of me. Heat and pain lanced through me, forcing me to my knees. I coughed up blood, and with each word, I started to disintegrate with them. I cried out, looking around as smoke from the burning village continued to rise to the sky; I could smell the pungent scent of certain herbs that I was sure were forbidden by the coven to be used in witchcraft rituals.

"Stop, stop it!" I screamed as hands touched me, sending memories into my mind. "No! I don't want that!" I sobbed as one after another sliced through me with nails and sharp bones. Their skin was decomposing as they touched me.

"Find our grimoires, you must. They hold clues to what he's done, and how to undo the curse, sweet child. You fear us, but we are a part of you," the first woman said with her eyes now clear of blood. "You're our last hope, this ends with you."

"What does that mean?" I asked, even as I felt the scratching of bones through my flesh.

"Wake up, Lena," she said softly, her hands touching my face.

I shoved her away and started to run from her. There were ashes everywhere. The sky was thick with smoke, and my bare feet slipped through the mud and ash as I ran from the woman who seemed to be gliding as she chased me. As if she was straight out of a horror movie.

"Lena!" she shouted.

"Magdalena, wake up!"

I sat up in bed. My body was covered in a sheen of sweat and my eyes were wet from crying. I looked around, looking into my mother's eyes as she touched my cheek comfortingly.

"Lena," she whispered as she hugged me to her.

"Mom, what are you doing here?" I whispered even as I wiped my eyes.

"I left the coven," she admitted. "If they won't accept you, then I won't accept them. Grandma is here as well," she replied as she wiped the hair from my face. "I didn't throw you away. I needed to stay long enough to make sure Helen didn't succeed in stripping your powers."

"She can actually do that?" I asked, still shaking off the nightmare.

"With the coven's support, it's possible, but Tabitha has moved against her, and put her in her place," Grandma said as she moved into the room, her eyes wide as she hiked a thumb over her shoulder, indicating the front of the house. "Seems like you attracted Fae, and they've taken up residence in our front yard."

"They're with some witches from the Guild," I said wrinkling my nose.

"What?" my grandmother whispered, wringing her hands. "Magdalena, no," she mumbled. "How? How did they find you, or did you bring them here?"

"I didn't bring them here, and it's a long story. Why are you here?" I asked, hating that they were. I was happy that they had chosen me over coven politics, but leaving the coven had severe consequences. "Please tell me you can go back."

"Why would we?" Grandma asked, her blue eyes smiling. "Missy, you're our blood. What happened with Benjamin happened because we couldn't help him," she said softly. "You don't think we wanted to? We've been a part of this coven since we were born, but this happened to you because of Helen using the coven laws to her own advantage and not because of anything you did. We made a choice, Lena. We chose you; our bloodline will continue to flourish with or without the coven. Fitzgeralds always stick together."

"But you shouldn't have had to choose, Helen doesn't own the coven," I replied, shivering as something inside of me stirred. My mind was replaying something from the dream, along with a chant.

"Lena, are you well?" my mother asked, her hand moving to my forehead before I could reply. "You're feverish," she said, already removing the cloak she wore and heading into the kitchen as I followed. She smiled as I groaned at the types of herbs she was selecting out of the cupboard as grandma started the stove.

"I'm fine, I promise. We have bigger problems, like the Fae camped out in the front yard?"

"They can't come in here," Grandma said, as she joined my mother in breaking up the herbs and packing them into the diffusers.

"One already did, and I'm not drinking that," I replied. Oh, hell no. Grandma was badass in the kitchen, she could cook a lot of things, but she'd also several of the recipes for the nasty-tasting potions and tonics we'd sold at the store.

"No?" she laughed, and my mom shook her head with a soft smile. "You're so much like your mother was at your age. I think 'no' was her favorite word."

"No offense, Grandma, but tonics are really not your strong suit," I mumbled, even though I was smiling. They weren't willing to leave me on my own, and they'd come for me, after all. "Will Kendra be safe at the abbey?" I asked, watching as their smiles faltered, giving them away.

"Kendra will be fine, she's a Fitzgerald," they replied together, as if they'd rehearsed it.

"And us, will we be fine?"

"Guild witches and the Fae are camping together in the front yard, and demons are hunting us; Lena, nothing is going to be fine ever again. We will survive this, though, we are Fitzgeralds. We haven't come this far to be taken down by a few demons, or a Warlock from the Guild."

"You guys didn't talk to them?" I asked, and watched as my mother blushed. "Mom?"

"The older gentlemen seemed willing to talk, but we had no idea who he or the others were. We used a protection spell to get into the cottage. Oh, and by the way, someone has put extra rune stones around the cottage. Is there something you want to tell us?" she asked, her light blue eyes held mine and I realized she already knew. Kendra must have been able to see through my eyes, as I had through hers. Shit.

"I went through Harvest, with Lucian," I replied.

"Going through it, Lena, you're not done. Not until the moon phase is complete. In a week or so, we'll test you for pregnancy."

"I'm on birth control," I replied to my mother.

"You think they didn't consider that maybe someday there would be a better way to prevent pregnancy?" Grandmother responded. "The Harvest bypasses any herbs or medicine, the same with ridding the uterus of unwanted pregnancy. It's a spell, Lena, one that ensures you conceive a child. Even if a witch takes measures to prevent it, they wouldn't be able to counteract the spell.

The Harvest and the Awakening spells are performed with very strong magic, and the help of the entire coven. No birth control could override that."

"What?" I whispered as my jaw dropped. "No, no, just no!" I replied. "I can't do that, have Lucian's baby, not me. He accused me of being sent by the coven to steal his sperm!"

They laughed, as if it was funny. It wasn't funny. I'd told him I was on birth control, and then he jumped me a bunch of times and I'd jumped him a bunch of times! There'd been no protection from pregnancy! He'd even asked if I was on the pill, and I'd told him yes!

"He chose to sleep with a witch in the midst of Harvest. I am sure he knew the risk; he's been around our coven long enough to know what the goal of the spell was, so he shouldn't be surprised when a baby arrives, and if he told you otherwise…" Grandma made a tsking sound with her tongue. "Either way, it's a good match, a very powerful one."

I wasn't listening. For the first time in my entire life, I was praying for my period, literally willing Mother Nature to knock at my door. This wasn't happening to me, I was having nightmares, and strange dreams, and now this! I looked out the window, watching as the sun rose above the mountains.

"I had a really strange dream," I whispered, and explained it to them. Every single detail, and I watched as they shook their heads.

"Considering that you've always had nightmares," Mom whispered, "it could just be more, but Kendra told me she's been having nightmares, and many of the newly Awakened witches said they'd been having nightmares, too, and just like you, they forgot them soon as they woke up."

"Yes, but Mom," I replied, watching as the sun continued to rise. "I'm awake, and this one I remember."

CHAPTER
forty

The sun had just set when I saw the Fae disappear and decided it was the perfect chance to get to Lucian's house without giving them any opportunity to ask me any questions or offer more help.

As I got closer, I noted his house no longer showed any sign of the violent sex-fest Lucian and I had that tore apart much of the lower level of his home; it was as if magical fairies had fixed it, which realistically could be the case. I knocked once and waited; when there was no answer, I knocked again.

When he finally opened his door, I paused; words got lost as I took in his naked chest and sleepy gaze. His hair was tousled, and his jeans hung low on his sexy hips. That pesky happy trail made words near impossible to form.

"Can we talk?" I babbled after forcefully removing my eyes from his sleek muscles and seductive body. The man was made by the Gods, he had to be. He was sex incarnate, and it was the only thing my body seemed to crave when he was near.

"You sure you don't want to use that mouth to do something else?" His voice was a sexy rumble, and his hand slowly moved down his chest to where his cock was hardening. Obviously his body craved mine as much as mine craved his.

"Lucian," I whispered as a blush colored my cheeks and my eyes grew hooded from the lust that hit me like a Mack truck. "We really need to talk."

I couldn't think around him, but I had to be honest with him. He wasn't going to be happy when I told him the truth, considering how pissed off he'd been when he'd thought I had tried to steal his sperm. I chewed my bottom lip as I considered the best way to inform him that I may or may not be carrying his child.

I felt like a thief, and the mere idea was making me sick. He deserved my honesty, and I needed a few answers of my own. Like had he slept with Elaine when she'd left his house before I'd shown up and Lucian and I wrecked it? Had he known that we had an audience when we had sex at his club?

"We can talk after we fuck," he said, already pulling me inside the entryway.

"I didn't come here to fuck…" I paused as I entered his house to find Layton and Bane seated at the table with their phones in their hands.

"Aw shit, should we make popcorn, or save the china?" Layton asked with a cocky grin as he took in the soft blue summer dress I'd worn, and my bare feet. "Come on baby, let's see you lose that inhibition again, last time was fucking hot. What do you think we should call the video, Bane? Witches Gone Wild?"

"Leave us," Lucian said, his eyes commanding obedience from the two. He held his hand out for me when they were slow to do as he'd demanded. "Come," he ordered, the single word holding more meaning than it should have.

I hesitantly placed my hand in his as he led me up the stairs and away from the curious eyes of his men. Once we were inside his room, all thoughts of talking disappeared and I had to seriously focus to make myself get the words out.

"The pill didn't work, Lucian," I stammered, "I found out that the spell the coven casts during the Harvest doesn't just make our sex drive go into overdrive. It also makes anything we do to prevent pregnancy useless. I didn't know they did that. I honestly just wanted you, to be with you," I whispered as he released my hand and turned to face me.

"You came here to tell me you could be pregnant with my child?" he asked. His posture had changed to a guarded look that made my stomach sink. "Is that what you're telling me?" he continued softly.

"I'm telling you it could be a possibility. You deserve to know; I owe you that much. My mother and grandmother explained it to me today."

He nodded but he didn't seem worried in the least that I could be carrying his child. I started to say something but he stopped me with a jerk of his head and a sexy grin that made the butterflies in my belly swirl and take flight.

"I'm not an idiot, Lena," he said after a moment of awkward silence had passed. "You don't have to be worried about being pregnant with my child, though; I can't have them."

"But in the club…"

"If you'd known I couldn't make pretty little babies, would it have changed your mind about coming to me?" he asked.

"No," I mumbled. "I told you when I first met you that I don't want children," I replied carefully. "I wanted to be with you since the moment you kissed me outside the main house. I don't understand; at the club you were angry at me. You accused me of stealing your sperm."

"I accused you of trying to," he amended. "The coven had been pushing for me to attend the Harvest because of my bloodline; I wouldn't put it past some of those elders to send someone to accomplish their end goal. I made it painstakingly clear that I wanted nothing to do with the Harvest. Yet you came into your powers in my bed, so you can see where I'm justified in assuming they knew where you were."

"You called me a liar outside my door after you were fully aware that I hadn't lied to you."

"I wanted inside your house; it pissed you off enough that you opened the door, didn't it?" he smiled.

"Did you fuck Elaine before I, uh, showed up and destroyed your house?" I asked hesitantly.

"No, she tried to take advantage of us being apart to slither her way back into my bed. I was kicking her out of my house when you saw us together."

"At the club, were you aware of us being watched?" I accused, feeling the anger all over again that came from being humiliated.

"No, I was too busy to care. I had no idea she turned the glass, nor do I care if they watched me claim what is mine. I couldn't give a fuck if they watched me tear apart your sweet flesh and make it mine. I don't give a fuck if you care, because everyone in that crowd now knows you are mine. I'm not embarrassed about what we did, are you?"

"No," I responded honestly. "Still, I would have been a lot happier if that first time would have been private. If I wanted them to watch me get fucked, I'd have requested it."

"Good to know," he smiled as he looked down to where my breasts were heaving with my effort to expel the questions that had eaten away at me. "Miss me?" he asked, his hands slipping around my waist as he pulled me closer to his massive body, and the erection that was now proudly tenting his jeans. When I didn't answer him, he growled. "I asked a question, I expect an answer," he demanded.

"Yes," I answered and moaned as I felt his hard cock press against my belly.

"Good, because I've barely been able to think of anything other than getting you back into my bed ever since you left it," he growled as he pulled at the ties of my dress's shoulder straps. "Are you ready to give me control, Magdalena? Submit to me," he whispered as he lowered his mouth to kiss my naked shoulder.

His hands pulled on the dress, until it pooled on the ground at my feet. He stepped away from me and I had to fight the urge to move closer to him. The thin silky panties I wore were sheer, and did little to hide how wet he'd already made me.

"I asked you a question," he whispered as he began to slip from his jeans, exposing that he was once again commando, and his massive cock was hard and ready to give me what we both knew I needed.

"Yes," I replied, and waited to see what he would do with my answer.

"Get on the bed, and touch yourself for me," he ordered, and I hesitated, which earned me a swat on my ass that pulled a hiss from my lungs. "Do as I told you or you will be punished for disobedience, little witch."

I silently moved to the bed and crawled onto it, resting on the stack of pillows as I allowed my legs to bend at the knees while I slipped my hand into my panties. He smiled and made a tsking sound with his tongue.

"Get rid of the panties; I want to see your flesh as you finger it for me," he ordered, and I absently followed his command. Once I'd pulled them off, I tossed them at him and watched as he caught them and smiled victoriously. "Relax, and show me how you've pleasured yourself in my absence," he ordered. He'd only been gone a few days, or so I'd thought. It was hard to know since I'd been hiding in the cottage, but I hadn't missed the fact that he hadn't come to my bed. I had found plenty of release by my own hand, and somehow, he knew it.

I once again let my knees fall apart, giving him a seductive view of my glistening flesh. Just the thought of fucking him made me wet with need. I rubbed my fingers gently over my clitoris and rocked my hips to create friction. He ignored it, which caused me to hesitate as he gave me his back as he moved towards the other side of the room.

"I didn't tell you to stop," he rumbled, and I started to rub my clit again as I watched him open the door to his closet and disappear into it. When he reemerged, he was carrying a black box, larger than a shoe box, but it piqued my curiosity as he set it on the bed and retrieved a chair. He didn't touch the box again as he sat before the bed, watching my leisurely exploration of my pussy. "Good girl," he crooned as I slipped a finger inside and pulled it out slowly.

"I need you," I replied, watching as he stood up and sat on the bed as he pulled the box closer.

"Not yet," he replied as he leaned over and moved my hand away from my pussy as his tongue slipped out to clean the mess I'd made. "First, you are going to learn a few things. Like how it feels to be filled," he said hoarsely. He pulled out a little jeweled plug and smiled when I shivered. "I want you to turn over onto your stomach, stick your ass in the air, and spread your legs for me; show me what's mine, little one."

I did as he said, as I had a pretty good idea of what he planned to do to me. I moaned as he pushed the shiny plug into my pussy, using it to fuck me gently as he kissed the inside of my thighs. His mouth slowly moved to my naked flesh as he sank the jeweled plug deep into my pussy.

"Such a greedy pussy; it begs to be fucked, doesn't it?" he growled as his tongue licked a pattern around the plug as he held me open for his slow seduction.

"I need your cock, now," I growled in response and cried out as his hand slapped my naked ass, creating a deep burn as his other worked the plug.

"My rules, Lena, and I have no plans of letting you come anytime soon," he replied as he pulled out the plug and pressed it against my ass. "Relax, or this will hurt," he ordered.

It was easier said than done, and we both knew it. I felt it press against my ass, even as he pushed at the entrance. It was uncharted territory and the more he pushed, the more it burned. It didn't deter him, nor did my groans of pain as he pushed it all the way inside. I whimpered as it filled my ass, burning with a foreign sensation that bordered on pain and pleasure.

"Good girl," he crooned as he stepped back, taking in the sight of my ass filled with his jewel-tipped plug.

I wasn't sure I liked it, or if it was because it felt wrong allowing him to touch me there. It was something I'd never even considered doing until now. I was still on my knees with my ass presented to him when he moved closer, using his fingers to fill my pussy. The combination was heady and explosive. I moaned as he filled my core with two fingers as he pushed against the plug.

"You're already so close to coming, aren't you, Lena?" he asked, and I noted that he was using my name, a lot. It probably had something to do with taking control over me.

"It hurts," I whispered as he pulled the plug out halfway and pushed it back inside.

"Imagine how it's going to feel when I fuck it for the first time?" he whispered, and pushed it back inside. He turned me over onto my back and pushed my legs apart. "I need you wet enough to fit me as well as the plug inside this tight body. I find that you make me lose control, something that shouldn't happen in *my* bedroom," he growled as he pulled out a pink silicone dildo, which was smaller than his own cock. "You like?" he asked, noting the color and smiling as he slapped it against my pussy. "It's the color of your flesh after I've fucked it. I saw it in the club's warehouse and had a bit of trouble thinking of anything besides pushing it inside your pretty pink pussy."

I moaned as he pushed it against my pussy and slipped it inside barely more than an inch. I felt unnaturally full, and ached for him to remove the other. He leaned over, licking and sucking on my nipple and allowing his teeth to graze the raised peak as he pushed the dildo inside me until I was full.

"Fuck!" I yelled as I tried to lift myself up, only to be pushed down hard as he began to move it inside of me. He was doing it achingly slow, and I rocked my hips to adjust to the fullness.

"That's it, my sweet girl, fuck it for me," he growled as he claimed my lips hungrily. His kiss consumed the pain the fullness created, turning it to pleasure as he used his toys to fuck me. When his mouth pulled away from mine, it lowered to my belly, kissing the sensitive flesh as he moved his mouth lower. The dildo started to vibrate and I cried out as my body began to tremble from the impending orgasm that he withheld from me. Every time I got too close to coming, he'd pull it out and watch me as I struggled to claim it for myself.

"Bastard," I seethed somewhere around the fifth failed orgasm, and he laughed huskily.

"I said I needed it wet, not sated. When you come, Lena, it will be with my cock buried in this sweet flesh. I would have preferred tying you up, putting a ball gag in that sweet mouth, and fucking you while you screamed around it, but you seem to undo me before I am ready. I find myself out of control, and in need of you before I should. This greedy little pussy needs to come, doesn't it?" he asked as he withdrew the dildo and shifted himself between my legs, rubbing and teasing his massive cock against my opening.

"So fucking wet," he growled as he pushed the large head of his cock inside and pulled it back out. "Beg for it," he demanded and I threw pride out the window, doing just as he'd ordered. I was on fire, and he was the one thing that could soothe the ache he'd created. "Good girl," he crooned, and I almost lost it as I convulsed with just his words.

He pushed inside of me and I moaned at the fullness, and the pain that rocked my body at being so full. I watched the pain on his face as he tried to force his massive cock into my wetness, but as much as he tried, he wouldn't fit with the jeweled plug in me at the same time. I could hear him grind his teeth as he struggled to push even more inside. Sweat beaded at the back of my neck as he lifted my legs and secured them around his hips, finding another inch buried in my tightness.

"Bloody hell, Lena, so fucking tight," he whispered breathlessly as he rocked his hips and found a tempo that allowed him to gradually fill me with the full length of him. I was crying out, screaming his name as my fingers scratched down his back as pain and pleasure fought to take precedence. It was painful to be this full, and yet I didn't want him to stop, didn't want him to remove the toy, either. I liked being dirty with him, being his sexy little plaything behind his bedroom door. He undid me, made me want things I never would have thought possible.

"Move," I begged as he tried to allow me time to adjust to the sheer magnitude of being fully filled this way. "Move, you bastard," I pleaded, and felt him trying to remove the plug. "No! Please, just move, make me yours, Lucian."

"You undo me," he whispered as his mouth found mine, even as he began to move inside of me.

I climaxed without warning, shattering to the stars as a kaleidoscope of colors exploded behind my eyelashes. The extra lubricant gave him more to work with and he attacked me with vigor, pushing my legs up as my head thrashed from side to side as sweat beaded at the back of my neck.

"So fucking beautiful," he crooned as he looked to

where our bodies were joined, and then without warning, he pulled out and removed the plug as he lay beside me, turning me onto my side as he entered my pussy again. "I just want you, nothing else this time, little one. Just you and your sweet noises as I fuck you," he whispered against my neck as he lifted my leg and filled me full of his cock.

His arms wrapped around me as he took me slowly, moving us around the bed into intimate positions that forced us to be slow and close. After a while, he pulled me on top of himself, and watched me come undone. He smiled and pinched my nipples hard. He came with me as I cried out his name; the combined orgasms rocked us until we were nothing but a mess of limbs tangled together, and then, we slept from the exertion of multiple releases.

Throughout the night he would wake and begin his sexual conquest of me again. It wasn't until the predawn hours slipped by that I came to the conclusion that getting any real sleep with him near wasn't an option. It was impossible because it wasn't just him waking me up for more; it was me waking him up to give me more. Together we were insatiable, driven by a need to get closer even though there was no possible way to accomplish it. This man was burrowing deep beneath my skin.

I left him in his bed and quietly dressed in the dress I'd arrived in, then headed to my own bed to be able to get some much-needed sleep as dawn broke over the ridge.

By 8 A.M., my entire world came to a halt and unraveled.

CHAPTER
forty-one

I awoke from a dead sleep to the sound of terrified screaming inside my head. I blinked, trying to dispel the sleepy fog that clouded my brain. I felt genuinely scared, and a sense of dread without understanding what was going on. I could hear Kendra, but looking around my small bedroom, I couldn't find any sign that she'd been here. I sat up and considered going back to sleep when something triggered the connection I shared with her, and my mind tried to make sense of what I was seeing.

I could feel her panic, her sense of fear and helplessness, which made no sense. Kendra was at the abbey, safe from anything that could hurt her.

"Lena, run and hide! They're hunting us; you have to hide," she whispered through trembling lips.

"Kendra, calm down," I whispered aloud, as if she was in the same room. My eyes tried to focus on the strange scene I was seeing through her. "What…" I shrieked as what I was seeing came into view, allowing me to take in the morbid details of hacked and dismembered bodies. Familiar faces with lifeless eyes stared back at me. I screamed hysterically as her panic and mine met and collided in sheer terror.

The windows rattled as I tried and failed to contain my emotions at what I was seeing. The abbey looked like it had been attacked, and she was hiding in the corner among the dead who had been indiscriminately slaughtered. It was just like a nightmare I'd had; only this time it was real. I didn't even pause to figure out how I knew I'd had the fucking nightmare; I couldn't, as I watched a monster rip one of the elders apart as Kendra screamed and gave away her position amongst the bodies.

"No! Run, Kendra, run!" I screamed, panic-stricken as I watched the creature approach her, even as a younger version of Lucian materialized in front of Kendra and slapped her as she screamed hysterically. I felt it all the way to my bones, as if it had been me instead of her who was being assaulted. "No! Leave her alone, oh God, no!" I could hear footsteps moving closer to me but I was no longer inside my bedroom, I was with her, watching as the horror unfolded.

The man had dark hair and indigo eyes, a shade lighter than Lucian's, but the runes and tattoos on his body looked the same. As if he'd slipped into a Lucian suit, just for this task. I wasn't sure how I knew it wasn't Lucian, only that it wasn't him. Details were off, such as the tattoos of the people on his arms, whose hands were covering the wrong parts of their faces. I'd spent all night learning every detail about his beautiful body and knew it wasn't him.

"Run! Dammit, fight, Kendra, fight him!" I screamed as I felt blow after blow land on her body as he hit her. I could taste blood, and feel the taint of evil as it filled the abbey. She slipped in blood and the creatures laughed at her, even as the Lucian wannabe pinned her to the blood-slick floor and smiled as he forced her legs open and revealed her state of undress from her recent encounter with her Harvest partner. "No, let her go!" I screamed as I jackknifed from the pain as she was assaulted. Pain ripped through me and I coughed and choked from it as I rolled in a ball and sobbed. I had to remind myself that it wasn't my pain I was feeling, but hers.

"Slut, I'm surprised he allowed you to fuck anyone else," the man seethed as he pulled out of her and rose to his full height, yanking her upwards by her hair painfully. "I'm going to enjoy hearing you scream for me. Put her with the others, we leave now," he ordered the creatures as he smiled coldly. "Someone is watching us, find out who it is," he sneered as he licked Kendra's blood from his fingers. The moment his fist collided with her face, the connection broke and I screamed at the emptiness I felt, as if his blow had killed her, snapping the bond to an empty void where I felt no connection to my sister.

Hands shook me; my mom screamed my name as I wiped at tears as sobs tore through me.

"Magdalena, what is it?" my mom whispered with worry.

"Lena, wake up!" Lucian snarled and I snapped my eyes open and screamed.

"The abbey, oh my God, they killed them all, everyone!" I sobbed at the faces that looked at me as if I'd lost it. The Fae who had been camped on my lawn watched me carefully from the doorway. They'd probably heard my hysterical screams and gotten Lucian.

"That's impossible; I have people there watching it," Lucian admitted, but I felt it. His eyes looked me over as I trembled from the loss of my sister.

"I saw it through Kendra, they're dead, d-d-demons got them. Those things had to have been demons," I stuttered as I trembled violently.

"Ryder," Lucian said, his hands released me as he sat back. "Bring them," he growled as Lucian vanished right before my eyes. I shook my head; that wasn't right. Witches couldn't do that, right? Ryder grabbed me and I felt the sensation of time and space shifting around us and then we were inside the abbey and I slipped and landed on my hands and knees in *blood*.

"No!" I sobbed as the carnage was revealed. There were bodies littered everywhere, staring lifelessly at the ceiling as I tripped over them in my rush to find my sister. "Kendra! Answer me, oh God," I cried as I slipped in the blood, finding her phone where she'd been hidden from her attackers. "No, please, no-o-o!" I screamed.

"Magdalena, come with me," Synthia whispered as she struggled to pull me away from the destruction.

"No, she's here, she has to be here!" I screamed and pulled away from her. I caught sight of a leg that was partially hidden behind one of the couches and lost it. It wasn't attached to anything; I could see that from where I stood. I could hear my mom and grandmother screaming over my own horrified sobs, and I moved towards the leg, only to find Ryder blocking my path. He shook his head even as Synthia tried to get me to understand her words.

"You don't want to see her like this," she repeated. "Keep the memories you have, Lena, not the ones you will have if you see her now."

"Let me go! That's my sister!" I wept, "These are my people! Oh God, who would do this?" What kind of a monster would tear people apart or kill on this kind of scale? It was a fucking massacre, and everywhere I looked, bodies littered the abbey floor.

"She's not here," Lucian said as he helped them move me backwards, towards the doors.

"Let me go!" I yelled as the elements shook the abbey even as one of the creatures I'd seen through Kendra's eyes stepped out of the hallway, his eyes glowing blood red as he smiled and dropped the arm he had been holding. Thunder boomed outside, and before I had even considered my move, the silver eyed demon-fae guy was there, ripping the monster's heart out with one hand and severing its head in one fluid motion.

I screamed as a sob tore through me. Demons, demons had my sister. She couldn't be dead. She just couldn't be. I'd feel it if she was. I refused to believe that Hecate would take my sister; I'd already lived through so much, how could she be so cruel as to allow this to happen? I struggled against the arms that held me, and I heard Lucian give Ryder permission to 'Shut her down,' whatever the hell that meant.

My hands clamped against my ears as I wailed in disbelief at what my mind was trying to tell me. "Kendra!" I sobbed as I doubled over with pain from the loss, this wasn't happening. It just couldn't be. I'd already lost so much; I couldn't lose her, too. I wouldn't survive it. I wasn't strong enough. I'd been strong for too long, barely able to build the wall to hold the pain that threatened to consume me daily, I'd been barely breathing! This? This would destroy me; it would destroy the coven! I screamed louder, unwilling to hear or see anymore.

I felt Ryder touching me, his hands cradled my face even as I tried to get away from him, then he whispered in a gentle voice even as blackness rushed up to devour me.

"My…sister," I whispered as the blackness took hold and everything shut off.

~~*

~Lucian

I watched as Lena went down, fighting against Ryder's hold as she struggled to understand the destruction inside the abbey. I moved with him as he took her outside, and placed her beside her mother and grandmother on a large blanket he'd glamoured.

I was staring down at her when the woods surrounding the abbey began to fill with my men as well as the demons under my control. They moved from the thick forest, numbering in the thousands. It didn't go unnoticed by Ryder who looked at the army who converged on us.

The fucking bloodbath in the abbey shouldn't have happened. I'd been distracted, and Lucifer had been here; his stink permeated the abbey. He'd taken Kendra, probably mistaking her for Lena. He'd seen us in the club together; he knew she was more than a casual fuck.

My men moved closer, depositing the witches who'd escaped to the safety of the forest at my feet, which was somewhat a relief knowing that Lena wouldn't be alone and that the coven was contained. For the most part.

"Found these ones hiding in the forest," Phayden said, his red eyes shifting from me to the abbey. "Got started without us?" he questioned and I growled.

Helen and her spoiled of a bitch little daughter weren't among the bodies, nor were they with the crowd that had escaped into the forest, neither was Devlin.

"Spread out, look for any other survivors. Do not harm them, and find Devlin. He was stationed outside the abbey to observe this place and he's missing," I growled, watching as the demons moved into efficient groups and spread out as they reentered the thicket for any more survivors. Ryder watched as the demons disappeared and turned to look at me with something akin to suspicion.

"You control hellhounds, and you sure as fuck are not the right hand man to Lucifer. You told me that you and your people weren't Lucifer's demons either; who the hell are you, Lucian?" he demanded.

"Think bigger. Right hand man is nothing more than an illusion, keeping him out of too much trouble is only part of my responsibilities. Looks like he's chafing at his restrictions and wants to challenge me," I replied as I kneeled down and looked at the girl Lena considered a friend, Kat. "What happened here?" I asked as she cried, loudly and noisily.

I pinched the bridge of my nose before using compulsion and snapping her to attention. I knew Ryder watched, trying to pinpoint exactly who or what I was, but I didn't care. I didn't have time to, either.

"What happened here?" I demanded and she ground her teeth together and winced as pain shot through her mind, which is how Lena should have responded, instead of being able to think for herself.

"Helen let them in, she let those creatures into the abbey. Helen opened the back doors to let us out, as if she felt bad for letting the monsters inside, but when Tabitha tried to escape with us, she sealed the doors and we couldn't get them open again. The screams, oh god, the screams were so horrible. She killed them, by letting those creatures inside, she sent everyone who was left in the abbey to their deaths, they're all dead!" she cried and hiccupped. "We couldn't save them so we ran and hid before they could come after the rest of us. We'll leave this place, start over, those who survived are agreed. We have to."

"No, you won't," I whispered as I stood back up, my eyes moved to Lena where she slept peacefully without the pain that was tearing her apart just a short while ago. I wasn't willing to lose her, or to allow the coven to run this late in the game.

So Helen had had a hand in this massacre of her own fucking people. I'd noted the doors in the back already; they were covered in blood and had been magically sealed shut. She'd sealed them in, stealing the only chance they'd had at surviving the horrors that were visited on this place. Kat's retelling of Helen's actions meant the bitch had knowingly assisted in the killing the high priestess, along with most of the elders who argued against her taking Tabitha's place when the time came.

This was on me, I'd allowed Lena to distract me and in doing so, I'd been ill prepared for Lucifer's attack. He'd descended on the abbey with a fucking army which was no easy feat. There'd been no ripple effect from that many demons escaping hell at the same time.

"Found Devlin, they got him pretty fucking good. He stayed conscious long enough to tell us it was Lucifer who did this. They caught Devlin as they were leaving and gutted him good. He said Lucifer looked a lot like you and he was bragging that Lena would think it was you who was killing her coven, and that she'd believe it was you raping her when he got her to the in-between. I know he left Dev alive as a message and a jab at you. You think he knows he took the wrong twin?" Spyder asked, his senses were hungrily seeking the carnage behind the abbey walls. We could all sense the souls that were escaping their bodies, seeking entrance into the world beyond this one.

"Doubt it, he's still high off the bloodlust," I snapped. He'd thought to take her in my form? How had Lena discerned that it hadn't been me who'd been here? Not once since seeing this mess through her sister's eyes had she turned accusing eyes at me.

I ignored the answer, knowing it was because I'd let her get too fucking close to me, it had been a mistake. I allowed my armor to form around my body as I beckoned to the fleeing souls, calling them to me with whispers of sweet revenge for what had occurred to them.

Ryder and his crew watched as I absorbed the souls and took them inside of me. I wouldn't feed from them, but I would allow them to be present when I took Lucifer's head. The rush of power from them joining the staggering numbers of souls I already contained sent a ripple through the abbey, and I remained guarded as I watched Spyder ordering my men to collect the dead and pile them together. My men walked freely into the abbey and I wondered if Helen was the one who had brought down the wards when she allowed Lucifer and his demons inside. I would have to question her and Cassidy once my men found them, if they ever did. Those bitches could be with Lucifer, or if he double crossed them, they might be running for a very long time.

Kat said the coven intended to run from this place of death and I knew she spoke true. I couldn't allow it, not with Katarina being so close, and with her newly awakened powers, the seal was about to be awakened as well. I couldn't chance the repressions that would come from it.

No, it was embedded in their collective coven psyche to survive, to run and hide from the monsters that hunted them. Katarina wasn't among the dead, if she'd been, I would have felt the seal going to the veil with her. I hadn't felt shit.

"Check everywhere and make sure no one is hiding inside the abbey," I ordered. "Ryder, put the survivors to sleep while I figure out what to do, please," I said to the man who watched me coldly as the souls continued to arrive and settle into my armor. I pushed power into them, knowing he sensed the magnitude of it as I absorbed the armor and returned to human form.

"Bane, Benjamin is just beyond that thicket watching us." I nodded to one of the densest parts of the forest that surrounded us. "He was present for this, get him and figure out what his damage is," I said as Bane mentally tracked the kid and locked onto him. "See what he knows and why he chose to show his face here after all this time."

"With pleasure," Bane hissed, and apparated into the shadows of the forest.

"We need a plan, they will run from this," Spyder said as he surveyed the sleeping witches.

"How do we stop them from running again?" Deviant asked as he moved closer.

"We need to reconstruct the scene. The abbey is old and they use a boiler to heat the common rooms and the residential areas. The weather is just beginning to turn and I am sure they would have had it in use. Make it look like the boiler exploded in the early morning hours. Have it appear as if the bodies of those who died were burned beyond recognition in the resulting fire," I said turning to

Ristan who nodded that it could be managed. "This should only destroy a portion of the abbey and hide what really happened here today." My eyes drifted to Lena, where she slept unaware of what was about to happen. I felt my gut as it dropped and hid the wince and anger that my next words brought with force. "I want their minds wiped. Give them new memories of what happened. We need to reset the past few months and adjust their memories of our presence here."

"That's only a fucking Band-Aid and you know it. The stronger ones eventually get the memories back; they'll know who wiped their minds when they do. And her," Spyder said nodding towards Magdalena, "What about her? When that demon attacked her, we guessed that their bond was unusual, but until this morning, none of us realized how strong of a bond she really has with her sister, you don't think she won't miss that?" he snapped.

"Not if she doesn't know she does. She won't look for it if she doesn't know it existed."

"And when she does? She'll be a powerful enemy when she figures out you made her forget. She'll reach for Kendra, maybe not right away, but she will. The moment she pokes at it, this will all unfold."

"Lena won't reach for Kendra, nor will she be able to. Kendra is with Lucifer, probably passing through the Gates of Hell as we speak. If not, he's in the void that is the in-between, and nothing can get through it and he knows it. Lena won't feel her unless he brings her back to this world."

The ground trembled and I looked at Lena, who had moved her hand beneath her cheek and slept still.

"That's not good," Deviant said as he watched the ground.

"Go check the Hell Gate, and send Kallum into hell, see what the chatter is. We need to get ahead of Lucifer, see what he's planning. If he has Katarina, we're definitely running out of time." I turned to Ryder. "Wake Kat up, I need to know if Lucifer took more than just Kendra with him," I demanded.

"What the fuck just happened?" he demanded.

"I'm trying to figure that out, wake her, quickly," I said impatiently. The moment her eyes opened I pushed power into the words. "How many women were taken from here?"

"Several, I think," she whispered as she gasped for air.

"Bloody fucking hell," I seethed and smashed my hand into the wall. "Put her to sleep again, Deviant, go check the gate, now!"

"We may have a problem," Phayden interrupted as he materialized next to me, holding out a stack of photos. He handed them to me and I flinched as photos of myself and my men were revealed, along with research about me. I wasn't a fucking Blackstone. I'd only said I was; it was who I had pretended to be to get closer to Katarina's coven. "Found that in a room that looks like it was the high priestesses."

I looked around the chaos and shook my head as I wondered how much the sharp old woman had been able to figure out before they'd killed her. Luckily, she wouldn't be sharing the information with anyone.

I felt the displacement as Deviant stepped from the shadows and shook his head. "Gates are open, but only a sliver. Not enough for demons to escape through without help. Kallum is on his way to hell, so he's going to be quiet for a while until he feels it's safe enough to get word to us."

"This is off," Spyder said.

"It's all fucking off, but I'm sure that's how it's supposed to be if Katarina is playing games again. Too many times she has upped the ante and others have paid the penalty for it," I mumbled. "We don't have long to control the scene, and I am not seeing any way around moving forward with this course of action. We can't chance losing them, and if Katarina is part of the survivors, she won't leave them behind. We'll use them if she is here, and if Lucifer has her, at least we know she's not running and we can only hope that he kills her for us. Gods forbid he discovers that she has the seal."

"And Lena? If you get too close to her and she remembers being with you?" Spyder asked, and I flinched. "You'll explain it to her, or make her think she's crazy?"

"Girls fantasize its normal. That's what I'll make her think. As seductive as the idea of keeping her is, I can't see it happening." I shook my head as I thought through the events of today and several different implications came to mind. "The more I think on this, I am fairly certain that Lucifer taking Kendra was a fuck up. Helen wanted him to kill Lena. The price was the high priestess. I think Helen hadn't given him Lena's details yet, or he wouldn't have mistaken Kendra for her. No, I think he saw Lena with me at the club a while ago and he knows she means something to me. Him happening upon Kendra was dumb luck and he was capitalizing on it. Lucifer would believe his pact with Helen is fulfilled as him taking Lena would mean she is as good as dead. The fact that he would be thumbing his nose at me would just be a bonus to him. For her protection as well as the covens, she gets wiped too," I expelled a frustrated breath, hating the idea. "I want the entire town spelled, and kept asleep until everything is in place. I also don't want the coven or the townspeople to remember Magdalena returning. Lucifer can't know he has the wrong woman.

I detested all of it, but was the only way to curtail the damage Helen and Lucifer had caused. I hated knowing that when the memories I was about to create in Lena's mind crumbled, she'd hate me. She'd hate me for leaving Kendra alone with Lucifer, for taking away her chance to find her sister. And Lena would search, the others would run, but my girl, she was a survivor and a fighter. She'd die trying to save her sister before she gave up looking. That wasn't something I was willing to let happen. "When they wake, they'll be faced with the devastation of the accident, but they'll be okay. Accidents on a massive scale are easier to deal with, than to know something hunted them down and slaughtered them in the one place they'd assumed was their sanctuary."

"I'll wake her when you're ready," Ryder said as he nodded towards Lena's sleeping form. "I assume you plan to be the one to steal her memories."

"Indeed," I said begrudgingly.

"And how do you intend to keep them safe if they're unaware of what is happening here?" Synthia asked.

"I intend to have a little help from my friends," I whispered as I picked up Lena's sleeping form and cradled her soft curves against my body. "I know you have a soft spot for witches. I intend to put it to good use."

CHAPTER
forty-two

We cannot learn without pain. ~**Aristotle**

~Lucian

I held her cradled in my arms. I was unwilling to allow any of the others to take my slight burden from me. With everything going wrong, she was my right. She was the softness to all of my hard edges. Never had I felt this way about anyone, not even Katarina and I'd loved her more than I'd ever thought I could love another being.

"Hate to point out more flaws in this plan, but Tabitha is among the dead," Spyder said, his eyes on the lifeless corpse of the high priestess. "That's something that won't be missed when they wake."

"Sarah can easily take her place. She's from one of the original bloodlines. She's nurturing and is probably the most powerful witch this coven has right now, other than her granddaughter. We can perform the spell to make it happen if Alden is willing to help us cast it," I said looking directly at Synthia, knowing she had sway over the Guild elder in question.

"I can make that happen," she mused. Her eyes moved to the sleeping form that had moved her head into the crook of my neck. "She's strong, you sure this is even going to work on her?" she asked.

"I'm sure it will," I replied as I looked at Ryder. "I need a little help remodeling her mother's manor house. Much of it was gutted in a fire; think you can make it look the same as it did before?"

"I would have had to have seen it myself to be able to replicate it to what it had been before the fire," he said as his eyes moved to Synthia. "If there are some pictures of the house, I can do a better version and perhaps you can give them some sort of memory that they had some upgrades done to the house. From what I have seen of it, the house is old and could probably use some improvements."

"I'll have Layton pull up the details we have on file," I replied. "We were doing a lot of reconnaissance of all of the homes belonging to the members of the coven and we have some pictures that were taken just before the opening ceremony. I need you to follow me, and wake Lena up," I said through clenched teeth. The idea of her forgetting me was making this shit near impossible to follow through with. "Please," I asked, offering him the respect I felt he deserved for helping us even though he didn't have to. They'd made a choice to, and that had earned a notch of respect.

Not a lot of beings could say they had my respect, much less earned it.

"I'm going to need a few moments after you fix her

room," I replied knowing it made it me look weak, but unable to give a shit. Mentally, I called to Layton and watched as he materialized with the photos. "Give the photos to Ryder, and make sure the deed to the store is returned to the Fitzgerald's, it will give them some semblance of security and purpose."

Cold bastard that I was, I'd planned to use it to barter with Lena. Now, it seemed empty. She'd hate me once she figured out everything out, and what could have been between us, would wither and die along with the fire she'd felt for me. In the end, I was saving her life, and that was worth more than what could have ever been between us.

Even the devil had a conscience when feelings were involved, which I wouldn't make the mistake of allowing to happen again.

I transported Lena to Kendra's room after Ryder had been given the images and I knew he followed close behind us. Lena moaned as we materialized in the shadows of the room. Ryder sifted in and looked at one of the pictures of what the room was supposed to look like. All things considered, the damage to the bedrooms wasn't bad, apart from the smoky smell. Ryder waved a hand and new paint brightened the walls. He checked out each piece of furniture, each knickknack or picture and fresh replacements would take the place of the smoke damaged items. He flipped open the jewelry box on the dresser and seemed satisfied with his work.

I sat on the newly glamoured bed and held her sleeping form in my arms tightly. I would have Layton retrieve Kendra's and her mother's things from my house and bring them here as soon as possible.

"You're sure you want to make her forget you?" Ryder asked carefully, his eyes holding no malice or intent to use her against me as many would. Most looked for ways to get to me or looked for weakness; he didn't.

"You have another fucking plan you been holding out on?" I snapped, hating that I had no options other than what I was about to do. When he didn't offer one, I shook my head. "Letting her go is a kindness, she's deserves someone who isn't steeped in the blood of the dead. She deserves someone who can touch her without the blood of her ancestors on their hands. That's not me. I have to let her go, because it's the one thing I can control right now, and it's the only way to protect her."

"As you wish," he said, and whispered the words to release her from her sleep induced state.

Once we were alone in the room, I held her to me inhaling the sweet flowery scent of the homemade shampoo as I kissed the top of her head. I hated the twisting knots in my stomach at the idea of letting her go, but I'd spoken true. She deserved someone better, someone who could give her what she deserved in life. That person wasn't me. I considered leaving her some of the memories we'd had, but she would poke at them and the false memories would unravel faster than they usually did with the stronger witches. I couldn't allow that. Magdalena was smart; it had to be everything that I wiped away or nothing at all. She was too smart, too powerful and I needed time to find Katarina and get Kendra back from Lucifer. If she was still alive, which, I doubted after seeing the destruction at the abbey.

"I wish I had another choice, little witch," I whispered as I kissed her forehead and rested mine against hers. "It's the only way to keep you safe, and be able to watch over you and protect you," I explained to her sleeping mind, hoping she retained the memory of those words when she finally gained them back. "Wake up, Lena," I encouraged watching as her lashes fluttered as she began to stir from her slumber. "Wake up," I growled; knowing if I waited another minute, I'd lose what little willpower I had to follow through with my plan. I wasn't a good person, this shit was beyond me. I could easily subdue her, and keep her, but she'd been right when she'd told me she was a butterfly. I knew butterflies weren't meant to be captured. They slowly withered in captivity and died. Lena reminded me of a Palos Verdes Blue butterfly, beautiful and elusive. Rare among her own fucking species, she was one of a kind, and she deserved to be set free.

"Lucian," she whispered through a strained voice from screaming at the terror she'd faced earlier. Her eyes snapped open as her lungs filled with a silent scream as the horror rushed back to the fore.

"Nothing happened today, you're fine, Lena. Everything is going to be just fine…It's all going to be okay," I amended. I sure as fuck didn't want her remembering that word. "Kendra is safe." The lie stuck in my craw, and I swallowed it hard. Kendra was taken because Helen let Lucifer into the abbey. It was a fuck up that Lena had nothing to do with, however, she would find a way to blame herself for it, for goading Helen into making the proverbial deal with the devil to accomplish her goals and Lena didn't need that shit on her, no one did. She deserved to be free from the burden until the time she remembered who she was. I held a small hope that if I had Kendra back by the time she regained her memories, she might forgive me.

I pushed more power into the compulsion and each lie I forced on her. Her eyes rose to mine and she shook her head, sending her beautiful hair cascading across the silk sheets. Her lips curved into a soft smile as she held my stare, as if she'd been momentarily distracted by the sight of them. It lasted no more than a moment before she frowned and looked at me, and noted the look of sadness in my eyes. I wanted to pull her to me. Undress her sexy as fuck curves and take her one last time, but I didn't have time and I knew she was still sore from the last bouts of sex we'd indulged in. I couldn't get enough of her, as if she'd put a spell on me. I leaned down and kissed her gently, enjoying the throaty moan that slipped from between her lips as ours connected. I felt my heart thudding in my chest and forced myself to pull away from her.

"You don't know me, we haven't met yet," I whispered and looked at her. Her nose crinkled and she frowned as if she thought I'd gone crazy. She sat up slowly, shaking her head as her hands slowly moved beneath the shirt I wore. I pulled her hands away punishingly and pushed her flat onto the bed where I could loom over her, and looked into her beautiful eyes. "You don't know me; you never left Haven Crest after Joshua's funeral. You remained here and help run the family business with your mother. You remember everything you learned in college but you will assume it was taught at the local school, but you never attended college. You've been here the entire time, *Kendra*," I continued, even as my words turned sour on my tongue.

"I'm Lena." She hiccupped a sob as her eyes regained focus as she fought the compulsion. "Don't do this to, please, Lucian, don't do this. You can't, don't take this from me," she begged as tears slipped from her eyes and she pleaded to remain herself. She was fully awake now, her mind fighting to retain her memories.

"You're not, Lena left town. You're Kendra," I growled back, forcing my power into the words which caused her to suck in air as it ricocheted around her mind.

"I'm Kendra," she cried, her pain filled eyes lost focus and she stopped fighting against me, even as her hands fisted my shirt as if she was trying to hold on to me. "Lucian," she whispered as her eyes regained focus as she fought me. "Stop this; I'm strong enough to make it. I promise. Don't do this to me," she pleaded, her beautiful eyes filled with fire as she struggled to remain Lena, even though fighting it was hopeless. "Don't make me disappear."

"You're Kendra, and you've had no contact with Magdalena in years. She failed to show up for the Awakening and is lost to you. As far as you know, she's never coming home, don't look for her. She severed the bond, it's destroyed. The more you looked for her through the bond, the further she would run from you, so you don't even bother trying any more. You're the granddaughter of the high priestess now, you're happy. Very happy," I continued even as my throat constricted and tightened with each lie I fed her subconscious.

"I'm happy," she repeated.

"You'll be safe now," I whispered as I kissed her lips and pulled away.

"Lucian," Spyder said quietly from the doorway. When I failed to speak, he continued. "The manor house is finished; the accident has been staged and the rest of the abbey has been taken care of. No one will be able to identify what happened there today as anything but a boiler explosion and the local morgue has the burned remains of those who died." A sly smirk played at the corners of his mouth. "I also took the liberty of removing the records of Todd's death and his body will probably be found in the near future. I made it look like he was the victim of a car crash rather than a demon possession. The rest of the coven who survived have been settled back in their homes; the out of town harvest guests are bunked at the hotel, and their memories have been prepped to be wiped of today's events along with the other things you asked for. Once we cast the spell, their memories will be cleared and the new ones will be set in their minds."

"Good, now get the fuck out," I snapped, ignoring the tremble in my hands as I itched to touch her, to kiss her and hold my body against her softness. I was fucking pathetic, and she was a weakness I couldn't afford. So why the fuck was it killing me to let her go?

"I want you," she whispered seductively, and I blinked at her words. Blue fire lit in her eyes as she looked at me. My Lena was in there, fighting to overcome the compulsion, and greedy for the exact same thing I wanted: Us.

"No, you don't, Kendra," I whispered after I'd cleared my throat and swallowed the answer she'd wanted. The one I'd wanted to give her in return. "You are Kendra, Lena is gone!" I forced everything into it and watched her mind gave in.

She sucked in air and gasped to bring it into her lungs as she shook her head violently. Tears slipped from her eyes and I kissed them away, unable to stop myself. Her hands clung to me, even as she continued to gasp for air.

I ran my hands over her tattoos, removing them as I went along. Kendra didn't have tattoos, so this would complete Lena's camouflage. It was also my last 'fuck you,' to the tattoo artist who'd carelessly taken what rightfully should have been mine. I picked up her foot and slowly traced a rune into her sole, one that would make her safe from possession; this one would be stronger than the devil's trap that she used to have on her pubic bone. Her transformation to Kendra was too easy. It shouldn't have been. I only had to stop by the cottage, collect her belongings and the cat, and it would be finished. I gently placed her foot on the bed and swallowed hard.

"I'll miss you, my sweet witch," I whispered before I pushed the rest of the fabricated memories in to her mind, and buried the ones we made together behind a steel wall, along with who she really was. I watched as Lena disappeared from me, her eyes lost focus and she succumbed to the compulsion and power within my words. "You'll probably hate me when you remember what I have done tonight. Kendra," I fucking choked on her new name, it was so fucking wrong. Kendra was weak, Lena was strong. They were so different from each other, and I fucking hated that I was forcing Lena to disappear, but I knew I had to do it to keep her safe.

Lucifer thinks he stole Lena; as long as he believed that, he would leave the real one alone. "You can breathe now, sweet girl. The pain from Joshua's death is lessened, it will hurt, but you won't feel the pain anymore. You're no longer weighted down by grief. You're free my butterfly. You can fly, now," I whispered and watched as the light faded from her eyes. "Sleep. When you wake up everything will be okay. You'll be okay, Kendra. You'll have a life again, the one you should have had before it was taken away from you by the pain you were forced to live through."

"Everything is ready," Ryder said from the doorway, his eyes took in Lena's ashen color and tear streaked face. "If she's as stubborn as Synthia, she'll come after you when she regains her memories."

"I know," my reply was clipped, I was unwilling to release her hands from where she clutched my shirt, and I held her to me. "She'll hate me for hiding what happened to her sister, but she'd pay with her life if she goes after Lucifer and that's something I am not willing to allow."

"Their house is repaired, and I was going to take care of the damage you and Lena did to yours, however, it looks like your people beat me to it." He fought a smile that twitched in the corners of his mouth, as he knew full well how the damage to the house happened. "I was advised by Spyder to move out most of the personal items, which are now stored in some hidden rooms that he showed me. If the house is observed from the outside, it will appear newly renovated with minimal items inside. He said you were undecided on whether you wanted to be so close to her. Memories and all," he stated.

"Thank you," I mumbled, waiting for him to announce what the price would be for all of this help. No one ever gave without taking in my world, not even me. When he failed to name his price, I asked. "Name it."

"Name what?" he countered as he crossed his arms and leaned against the door, watching me.

"Your price, the favor, don't fucking play with me," I snapped, my tone overly harsh as his toying with me wore down the last of my patience.

"Nothing," he said as he looked from me to Lena. "You've paid enough today, Lucian. You let her go, which was surprisingly unlike you. If Synthia is my weakness, Lena is yours. Don't let your enemies see it, because they will use it against you. Witches have a way of burrowing in and getting underneath our skin. We're alike in this, I won't ask shit from you, because I know exactly what it is going to cost you to stay away from her."

My eyes moved from him to where Syn sifted in, feeling his discomfort. "Alden is waiting to perform the spell that will transfer the high priestess's powers to Sarah. However, he does have one condition."

I snorted, and looked at her.

"Oh he does, does he?" Ryder asked before I could, his brow lifted in silent challenge.

"He'd like to remain here. He wants to know more about them. He can't do that if they think he's from the Guild. They'd never allow him to get close to them. It will however allow us to have eyes on the inside, as long as we feed them a memory of him being a friend to the coven. He can also bypass the wards in the lower level of the abbey. They have rooms that are heavily warded, stronger than any I've ever encountered to date. They buzz when Adam and I tried to get close, but they don't sense Alden as a threat, he's able to move beyond the wards without them sensing him. I'm pretty sure if I would have tried to push past them, they would have brought the abbey down on our heads. Pretty sure it's a failsafe, kinda like the ones we had inside the Guild."

"It sounds like your uncle will have quite a bit of exploring to do," I agreed.

"Your guy Layton used compulsion on some of the witches to see if they knew what was down there, they didn't know anything. Most said they didn't even know there was anything beneath the abbey," Synthia said.

"No, they probably wouldn't," I admitted. "Perhaps only Tabitha and some of the elders knew what was down there." I scratched my head in frustration and tried to stop my mind from gravitating towards thoughts of Lena. I needed to get back on track, back to what I came here to do. Hunting down Katarina. Unless she was with Lucifer, which considering how the earth quaked just a little while ago could be a very real possibility. One thing I knew about Katarina, she would do anything to remain in the game long enough to try and get to me; it was something I always counted on.

"Is she going to be okay?" Synthia asked, nodding at Lena.

"She's a fighter; she'll be hell on sexy little heels when she regains her memories though. In the end, she'll understand, but I am fairly certain she'll still hate me for not allowing her to have a say in hers or Kendra's immediate future. But yes, she'll be okay. I've done everything I can to make sure she will be," I muttered as I stepped away from the bed and away from the little witch who had slipped beneath my skin.

CHAPTER
forty-three

Fate whispers to the warrior, "You cannot withstand the storm." The warrior whispers back, "I am the storm."
-Anonymous author

-Magdalena...Kendra
One Month After Mind Wipe

"Kendra? We'll be late,"

my mother called up the stairs as I stared at my reflection. "Everything alright?" she continued.

No, nothing was all right. Everything was *too* right. I felt like an alien had taken my place. I groaned as I pulled on a dress, hating that it was so tight. My boobs were out of control, and nothing in the closet or drawers fit me correctly. They were all uncomfortable and even though the styles were what I always wore, I just didn't feel like myself in them anymore.

"I'm coming!" I called down as I raced into Lena's old room, yanked open the closet door and pulled out a white silk dress that had a rainbow of butterflies in every color that fluttered from the hemline, up to the waist. I held it up to my chin in front of her stand up mirror, and decided it would probably work. I stripped off the too tight dress I was wearing and shimmied into the other, as I grabbed shoes and moved towards the stairs. The dress wasn't tight, it fit perfectly. Right along with the small heels I'd pilfered, and a matching white wrap that I slipped around my shoulders as I raced down stairs.

"There you are, I was beginning to think you'd changed your mind," mom said, her eyes noting the dress. "Is that new? I haven't seen you wear it before."

"Sure," I lied, not wanting to see her be sad when I said Lena's name. Lena hadn't even bothered to let us know she was alive; why should we continue to be upset about her being gone? Bitch was probably out having a life while I was trapped in this town with a mother who had been sad most days, because one child had been killed in a war, while another chose to be gone from her life.

I frowned as I thought on it for a moment as she hadn't been as sad, since Alden started coming around. The first time he showed up, he quietly explained that he felt I was stronger than the rest of the newly awakened witches and therefore it was really important that I learned to control my powers as quickly as possible. He had been giving me lessons in control every day and since he'd been coming around, I had seen what had been going on between my mom and him.

"You look beautiful, Kendra," she said and my brain itched, but I ignored it. Lots of things had been itching my brain for weeks now and so far, I had done my best to ignore it. Some days were worse than others.

"I still can't believe they found him down a ravine," I

said, switching subjects to Todd's death which had come as a shock so soon after we'd lost so many to the accident up at the abbey a few weeks ago.

"His poor mom," she said softly, knowing exactly what Todd's own mother was going through. She picked at a stray strand of hair that had taken up residence on her sweater and looked at me oddly. "You didn't put on make-up."

"I put on mascara," I said offhandedly. "Besides, it's a funeral, not a party."

"It's just so unlike you," she replied and shrugged. "Oh well, grandma's waiting in the car. She's dead set on driving us."

"And you don't like the idea because you made more secret plans with Alden?" I teased. I knew they'd been hanging out together and trying to hide what they were doing, and I was surprisingly okay with it. He seemed pretty nice, respected my mom, not to mention, their little sneaking around gave me time to do other things without her constantly in my space.

"Kendra, you knew?" she whispered as she covered her mouth with her hand.

"Duh, Mom," I laughed. "It's nice to see you putting yourself out there again. With dad being gone, and everything going on, it's nice to see you smiling again."

"There's nothing romantic going on, we're just friends," she said primly. Lordy she was a bad liar and I smiled.

"If it turns romantic, I'm okay with it," I admitted.

"You want to watch *Breakfast at Tiffany's* with me tonight?" she asked and I cringed.

"No, not especially," I laughed. "I have plans tonight with Kat and Dex, and I overheard you making plans too, so go out and have fun. I'll be okay."

"It's nice to have someone my own age to talk to," she blushed and I felt a small tug of jealousy. She was my mother, and even though I hated the idea of her dating again considering her history with my father, I wanted her to be as happy as I was.

"I'm glad you're happy," I said as we walked down the drive towards the car and my eyes drifted on their own to the old mansion that was on the property adjoining ours. "That thing is creepy," I whispered, but my body reacted differently. I'd spent over an hour staring at that damn place last night, which seemed to make my brain itch even more that it already was.

"It doesn't bother you? Your dad…" I shook my head.

"Dad is an asshole, he left us and he certainly doesn't deserve us," I snapped. "He left us when shit got hard, and for some reason, I just don't see Alden doing the same thing. A car horn blared from the end of the driveway where my grandmother waited and I cringed. "That power has gone to that lady's head, I swear it," I whispered as mom covered a laugh with her hand.

"We're dallying and it's rude," she mused as we headed for the car. Once we were seated and belted, I sat in the back and listened as mom and grandma argued about which route was faster to get the coven's cemetery, and other coven business that I drowned out as my mind replayed the dream of the indigo eyes that haunted me.

When we finally arrived at the cemetery, I realized I had forgotten the flowers in the car and signaled to my mother that I was going back to grab them as she reached out and hugged Todd's mother. I felt bad for his mom, but the asshole had cheated on Lena, which had driven her away. It sucked that he was dead, but I couldn't find it in myself to forgive him for pushing her away from us.

I rounded the corner of a van and hit a brick wall, literally. I fumbled to catch my balance as I started to fall to the ground, only to be caught mid-air and pulled upright. I started to growl, but the moment my eyes held his, I lost all coherent thought. He stared back at me, as if he was searching for something to say, and failing.

"I…uh…wow," I mumbled and stepped away from him. His touch set me ablaze, and I had to get distance from him to be able to speak. His eyes took in the dress and he looked taken back.

"Butterflies," he whispered as he eyes lifted from the dress to my face.

"Got something against butterflies?" I asked tartly, noting that I'd gone on the defense pretty quickly. The itching in my brain had intensified to the point of being painful and I noticed his posture stiffened as he watched me.

"Not at all," he said carefully. "I find them most exquisite when they take flight."

"Indeed," I said as I brought my hand up to touch my face. What the hell did he have in his shirt, a freaking steel sheet? "You should really watch where you're going," I mumbled, noting nothing was bleeding or broken.

"The same could be said about you," he countered.

"This funeral is invite only," I said evasively. I had a good idea who he was, even though I hadn't seen him before. Everyone in the coven and in town couldn't shut up about him.

"I was invited by the high priestess."

"You must be Lucian, then," I replied as I narrowed my eyes on him. I didn't like him. He had been throwing an awful lot of money around, as if he thought we could be bought. We couldn't.

"Indeed," he answered smoothly as he smiled. "You must be Kendra," he spit my name out like it was a curse.

"In the flesh," I replied with a cocky smile. "You can go, now," I added, as I moved to the side to allow him to pass, as if I could stop him if I wanted to.

"You're dismissing me?" he asked in surprise.

"I am," I winked and moved towards the car.

"I don't get dismissed, I do the dismissing."

"Really? Because I'm pretty sure you just got dismissed, by me," I replied with a wide grin, enjoying his annoyance over being dismissed by a little girl, one who wasn't impressed with his fat bank account, his good looks or his fancy suit. He was really delicious, and beyond yummy though.

His eyes challenged me, even as he walked me backwards towards the empty parking lot. I allowed it, but only because I needed to know more about it him to be able to judge if he was going to be trouble.

"Scared?" he asked.

"Excited," I quipped.

"You should run," he growled from deep in his chest.

"Not a chance, I don't run," I countered even as I felt my backside hit the bumper of a sleek car. I had no idea he was this hot, nor did I care. He was an outsider, one the elders had chosen to let in. They were too trusting, and I wasn't. He'd come here for a reason, one I intended to get out of him.

"You're playing with fire," he warned.

"Maybe I like the burn," I said, and his eyes grew hooded.

"You have no idea how hot it can get, little girl," he growled as he stepped even closer.

"No, I don't," I replied honestly as I wetted my lips and smiled. "But, I'm not afraid to find out," I continued, knowing he was getting both angry and turned on by our encounter. I wasn't sure why I was goading him. Men like that were way too much trouble and usually only looking for a quick thrill and spill. Not that that was a bad thing, but men like him probably had a fleet of women hanging on them, or waiting in line for a turn with him. No thanks; I didn't stand in lines for any male.

"Is that so?" he asked as his eyes moved to where my tongue had jutted out to wet my lips. "Consider yourself warned." He boxed me in, and before I could think better of it, he smiled coldly. "Do you like to play games?" he asked.

"I like to win," I replied easily as I refused to break eye contact with him. Somehow, it felt important to keep my eyes on his, as if I failed to do so, I'd lose this battle of wills.

"You won't win against me; no one ever does. I have no mercy," he continued.

"Do I look like I need mercy?" I countered, allowing the air around us to ruffle the leaves along with my hair, in a small display of my power.

"You look like you need to be taught some manners," he replied.

"And you think to teach me? Don't think so. Now, if you'll excuse me, I have flowers to retrieve and my respects to pay to Todd's mother. I'm sure we'll be seeing each other soon enough, Blackstone. I look forward to it."

"Count on it, witch," he replied tightly as he moved away from the car, straightening his jacket and watching me as I tried not to run to my grandmother's car to retrieve the wilted roses.

I wasn't sure how I knew it. I could feel deep in my soul, that he wasn't human. He wasn't one of the undead or a demon either. He had a pulse, one that had kicked up right alongside mine as he'd gotten close to me. I planned to make him my business, and figure out exactly why he was here, and what he wanted.

I moved back to the funeral and stood silently beside my mother, who turned and smiled at me as I looked across the casket, to where Lucian stood. His eyes were locked on mine, and a cocky grin was plastered across his full lips. One I planned to remove right along with him and his club. This town wasn't for sale, and I'd make sure I got that message across to whatever the hell he was.

The funeral and ceremony went off without a hitch, and Todd was returned to the leyline, where his soul was freed to give the coven power, as well as to be reborn if it was meant to be. I wasn't sad that he was dead, which bothered me, but I didn't have time to dwell on it either. I kissed my grandmother and mother goodbye as I joined Kat in her car with a few of our other friends.

We headed out to the abandoned church that was about two miles outside of town and got out of the car; my mind couldn't shake the niggling feeling that I knew Lucian, but I didn't have the first clue as to where I knew him from.

"Are you having second thoughts?" Kat asked, her crystalline eyes held mine as she watched me.

"No, are you?" I asked, countering her and turning it back on her.

"No, demons are real and we have to protect the coven. I'm all in."

"Good," I said, watching as the others who had been awakened with us, filed into the empty church. "It's time to train."

"You think the coven is on to us?" Dexter asked, his eyes moving from me to Kat. "Your mother hasn't seemed to notice, but your grandmother, she's smarter than most."

"Blackstone and his men are here for a reason, and Carolina and Brian were attacked by demons less than forty miles away from our home. No one in the coven believed them except us and that's weird. Normally word of demons freaks them out and this time it's like they're all hiding their heads in the sand. No, now is not the time to sit down and let shit happen. We all have holes in our memories and I for one want to know what is missing up here," I said as I tapped my head. "It's time to protect the coven as our ancestors did in the times when it was needed. We protect our own, at all cost. Even from themselves when it's needed. If we're under attack, we need to be prepared to strike hard and fast, and it will take more than just magic to send them a message. If the demons are here, or coming for us, we'll be ready for anything they try."

Cries of agreement went up and I smiled as all of us gathered into a circle, held hands, and recited the spell from the grimoire Alden had given me. Along with the lessons in control, he had been passing along things the elders of the coven had kept hidden from us. He didn't have his head in the sand as the others seemed to be inclined to do, and I was thankful. The old man had even brought in a select few of his own coven to train us to fight, to prepare us for battle should a demon come to our doors. If demons were closing in on our coven, we'd be ready. I had no intention of meeting them unprepared or without skills to defend those I loved.

It was time for our coven to start fighting back, instead of waiting to be slaughtered or running. Too many lives hung in the balance, and too many times, the bad guys won the battle. Things weren't adding up and the older witches of the coven seemed oblivious to what was happening around us. We'd told them of demons, they'd ignored it. We gave them details of the attack; they'd brushed us off as if we had been spinning tales instead of stating facts. No more.

I looked around the circle at the nervous witches, and smiled reassuringly as the pages of the grimoire started turning on their own. Eyes widened, and power moved through the circle. The fire crackled and the clouds moved to reveal the full Harvest moon. It was time to unite this coven, and make it a force that monsters feared.

Whatever we faced, we'd face it together…Head on. In the last few weeks we'd come a long way, and we would only move forward. There was no looking back, not now, not ever. There would be no more running, no hiding from the enemies of old, for this coven. This was our time, and we would be prepared for whatever came looking for us.

~The End For Now~

About the Author

Amelia lives in the great Pacific Northwest with her family. When not writing, she can be found on her author page, hanging out with fans, or dreaming up new twisting plots. She's an avid reader of everything paranormal romance.

Stalker links!

Facebook: https://www.facebook.com/authorameliahutchins
Website: http://amelia-hutchins.com/
Amazon: http://www.amazon.com/Amelia-Hutchins/e/B00D5OASEG
Goodreads: https://www.goodreads.com/author/show/7092218.Amelia_Hutchins
Twitter: https://twitter.com/ameliaauthor
Pinterest: http://www.pinterest.com/ameliahutchins

Now for an exclusive peek at S.L. Jennings highly anticipated Born Sinner coming summer 2016!

S.L. Jennings Stalker links!

Amazon: http://www.amazon.com/S.L.-Jennings/e/B009YPO1WU

Goodreads:https://www.goodreads.com/book/show/30142491-born-sinner

Instagram: https://www.instagram.com/s.l.jennings/

Twitter: https://twitter.com/MrsSLJ

Facebook: https://www.facebook.com/authorsljennings/?fref=ts

BORN SINNER

S. L. JENNINGS

COMING SOON

Chapter One

It's cold tonight.

But not just any kind of cold. The kind of cold that seeps into your pores and leaves a dusting of frost on your bones. The kind that chills your blood, making it congeal in your stiffening veins.

I've walked the same route to work every night, saying silent prayers for safety. Dope dealers and prostitutes scurry from the flickering harshness of broken streetlights like cockroaches, dodging undercover cops and the prying eyes of passersby. No one speaks to each other unless they want something, and even then, they settle for swift words in clipped tones. I'm invisible here. No one wants anything from me. And even if they did, I have nothing to give.

"Watch it, bitch," an asshole in an ugly green parka barks out as he nearly mows me down, loud enough to drown out the hip-hop music blaring from my earbuds. It's begun to snow, and instead of focusing on his steps, he's resorted to walking through anyone who stands between him and warm, dry shelter and his next drink.

"Excuse you," I sneer, glaring back at him from over my shoulder.

"Yeah, fuck you," he spits, casting his middle finger to the heavens.

I feel it inside of me. The heat of his hatred. The blackness of his soul. His eyes are empty, glazed depths of sorrow and poison. His yellowed, clammy skin is merely a vehicle for the chemical waste wrapped around weakening bones.

I find the whispers flooding my mind before I can resist them, the voices so distinct that I can no longer hear J. Cole's lyrical diatribe rattling my skull. I should fight them, but I don't. I don't want to. Not this time. I've been fighting pricks like this my entire life. At some point, you learn to fight back.

Electric synapses fire with the command, and my lips part to utter a single word.

"Fall."

He doesn't even see the patch of ice before the heel of his scuffed boot skates across it. Arms flail violently as he tries to regain his balance, but it's too late. He's airborne— suspended in time like the feather-light snowflakes swirling around us. And before a single, blood-curdling scream is ripped from his throat, he hits the piss-stained sidewalk with a deafening crack.

I exhale through the taste of metal in my mouth, and keep walking, leaving pain and chaos in my wake. I turn up the music as loud as it'll go to drown out the desperate cries for help.

I never said I fought fair.

"You're here early," Lily smiles when I enter the dingy corner store where we both work. Beautiful and blonde and bright, she's much too angelic to be working in a dump like this.

I peel off my fingerless knit gloves and rub my palms together before stowing my earbuds in my coat pocket. Eduardo, the store manager and the owner's nephew, is too cheap to turn up the heat. "Bored, and Sister had a date. Thought you could use the company. Busy tonight?"

Lily's sky blue eyes scan the shelves and racks of chips and six packs. "Not really. But I'm glad you came in." She smiles again. She's always smiling, always ridiculously optimistic. And while that would annoy the crap out of me with anyone else, I genuinely enjoy her sunny disposition. It's a welcomed change from the doom and gloom of our little slice of purgatory outside.

I step around the counter, halfway encased by bulletproof glass. Eduardo was also too cheap to spring for one that at least touched the ceiling, but some protection is better than none. "You here by yourself?" I frown. Even with the added security of cameras and an alarm system, working the night shift at any establishment in this part of town isn't safe. Especially for someone like her.

"Logan is stocking in the back. I'm fine, really. You worry too much."

I shake my head. I wish she worried more. Lily doesn't know the horrors I've seen—the horrors I've created. To her, I'm just a troubled girl with a dark past that she wants to love and nurture. But in reality, I'm a troubled girl with a dark past whose thoughts and words are weapons. And while she is one of the only people I can call friends, she can't know about me. No one can. Or else I'll end up just like my mother.

I stash my coat and bag under the counter and slip on the ugly, maroon vest we're forced to wear. It's not doing me any favors over my black sweater and ripped, faded jeans, but somehow Lily still looks svelte and glamorous in it. I've asked what she was doing working in a rotted out neighborhood on the south side of Chicago—she looks like she comes from money, even though she swears she's not. But something about her won't let me believe that.

There's a stain that poverty leaves on all it touches. It coats your palms when you're cold. It bleeds onto your lips when you're hungry. It paints your skin when you're sick. You can try to scrub it away, but the result is always the same. You're one of society's forsaken.

Lily has never worn that stain. I would have recognized it if she did.

A bell jingles from the doorway, startling us both. I nearly gasp audibly when I see who it is.

"God, not this guy again," Logan bristles behind us, holding a cardboard box full of Pop Tarts. Lily and I didn't even hear him approach.

"What?" My voice is barely a whisper. The wind has been knocked out of me.

"That dude gives me the creeps," he shakes his head, sending muddy brown curls dancing across his forehead. He drops the box and moves in closer, whispering, "I seriously think we should tell Eduardo about him. He comes in every night and buys the same exact thing... especially when *you're* working." He points his gaze at me.

"So? Maybe he works the night shift too?" I shrug.

"The night shift at a slaughterhouse. He could be a rapist or serial killer. You really want someone like that stalking you?"

I roll my eyes. "He's not stalking me, Logan."

"You don't know that, Eden. He gives me a bad vibe."

"Well, I think it's cute. Romantic, even," Lily chimes in, reaching up to ruffle Logan's shaggy brown hair. I wish I could have warned her not to do that. His greasy mop probably hasn't been washed in weeks.

"Whatever. The fucker is trouble. Just *look* at him."

And as if some biological instinct hooks itself within muscle and bone, transforming me into a lust-strung marionette, I do.

The first time he came in, nearly six weeks ago, he scared me. It was after three in the morning, and I didn't hear the door chime. At least I don't think I did. I had been engrossed in a new paperback and my Kendrick Lamar playlist, and didn't notice him until he was silently standing before me. No sound of footfalls or the rasp of his breath. He just stood there, watching me, waiting for me to notice him. I nearly shrieked and fell over from my stool.

The next night, I was stunned once again by his presence, but this time, the flavor of my curiosity was something different altogether. I actually let myself *look* at him, while silently praying that he couldn't see *me*.

He was tall and built like someone who trained religiously. I thought maybe he played for the Bears or maybe even the Bulls, but the way he moved was almost too lithe and graceful to pin him as an athlete. Yet, there was something uniquely feral about it. And his face… hard and menacing, yet unquestionably pretty. Like he knew he was gorgeous, yet didn't want to be. Still, even the dark scruff on his chiseled jaw seemed precise and elegant.

When he approached the register, I tried not to stare at him, but I wanted to see his eyes. I needed to know what darkness lurked behind this massive beast of a man. But he wouldn't look at me. He simply slid his Arizona Iced Tea and pack of mints across the counter and waited silently for me to ring him up.

I couldn't breathe. The air had been sucked right out of the room. I felt lightheaded and my fingers began to shake violently. The whispers began to snake their way into my skull, urging me to say the words. *Look at me. Look at me.* But my tongue had turned to lead that not even my mind's compulsion could move.

I was grateful. I had a feeling his gaze could turn me to stone.

He came in everyday after, buying only his canned iced tea and wintergreen mints. Sometimes it was at the start of my shift. Sometimes toward the end. He never spoke, never met my eyes. I'd watch him from across the store and mentally record his movements and the way his dark clothes seemed to stretch around his body like a designer glove. Something about him was dangerous, but not in the criminal way. But in the way that made my senses hum with anticipation and fear every time I heard the entrance door chime. The way that made me afraid of myself.

Tonight is different though. He's dressed in similar clothing. He goes straight to the back for tea and mints. And he doesn't meet my eyes. That's nothing new. But there's something else…something off. I can feel it in the way the air seems to pulse with excitement around his frame.

It's 10:40 p.m. I'm not scheduled until 11. How would he have known I had come in almost half an hour early? I look to Logan whose dark eyes are trained on the mysterious stranger/my would-be stalker.

The man approaches the register with unhurried steps, although I can tell that tension grips his shoulders like a vise. I make a move to the counter to ring him up like I do every night, but before I can take a full step forward, Lily darts into my path, beating me to it.

"I've got it," she smiles sweetly. "Still my drawer and I don't want to mess up tonight's count."

Right. Although, that's never mattered before.

A voice echoes in my head, but I shut it down before I can make out the words.

Lily rings up the items swiftly without her usual friendly chatter. But just before the man can escape our intense scrutiny, she plasters on a smile and asks him, "Will there be anything else?"

I hold my breath as he slowly lifts his chin to face her, giving me a full view of the man who's haunted my daydreams everyday for the past six weeks.

Gray. His eyes are gray, but the most stunning shade I've ever seen. As if they were plucked from the crying heavens, coated in stardust and cast in steel. His eyelashes are thick and dark, much like the hair that layers his chin and surrounds full, sensual lips. A marled charcoal beanie sits atop his head, allowing just the tips of his hair to tease me.

He's too beautiful to be cold, but I know, without a doubt, he's frozen solid to the core. Still, every cell in my body is engulfed in flames just by his proximity. I'm almost certain I could melt the bulletproof glass just by squeezing my thighs together.

He squints for one quick fraction of a second, and before I can even decipher the inflection, he turns and stalks out the store. I'm speechless…scared. But not of him. I'm scared of the way my body burns for this complete stranger who has never even spoken to me.

"I told you…*totally* psycho," Logan proclaims after a long stretch of uncomfortable silence. "He's probably that guy that called and asked for your schedule earlier today, Eden."

I hear him. I just don't want to. "What did you say?"

"Yeah. Eduardo answered. Some guy wanted to know what your hours were."

I frown. "You sure he was asking about me?" I've never been the topic of interest. And I've worked damn hard to keep it that way.

"Pretty sure. He asked for the girl with the silver hair, tatts and a nose ring. You're the only one around here that fits that description. We didn't tell him anything, of course. But still… someone was looking for you."

I touch my short, black polished nails to my dove gray locks reflexively. To the outside world, it's a fashion statement. But the truth is, my once jet-black hair started losing its pigment years ago. It was just a few strands at first. But then almost overnight, I had the mane of an 80 year old.

I turn away from his questioning glare and pick up the box of Pop Tarts, if only to fight the urge to wring my hands. "I'm going to restock these," I murmur, stepping from around the counter.

"Hey, Logan, why don't you take off a little early? I can stick around to keep Eden company," I hear Lily say as I stuff processed strawberry pastries into wire racks.

"You sure? What if that guy comes back? Maybe I

should stick around just in case…"

"No, no. Us girls can take care of ourselves, I promise. And if he comes back, we have Eduardo's taser behind the counter."

I don't have to look up to know that Logan's face is screwed in uncertainty. He wants to go; it's Friday night. But he also wants to be a decent human being. At least that's what he wants Lily to believe.

"Well…ok. If you think you two will be alright." The promise of a cheap beer and a joint win out over chivalry. I could make him stay if I really wanted to, but I won't. I don't like being in his head. I don't like the bitter taste of his blood on my tongue.

"We will. Now go and have a good time."

I take my time shelving junk food and barely lift my head when he bids us goodnight. I want to like Logan, but his soul is murky, his thoughts impure. I don't know what they are specifically, but I can feel the intensity of them. Lust. Indulgence. Aggression. He wants to be a good guy, but this city's consequences have poisoned his heart and compromised his morals. He is merely a prisoner of this man-made hell.

"You feeling ok?"

I swallow a shriek and grip my chest in surprise as I stagger backwards. "Shit, Lily! I didn't even hear you. Are you trying to kill me?"

"Sorry," she chuckles. "Almost done?"

"Yeah. Two minutes."

"Ok. Come up front when you're done. Something I want to—"

Her head whips to the glass double doors, but from my crouched position on the floor, I don't see anything. "What is it?"

"Nothing." But she doesn't look my way. "Hey, do me a favor and run to the back for more potato chips. Do it now."

I glance over at the chip display. "It's fully stocked. I think Logan beat me to it."

She doesn't acknowledge my words. Instead, she moves swiftly to the front of the store. But before she can make it, the door chimes. Someone's here.

The voice is deep, the accent Russian. There's a second set of footsteps following the first. Then a third. A cold dread sweeps through the store, a bone-chilling sensation that makes me shiver from my spot on the dingy linoleum. I force myself to my knees, hoping to get a view of the entrance. I've only had a couple run-ins with the Russian Mafia, and this can go only one of two ways: they respectfully pay for their stuff and leave, or they cause a ruckus, emboldened with vodka and recent violence, and get grabby with Lily.

I look to my friend, who looks cool and calm as if a doting grandma was eyeing her from the doorway. "Anything I can help you gentlemen with?"

The first one—the bigger, scarier one—replies to her in his native tongue. She shakes her head. "I'm sorry, I don't know what you're saying."

The man frowns, causing his bushy black eyebrows to hood his dark eyes. "The girl. Where is she?" he says in a thick accent.

"I'm the only girl here," Lily smiles, the lie painting her pink-glossed lips. She casually makes her way behind the counter without the slightest inkling of urgency in her step. "But if you'd like to leave a message—"

"Don't play with me, *d'yavol.* Give us the girl, and we might let you live."

Holy. Fuck.

My eyes scan the small space around me, searching for anything that can be used as a weapon, when a set of Italian leather shoes come into view.

"Hello, Eden."

Horror coils my stomach. But before I can run, fight back, respond—something—there are strong hands roughly gripping my arms and pulling me to my feet.

"Here she is."

His hands yank me towards the front of the store, despite my violent protests. "Let me go, asshole!" I demand, putting all my strength into fighting out of his grasp.

"You will come, *сýка*. The master awaits." The Russian thug drags me as if he doesn't even register my one hundred and twenty pounds.

"Let her go," Lily orders, squaring her shoulders. "Or you won't make it home for *borscht*. I can promise you that."

"Too late, *d'yavol*," replies the slick-haired monster on the other side of the counter. "You had your chance to kill her. Now we've come to collect."

It happens so fast. Too fast for my unreliable, human eyes to fully believe.

Lily flips completely over the enclosed counter, unsheathing razor sharp daggers in each hand. The Russian staggers back, but not before she slices him across the chest. Bright red blood spurts onto the bulletproof glass, but it doesn't slow him down from producing a machine gun from inside his floor length wool coat and spraying bullets in Lily's direction. Luckily, she swiftly takes cover behind a shelf, moving impossibly fast to avoid being hit. The other Russian mobsters also pull out their weapons, ready to do battle.

"Come out, *d'yavol.* I have a big present for you." Blood soaks the man's entire torso, although there are no signs of him slowing down. He agilely steps around littered potato chips and puddles of soda, hoping to catch her, and essentially, kill her. I'm not sure whom I should be more afraid of.

"Come on, Vlad. We have the girl. Let's get out of here," says the other goon. He holds his gun with a shaking hand. Out of the three, he's the youngest, and most terrified.

"No! We will finish the job," the man called Vlad shouts, rounding the corner where Lily escaped. I'm only one aisle over, still trapped by some greasy pig bathed in cheap cologne. She has nowhere to run. And even if she did, she couldn't possibly dodge their bullets.

The sudden ear-splitting sound of breaking glass rattles my teeth as the entire storefront window explodes, raining down jagged, crystalized shards. The Russians train their attention and their guns on the entrance, but it's too late. It's him. The stranger. The dangerously handsome man who had been coming in every night for his fix of iced tea and mints.

Without missing a beat, he rushes in with two guns drawn. He hits the younger thug before he can even get a round off, sending him to the ground, before putting a bullet between the eyes of the asshole in stinky cologne. His corpse slumps on top of me, his dead weight trapping my frame to the dingy floor. Blood gushes all over me, staining my clothes and skin. The smell is overwhelming, and I struggle franticly to turn my head, just in time to vomit.

Strong hands yank me from the pool of blood and

my own waste, and swiftly drag me deeper into the store. Between the sounds of gunshots, the sight of blood and the sickness in my roiling gut, I'm disoriented. Shock and panic rally my rattled senses, and I begin to scream at the top of my lungs like a crazed lunatic. I don't even know what I'm saying or even why I'm screaming. I'm beyond reason, beyond feeling anything but intense dread. Hysteria is all I know.

The blow comes before I can even see it, let alone prevent it. It jolts my skull for only a moment before a dark heaviness cloaks me in oblivion.

Just before it takes me under completely, I look up to stare into twin pools of gray moonlight. Then everything shimmers before blurring into black.